Berkley Sensation Titles by Cheryl Holt

PROMISE OF PLEASURE
TASTE OF TEMPTATION

Taste
of Temptation

CHERYL HOLT

BERKLEY SENSATION, NEW YORK

THE BERKLEY PUBLISHING GROUP
Published by the Penguin Group
Penguin Group (USA) Inc.
375 Hudson Street, New York, New York 10014, USA
Penguin Group (Canada), 90 Eglinton Avenue East, Suite 700, Toronto, Ontario M4P 2Y3, Canada
(a division of Pearson Penguin Canada Inc.)
Penguin Books Ltd., 80 Strand, London WC2R 0RL, England
Penguin Books Ireland, 25 St. Stephen's Green, Dublin 2, Ireland (a division of Penguin Books Ltd.)
Penguin Group (Australia), 250 Camberwell Road, Camberwell, Victoria 3124, Australia
(a division of Pearson Australia Group Pty. Ltd.)
Penguin Books India Pvt. Ltd., 11 Community Centre, Panchsheel Park, New Delhi—110 017, India
Penguin Group (NZ), 67 Apollo Drive, Rosedale, North Shore 0632, New Zealand
(a division of Pearson New Zealand Ltd.)
Penguin Books (South Africa) (Pty.) Ltd., 24 Sturdee Avenue, Rosebank, Johannesburg 2196,
South Africa

Penguin Books Ltd., Registered Offices: 80 Strand, London WC2R 0RL, England

This is a work of fiction. Names, characters, places, and incidents either are the product of the author's
imagination or are used fictitiously, and any resemblance to actual persons, living or dead, business
establishments, events, or locales is entirely coincidental. The publisher does not have any control over
and does not assume any responsibility for author or third-party websites or their content.

TASTE OF TEMPTATION

A Berkley Sensation Book / published by arrangement with the author

PRINTING HISTORY
Berkley Sensation mass-market edition / June 2010

Copyright © 2010 by Cheryl Holt.
Excerpt from *Dreams of Desire* by Cheryl Holt copyright © by Cheryl Holt.
Cover art by Sam Montasano.
Cover design by George Long.
Cover hand lettering by Ron Zinn.
Interior text design by Kristin del Rosario.

ISBN: 978-0-425-23514-0

BERKLEY® SENSATION
Berkley Sensation Books are published by The Berkley Publishing Group,
a division of Penguin Group (USA) Inc.,
375 Hudson Street, New York, New York 10014.
BERKLEY® SENSATION and the "B" design are trademarks of Penguin Group (USA) Inc.

PRINTED IN THE UNITED STATES OF AMERICA

10 9 8 7 6 5 4 3 2 1

Taste of Temptation

Prologue

❧

"THIS is my most famous remedy of all."

"What is it called?"

"The Spinster's Cure."

Phillip Dudley, who—when selling his wares—used the false name and character of Frenchman Philippe Dubois, smiled at his pretty, auburn-haired customer. She looked bedraggled and exhausted, as if she desperately needed whatever he could convince her to buy.

"The Spinster's *Cure*?" she asked. "What does it do?"

"It helps an unwed female find a husband. You've never heard of it?"

"No, sorry."

He filled a vial with the red liquid and, as if the concoction was exotic and rare, gently placed it in her hand.

"You should try a sample. It would be extremely beneficial to your condition."

She scowled. "My condition! What do you imagine is wrong with me?"

"You're lonely, Miss Hamilton."

"I am not," she scoffed.

He peered into her striking green eyes, certain she was lying.

He was a renowned charlatan who had a knack for guessing a woman's hidden thoughts and feelings.

"You shouldn't pretend with me, *cherie*," he said. "How old are you?"

"Twenty-four."

"How can you insist you're not lonely? Despite your advanced age—"

"Advanced! You talk as if I have one foot in the grave."

"Face it, mademoiselle. You are no longer in the first blush of youth, yet you wear no wedding ring. No husband has been chosen for you. How can this be?"

"I've had a bit of trouble lately—not that my personal affairs are any of your business—but my father is recently deceased, so I'm busy caring for my two younger sisters. There's been no time to worry about marriage or anything else."

"If you could have one wish granted, I am positive you would ask for a handsome husband, a home of your own, and children to mother."

She gaped at him, amazed that he could be so astute, when he had simply voiced what most women craved.

"How did you know?" she marveled.

"I am Philippe Dubois," he answered, sounding pompous and wise. "It is my job to know."

He wrapped her fingers around the vial.

"You must drink this potion," he instructed, "while staring at your true love. You will be married to him in four weeks. *Je guarantee!*"

"You're joking."

"Not about this. *Never* about this."

She gazed at the vial, running her thumb over the cool glass.

Her yearning was palpable. She wanted the potion to be real, wanted it to magically alter her circumstances, but she wasn't prone to superstition or fantasy.

In the end, logic won out.

"I don't think so."

"But you must!" He grabbed her hand and held it, palm up, tracing down the center. "This line right here?"

"Yes."

"It tells me that your dreadful fate is set. Drastic intervention is necessary to change it."

"I don't want my fate to be altered."

"You're not serious, *mon amie*." He studied her shabby dress and tattered cloak. She wore the trappings of gentility, but her threadbare attire indicated she was experiencing tremendous financial difficulties. "You would go on as you have been? Why continue to struggle and toil, when you can drink a dose of my Spinster's Cure and fix what is wrong?"

"I don't have any money to pay you for it."

She tried to give it back, but he wouldn't take it.

"For you, it is free. When you are happily wed—as I promise you soon will be—you will come and reimburse me."

"You're mad," she protested.

"Not mad," he responded. "I know of what I speak. Just you wait and see."

Chapter 1

❦

"MICHAEL! What are you doing?"

Captain Tristan Odell glared down the hall at his younger half brother, Michael Seymour.

"Tristan," Michael casually replied, "I didn't realize you were home."

"Obviously."

Michael—the recently installed Earl of Hastings—had his arms wrapped around a very fetching housemaid, his lean, lanky torso pressing her against the wall. Not that she appeared to mind.

She was buxom and plump, her abundant breasts scarcely constrained by corset and gown, and thus, the exact sort of female Michael relished.

A love bite was plainly visible on the girl's neck, so mischief had been brewing. If Tristan hadn't walked by, Michael would have lured her into an empty parlor, would have had her skirt thrown up and her drawers tugged down in a fast attempt to lose his virginity.

It was hell, trying to keep the eighteen-year-old boy in line. With his golden blond hair and big blue eyes, his broad shoulders and six-foot frame, he could have been an angel painted on a church ceiling. Women took one look at him and promptly forgot every lesson they'd ever been taught about decency and decorum.

"What's your name, lass?" Tristan asked the maid.

"Lydia, Captain Odell."

"Be about your duties, Lydia, and I don't want you to sneak off with the earl ever again."

She glanced at Michael, expecting him to counter the edict, but Michael merely grinned, a shameless, unrepentant rogue.

"Yes, Captain Odell," she sullenly mumbled.

"I don't care what he promises you," Tristan warned. "I don't care if he offers you money or plies you with gifts. You are to refuse. Do I make myself clear?"

"Yes, sir."

"If he pesters you, and you can't dissuade him, come to me at once."

"I will."

"For if I stumble on another tryst, you'll be fired immediately. I won't give you a chance to explain. You'll simply be turned out without a reference."

The threat of termination got her attention. She curtsied and left, but she was mutinous, and Tristan knew it was only a matter of time before she'd be searching for other employment.

"You!" Tristan pointed an admonishing finger at Michael. "In the library!"

Tristan spun and marched off, as Michael complained, "You're such a scold. You never let me have any fun."

"This isn't *my* fault."

"The way you carry on, one would think you were my mother."

"Don't bring your poor mother into it. If she hadn't died when you were little, she wouldn't last long, watching you now. Your antics would be the death of her."

"My mother would have loved me," Michael confidently claimed. "She would have thought I was marvelous. All women do."

Tristan rolled his eyes and plopped down into his chair behind the massive oak desk. Though Michael was the earl, he slouched—like the recalcitrant adolescent he was—into the chair across from Tristan.

The prior earl, their philandering father, Charles Seymour, had passed away six months earlier, orphaning Michael and his twelve-year-old sister, Rose.

There were several relatives who could have stepped in as guardian for the two children, but for reasons Tristan couldn't fathom, Charles had chosen him.

Tristan was Charles's oldest, but illegitimate son, the product of an illicit romance between Charles and Tristan's Scottish mother, Meg. Charles had owned a hunting lodge near Tristan's village and had visited every autumn. As a wealthy, urbane aristocrat, Charles had possessed the same charisma as Michael, and pretty, foolish Meg hadn't stood a chance.

She'd died when Tristan was a baby, so she'd been unavailable to insist on continuing contact with his father. As a result, Tristan had only seen Charles a few times, and he'd been given scant fiscal support.

Tristan had made his own way in the world, had embraced his love of sailing and the sea. He owned a small shipping company and sailed as captain of his own merchant vessel. He was never happier than when he was out on the water and flying over the waves, so it had come as an enormous surprise to learn that he'd been roped in by Charles, cast as mentor and protector to his half siblings whom he'd never met.

At age thirty, Tristan had never been married and had no children of his own, so he knew nothing about parenting. He was floundering like a blind man, groping about in the dark.

Yet he wasn't eager to be compared to his negligent father, so he took his responsibilities seriously. When he'd received the letter advising him of his guardianship of Michael and Rose, he'd grudgingly traveled to London to assume his duties.

Michael and Rose weren't overly distraught at Charles's demise. Nor did they seem to miss him. Apparently Charles had been as absent in their lives as he'd been in Tristan's. They viewed his passing as one might that of a distant family friend.

"Well"—Tristan struggled to look fatherly—"what have you to say for yourself?"

"She's very fetching? She's loose with her favors? You're a stick in the mud?"

Tristan snorted with disgust. "You're hopeless. I have no idea why I lecture you."

"Neither do I. It's a waste of breath."

"It certainly is, but you must heed me: You don't want to gain a reputation as a fellow who tumbles his servants. Those kinds of men are regarded as swine."

"I don't feel like *swine*. I feel randy as the dickens."

"You have an obligation to your employees. You can't frivolously ruin them—even if they beg you to."

Tristan glowered, stupidly expecting to elicit some evidence of remorse, or at least a hint that Michael recognized his behavior to be rash and wrong. He was a peer of the realm, so he should set an example, but as Tristan had quickly learned, Michael acted however he pleased.

He'd been raised by nannies and governesses—pushovers all—who'd been dazzled by his delightful smile and charming manners. With his being eighteen and horridly spoiled, there wasn't much Tristan could do but peck like a hen while keeping a tight rein on Michael's fortune, a staggering array of money and property that he wouldn't completely control until the age of twenty-five.

"I've enlightened you as to women"—Tristan's cheeks flushed with embarrassment—"and the urges we men suffer because of them. You have to be cautious."

"It was just a kiss," Michael contended.

"Kissing can swiftly lead to more, and trust me, a low-born female like Lydia is a mercenary. If you impregnated her, you'd end up supporting her for the rest of your life."

Bored with the topic, Michael yawned. "Quit nagging. I like you, Tristan, but honestly, you can be positively tedious."

Michael flashed an imperious glare, filled with youthful disdain. Tristan had sailed around the globe, had whored and debauched in cities from Bombay to Shanghai, so he was in no position to chastise, but he felt compelled to guide Michael in his carnal conduct.

Michael was an *earl*. There were standards to be maintained, as their father had pointed out in a letter he'd written to Tristan on his deathbed.

Watch over Michael and Rose, Charles had penned. *Be kind to Rose. Dote on her as I never did. Be stern with Michael. Teach him the lessons I never bothered to impart. . . .*

The words were powerfully binding. Tristan was desperate to do right by Michael and Rose, desperate to make his father proud—a situation to which he'd never aspired when the man had been alive.

"I've explained the mechanics of sexual activity," Tristan reminded Michael, "and I hope you've paid attention."

"Oh, yes"—Michael grinned wickedly—"and I can't understand why you're working so hard to prevent me from practicing what you described. It can't be healthy to be so physically frustrated."

"You have to wait till you're married."

Tristan nearly choked. Had that sentence come from his own mouth?

"Ha! I don't know why you're so determined to keep me in the dark."

"It's not the *dark* I'm worried about; it's the baby that arrives nine months later."

At all costs, Tristan would thwart Michael from siring

any bastard children. Being a bastard himself, it was a sore subject for Tristan, but he couldn't get Michael to grasp why it mattered.

"I wish you'd take me to a brothel," Michael blurted out.

"A brothel?"

"Yes. If I could dabble with whores occasionally, I'd be—"

Tristan was saved from the conversation by a knock on the door. Michael's cousin, Maud Seymour, poked her nose in. She was a few years older than Tristan, a fussy, unremarkable widow with mousy brown hair and unmemorable gray eyes.

For more than a decade, she'd resided in the mansion, with her daughter, Miriam, who was now sixteen-years-old. She'd served as the earl's hostess, as well as a detached mother-figure for Michael and Rose.

She was the ultimate hanger-on, the dreaded poor relative who'd come for a visit, ingratiated herself, and never left.

She was used to running the household, having had no supervision from Tristan's father over the accounts or servants, and she'd been furious over Tristan's barging in and seizing control. Tristan tried to be cordial, anxious to build a rapport rather than fight over territory.

He didn't care about the house or servants. He cared about Michael and Rose and ensuring that their futures and fortunes were secure.

"Yes, Maud, what is it?" he asked.

"An applicant is here to interview for the position of Rose's governess. A Miss Helen Hamilton."

Tristan bit down a curse. He'd forgotten about the interview. Rose had been without a governess for almost two years, and while she insisted she didn't need one, Tristan insisted she did.

He'd immersed himself in the search, but he couldn't find the exact person he wanted.

Rose was a lonely, sweet girl, and so far, the candidates

had seemed too old or too grumpy or too lazy to be allowed to watch over her. Maud claimed he was finicky, and he probably was, but he had to keep stopping himself from asking why, when she'd been in charge for so long, the post had remained unfilled.

Finances weren't a problem, and Tristan suspected that Maud didn't like Rose enough to trouble herself with hiring someone.

"You don't have to bother with it," Maud told him. "I'm happy to talk to her for you."

"I don't mind meeting with her," he stated. "It's my duty to Rose."

"You're so conscientious," Maud simpered, flattering him. She was practically batting her lashes. "It's so refreshing to have a man about the place who enjoys being in command."

"What am I, Cousin Maud?" Michael inquired. "I'm a man."

"You," Tristan needled, "are an arrogant boy who's barely out of short pants."

"You think I'm a boy," Michael retorted, "but if you gave me half a chance with the ladies, I'd show you that I can—"

"Michael was just leaving." Tristan cut him off, terrified of what risqué comment he might make in Maud's presence.

"Yes, Maud," Michael agreed, "I'm leaving. The maids are having tea down in the kitchen. I promised I'd join them."

"He's not going to the kitchen to chat with the maids," Tristan said. "He's going to his bedchamber to contemplate his many deplorable character traits."

"I don't have any deplorable traits," Michael boasted. "I'm flawlessly wonderful. Ask anyone."

Tristan rolled his eyes again. "Maud, escort him out, then send the applicant down to speak with me."

Maud and Michael departed, and Tristan sat, listening as their footsteps faded.

"A brothel, indeed," he muttered to the silent room.

If Michael started frequenting whores, his name would be permanently sullied, which Tristan couldn't permit.

His father's deathbed letter had contained the request that Tristan arrange brilliant marriages for Michael and Rose, to partners befitting their station. If Michael developed a reputation as a philanderer who had bastard children scattered hither and yon, no sane father would have him as a son-in-law.

More footsteps sounded in the hall. They were dainty and hesitant, and before he could fully shift his thoughts from Michael and his budding sexuality, the interviewee entered.

On seeing her, he frowned.

She was very pretty, petite, slender, and willowy, with a gorgeous head of auburn hair and big green eyes. Her skin was creamy smooth, her cheeks rosy with good health, her lips red and lush as a ripe cherry.

Her manner was pleasant, her dress neat and trim. She seemed to glide rather than walk, providing evidence of education and breeding.

No doubt, she'd be perfect, a cheery, competent, and interesting person whom Rose would adore. He detested her on sight.

He'd specifically informed Mrs. Ford at the employment agency that he wouldn't consider any attractive, young females. Not with Michael in a constant state of lust. Was Mrs. Ford blind?

"Is this the library?" She peered around at the walls and walls of books stretched from floor to ceiling, and she chuckled. "Of course it is. That was a silly question, wasn't it?"

She focused those beautiful green eyes on him, and he felt as if he'd been hit with a bolt of lightning. She seemed to know things about him that she had no reason to know, seemed to understand what drove him, what he wanted, what he needed, and the sensation was so bizarre and so alarming that he actually shuddered.

"May I help you?" he queried.

"I'm looking for Captain Odell."

"You've found him." He stood, certain he appeared persnickety and overbearing. "And you are . . . ?"

"Miss Helen Hamilton. I've been sent by Mrs. Ford at the Ford Employment Agency to—"

"Yes, I'm aware of why you're here." He gestured to the chair that Michael had just vacated. "Sit."

At his sharp tone, she faltered, then forced a smile and came over, carefully balancing on the edge of the seat, her skirt demurely arrayed, her fingers clasped in her lap.

They stared as if they were quarreling, but she didn't cower as he wished she would. He was eager to expose a chink in her armor so that he would feel justified in rejecting her.

"Well?" he asked.

"Well, what?"

"Where are your references?"

"Oh, those." She waved an elegant hand as if a prior endorsement was of no consequence. "I didn't bring any."

He breathed a sigh of relief. No references, no job.

"Then we needn't continue this discussion. I can't imagine what Mrs. Ford was thinking."

"Would you hear me out?"

"No."

As if he hadn't declined to listen, she began extolling her virtues. "I could have penned some fake letters, but I didn't because I'm too honest."

"Are you?"

"Yes. You see, I've never been a governess before. However, I've had excellent schooling. My studies included languages, art, science—both biological and geological— history, penmanship, and I'm also trained in the finer graces such as dancing, painting, and—"

He held up a hand, stopping her. "Thank you for coming."

He pointed to the door, indicating she should leave,
but she didn't. Her gaze brimmed with hurt, and perhaps a flash of desperation, and he felt as if he'd kicked a
puppy.

"I speak French, Italian, Latin, and a bit of Spanish."

"No."

"I sing like an angel."

"No."

"I can play pieces by Mr. Mozart on the pianoforte."

"No."

"Please?"

"Good day, Miss Hamilton."

"Mrs. Ford said I was exactly who you were looking for."

"Mrs. Ford was wrong."

She scrutinized him, her head tipped to the side as if
he were a curious bug she was examining.

"Why are you acting like this?" she stunned him by
asking.

"What did you say?"

"Have I offended you?"

"No."

"That's not true. From the moment I arrived, your dislike was palpable. Tell me what I've done so that I can
apologize, then we'll move on and conduct ourselves like
rational adults."

"I have no desire to continue."

"But . . . why?"

"My reasons, Miss Hamilton, are none of your business."

His comment fell into the room with a heavy thud, his
discourtesy blatant and mortifying. Despite his low antecedents, he was a gentleman, and he hated upsetting her,
but he wanted her to go away.

She seemed to deflate, appearing vulnerable and de-
fenseless, a tragic figure who could benefit from a steady
male influence, and he was irked to find himself won-

dering what it would be like to be the man who supplied it.

"May I be frank, Captain Odell?"

"No, you may not."

Once again, she blathered on without permission. "Mrs. Ford urged me not to mention it, but my father was Captain Harry Hamilton of the Forty-Seventh Dragoons."

Tristan recalled a scandal that even he—being far out to sea and away from England—had heard about: a torrid affair, a duke's mistress, a duel in which the dashing Captain Hamilton had recklessly perished.

"If Harry Hamilton was your father, then you most especially would not be appropriate for this position. I wouldn't want you within a hundred yards of my ward."

"I'm twenty-four years old, Captain Odell. I have two sisters. Jane is eighteen, and Amelia is only twelve—the same age as Lady Rose. We're all alone in the world, and I can't provide for them. I need this job."

"I'm sorry, but no."

"I'll work for free, for a whole month. Give me a chance to prove myself."

"It wouldn't do any good."

"Weren't you in the navy when you were younger?"

"I was."

"Then I'm begging you, as a favor to my father, a fellow soldier who served his country honorably for decades. Help me save my sisters."

She reached out to him, trembling, beseeching him, and Tristan was too moved to reply. He simply shook his head.

To his horror, tears welled into her eyes, and he nearly leapt over the desk and shielded her face so he wouldn't have to see them.

Though he was a tough, swashbuckling sailor, he was a sap for a woman's tears, and he couldn't bear to know that she was so unhappy. Her woe made him want to assist her, to watch over and shelter her and her destitute siblings, and he bit down on all the comforting words that were fighting to burst out.

"Go now," he said very quietly.

Rudely, he grabbed a stack of correspondence and pretended to read it, effectively dismissing her.

He could sense her studying him, her probing attention wretched and intent.

Ultimately, she sighed and left, and he collapsed back into his chair, feeling like a heel. He wasn't generally so callous, and he was chagrined that he'd been cruel to her. But London was a brutal place, and there were too many poverty-stricken females. He couldn't save any of them, and he wasn't about to try.

It dawned on him, though, that he could have slipped her a few pounds to ease her immediate plight.

Eager to catch up with her, he hurried out to the hall and proceeded to the foyer when—to his disgust—he ran into Michael and Miss Hamilton.

Michael's arm was around her waist, and she was pressed to the wall, much as Tristan had witnessed earlier with the housemaid, Lydia.

So . . . Miss Hamilton was not only the daughter of a notorious scoundrel, but she was loose and indecent, too. Had she come specifically hoping to bump into Michael? He was definitely rich enough to solve her problems. Had seduction been her scheme all along?

"Michael!" he snapped. "Unhand her at once."

Michael chuckled and stepped away, while Miss Hamilton stumbled, struggling to right herself.

"She tells me," Michael said, "that you didn't feel she was suitable to be Rose's governess. She must be joking. *I* think she'd be spectacular."

Michael's naughty gaze roamed down her torso, and she blushed furiously.

"Weren't you going to your room?" Tristan asked him.

"Why, yes I was."

Michael strolled away as Miss Hamilton peered at Tristan, her expression unreadable. He couldn't decide if she was embarrassed at being molested or at being discovered.

For the briefest moment, it looked as if she might explain or defend her behavior, but instead, she spun and stomped out.

Chapter 2

ಠ

"HELLO, lovely lady. Who might you be?"

Helen glanced up to find a young, blond god blocking her way. He was probably the most handsome man she'd ever seen, with the exception of offensive, arrogant Captain Odell, whose company she'd just fled.

While this fellow oozed charm and urbane grace, Odell was his total opposite: dark and dangerous and smoldering with temper and bad humor. His black hair had matched his black personality. He'd worn it longer than was fashionable, pulled back in a queue and tied with a strip of leather, and he'd had a gold earring in his ear—an earring, for goodness sake!—giving him the air of a pirate or a bandit.

Mrs. Ford had warned her that he could be difficult, but the woman had no idea! Helen had never met a more obnoxious buffoon in her entire life. It was no wonder he couldn't hire a governess for Lady Rose. Who would work for the despicable oaf?

Though he'd been sitting in a fancy library and attired in a gentleman's coat and trousers, expensive clothes couldn't conceal his genuine character. He was a brute. He had a heart of stone beating under his ribs.

No, not a heart of stone. He had no heart at all. He was an unfeeling, uncaring monster.

"Excuse me," she muttered to the blond god, "but I was just leaving."

"So soon, and without our being introduced? I never allow a pretty female to cross my path without learning her name."

She didn't know who he was, but she suspected he was the new earl. Mrs. Ford had warned her about him, too.

"Miss Helen Hamilton."

"You don't mind if I call you Helen, do you?"

"Actually, I do."

He was between her and the door, and short of physically pushing him aside, she couldn't escape.

Wasn't that just her luck? One man in the dreaded house had forced her through the most horrid appointment in history, and the other imagined himself to be Don Juan.

"I really should be going."

"Didn't you speak with Captain Odell? I assume he's given you the job, and I'm delighted that you will be joining our staff."

"No, he didn't give me the job."

"He didn't? Why not? You'd be perfect. Is he insane?"

"Yes, he is."

She probably should have kept her mouth shut, but Odell had infuriated her beyond measure. He couldn't begin to guess what it was like to be poor and afraid, to be out of options but having others depending on you.

Helen had never been employed and had few viable skills. It had been the ultimate humiliation to attend an interview, but then, to be insulted and abused by the interviewer—when she hadn't a clue why she'd received such uncivil treatment—was too hideous to abide.

To her great dismay, tears flooded her eyes. She couldn't hold them at bay. She hated to be so maudlin, but after suffering so many catastrophes, who wouldn't be? The weight of the world seemed balanced on her shoulders, and she couldn't remember the last time anything had gone right.

"My darling girl," her gallant swain said, "what is it? What's wrong?"

"I . . . I . . . needed the position, and I'm a tad over-wrought at it not being offered to me."

He appeared stricken and reached an arm around her waist as if to hug her, but the library door opened and Captain Odell marched out.

On seeing them, he stormed over.

"Michael," he snapped, confirming that her admirer was indeed Lord Hastings, "unhand her at once."

"She tells me," Lord Hastings mentioned, "that you didn't feel she was suitable to be Rose's governess. She must be joking. *I* think she'd be spectacular."

The two of them had a brief spat, but Helen was too upset to listen. She had no idea why the earl had flirted with her, but Odell was glaring as if she were a harlot.

The earl skittered off, and Helen stared up at Odell, searching his blue, blue eyes for a hint of kindness or understanding. She wanted to explain what had happened, or to defend herself, but what was the use? He would never believe her.

Without a word, she turned and hurried out. If he thought she was rude or impertinent, she hardly cared.

Her cloak and bonnet were where she'd left them, on a chair in the foyer, and she scooped them up and walked out onto the stoop.

She stood on the steps, tying her bonnet and gazing down the street. Carriages rumbled by. Maids and foot-men scurried past. Everyone had something to do, some-place to be.

Helen had nothing at all, except her sisters, Jane and Amelia, who were waiting for her in the dilapidated room they'd rented with the last of their money. They'd sent her off to the interview with fond wishes, certain of her success.

They were so optimistic, so sure of the future, and their positive attitude was Helen's fault. She'd shielded them from learning the exact depth of their plight, but after this debacle, there was no way to keep them from noting the cliff upon which they were perched.

As the daughters of Captain Harry Hamilton, they'd ridden out many storms in their chaotic lives, had been buffeted by poverty and plenty, by scandal and infamy.

Through years of tumult, the three of them had persevered, but after Harry was killed in the duel, they'd been on a downward spiral that couldn't be halted.

The angry duke of Clarendon hadn't been satisfied with merely murdering their father. He'd craved even more revenge. Creditors had come forward; bank clerks had swarmed. The Hamiltons' home had been seized, their possessions sold, nearly all but the clothes on their backs taken from them.

They'd traveled to London, throwing themselves on the mercy of relatives, who'd shunned them. People who should have behaved better declined to provide shelter. Only Amelia's thrifty hiding of their mother's jewelry had saved them from starvation on the streets, but that money was long spent.

"What to do? What to do?" she murmured.

She'd gone on dozens of job interviews, pleaded for assistance, and begged for handouts, but to no avail. Harry Hamilton was notorious, so his daughters were, too.

They were destitute and desperate, and the notion of returning to their boardinghouse, of telling Amelia and Jane that there was no job, that Odell hadn't liked her, after all, was too depressing to consider.

Her stomach rumbled, reminding her that she hadn't eaten since the previous day. They'd had a few scraps of food remaining, and she'd let her sisters have them, pretending she wasn't hungry and insisting she'd dine like a queen the moment Odell hired her.

She snorted with disgust, then reached in her reticule, hunting for a kerchief to dab at her eyes, when she stumbled on the vial the peddler, Mr. Dubois, had given her.

What had he called it? The Spinster's Cure?

He'd claimed it had magical powers.

"If only it were true." She sighed.

A rich husband would definitely come in handy, but there was no magic in the universe strong enough to fix what was wrong.

Her stomach growled again, protesting its empty state, and she held the vial toward the sky. The liquid appeared to be red wine, which she imagined it was. She pulled the cork and sniffed the contents, detecting a cherry flavoring.

Eager to quell her hunger pangs, as well as to have a bit of fortification for the long walk home, she tipped the dark fluid into her mouth.

She'd started to swallow, when suddenly, the door of the mansion opened behind her. She whirled around, and to her horror, she was face-to-face with Captain Odell.

"Are you still here?" he complained.

"Odell?"

She coughed and sputtered, banging her chest, absurdly panicked about having ingested the potion while looking at him. Frantic thoughts rattled her: What if the tonic was real? What if she'd pitched herself onto a new and unexpected path? What if—God forbid—she ended up married to the arrogant oaf?

The liquid slid down with ease, landing in her belly like the kiss of death. There was the oddest calm in the air, as if the entire world had stopped to mark what she'd done. Fate seemed to be readjusting lives and fortunes.

She gazed at him until she was mesmerized, drowning, not able to tear herself away.

Here he is . . . here he is . . . finally . . . a crazed voice whispered in her head.

With his being so handsome, so masculine and tough, she didn't suppose life had ever thrown him for a loop. He was the type who'd brazen it out, who fought and scraped and always came out on top. He'd never be scared or weary, would never be anxious or sad.

His shoulders were very broad, the kind a woman could lean on in times of trouble, and for a wild, insane instant, she nearly hurled herself into his arms and begged him to never let her go.

Luckily, before she could make an even bigger fool of herself than she already had, she noticed he was studying the empty vial clasped in her hand.

"Are you a lush, too, Miss Hamilton?"

"What?"

"From your behavior with the earl, it's clear you're a flirt. Are you a secret drunkard, too? I feel we've dodged a bullet. I'll have to speak with Mrs. Ford to ask why she'd send someone with so many vices."

"You think I'm a flirt? You think I'm a drunkard?"

He smirked, pointing to the vial. "The evidence does seem incontrovertible."

He was so smug, so patronizing. If she'd been a man, she'd have pounded him into the ground.

How dare he criticize! How dare he scold!

She was the granddaughter of a baron on her deceased mother's side. True, her mother had been disowned and disinherited when she'd eloped with Harry Hamilton, but that fact didn't change ancestry. She had aristocratic blood flowing in her veins, while he was a barely acknowledged Scottish bastard son.

He might have been temporarily elevated into the ranks of Polite Society so that he could fraternize with his betters, but despite her current difficulties, she was one of those *betters,* and his conduct toward her was outrageous.

"For your information," she seethed, jabbing a condemning finger at the center of his chest, "I am not a flirt."

"Oh, really? You couldn't prove it by me."

"The earl of Hastings is a menace. I am a decent female who visited you with honorable intentions only to be accosted by him, and I lay the blame for his lechery solely at your feet. What sort of guardian are you, anyway?"

"Now just a damned minute, you little—"

"It's Miss Hamilton to you, and I am not a drunkard, either. That vial contained a love potion."

"A *love potion*?"

"Yes. A peddler insisted I try it, but I drank it because I'm starving. I haven't any idea why I must explain myself to you, but I feel compelled to confide that I haven't had anything to eat for the past two days."

"A likely story, shared to elicit sympathy, but it hasn't."

"I gave my remaining food to my sisters. But do you know what?"

"No, but I'm sure you'll tell me."

"I was advised to swallow the potion while staring at the man who is destined to become my husband."

He was a sailor, and as she'd suspected, he was superstitious as the dickens.

He blanched.

"Meaning what precisely?" he haughtily inquired.

"Meaning I curse you."

"Curse me?" He gulped with dismay.

"Yes. I hope I've actually set off some magic and that you wind up wed to me. It would be your worst nightmare, and it would serve you right for being such a horse's ass!"

She whipped away and started off.

"Miss Hamilton!" he barked. "Get back here this instant."

He'd shouted the command in his most stern, ship-captain's tone, but she ignored him and marched on, which she was certain would annoy him into infinity.

Chapter 3

❦

"WHAT was Captain Odell like?"

"Very handsome, very charming."

Helen nearly choked on the lie, but as usual, she was determined to conceal the grim realities of their situation, although Jane seemed to understand the extent of their plight. With her being eighteen, and Amelia only twelve, Jane was complicit in hiding the truth from Amelia.

Amelia was the eternal optimist, being constantly positive that prosperity was just around the corner.

"Why didn't he hire you?" Amelia's concern was heartbreaking.

The three sisters were spitting images of their deceased father: slender, auburn-haired, and green-eyed, with his amiable temperament and penchant for conversation.

"Oh, he liked me very much, Amelia. He'd simply found someone else right before I arrived. She was older and more experienced." At Amelia's worried expression, Helen added, "He was terribly sorry for putting me to the trouble of coming so far, and he offered to send me home in his carriage, but the weather was so pleasant that I decided to walk back."

This last was a bit much for Jane, and she spun away and went to the grimy window to gaze outside.

"Was Lord Hastings in residence?" Jane asked, her finger tracing over the dirty pane.

Jane was fascinated by the antics of aristocrats like Hastings, and in a fairer, more sane world, she'd have moved in their circle. Not in the direct center of it, but certainly on the edges. Though she never complained about how things had gone, she suffered pangs of envy, and Helen couldn't blame her.

The sins of their parents, and the injustices of society, had combined to wear them down till there was nothing left.

"Actually, I met the earl."

"Really? Was he as attractive as they claim in the papers?"

"More so, I'd say. He was tall and blond and extremely gallant. I liked him very much."

She wasn't aware that she had such a knack for fabrication, and she wondered where she came by it. No doubt, it was a trait inherited from her father, who'd been a renowned charlatan and rogue.

"I wish I'd met him, too," Jane murmured, and there was such longing in her voice that Helen could barely keep from weeping.

"I'm sure you will someday," Helen fibbed with false cheer. "Once this bad spell is behind us, there's no telling where we might bump into him. At a ball. At a supper. Since I know him, I'll be able to introduce you."

"I'd enjoy that." Jane glanced over her shoulder. "What now?"

"Now, I'll . . . I'll talk to Mrs. Ford and have her schedule another interview. There has to be someone in this blasted city who needs a governess."

"Who better than you?" Amelia loyally said.

"Precisely," Helen agreed.

"You have to let me try, too," Jane insisted. "I'll come with you to Mrs. Ford's. I'm old enough to work."

"We've been through this, Jane. If you take a job, there's no going back. After we've returned to our prior status, it would be a black mark that would keep you from making a good marriage."

Jane stared and stared, and Helen could practically hear her sister's cynical retort—they would never return to their prior status, there would never be a good marriage—but thankfully, Jane didn't mention the depressing prospect in front of Amelia.

Helen was saved from further discussion by angry footsteps pounding up the stairs. As their landlord hammered on the door, she cringed.

"He's been up three times," Amelia whispered, "looking for you."

"Did he say what he wants?"

Amelia shook her head, but Helen knew what he sought: rent money she didn't have.

"I'll talk to him, then I'll be right back. Put on your bonnets, and we'll go for a walk after I'm finished."

She forced a smile and slipped into the hall. On seeing her, the exasperating man nearly shouted her penury to the entire building. She motioned him to silence, then proceeded to the rickety staircase and marched down. He had no choice but to follow.

As she reached the foyer, he wasted no time in getting to the point.

"Where is my money, Miss Hamilton?"

"I need a few more days, Mr. Beasley."

"You've been saying that for three weeks."

"I know, but I should land a job any minute."

"What happened this morning? I thought you had a position starting."

"The interview wasn't as successful as I expected."

"Meaning they learned you were Harry Hamilton's daughter and they sent you packing."

"There's no need to be cruel, Mr. Beasley—or to speak ill of the dead."

"I don't care about the dead, Miss Hamilton. I care about the living—namely *me*, and I'm not running a bloody charity. I'll have my money by nine o'clock tomorrow morning, or I'll toss you and your sisters out on the street. Don't make me."

He stomped off, and Helen collapsed against the banister, her knees giving out. She sank onto the bottom step, her head in her hands. She was frozen in place, paralyzed by indecision and fear.

Visions danced in her mind—of the comfortable house her father had owned in the country, the gentle way of life to which they'd been raised. While they'd never been wealthy, there had been servants, and the occasional new gown, and beaux who came calling, and parties and suppers and neighborhood soirees.

All gone. And she had no idea how to get them back.

Gradually, she realized she was being watched, and she glanced up to see a woman named Josephine—Jo to her friends—who resided in the building. She was always cordial, always stopping to chat and ask how Helen was faring in the big city.

She was about Helen's age, but she had a rough edge, evidence of the hard existence a female endured in London. She dressed in flamboyant clothes, with bodices that were cut too low, and sleeves that showed too much skin.

There were rumors that she was a doxy, that she entertained gentlemen in ways Helen couldn't imagine. Under different circumstances, Helen wouldn't have fraternized with her, but Jo was courteous and kind, and in light of Helen's predicament, she was in no position to judge.

Jo had a satchel sitting on the floor next to her, and she was wearing her cloak and bonnet. She peeked outside as if waiting for a carriage to arrive.

"Are you leaving us?" Helen inquired.

"Yes, I've accepted a new situation. It comes with room and board."

"How lucky for you."

"Isn't it, though?" There was an awkward pause, and she said, "I couldn't help overhearing you and Mr. Beasley."

"We weren't exactly in a spot that encouraged private conversation."

"What will you do?"

"I don't know. We're a bit desperate."

Jo nodded, studying Helen, taking her measure. "Might I make a suggestion?" she eventually asked.

"Any advice would be greatly appreciated."

"You seem out of your element, what with trying to get by on your own. You're not very good at it."

"That's putting it mildly."

"So I was thinking of another option. It's not what you're expecting—you being a lady and all. Promise you won't be offended."

"Considering the condition of my empty purse, there is nothing you could say that would upset me."

"You might be surprised." Jo chuckled.

Helen assessed Jo's brazen outfit, her exposed cleavage, and she chuckled, too.

"Perhaps you'll embarrass me," Helen admitted, "but I won't swoon."

"There's the ticket. It's a cruel world out there. You need to buck up."

"Yes, I do."

"Are you aware of my true line of work, Miss Hamilton?"

"I believe it might have been mentioned to me."

"Previously, I found my own customers out on the streets, but I'm moving to a house being operated by a new madam."

"And this house, it's a . . . a . . ."

Helen couldn't finish, and Jo bluntly said, "It's a brothel, Miss Hamilton."

At having the word so blithely uttered, Helen gasped. "Are you proposing that I . . . that I . . ."

"No," Jo quickly replied. "My employer is Lauretta Bainbridge. Have you ever met her?"

"We wouldn't have crossed paths."

"For years, she was mistress to Viscount Redvers."

"Lord Redvers? Gad, I know *him*."

"Gossip has it that he split with her when he married. His bride insisted on it."

"I can certainly understand why."

Lord and Lady Redvers were acquaintances of the peddler Philippe Dubois. They had stopped by when Helen had been chatting with him by his wagon. The viscount had been gruff and grumpy, while the viscountess had been sincere and friendly. She'd asked Helen to call her by her Christian name, and Helen had liked her very much.

Hopefully, the licentious viscount would prove himself worthy of his gracious, pretty wife and his philandering would be a thing of the past.

"Anyways," Jo continued, "what with Mrs. Bainbridge being dumped over by Redvers, she needs to support herself, so she's started her own place."

"What has that to do with me, Jo? I could never . . . well . . . you know."

"What if she could wrangle you a post as mistress to some rich nabob?"

"Mistress!"

"You wouldn't be a working girl like me. You'd be in a class high above it."

"But mistress!" Helen exclaimed again.

"Don't look so shocked. You'd have your own home and income. Your expenses would be paid, and you'd have an allowance for clothes and such."

"It sounds so tawdry."

"Why would you say so? Women enter into arrangements like it all the time, and Mrs. Bainbridge could negotiate the terms for you."

Helen was aghast. "People actually contract over this sort of affair?"

"Yes, Miss Hamilton. Occasionally, you must endure the unpalatable to make ends meet, but in the process, you have to protect yourself. Negotiations are customary."

"I shudder to imagine it."

"View it as a bridge to getting back on track. You haven't done much of a bang-up job so far."

"No, I haven't," Helen dejectedly concurred.

With each of her decisions, she and her sisters had dropped a few rungs down society's ladder until they were wallowing at the bottom with a kindly, well-meaning whore.

Still . . . to be a mistress! It would be so wrong. Despite the low morals of her father, she'd been raised to behave better.

"I couldn't, Jo."

"Why couldn't you? You'd be providing shelter for your sisters. From where I'm standing, you don't have a way of doing that as of nine o'clock tomorrow."

"I know, I know."

Jo laid a comforting hand on Helen's shoulder.

"I fear for the three of you, Miss Hamilton."

Footsteps echoed at the top of the stairs, and Helen peered up to see Amelia on the landing.

"What is it, Amelia?" she asked.

"I'm sorry to interrupt, but we ate the last of the cheese. Did you bring us any food?"

"No."

For the briefest instant, Amelia appeared crushed, but she was a brave child and she hid her dismay.

"It's all right," Amelia claimed. "I'm not hungry. We were just curious."

She turned and trudged to their room, the shutting of their door reverberating through the drafty building. Helen stared at Jo, ashamed and at a loss as to how to carry on.

"Why don't you talk to Mrs. Bainbridge?" Jo said. "It can't hurt. See what she says. You never know. She might find you a grand match and all your problems would be solved. Think how it would ease your mind."

Helen thought of Jane and Amelia, of having to explain why they were being thrown out on the street, and she simply couldn't bear it.

She sighed. "Maybe I should."

"Some handsome gent will snap you up in a trice. I don't doubt it for a second."

"HELLO, Lauretta."

"Hello, Captain Odell." She smiled her sexy, seductive smile, then focused on Michael. "You must be Lord Hastings."

"I'm very pleased to meet you." Michael swept up her hand and kissed it.

"Ooh, such lovely manners for one so young. How delightful!"

"You haven't told anyone that we were coming, have you?" Tristan asked.

"Absolutely not. My word is my bond, Captain."

Though Tristan had initially scoffed at Michael's suggestion of going to a brothel, he'd once again caught Michael sniffing around Lydia. Suddenly, the notion of regular visits didn't seem like such a bad idea. The harlots would tamp down his salacious impulses, *and* they would teach him the ins and outs of intercourse so that Tristan didn't have to.

He'd known Lauretta Bainbridge for years, through his thorough acquaintance with the seedier side of aristocratic London. When she'd split with Viscount Redvers, she'd taken over an establishment run by a prior madam who'd fled the city for unknown reasons.

Lauretta catered to the upper echelons of high society, so she'd been the obvious choice to supply Michael with the lessons Tristan was desperate for the boy to receive.

She circled Michael, as if assessing a fine piece of horseflesh, and she stopped in front of him and stroked a palm across his chest.

"This will be so enjoyable."

"Will you . . . ah . . . deal with him yourself?" Tristan inquired.

"He'd probably like someone nearer to his own age." Lauretta was in her thirties.

"Someone pretty," Michael said.

"I employ the prettiest girls available anywhere. I select them myself for their poise, beauty, and skill."

The door opened, and two whores burst in. They were bubbly and giggling, dressed in corset, drawers, and spiky heels. One was blond and the other brunette. They were busty and curvaceous, and Tristan felt a carnal stirring of his own, wondering if he shouldn't partake, too.

Since arriving in London to watch over Michael and Rose, he'd lived like a saint. He was in a damned brothel. Why not indulge?

"This is Jo," Lauretta said, "and this is Peg. Girls, this is Lord Hastings."

"How do', milord," they chimed in unison.

They gave a naughty curtsy, torsos leaned forward so that Michael had a full view of their breasts. His attention was instantly captured, and Tristan could see that he'd be in excellent hands.

"How long will they be?" Tristan queried.

"His lordship can stay till morning, if he likes."

Lauretta's reply caused a bout of simpering and cooing by the two lusty whores.

"Let's just do three hours for his first visit. That should be plenty."

Michael grinned. "I can come back again on Saturday, right?"

"Yes, Michael," Tristan agreed, "every Wednesday and Saturday, till you're bored with it."

"Don't worry, Tristan"—he eyed their shapely torsos—"I won't get bored."

He extended an arm to both girls, and they hurried over, one on each side, and led him out.

Tristan sighed, feeling as if he'd pushed a baby bird from the nest. There was an awkward moment, where he debated if he should leave or request a whore of his own. Lauretta—the consummate saleswoman—jumped into the breach.

"What about you, Captain? Should I prepare a room for you, too?"

At her offer, Tristan considered, then shook his head. "I don't think so."

"Are you sure? It can't be healthy, hanging around that prude Maud Seymour."

"Lauretta! What sort of comment is that?"

"Rumor has it that she's set her sights on you."

Tristan had often suspected it to be the case. Not that he'd admit it.

"Why would you suppose so?"

"Because she's a mercenary, and you control the earl's money. She knows where the bread is buttered." She winked. "She plans on marrying Hastings to her daughter, Miriam. You realize that, don't you? It would be awful to have him caught in a peccadillo from which he couldn't extricate himself."

"She'd try to trap him?"

"I wouldn't put it past her. Would you?"

No. "Where do you hear these things?"

"I run a brothel, Captain. You'd be surprised what type of information is bandied about."

"I appreciate the warning. I'll have a chat with Michael; I'll advise him to be careful."

"Good—but let's get back to my original question. You've been working so hard. Won't you let us relax you?"

"I'm not much of a one for prostitutes."

"Since when?" She laughed and laughed.

"I must be growing old, but I'm bothered by the casual nature of it. It seems so . . . pointless, I guess."

"Maybe you should marry and settle down."

"Matrimony is not in the cards."

He was a seafaring man, gone for months and years at a time, and he'd return to that existence once his duties to Michael and Rose were concluded. His itinerant style of life wasn't conducive to marital harmony.

She studied him with a shrewd expression.

"If you're reluctant to wed," she said, "there's an alternative."

"What is it?"

"How about a mistress?"

"A mistress?"

"Yes."

He'd never kept one, though it was common practice for a gentleman of means. For a price, the situation supplied many benefits: a fetching, trainable female; regular sexual congress; and feminine companionship without a wife's nagging.

Still, Tristan wasn't in the mood to make such a commitment.

"No, thanks."

"I have someone in mind who'd be perfect for you."

"Really? In what fashion?"

"She's very attractive and highly educated, so you'd actually be able to carry on a conversation."

"Always an advantage."

"Plus, she has the sweetest manners and disposition. Would you like to meet her?"

"When?"

"Now. I've arranged some interviews this evening for a few of my more discerning guests. She'll be snatched up immediately, and I'd hate to have you miss out. Would you like an introduction?"

He shrugged. "Why not?" He decided out of curiosity more than anything else, being oddly interested in seeing what kind of female would approach Lauretta Bainbridge for assistance. Only the most desperate one, he was sure!

They started down the hall, Lauretta filling him in on the woman's personal details. She was former gentry who'd suffered a terrible run of bad luck, and she was anxious to improve her lot by allying herself with a wealthy gentleman. And, of course, she was chaste as the day was long.

Tristan snorted at that, not for a second believing he'd

stumble on a virgin in a bawdy house, but despite his misgivings, he couldn't deny that his ardor was flaring.

Why not? a niggling voice prodded. He wasn't a pauper. His business made him money hand over fist, and combined with the fees he was paid for supervising his half siblings, he was becoming richer by the minute.

He had the coin to buy whatever he wanted. A mistress, perhaps?

They climbed to the next floor, and Lauretta knocked, then opened the door to a blue bedchamber, complete with blue walls, drapes, and furnishings.

An auburn-haired woman sat on a divan, and as they entered, she spun around. Their gazes locked, recognition dawned, and his mouth dropped in shock.

"Miss Hamilton?" he wheezed.

"Captain Odell!"

She leapt up and hurried behind a large chair, using it as a shield as if he might attack her.

Ever since she'd walked out of Michael's library, he'd been fretting over her. She'd prevailed on his better nature, had begged him to have mercy on the children of a deceased soldier, but he'd ignored her plea.

What sort of man was he?

He'd been plagued by the answer to that question, but if she would involve herself in such a dangerously idiotic scheme, why had he worried about her? She was an enticing mix of naiveté and trouble, needing aid but not deserving it, and his fury soared.

"What in the hell are you doing?" he barked.

"You two know each other?" Lauretta asked.

"No," Miss Hamilton said at the same moment that Tristan said, "Yes."

She wasn't attired as scandalously as a whore, but she was definitely wearing a gown that was more risqué than the one she'd had on earlier in the day. It was cut very low in the front, her corset laced very tight to present a spectacular amount of cleavage he hadn't noticed during her interview.

Her hair had been styled into fat ringlets that dangled on her shoulders. Her lips, eyes, and cheeks had been enhanced with cosmetics. She was pretty as a picture, a ravishing, refined beauty who exuded charm, grace, and just enough innocence to tantalize a man's fantasies.

What would it be like to lie down with her, to thrust himself between her smooth, shapely thighs?

"Are you insane," he snapped, "offering yourself like this?"

"I told you my condition was dire," she snapped right back. "Did you think I was joking?"

"Let me get this straight: This morning, you hoped to be governess to an impressionable young girl, but this evening, you're selling yourself to the highest bidder?"

"That about covers it," she retorted. She glared at Lauretta. "Would you get him out of here?"

"Are you positive? He's a brilliant prospect, and he could—"

"I loathe him," Miss Hamilton interrupted.

"Oh."

Lauretta was speechless, and Tristan was a bit undone himself.

He couldn't remember when he'd last been so thoroughly insulted, and the derogatory comment rattled loose a choice he'd never intended to make.

"I'll take her," he curtly fumed.

"What?" both women asked.

"I said, I'll take her."

He grabbed Miss Hamilton by the arm and started out.

"Captain Odell . . . Miss Hamilton . . ."

Lauretta was confused, uncertain if she should stop him or not.

"I don't want to go with him!" Miss Hamilton insisted, but he kept on.

"Captain Odell," Lauretta called, "perhaps we should discuss this."

"There's nothing to discuss except the contract. I'll have my clerk come by tomorrow to hash out the details."

"But . . . but . . . I can't have rumors circulating that she went with you against her will. We've had some gossip lately about our procedures. Word might get back to—say—Lord Redvers, and he'd be angry."

"Miss Hamilton is very happy," he replied. "There's been no coercion."

"Ha!" Miss Hamilton huffed.

"If anyone complains, send him to me. I'll take full responsibility."

"Mrs. Bainbridge!" Miss Hamilton wailed, but Lauretta must have recollected the finder's fee she'd be paid. She pulled herself together and smiled.

"This is for the best, Miss Hamilton. Trust me. In the end, you'll be glad."

Tristan stomped to the stairs and marched down, his grip on Miss Hamilton tight as a vise.

Chapter 4

❧

"WHAT, precisely, were you planning to tell your sisters?"

"I hardly see how that's any of your business."

"Since I just bought you like a hog at a fair, everything about you is my bloody business."

"Don't curse at me."

"Then don't act like a fool. I can't abide an imprudent woman."

"If that's the case, we won't get on. I don't have a prudent bone in my body."

"I won't argue with that. You're crazy as a bedbug."

After a tense, uncomfortable carriage ride, he'd brought her to Lord Hastings's mansion in Mayfair. The house was quiet, everyone abed, and they were ensconced in a front parlor, a candle lit, the door closed so that they were sequestered in a most improper fashion.

Helen sat on a sofa, watching as he went to the sideboard and poured himself a tall glass of liquor. He leaned against the cupboard, drinking, observing her as if she was a lunatic he'd rescued from an insane asylum.

"You're broke and you're in trouble," he fumed, "yet

you imagine you can solve your dilemma by becoming a courtesan?"

"It seemed like a good idea at the time."

"A good idea!" he shouted.

"Will you be silent?" she hissed. "I don't want a servant to come down and find me in here alone with you."

"How can it matter if you're with me? You're my mistress, remember? I'm allowed special privileges."

"I don't care what happened with Mrs. Bainbridge; I will *not* be your mistress."

"Oh, really?"

"Yes, really, so you needn't bother contacting her. Whatever terms you offer, I will refuse."

He scowled. "Are you claiming you'd give yourself to a stranger, but you won't consider an arrangement with me?"

"Yes, that's exactly what I'm claiming."

"Why is that?"

"Because you're bossy and cruel, and I can't stand a man who thinks he knows everything."

"It doesn't take much intellect to come across smarter than you."

"See what I mean? You're a vain brute, which I can't abide. I've put up with plenty of male nonsense in my life, what with my father and his problems, and I won't tolerate any from you. So if you've said all you need to say, I'll just be going."

She stood, determined to march out, appearing much more brazen than she felt. It was the middle of the night and pitch-black outside. The notion of traipsing through London was terrifying, but the prospect of staying with Odell was even more odious.

What were his rights to her? Did he *own* her? Could he prevent her from leaving?

She wasn't sure, but she was anxious to escape his horrid presence, hurry home, and lick her wounds.

She couldn't even sell herself in a brothel and have it

turn out as it was supposed to! Was there any endeavor at which she wouldn't fail?

"Sit down, Miss Hamilton," he said.

"No."

She took a step toward the door and he shouted again.

"Sit down!"

"Is that how you talk to the sailors on your ship? It may cow them into obedience, but it has no effect on me at all. I suggest you lower your voice and mind your manners."

In reply, he glowered so maliciously that, despite her bold statement, she stumbled to a chair and plopped down.

"Here is what we shall do," he pompously announced.

"*We* shan't do anything. I'm going home, and if I'm lucky—which I haven't been so far—I'll never set eyes on you again."

"You're not leaving, Miss Hamilton. By your actions, you've proven yourself incapable of rational decision-making."

"I was merely trying to provide for my sisters."

"By selling yourself in a brothel?"

"You were there, too, Mr. High-and-Mighty. Did you stop by for a cup of tea?"

His cheeks flushed. "I had . . . personal reasons for being there. I needn't explain myself to you."

"Having a quick tumble, were you? With who? Mrs. Bainbridge?"

"Miss Hamilton! Must you constantly be impertinent?"

"Yes, I must."

"I'm prepared to do you a favor, so be silent and listen."

"What is it? I'm absolutely on pins and needles waiting to hear."

"You will work for me."

She inhaled sharply. "I will not be your mistress!"

She jumped up, ready to march out again, and he stomped over, so that they were toe-to-toe. He was very tall, and very irate, and it was definitely a sight, having all that male umbrage lorded over her.

She'd never previously had to deal with a furious man. The bulk of her experience had been obtained through occasional visits by her father when she was a girl. He'd always been full of fun and mischief and grandiose plans that never came to fruition. He'd never raised his voice or waxed indignant on any topic.

How was she to handle a very angry, very arrogant Captain Odell?

She had no idea, but she didn't retreat. Feminine instinct told her to stand her ground, to show she wasn't afraid of him—and she wasn't.

She seemed to know things about him that she had no means of knowing—the most relevant being her certainty that his bark was much worse than his bite. He might grumble and nag, but he would never hurt her.

"You will work for me," he started again, "as my ward's governess, the position for which you interviewed this morning."

"I'm sure this will come as a huge surprise to you, Captain, but I don't want the job."

"You don't want it?" He looked as if he might faint.

With his having purchased her from Mrs. Bainbridge, she had an inkling of his ruse. He was offering honest employment, but if she accepted and moved into the mansion, she had no doubt that he'd attempt carnal mischief.

"No. So . . . if you'll excuse me? It's a long way back to our boardinghouse, and my sisters will be worried."

She tried to step by him, but he grabbed her arm and snarled, "Just a damned minute!"

He whipped her around to face him, and she bumped into him so that her chest was pressed to his, their legs tangled together.

For a brief instant, they were frozen in place, and to her astonishment, there was a charge of energy flowing between them. Their proximity made the air sizzle with excitement. Her anatomy was enlivened. Her pulse raced, her cheeks heated, then—as if he'd been burned—he released her so swiftly that she nearly fell.

They glared, breathing hard, as if they were quarreling, and she supposed they were.

"You are the most obstinate, exasperating woman I've ever met," he seethed.

"And *you* are the most irritating, annoying man."

He was about to hurl another insult, but he reined himself in, visibly tamping down all the rude remarks he was yearning to hurl.

"We've gotten off to a bad start," he stated, "so let's begin again."

"You can say whatever you wish, but I will not be your mistress."

"Miss Hamilton! Why must my every comment precipitate a battle with you?"

"Because I'm fighting for my life, and I intend to go down swinging."

"Well, shut up for once. I'm trying to help you."

"A likely story."

"Miss Hamilton!" His patience was exhausted. "Don't speak! Don't complain! Just listen!"

He dragged her to the sofa and pushed her down onto it.

"There is a tender of decent employment on the table," he said. "Accept it immediately."

"No."

"Why on earth not?"

"I don't trust you."

"I don't care. Simply say *yes*. Stop being such an ingrate."

"Since the moment we met, you've been a total beast. Why should I imagine you're serious? Why would you suddenly be kind to me?"

"I have decided—as you so prettily put it—to have mercy on the destitute children of a fellow soldier. I had planned to tell you this morning. That's why I came outside, but then I caught you drinking, so I changed my mind."

"I wasn't drinking!" He frowned, dubious, and she insisted, "I wasn't!"

"I'll believe you—for now."

She threw up her hands. "Oh, for pity's sake."

"But so long as you're working here, I won't allow such misbehavior. I'll expect you to be a model of decorum at all times."

She wanted to continue protesting her innocence, to call him a conceited bully, an overbearing lout, but the most exhaustive wave of weariness swept over her.

She was only twenty-four, but she'd been swimming upstream since she was a young girl. Her mother had died when Amelia was born, when Helen herself was just twelve, and the family's burdens had fallen on her shoulders.

She had raised her sisters, had held on to their home. *She* had juggled the creditors and paid the bills. She had struggled and struggled, but it had all been for naught.

There was nothing left of what had been, and Odell was tossing her a rope, offering to pull her out of the ocean of debt and despair where she'd been drowning. The chance she'd been seeking had arrived, and she needed to close her mouth and do whatever he said.

For Jane and Amelia, she told herself. She could endure any torment in order to know that they were safe.

"I will remain so piously sober," she vowed, "that you'll think I'm an evangelical missionary."

At hearing her acquiesce, he reverted to his smug self. "Good. Now we're getting somewhere."

"What will my salary be?"

"We'll discuss it tomorrow."

"Fine." She nodded sweetly, the very picture of accommodation. "Will the position come with room and board?"

"Of course."

"What about my sisters?"

"How old are they?"

"Jane is eighteen, and Amelia is twelve."

"My ward, Rose, is twelve as well. Amelia will be her companion, and you can school them together."

She scowled, wondering if it was some sort of trick,

but he seemed sincere. Why would he act so magnani-
mously?

"What a lovely gesture," she replied, stunned by his generosity. "Amelia has been so lonely since we moved to London. She'll be excited to have a friend."

"As will Rose."

"They'll get on like thieves in a thicket."

"Yes, they will."

"What shall we do with Jane? You won't demand that
she serve as a maid, will you?"

"No."

He scoffed as if it was the most preposterous question
he'd ever heard, and she breathed a sigh of relief. No matter how bad things became, Helen was determined to see
her sister wed to a husband befitting her prior station.

"What will she—" Helen tried to say, but he interrupted
her.

"Once again, we'll figure it out later. In the meantime,
let's get you home. I'll send a carriage to fetch the three
of you at ten o'clock in the morning."

Helen stood, and she gazed at him, overcome with such
powerful emotions of gratitude and joy that she could
barely keep from grabbing him and pulling him into a
tight hug.

"Thank you," she murmured.

"You're welcome."

"You'll never regret this as long as you live. I swear it."

"I regret it already."

She glowered at him. "You won't even know we're here."

"I seriously doubt it."

They headed for the door, walking side by side, when
he glanced down at her.

"Always remember," he warned, "that I'm responsible
for my wards. They're impressionable children, so no
flirting and no drinking."

Just when she thought he was being marvelous!

"Do be quiet, Captain Odell. You insult me with your
complaints about my character."

"I'm taking a huge risk by hiring you."

"No you're not, but be quiet anyway."

They started out again, when he paused, looking uncomfortable.

"I need one other thing from you," he said.

"What is it?"

"The . . . ah . . . curse you leveled? Would you please lift it?"

She smirked, delighted to have the upper hand for a change. He was a sailor; she'd known he'd be a superstitious devil!

"I have no idea how. You'll have to take your chances."

MIRIAM Seymour, Michael's sixteen-year-old cousin, knelt on the floor, her eye pressed to the keyhole so she could spy on Captain Odell.

"You will work for me," Odell was saying, "as my ward's governess . . ."

At his remark, Miriam bit down a gasp of astonishment. She couldn't see Odell, but she could clearly see the woman to whom he was speaking. She was very beautiful, and thus, the exact opposite sort of person Miriam and her mother, Maud, would ever want in the house.

Miriam had discovered the pair after coming downstairs in a failed bid to bump into Michael. She was dressed in nightgown and robe, her hair down and brushed out, and she'd been hiding on the landing, waiting for him to return so she could descend and pretend she couldn't sleep and was retrieving a glass of warm milk.

With Michael having known her since she was a baby, he treated her like a little sister, and she was desperate to have him view her in a different light. He didn't realize it was time to pick a bride, and he remained oblivious to the obvious solution: He should marry Miriam and keep his fortune in the family.

Why *shouldn't* she be his countess? It made perfect sense.

When the front door had been flung open, she'd huddled up above, expecting Michael to enter, but being shocked to find Odell dragging in a protesting, recalcitrant female.

For a purported *governess*, she was extremely uppity, having no concept of her lowly status or of the captain's elevated role in the Seymour household. She was very rude, arguing with him as she prepared to stomp out against his wishes.

"Just a damned minute!" the captain barked, as Miriam leapt away and raced for the stairs.

She burst into her mother's boudoir, hastening through the sitting room to the bedchamber beyond.

"Mother! Mother!" she panted as she hurried in.

"My goodness, what is it?"

"You'll never guess."

"What? What? Is it Michael? Were you finally able to wrangle a kiss?"

Miriam stumbled to a halt, hating to witness her mother's excitement and that she was about to dash it. Maud always told Miriam that she had no feminine wiles, that she didn't know how to flirt or entice.

The criticism hurt. Miriam was trying as hard as she could with Michael, but she couldn't help it that she was poor, quiet, and plain, while he preferred girls who were rich, vivacious, and attractive.

"No, I didn't see Michael. He's not back yet, but you'll never believe what I *did* see."

Maud yawned, her enthusiasm for the chat having vanished in an instant.

"Tell me, then let me get to bed. I'm tired of dawdling up here, hoping that you've managed to push matters forward with Michael."

"Captain Odell has hired a governess for Rose."

"What?"

Maud threw off the blankets and scrambled to the floor, her mob cap bobbing, her robe rippling behind her.

"He's hired a governess," Miriam repeated.

"When?"

"She's with him in the parlor—even as we speak."

"Are you sure?"

"Yes. I listened at the keyhole. I heard them very clearly."

"The wretch didn't consult me!"

Since the captain's arrival, it had been Maud's constant lament.

For years, she'd run the properties and supervised Michael and Rose with very little interference. With Odell appearing on the scene, she couldn't so much as suggest a servant dust a table without said servant scurrying to the captain to ask if Maud's order should be obeyed.

"It's awful how he ignores you," Miriam commiserated, "and he should have sought your opinion, because I can't imagine where he found her. She looks as if she's been trolling for customers at Vauxhall Gardens."

"Miriam! Honestly."

"Well, she does. Wait till you see her."

"Is she pretty?"

"Very."

"She seems to be a woman of low . . . morals?"

"Yes. How could he bring her into the house? It's an insult to us."

"It certainly is. Was the captain interested in her in a manly way?"

Miriam thought of how the captain had yanked the woman inside, how he'd kept her close and loomed over her, and Miriam wished that, someday, a similarly handsome fellow—Michael, perhaps?—might manhandle her in the same rough fashion.

"Definitely. He was definitely *interested*."

"Ooh, this is bad," Maud muttered and began to pace. "This is very, very bad."

"What shall we do?"

"I don't know, but I'll think of something."

"You won't let her stay, will you?"

"Absolutely not. With the misery I intend to heap on her, I'll have her out of here by tomorrow afternoon."

*   *   *

"THIS is where you live?"

"Yes. Why?"

Tristan peered out the carriage window, staring at the dreary, dilapidated buildings lining the dark street. There were no street lamps, no candles burning in any of the windows.

He turned toward Miss Hamilton. She was illuminated by a beam of moonlight, and appeared delicate and ethereal, like a wraith from another world. For a fleeting moment, he was disturbingly drawn to her, as if he might like to kiss her.

He hadn't a clue from where the peculiar impulse had sprung, and to his horror, he recalled the love potion she'd drunk, the curse she'd imposed. Frantic questions careened in his head: Was the potion taking effect? Was a supernatural force causing an attraction to form?

He shook off the absurd perception, remembering he'd just been in a brothel, and his arousal hadn't had opportunity to wane. That was all. His heightened regard had nothing to do with curses or potions or anything else. It was a purely physical reaction to a beautiful female.

Still, he slid over, squashing himself into the corner, trying to move as far away as possible given the small confines of the carriage's interior. He glanced out again, letting his temper flare, convinced that a bit of fury would distract him from his fascination.

"You rented a room here?" he fumed.

"Don't scold as if I did it on purpose. My funds are completely depleted; it wasn't as if I had a lot of choices."

"You trotted off, leaving your sisters alone? Are you mad?"

"They locked up behind me."

"Well, that certainly has me relieved."

"And nobody *trotted* off. I was keeping a scheduled appointment."

"You were pitching your wares in a damned brothel!"

"Don't mount your moral high-horse. You continue to forget that I met *you* while I was there."

He snorted with disgust. "Your mind works in the strangest ways."

"Doesn't it, though?"

A coachman opened the door and lowered the step, and Tristan gazed out, fretting over her walking to the stoop and climbing the stairs. The very idea raised the hairs on the back of his neck.

She clambered out and Tristan descended after her, but she strutted into the building without pausing so he could escort her.

Was the crazed woman trying to be robbed? Raped? Murdered?

He didn't understand how she'd survived so long. The Good Lord, in His infinite wisdom, watched over idiots and fools, so He likely had a full-time job watching over *her.*

"Wait for me," he grumbled to the outriders, and he marched after her and stumbled into the shadowy foyer.

The air was very cold, and the place reeked of decay and mold and tormented lives. He actually shivered with alarm, imagining her and her sisters passing their days in such a terrible spot.

"Miss Hamilton?" he said. "Where are you?"

"Are you still here?" she asked from up above him, and he realized she was already halfway up the stairs.

He'd told her that he'd send a carriage for them in the morning, but he was overcome by dread, as if—should he leave her behind—something might happen, that she might be harmed or he might never see her again.

To his dismay, it dawned on him that he was anxious to have her close by so he could keep her out of trouble. He didn't dare permit her to be off on her own and unprotected. Not for another second.

"Are your sisters asleep?"

"Amelia probably is, but Jane is likely awake. Why?"

He started up the stairs, not inclined to let her go any

farther by herself. He found her on the landing, and he neared until his body was touching hers.

He could feel her warm breath on his cheek. A wayward strand of her soft hair tickled his chin. He could smell her, and it was an enticing scent of clean skin with a hint of flowers underneath. The odor tantalized his male sensibilities, making him contemplate behaviors he had no business contemplating.

"Let's get your things," he whispered.

"Why?"

"You're all coming with me."

"Now?"

"Yes, Miss Hamilton. Now. There's no reason to delay."

"But . . . I owe rent to the landlord."

"I'll handle it tomorrow. Let's go!"

Chapter 5

"HOW was your evening?"

"Perfect."

Michael stared at Tristan, his expression blank, trying to look like an innocent who had just been deflowered, but it was scarcely the case.

Tristan was very old and very stuffy, and he yearned to believe that Michael was a naïve boy, so Michael wouldn't shatter his illusions. But for the prior two years, Michael had been sneaking off to brothels with his friends. Several of his acquaintances already kept mistresses, and Michael couldn't fathom why Tristan was so prim on the subject.

He was relieved that Tristan had allowed visits to the brothel. Michael could now go as often as he liked, and he wouldn't have to lie to Tristan about what he was doing.

Though he'd only known Tristan a few months, he liked him very much, and wanted them to be close. He didn't want them fighting over money or morals.

"I apologize for leaving you there all night," Tristan said.

"You shouldn't. It was very . . . exhilarating."

"I trust the two ladies . . . ah . . . taught you the pertinent details?"

"They were very adept at their instruction."

"Well . . . good."

Michael bit down a laugh. Tristan was usually so composed and unruffled, and it was humorous to see him flustered. Michael would have liked to give him a blow-by-blow description of the event, but he doubted the poor man could withstand such a salacious conversation.

He hadn't been to bed, and he should have been exhausted, but he wasn't. The episode had enlivened him, and he was alert and eager to face the day. Miriam had cornered him, inviting him to accompany her on a ride in the park, and he'd said yes.

"Why didn't you come back for me?" he asked. "I was watching the clock, expecting you to storm in and scold me for having so much fun."

"I couldn't get over there."

"Why?"

"We had a situation arise. Since this is your home, and I am simply the trustee, I need to discuss it with you to be sure you're amenable with my decision."

It was an odd game they played. Michael was Earl of Hastings, the owner of the title, fortune, and property, but Tristan had all the actual power. Tristan constantly took action on his own, but he was gracious enough to seek Michael's opinion and pretend that it mattered, when they both knew that, in the end, Tristan would do whatever he wanted.

Michael was only mildly begrudging of the arrangement. On the one hand, he wished his father had trusted him with real authority. On the other, he was glad he hadn't yet been forced to assume so much responsibility, and he supposed there was some justice in Tristan being in charge.

After all, Tristan was Charles Seymour's oldest son,

and in a fairer world, Tristan would be earl, instead of Michael. For the moment, Michael was happy to let him run things. Over the next few years, as Michael came of age, he would have plenty of chances to succeed—or screw up royally!

"What happened?" he inquired.

"I'm certain you recall Miss Hamilton."

"I'm sorry, but I don't."

"She was here yesterday, interviewing to be Rose's governess."

"The attractive redhead?"

"Yes."

"Tell me you realized your mistake and hired her."

"I have."

"Marvelous. You're so stubborn; what changed your mind?"

"I learned she was in a terrible spot—mere hours away from being tossed out on the street with her two sisters."

"How awful for them."

"I brought the three of them to live with us. Is it all right with you?"

"Are the others as pretty as she is?"

"Exact copies."

Michael grinned. "Then I'm delighted. We can always make room for some pretty girls."

At the cheeky comment, Tristan glowered. "You should also know that they're a tad notorious."

"Notorious women? I'm more thrilled by the second."

"Others might not approve of our empathy or hospitality. There might be gossip."

Michael shrugged. "Why would I care?"

"I was hoping you'd say that. It seems their father was an infamous scapegrace, renowned for his peccadilloes. He was shot in a duel by the duke of Clarendon."

"Their father was Harry Hamilton?"

"Yes. Did you know him?"

"Of course. He used to chum around with Father on occasion. They got up to all sorts of mischief."

"That explains where Miss Hamilton comes by it."

"Comes by what?"

"None of your business, but I will expect you to act with the utmost decorum at all times."

"Why wouldn't I?"

"Amelia is only twelve—"

"Too young for me."

"She'll be Rose's companion."

"Wonderful. Rose needs a friend. Maud has kept her too isolated; she's lonely."

"My thoughts exactly. As to the other two—Miss Helen Hamilton and Miss Jane Hamilton—"

"How old is Jane?"

"Eighteen—the same age as you, which concerns me."

"You worry too much."

"Ha! From where I'm sitting, I don't worry nearly enough. You will behave yourself. I've allowed you regular visits to the whores, so that they can tend your masculine *needs*. There's no reason for you to bother Helen or Jane Hamilton."

"I won't. You have my word."

Even as he voiced the vow, he was awhirl with questions. Jane Hamilton was eighteen. Did she enjoy flirtation? Was she truly as fetching as her sister? It would certainly be intriguing if she was!

"Good," Tristan said. "Now get going on your ride with Miriam. The carriage has been out in the drive for the past hour. I'm sure she grows impatient."

Michael rolled his eyes. He often went to the park with Miriam, but it was ludicrous to say they *rode* together. Miriam was afraid of horses and of heights, so she trudged in a coach, a servant handling the reins, while Michael pranced along beside.

Although she fancied him, the feeling wasn't reciprocated. She was like an annoying sibling, and he could never be interested in a girl who was terrified of her own shadow.

He strolled out and marched down the hall to the foyer, where he was irked to see Miriam hovering, watching for him.

"Are you ready?" he asked.

"Yes. It's such a lovely day. I'm so glad you could make time for me."

"For you, Miriam, I can always make time."

In light of the designs she had on him, it was probably cruel to socialize with her. His amiability gave her the wrong impression, but what could he do?

She and her mother had lived with them for more than a decade. They were part of the family. It wasn't as if he could pretend she didn't exist, and he would never hurt her by telling her the truth: They would never become betrothed, despite how fervidly she wished it.

He'd extended his arm to escort her out to the carriage when footsteps sounded on the stairs. He stopped and glanced up to see a young lady, who had to be none other than Jane Hamilton, descending.

Her cloak and bonnet were worn, providing evidence of her penury, but she was extremely pretty—even more winsome than her sister Helen.

Their gazes locked, and it was the strangest thing, but his heart thudded with excitement. He felt as if he'd always known her, as if they were friends being reunited after a lengthy separation.

He shook off the peculiar perception, and he smiled up at her.

"Miss Hamilton, I presume?" he said.

"Yes."

Miriam stiffened with affront, and instantly he recognized that nothing in his home would ever be the same again.

The weeks ahead would be filled with drama, manipulation, and scheming, but from the looks of Jane Hamilton, she'd be able to hold her own against his plain, fussy cousins.

"Come down, come down," he told her, gesturing, urging her on.

She continued boldly, her stride not faltering, her gaze never leaving his. As she reached the bottom, she sauntered over, not evincing a hint of subservience or awe, which was shocking and refreshing.

Women constantly fawned over him; Maud and Miriam were particularly exasperating, and he was weary of false flattery and admiration. He and Jane Hamilton would get on swimmingly.

"Hello," she said, smiling too.

"Michael Seymour, at your service." He bowed flamboyantly. "Welcome to my humble abode."

"Humble?" she tartly responded. "I've already counted thirty-five rooms."

"Miss Hamilton!" Miriam hissed. "Where are your manners? You stand before the earl of Hastings! Show the proper respect!"

"Would you like me to curtsy, Lord Hastings?"

"No, but I would like you to call me Michael. Will you?"

"Only if you'll call me Jane."

"I will."

"Really, Michael," Miriam scolded, "I hardly think it's appropriate for one of her station to act so familiarly. Especially when she's just met you."

"I don't mind, Miriam, so you shouldn't, either." To his surprise, he didn't want the encounter with Jane to end. "Were you going out, Jane?"

"Yes. In the last few hours, so much has transpired that my head is spinning. I thought I'd take a walk to explore the neighborhood."

"You must come with us, instead," he insisted. "We're off to the park."

"Michael," Miriam fumed through clenched teeth, "could I speak with you privately for a moment?"

"No."

"There's something I must tell you." She leveled a glare at Jane that could have melted lead.

Jane was no fool, and she graciously offered, "If Miss Seymour would rather I didn't join you, I'm happy to decline."

"My cousin wasn't about to say any such thing." He scowled at Miriam, daring her to contradict him, but she never would. "Since you'll be staying with us, we must begin introducing you to our acquaintances. Today is as good a time as any."

Miriam couldn't bear it, and she muttered, "Michael, I won't be seen out in public with her. She is a servant!"

"No, she isn't," he sternly replied. "She and her sisters are my guests. They are here at my specific invitation."

He told the lie in order to thwart any nonsense from her and her mother. Miriam appeared as if she might explode, and Jane was unsettled, too. It was clear she understood that Miriam would be an enemy, and that she would need to tread cautiously.

"Were you aware, Jane," he asked, "that I knew your father?"

"Oh."

Emotion flared in her expression, dismay or despair, and he rushed to quell it.

"He was a jolly fellow. I liked him very much."

"Oh!" She brightened, and there were tears in her eyes. "Thank you for saying so. I loved him very much, and I never hear anything civil about him."

He patted her hand, giving comfort and support.

"Let's go, shall we?"

"Let's do," Jane said, while Miriam was too peeved to comment.

He escorted them both out, ignoring Miriam's pique, pretending that she wasn't having a tantrum.

Outside, the carriage and his horse awaited them. When a footman moved to help Miriam climb in, Michael stepped forward and did a bit of penance by assisting her himself.

When he turned to assist Jane, she was over by his horse, stroking its neck, whispering in its ear.

"What's his name?" she asked.

"Bandit."

"He's a beauty. I love horses. We had several when we lived in the country. Mine was named Dolly."

"You don't still have her?"

"No, they took her when we lost Father's property."

"Who took her?"

"Why . . . the duke's men. After the . . . ah . . . duel, he bought Father's debts, and he foreclosed. They trotted off with my horse while I watched out the window. I'd had her since I was a child."

There was an awkward silence, as a vivid scene entered his mind, of her standing in an empty parlor, while strangers out in her driveway made off with her most precious possession. He almost felt as if he'd been standing there with her, and he suffered no small amount of outrage on her behalf.

Suddenly, he was very, very glad that Tristan had brought her to their home.

"I'm sorry," he said. "I didn't know that had happened to you. I knew about your father's bad end, but I wasn't apprised of the other consequences."

She chuckled miserably. "Don't pay any attention to me. I'm still a little raw over all that's occurred."

"Who wouldn't be?"

"Michael," Miriam snapped, interrupting their tête-à-tête, "are you ready?"

"Yes, I'm ready." He smiled at Jane. "May I help you in?"

But even as he voiced the question, a brilliant notion dawned on him. "Or would you rather ride with me?"

"Ride . . . with you?"

"Yes. We have numerous mounts that would be acceptable for a lady."

"I would *love* to ride. It's been an eternity since I have!"

"Then ride you shall, and you may do so whenever you're in the mood. Simply send a servant out to inform the lads in the stable. They'll deliver an animal to the front door."

"I am so grateful. You've given me a wonderful gift."

He gestured to a footman, who hurried to the stable to have another horse saddled, but when Michael looked back at her, she was crying.

His heart made that odd thudding motion again and, at viewing her woe, he was stricken.

"What is it?" He stepped nearer, being assailed by her heat, her scent. He took hold of her hand. "Don't you truly want to ride? You don't have to."

"No, no, it's not that."

"What then?"

"You and Captain Odell have been so kind to me, at a time when kindness has been in short supply."

For a brief moment, the rest of the world fell away. There was no house, no carriage with Miriam seething inside, no servants hovering. There was just him and her, and the feel of her slender hand clasped in his own.

He swiped a thumb across her cheeks to dry her tears.

"Everything will be all right now," he murmured.

"Yes, it will."

"Michael," Miriam complained, "I hate to pester you, but what's the delay? Mother wants me home by four, so I really need to get going."

Michael glanced over at her. "I've learned that Jane loves horses. She's decided to ride with me—instead of in the carriage. We're having a mount saddled for her."

"She *loves* horses?" Miriam was aghast.

"Isn't it marvelous?" he said. "She and I have so much in common."

Panic flashed in Miriam's eyes.

*   *   *

"LET'S count all the ways we're alike."

"I'm betting it's a lot."

Rose Seymour gazed at Amelia, desperate to please her. She didn't have any friends, because Maud never allowed it. Maud was supposed to have acted in Rose's best interests, but she hadn't taken her role seriously.

Rose never went visiting; other girls were never invited over. She spent all her time in the nursery, and since she was too old for a nanny and hadn't had a governess in ages, she was always alone.

Yet suddenly, like a gift from heaven, Amelia had appeared. The minute Rose had the chance she would run downstairs and hug Tristan so hard that he wouldn't be able to breathe for a week!

From the instant he'd arrived, Rose had known he would be kind. That first day, he'd asked what she needed, but she'd been too embarrassed to tell him she was lonely and simply wanted some children with whom to play.

How had he guessed her deepest desire? She would be grateful forever!

"My father is dead," Rose stated.

"So is mine."

"My mother died when I was born."

"Mine too!" Amelia said.

"I have two brothers—Michael and Tristan."

"And I have two sisters—Helen and Jane."

They giggled.

"It's like we've been living parallel lives, without even knowing."

"Yes, it is."

"Do you think it was fated that we be together?"

"Absolutely."

Rose tugged Amelia to her feet.

They were in her bedchamber, and they walked over and stood in front of the mirror. They were the same height and had the same bodily shape, the only difference being that Amelia had auburn hair and green eyes, while Rose had blond hair and blue eyes.

Their hair was long, and they both had it tied with a ribbon.

"Look! We could be twins!" Amelia gushed.

"Let's pretend that we are. It will be our secret."

"We were separated at birth. You were raised here by your rich father, while I was sent away to poor relatives, and no one knew where I'd gone."

"You've been distressed and penniless, but my dashing brother Tristan found you for me."

"I like that ending very much."

They giggled again.

Rose leaned in, peering intently, taking in all the details.

Prior to Rose being introduced to Amelia, Tristan had told her that, recently, Amelia had had a very rough time of it, that she and her sisters needed some understanding and support.

He'd asked Rose to help him make Amelia feel at home, and Rose had been glad to assist.

She studied Amelia's dress, which was faded and excessively mended. It was too short, too, as if Amelia had grown taller, but there had been no money to purchase a new garment.

At the thought of it—of her dear companion in dire straits—Rose was furious. How could such a lovely person be forced to endure such hardship? Why was the world such a cruel place?

"Let me show you something," she said.

"What is it?"

"My cloakroom is full of dresses that I never wear. I want to give them to you."

"Oh, I couldn't," Amelia protested.

"If you would take them, Amelia, I would be very happy."

Rose smiled, and Amelia smiled, too.

* * *

"CAPTAIN, you know I hate to make a fuss, but for once, I really must say what's on my mind."

Maud struggled for calm, anxious to appear pleasant and cordial, but she didn't imagine she was succeeding.

"Your comment implies that you've been overly reticent in the past."

"I've gone out of my way to be amenable."

"Have you?"

It had been utter hell dealing with him for the previous few months, and she'd tried to be gracious, to politely accede to his edicts and whims, but it was becoming ever more difficult to be civil, to be silent.

She'd spent an entire decade ingratiating herself to Charles, Michael's father, so it had come as an enormous shock when his will had been read and she'd learned that Tristan Odell had been entrusted with everything, while Maud had been left with nothing at all.

It had taken six weeks for Odell to be notified of his guardianship, for him to travel to London and assume his duties. Once he'd arrived, he'd jumped in with a vengeance. Her allowance had been stopped, her access to the bank accounts rescinded, and her authority over Rose and Michael revoked.

It was galling and maddening, and with his giving a job to Helen Hamilton in the middle of the night, Maud had reached the end of her rope.

She and Miriam resided in the mansion, too, and they couldn't have their status damaged by an association with the Hamiltons. Nor could Maud bear that she wouldn't be directing Helen Hamilton in her role as part of the staff.

Enough was enough!

"Is there a problem?" Odell asked, exhibiting the implacable composure that drove her up the wall.

They were in the library, with him sitting behind the massive desk, which had been *hers*. Now, he'd claimed the desk and room as his own, and she stood across from him like a supplicant.

She pulled up a chair and sat without being invited. "You've gone a tad too far this time."

"In what area?"

"With bringing the Hamilton sisters into the house."

"Why is that?"

"What will people say?"

"Who cares what they say?"

She sucked in a deep breath, let it out slowly, fighting to retain her poise so she wouldn't shout at him.

"I realize you're a seafaring man, Captain, and from another country to boot—"

"I'm from Scotland, Maud. My father paid for schooling in Edinburgh. You talk as if I was raised on the moon."

"I'm not criticizing your antecedents, Captain."

"It certainly sounded like it."

The conversation wasn't proceeding as she'd hoped. He was in a surly mood, displaying his typical contrariness, and she wondered if she'd ever grow accustomed to it.

She had big plans for Tristan Odell. He had control over all the Seymour money, so he was the perfect choice to be her next husband. Yet if she could ever manage to coax a marriage proposal out of him, how would she abide that arrogant attitude?

Her first husband had been timid and easily manipulated, and she'd loathed him for his compliant nature, but she'd relished it, too. She'd never had to argue or cajole to get her way. With Odell, they'd battle constantly.

"You must admit," she said, "that you're not familiar with London's social rules."

"I bet I know more about them than you'd guess."

"We have two young ladies in our midst—that being Miriam and Rose, and we have to think of their reputations."

"That's your concern?"

"Yes."

"Thank you for sharing it. Will there be anything else?"

He picked up a quill and dipped it in the ink jar, as if eager to dive into his correspondence. He was dismissing her, but she wouldn't go until she'd made her point.

"As a matter of fact, there are a few other topics I'd like to address."

A corner of his mouth quirked up, as if he was trying not to laugh at her. "What have I done, Maud, that has you in such a dither?"

"I've spoken with the oldest Miss Hamilton."

"Helen."

"Yes. I advised her that I'd assigned her a bed in the servants' quarters, located in the attic in the east wing, but she informs me that you've already seen to their arrangements."

"I have."

"I also showed her the nursery, where she should be teaching Rose, but she insists the room is small and drafty, so you've given her permission to open up the morning salon instead."

"I have," he said again.

"She claims she may furnish it however she likes, that she may buy books and supplies, and even . . . a . . . pianoforte."

She hurled the last like an invective, but the extravagance was beyond the pale.

She, Maud, no longer had money to purchase her clothing at Madam LaFarge's exclusive shop, but Miss Hamilton was to have an expensive musical instrument. It was grossly unfair.

"I want Rose and Amelia to be comfortable during their lessons," he blithely replied.

"And that's another of my complaints. How can it be appropriate for Rose to be educated with a girl who is so far beneath her?"

"As opposed to your method of not educating her at all?"

A muscle ticked in his cheek, clear evidence that she'd made him angry, which she hadn't meant to do.

"I sense that I've aggravated you."

"You have."

"It wasn't my intention, Captain. Please forgive me. It's difficult for me, not being consulted. I ran this household for years; I'm aware of what's necessary and fitting."

He shrugged. "I'm not used to debating every little detail. You shouldn't count on me seeking your opinion before I act."

"Am I to have any authority?" She sounded pitiful, as if she was begging for leftover scraps.

"You may implement any decision you wish—so long as it doesn't conflict with what I want to have happen."

So . . . there it was. He was a tyrant; he admitted it. She'd suspected the truth, but she'd danced around it, pretending nothing had changed.

"May I know where the Hamiltons will be sleeping?" she tightly inquired.

"I've had the maids air out the suites overlooking the rear garden."

They were the prettiest rooms in the house, saved for the most important visitors. It was shocking; it was an outrage.

"She is a *governess*, Captain. A servant. She and her sisters are a trio of homeless waifs, inflicting themselves on our charity."

"You couldn't be more wrong, Maud."

"What do you mean?"

He grinned, as if he was a cat toying with a mouse.

"Haven't you heard?" he said. "None of this was my doing. Michael has invited them to stay—as his special guests."

Michael was the earl. He owned the mansion. If he'd

elevated their status, there was no gainsaying him. Further argument was a waste of breath.

Maud spun and marched out, biting her cheek so hard that, by the time she reached her boudoir, she could taste blood in her mouth.

Chapter 6

❦

"WHERE the hell have you been?"

Helen jumped a foot and whipped around.

"Captain Odell! What are you doing in here?"

"Waiting for you. What does it look like?"

She was exhausted, exhilarated, grateful, confused, conflicted, and overwrought. It was nearly midnight, her lengthy day over, and she simply wanted to tumble into bed.

Rose and Amelia were inseparable. They shared a bedchamber, and after hours of giggling, had finally fallen asleep. Helen had trudged to her room, welcoming the quiet and the dark, only to find Odell sprawled in a chair by the window.

Apparently, he'd been there for some time. He was drinking a glass of liquor, and the decanter on the floor next to him was half empty.

They'd been living in the mansion for an entire week, with Helen maneuvering the hazards that came with joining a new household.

There'd been plenty of gossip and innuendo about her arrival, and a housemaid—a sullen girl named Lydia—had been particularly crass in suggesting how Helen might have *earned* her beautiful boudoir. Likewise, the earl's cousin Maud Seymour had been grouchy and difficult.

Other than those two, Helen was starting to feel as if she might eventually fit in.

She was determined to prove that she was deserving of the captain's generosity, so she worked very hard, getting up at the crack of dawn, enduring long hours at lessons for Rose and Amelia, then even longer ones after that shopping, visiting, and sightseeing.

Through it all, she hadn't run into Captain Odell a single time, and the situation had bothered her much more than it should.

She kept expecting him to check on them in the schoolroom, or that she would be summoned to the library to discuss Rose. At the very least, she thought she might bump into him on the stairs, but he'd been conspicuously absent, as if he was deliberately avoiding her.

She'd considered asking after him, perhaps requesting a meeting herself, but she'd had to have consulted the butler, and it would have been awkward. And really, why should she presume to have a heightened association with the captain? Why suppose that he would *want* to have a private chat?

He'd rescued her from dire straits and had provided honest employment, and it was ludicrous to imagine he viewed her as anything other than a servant. Yet, to her astonishment, he'd brazenly entered her bedchamber, and she couldn't ignore the spark of joy that rippled through her.

She was very glad to see him—but she couldn't let him know. Nor could she let him remain. If he was discovered, her job would be ended before it had truly begun.

"Get out," she insisted.

"No."

"I mean it. You can't stay."

She marched over to the door and clasped the knob, ready to fling it open and point out how he should quickly exit, but he didn't move. Neither did she.

"I asked you a question." He stared at her till her pulse raced.

"What was it again?"

"Where have you been?"

"I've been with Rose and Amelia, calming them sufficiently so they could sleep."

"It took till midnight?"

"Young girls can be quite silly."

He studied her as if he didn't believe her, as if he suspected she'd been out gallivanting, and at the notion, she almost laughed aloud.

If she'd wanted to leave the mansion—which she didn't—where on earth would she go? The only people she knew in London, that being her mother's relatives, loathed her because of her father. Who else would she have sneaked off to see?

"I've been working like a dog," she declared, "simply to make you happy."

"Have you?"

"Yes. I've become a slave, eager to do your bidding."

At that, he snorted. "Come here."

He downed his liquor and set the glass on the floor, and he held out his hand as if she should walk over and grab it.

"Why?"

"Don't argue with me. Just do as I say."

"Tell me what you want first."

"When you get over here, I'll show you."

Was he planning to force himself on her? She didn't think so. He wasn't the type, yet he definitely had a purpose in mind, and she was certain the result would *not* be to her benefit.

"Come!" he commanded, growing adamant, and she was torn as to whether she should.

He was her employer. Did she have a *right* to say no? What if she did? Would he fire her? Would he toss her and her sisters out on the street?

She knew he wouldn't. Though he pretended otherwise, he was too kind. She'd learned his secret. He was practically brimming with chivalry, and he couldn't conceal his gallant nature.

She sighed with resignation. Truth be told, she didn't want to refuse him. She was intrigued by him, more than a bit smitten and insanely attracted, and she was anxious to ascertain his intent.

Hesitantly, she took a few steps, and the moment she neared, he pulled her onto his lap. Her bottom rested on his thigh, and she was off balance, leaned forward, her breasts pressed to his broad chest.

The position was thrilling and shocking, but she didn't try to move away. He was all male, and she was assailed by his masculine scents: horses, brandy, tobacco.

"Have you been drinking, Captain?"

"Not enough to keep me from sneaking in here."

"Why did you?"

"Why are you hiding from me?"

"Hiding? I haven't been."

"I never see you anywhere."

"Have you been looking for me?"

"Yes." He seemed irked by the admission. "You're never around when I need you."

"That's because I'm always busy."

"Doing what?"

"Taking care of Rose, you oaf. Isn't that why you hired me?"

"You never come to supper."

It was the strangest comment ever, intimating that he'd been expecting her to and that he'd been angry when she'd failed to arrive.

"Was I supposed to join you for supper?"

"Yes, and you will accommodate me every night from now on. You and your sister Jane. At eight o'clock. I dine with Lord Hastings, as well as Miss and Mrs. Seymour. You and Jane are to be seated at the table with them. You are guests, not servants."

"Technically, I am a servant. I *work* for you, remember?"

"You're a guest. Lord Hastings decreed it."

"But . . . but . . ."

"What?" he asked when she couldn't finish.

"Mrs. Seymour informed me that we were to eat with the servants, so you're placing me in a terrible bind."

He grumbled low in his throat. "You are not to listen to a word that woman says, do you hear?"

"Yes, I hear."

"If you're confused as to how you are to behave and what you're allowed, you're to come straight to me."

Compliance was easier said than done. Mrs. Seymour had ruled the house for years, but Captain Odell had burst on the scene and usurped her authority.

The staff members liked him very much and didn't like Maud Seymour at all. They were in general agreement that things were much better since he'd taken over, but there was no denying that he'd stirred a pot of bitter feelings in Seymour.

Helen was no fool. It was dangerous to antagonize Mrs. Seymour, and with Odell pulling her in one direction and Mrs. Seymour pushing her in the other, Helen had to be cautious. The captain would be obeyed and Mrs. Seymour ignored. What an impossible tangle!

She was so immersed in thoughts of Mrs. Seymour that she was completely caught off guard when Odell dipped under her chin to nuzzle her nape. He nipped at the soft skin on her neck. She yelped with surprise and struggled to escape, but he merely tightened his grip.

"You smell good." His warm breath tickled her ear. "Why is that?"

"Because I wash frequently?"

He barked out a laugh. "Yes, I imagine that's it. You bathe. How refreshing."

"Are you feeling all right?"

"No, I'm quite drunk." He assessed her, and he scowled.

"I don't like having whole days go by where I don't speak with you."

"Really?"

"Yes, really. So you'll attend me every afternoon at four, to discuss Rose's progress."

"I'd like that; I think it's very wise."

"You'll meet with me in the morning, too."

"For what purpose?"

"Do I need a *purpose*, Miss Hamilton? As you mentioned, you work for me, so I don't believe I'm required to state a reason."

"No, you're not."

Helen was awhirl with excitement. Ten, four, and eight. Every day! She'd see him constantly, and at the prospect, she was ecstatic.

She couldn't explain why, but with his having rescued her, she felt bound to him in a powerful fashion, as if they were meant to be together, as if they *had* to be friends.

He appeared to sense it, too. They couldn't carry on as employer and employee. He was her knight in shining armor, while she was his damsel in distress. A personal relationship had been formed. They couldn't fight it, and it was futile for them to try.

"So . . . we're to have regular appointments," she mused.

"Yes."

"Now that we have your business out of the way, what else did you want? Have you another matter you wish to address?"

She was still perched on his lap, her chest crushed to his, an arm flung over his shoulder.

He was very close—too close!—and she could see the blue of his eyes, the tiny black flecks in the irises. He'd cut himself shaving, and there was a nick from the razor under his chin. His pirate's earring dangled from his ear, and she would have liked to flick at it with her finger.

His intent focus was on her mouth, their lips only inches apart, and his torrid concentration was thrilling.

"Yes," he said, "there is a topic I'm interested in reviewing."

"What is it?"

"Have you ever been kissed?"

"Kissed?" Her shocked tone was prim and prudish.

"Yes—kissing. I'm sure you've heard of it. It's when a man and a woman—"

"I know what it is, Captain. I'm twenty-four years old. I'm hardly a young maiden just out of the schoolroom."

"Then what is your answer?"

"I've been kissed dozens of times," she lied.

She recalled her fussy, pedantic neighbor, Wesley Smythewaite, an erstwhile suitor who'd briefly courted her when she was eighteen.

It was back when she actually thought the world might proceed as it was supposed to, that she might eventually marry and have a home and family of her own.

Wesley had bestowed exactly two kisses, cool, dry pecks on the lips that had been totally unsatisfactory and had guaranteed little in the way of future passion. As luck would have it, fate had intervened, so the romance was ended.

Her father had gotten himself involved in one of his peccadilloes, and Wesley's parents had severed all ties with Helen. Wesley hadn't had the courage to stand up to them, to insist that he would wed Helen anyway, and Helen had learned a brutal lesson about the treachery of men.

They were all spineless cads—although Captain Odell certainly seemed as if he might be different. She suspected that if he made a promise, wild horses couldn't force him to renege.

"You expect me to believe"—he looked extremely dubious—"that you've been kissed *dozens* of times?"

"When I resided in the country," she lied again, "I was rather popular."

She'd been too busy raising her sisters—with a deceased mother and an absent, unreliable father—to engage in any amour. She'd lived like a nun in a convent.

"All the boys mooned over you?"

"Of course."

"Why am I not surprised?"

"I'm not a flirt, though," she added, "despite how it sounds."

"Oh, no, not a flirt, but pardon me if I say that I'm not going to request permission."

"Permission for what?"

"I wish to be next in line. I can't figure out why, and it annoys the hell out of me, but I can't help myself."

In a quick motion, he stood, coming to his feet with her cradled in his arms as if she weighed no more than a feather.

He marched over to her bed and dumped her onto it. Before she could gather her wits to protest or squirm away, he followed her down and stretched out atop her, his body covering hers, so that she was pinned to the mattress.

He was very large, much larger than she, so he should have been crushing her, but he didn't feel heavy. Her torso welcomed the naughty positioning, rippling with a wicked joy that he was so intimately placed.

She shifted under him, his legs dropping between her widened thighs. He was wedged tight, and no amount of wrestling could have dislodged him, which was fine by her.

"What are you doing?" she demanded to know.

"If you've been kissed as many times as you claim, you shouldn't have to ask."

He reached behind her head, and with a flick of his wrist, he'd extracted a comb from her hair so that it was loosened enough to fall around her shoulders.

"Captain!" she scolded. "You can't just . . . just . . . take down my hair."

"Why not?"

"Well . . . because."

He grabbed a fistful and pressed it to his nose, inhaling deeply of the auburn strands.

"I've been wanting to do that for a whole week."

"You have?"

"Yes. I love red hair on a woman. Whenever we're alone, you'll take it down for me. Or I'll take it down for you."

He talked as if he'd be popping in constantly, and the notion was as exciting as it was dangerous.

It was foolish to encourage him, but the imprudent part of her—the one she'd inherited from her scandalous father—would be delighted to attempt any rash behavior he suggested.

Fortunately, she possessed traits from her cautious, sensible mother, too, so she comprehended that they were courting trouble, and she said, "Captain, you're assuming that I'll let you visit again."

"I'm not *assuming*. I'm merely notifying you of how it will be between us. You're the one who drank that stupid potion. Deal with it."

"The potion! Are you telling me that you think it was—"

"Helen?"

"Yes?"

"Be silent."

At hearing him refer to her by her Christian name, she was too elated to object. She was sequestered with him, in the middle of the night, sprawled on her bed, and he'd just called her *Helen*!

Perhaps that blasted potion had been magic. Since she'd ingested it, she'd definitely changed, and if she went through much more of a transformation, there'd be nothing left of the person she'd been before they'd met.

Ordinary, pragmatic Helen Hamilton would be replaced by a licentious vixen who would do whatever he asked, who would be unconcerned over any fall from grace.

He dipped down and kissed her as he'd threatened he would, and she didn't try to stop him.

If he thought she was a chaste young lady, he certainly didn't show it. He trapped her in a viselike grip, while his mouth captured hers in a torrid embrace that made her pulse gallop and her senses soar.

He gave no quarter, took no care to ensure that she was amenable or content with his level of ardor. He simply leapt into the fray, intent on a demonstration of passion that was far beyond her limited understanding of how such encounters were carried out, but she wasn't about to complain.

He seemed thoroughly smitten, and when he was such a dashing, handsome man, she couldn't help but be flattered. She was eager to prove herself worthy of his attention, and she appeared to be skillfully participating.

For a female with no prior experience, she had an instinctual knack for carnal endeavor. She knew precisely what he wanted and how he planned to achieve it. Without restraint, she threw herself into the venture, and she was amazed to discover that the more enthusiastic her response, the more ardent he became.

His hands were everywhere, roaming across her face, her shoulders, her arms. Everything happened so rapidly, and with such a reckless abandon, that as she realized he was caressing one spot, he'd already moved on to another.

She opened her mouth to request that they slow down so she could catch her breath, but before she could speak, he slipped his tongue between her lips. He pushed it in and extracted it in a way that tickled her innards, pulled at her breasts and her womb.

They engaged in a merry dance that seduced and cajoled, and with scant effort, he had her overwhelmed and yearning for much more than she could ever have from him.

Their hips began to flex, their loins pressing together in a rhythm that matched the sparring of their tongues. They were proceeding toward a goal, though she couldn't have said what it might be. She was excessively agitated, raw with a need she recognized to be womanly desire, and she could only hope that he would guide her to the end of the road.

He'd fanned a flame that she never should have allowed him to ignite, but at that moment, she was so aroused that she would have submitted to any wild deed—so long as he kept the pleasure coming.

Luckily, he saved her from herself. Just when she feared she might explode, he eased the rocking of his hips, their bodily motion ceasing. He frowned, looking irked again, as if he couldn't remember why he was in her bed.

"I guess we've established something." He sounded grouchy.

"What is that?"

"You were telling the truth."

"I was? About what?"

"You've been kissed in the past."

"Told you so." She smirked, glad to know that she'd been sufficiently competent to have fooled him.

"You behave yourself."

"What?"

"You obviously like to dally, and I'd better not hear that you're cavorting with any of the footmen."

"Ooh, you vain beast!"

She tried to cuff him with a fist along the side of the head, but he was too quick. He seized her wrist, pried open her knuckles, and nuzzled her palm, sending a wave of butterflies swarming in her stomach.

"If you decide you're in need of kissing," he haughtily commanded, "I'll see to it for you."

"You're awfully sure I enjoyed it enough to do it with you again."

He scoffed. "You'll want it—and fairly soon, too—if I'm any judge, which I am."

He drew away onto his knees, and he rested his hands on her neck, then traced them down over her bosom to her breasts. For the briefest instant, he massaged them, as if calculating size and weight, and he pinched the nipples in the center.

The gesture had a blistering effect. Sensation shot from

the pointed tips to her extremities with such riotous force that she felt as if she'd been struck by lightning.

"Don't forget to meet with me tomorrow," he said.

"What? When?" She was completely flustered and couldn't decipher what he meant.

"You and me. Ten, four, and eight o'clock. Wear a pretty dress to supper."

"I don't have a pretty dress."

"Find one."

He stole a last kiss.

"You're to call me Tristan when we're alone."

He slid to the floor and walked out, without pausing to see if anyone was in the hall. He was gone so swiftly that it was almost as if he hadn't been there at all.

Frozen in her spot, she listened to his fading footsteps. Silence descended, the house settling, as if people were finally back in their own beds where they belonged.

As she exhaled a tortured breath, she wondered what would happen next. In a few short hours, she'd be with him in his library. How was she to act?

She hadn't a clue.

Chapter 7

❦

"CATCH me if you can!"

Jane kicked her horse into a gallop, laughing as she left Michael choking on her dust. She bent low over the animal's neck, whooping with delight as she careened off the lane that led through the park and hurtled down a narrow path in the woods.

She felt as if a fairy godmother had waved her magic wand and fixed everything that was wrong.

They were living in the grandest house in the city, at the heart of the social whirl of parties and balls. She was treated as a welcomed guest with no chores or responsibilities. Clothes had been delivered, a few gowns with all the trimmings, so she could dress the part of the young lady she'd always been.

She had her own boudoir, plenty of food to eat, clean sheets on the bed, coal for the fire, and maids to assist her. No one cared that her father was Harry Hamilton. No one cared about the duel or the angry duke who'd shot him. Suddenly, it was as if none of it had ever happened.

Best of all, Michael Seymour invited her to go riding every afternoon.

Of course, the ride was arranged by Miriam, who was pathetically blatant in her hopes of getting Michael off by himself, but Michael was adept at foiling her plan by having Jane accompany them.

With each passing day, he spent more time with her. She could hardly turn around without bumping into him. His lazy smile mesmerized her, rattling her with wicked possibilities.

Could life be any more strange? More wonderful?

The sun was up. The sky was blue. The temperature mild. Michael was cantering after her.

She was so very, very glad to be alive!

Her mount thundered up to the lake's edge, and she reined in as Michael rushed up behind.

His color was high, his glorious blond hair tousled, his eyes glimmering with merriment. He looked dashing and sophisticated, and on seeing him, her breath hitched in her lungs.

He was quite smitten, and there was no mistaking his burgeoning affection. As opposed to Helen, Jane loved to flirt and flatter, so she knew when a fellow was interested and when he wasn't. Michael was extremely *interested*.

She glanced over at him and tossed her head, her auburn tresses swishing down her back. Her new riding habit fit perfectly, outlining her trim figure, the feather in the cap making her appear fetching and carefree.

Michael liked beautiful girls, liked bold ones, and she could be bold as brass. Poor Miriam—with her timid manner and plain features—didn't stand a chance.

"I didn't think you'd ever arrive," she teased. "Can't that old nag go any faster?"

"You brazen hussy." He chuckled. "Didn't anyone ever tell you that it's unladylike to ride as you do?"

"They told me all the time, but I didn't listen."

"When we race, you can't keep beating me. Bandit and I are males. Our self-esteem can't survive the drubbing."

He trotted up till he was right next to her, and he whipped Bandit around so that they were facing each other, the horses' sides pressed together, her foot and stirrup tangled with his.

He was very close, close enough to lean in and kiss her. He hadn't yet, and she constantly sensed that he wanted to, but something was holding him back.

He peered about, noting what she had: They were hidden in the trees, safe from the curious scrutiny of passersby. What was to prevent them from doing whatever they wished? There was no one to see.

For a lengthy interval, he studied her, seeming torn over a weighty decision. She didn't move, anxious to learn what he might dare.

"You're so pretty," he said. He settled his hands on her waist, and with a quick lift, he pulled her from her horse and onto his.

She fought for purchase, laughing and grabbing at his coat. As she stilled, he brushed the sweetest, softest kiss across her lips.

"You naughty boy," she murmured.

"Aren't I, though?"

"It's about time you kissed me. I thought you'd never get around to it."

"Have you been expecting me to?"

"You know I have, you cad. Why did you keep me waiting so long?"

"I hate to rush my pleasures."

"Ah, a fellow after my own heart."

He kissed her again, his tongue in her mouth, as he held her tight. She hugged him back, her arms winding over his shoulders, so that she could run her fingers through his luxurious hair.

When he deepened the kiss, she drew him nearer, eager to feel his hands roaming over her body, to feel him caressing her breast.

It was the most spectacular moment of her life, and she whispered a fervent prayer, begging the Good Lord to make Michael realize what an ideal bride she would be.

And why shouldn't he realize it? Although she was

beneath him in ancestry, they were a perfect match. They enjoyed the same activities, had the same opinions, and possessed the same wry sense of humor. Why, they even had the same favorite color and favorite food.

Fleetingly, she worried that she should have protested his improper advance, but she couldn't be coy. He could have whatever he wanted, and if she refused to give it to him, he could receive it from a dozen other girls, so she would do anything he asked.

She didn't know how long they kissed. The embrace went on and on, growing more heated, more arousing when, from off in the distance, she heard someone calling his name.

"Michael! Where are you?"

With great effort, Michael yanked away. He'd been as absorbed as Jane, and he frowned, trying to figure out what was happening.

"Michael!" The voice came again, and they both recognized it at the same time.

"Miriam," he muttered. "Damn it."

"Gad, I'd forgotten all about her."

"So had I."

When they'd galloped off, they'd left her plodding along in the carriage. Usually when they barreled into the trees, they swiftly exited on the other side.

How long had she been waiting? What might she say about their protracted absence? What if word got back to Helen? She would have a fit! She'd never condone Jane's fraternizing with Michael, and she would ruin any relationship.

"We'd better go." Jane sighed.

"Yes, I suppose we should."

He lifted her and seated her in her saddle, then, with the agility of a circus performer, leapt to the ground. To her surprise, he scooped up some dirt, rubbing it onto his trousers, coat sleeve, and cheek.

"Why are you doing that?"

"We'll tell her I struck a tree branch and fell off, and that's why we were delayed."

"An equestrian of your ability? She'll never believe it."

"Yes, she will. She knows nothing of horses, and it would never occur to her to contradict me."

"No, it wouldn't."

He grinned, and she grinned, too, liking that they had a secret, that she was complicit with him—to his cousin's detriment.

He climbed back in the saddle, and he turned his horse, ready to proceed out to the lane. He leaned over, his hands on her reins.

"I want to be alone with you," he said, "when we have plenty of time to be together."

"I'd like that."

"Let me come to your room."

"When?"

"Tonight, after everyone is asleep."

Jane knew it was wrong and reckless, but knowledge didn't necessarily convey wisdom.

"I'll leave the door unlocked," she replied without hesitation.

"THEY disappeared for an eternity, Mother."

"What is your definition of *eternity*? Five minutes? Ten?"

"A half hour, perhaps longer."

Maud glared at Miriam. "You let them vanish for *half an hour*?"

"How could I stop them? It's not as if I could forbid Michael from going off with her."

"No, you couldn't."

"They do it every day. Michael invites her to come with us, then when we get to the park, he forgets that I exist."

Miriam had tears in her eyes, and if Maud had had

any maternal instincts, she might have hugged Miriam and told her all would be well, but she wasn't overly affectionate, and she wouldn't encourage Miriam with falsehoods.

Jane Hamilton was pretty, confident, and bright—the sort that would attract any gentleman's attention. She possessed every positive trait that Miriam lacked, and there was something sly about her that Maud didn't like or trust.

Jane was clever and dangerous. She assessed the house and furnishings in a covetous fashion, as if scheming over how she could arrange her affairs so she never had to leave.

"Did Michael say where they'd been?" Maud asked.

"He claimed he'd had an accident in the woods, that he'd fallen off his horse, which delayed their return."

"You believed him?"

"Yes. Shouldn't I have? Why would he lie to me?"

Maud couldn't understand how she'd birthed such a silly child.

When it came to her daughter, she was no fool, and she wasn't blind. Jane was extraordinary, while Miriam was absolutely ordinary, so what chance did Miriam have against such stellar competition?

If Miriam was to maintain her place in relation to Michael, Maud had to get rid of the Hamiltons, but the captain was irrationally enamored of them. How could Maud persuade him to send them away? And until she could devise a valid argument to sway him, how was she to counter their overrunning of the household?

"There's no alternative, Miriam. We have to take drastic measures. You'll have to begin riding lessons again."

"Oh, Mother, no! You know I can't abide horses. They're so big and so . . . tall."

"Do you want to marry Michael or don't you?"

"Yes."

"Then you must get over these absurd fears. They're unseemly."

"I'm not brave."

"You don't have to be brave. You just have to be smart."
Maud started out of the room.

"Where are you going?" Miriam's voice was an irritating whine.

"I need to talk to Captain Odell. He must curb Michael's behavior."

"Can the captain make him ignore Miss Hamilton?"

"No. Only you can do that."

"But . . . how?"

"If you have to ask, Miriam, there's no hope of your ever being a countess."

"CAPTAIN, may I speak with you?"

"Sorry, Maud, but I have a four o'clock appointment."

Tristan forced a smile and tried to walk on to the library, but she was blocking his way. Short of picking her up and setting her aside, he couldn't avoid a conversation.

"We must review our travel plans," she nagged.

"I don't see why. We'll simply climb in our carriages and go."

They were scheduled to make a trip to the Seymour family seat, and it would be Michael's first visit since assuming the title. Every year, the villagers threw a party to kick off the harvest. But with Michael being the new earl, the festival would hold additional meaning for all.

"Obviously, Captain"—Maud chuckled as if Tristan was very naïve—"you have no idea of the effort it takes to move us to the country."

"Yes, I do. I just don't care to fret over it. The servants are very proficient, and they know what is required to prepare. I'm sure we'll manage."

He continued on, but before he could escape, she clasped his arm so that, suddenly, he was strolling with her.

"There is one other matter we must discuss," she insisted.

"What is it?"

"It's rather private. May we step into a parlor?"

"I really don't have time, Maud."

"Well, it can't wait, so we'll have to hash it out in the hall where anyone can overhear." She halted and pulled him around to face her. "It's about Michael."

"Isn't it always?"

Maud constantly sniped about Michael. She seemed to not like him or Rose very much, and Tristan couldn't figure out why she'd stayed on for so long, when she found the two children so untenable. He recognized that she'd been tempted by the money and the lofty position that came with supervising them. Unfortunately, Rose and Michael had suffered from her lack of interest.

Michael had become an uncontrollable roué, and Rose had grown quiet and forlorn. At times, Tristan could barely keep from shaking Maud and demanding an explanation for her indifference.

"There was a bit of a . . . *situation* . . . today," she said.

"What sort of situation?"

"He was riding with the Hamilton girl—the one who is his same age."

"Jane, yes. He's mentioned her passion for horses."

"They raced off together and left Miriam behind."

"And . . . ?"

"They were gone for over an hour, with no one having any idea of where they were or what they were doing."

"Your point being . . . ?"

"They're both adolescents, Captain. I shouldn't have to spell out the dangers."

"You suspect Michael compromised her? Is that what you're claiming?"

"No. I merely think a word to the wise might be advisable. We wouldn't want her reputation tarnished. Nor would we want Michael ensnared in a peccadillo. It would create a horrid mess."

Tristan agreed. His father had specifically charged him with arranging a good marriage for Michael. He would wed a woman of the appropriate rank and station. Jane Hamilton would never be the bride Tristan would select.

"Don't worry, Maud, I've spoken to Michael."

"You have?"

"I made myself very clear. He understands the risks posed by Jane Hamilton, and he would never be so foolish as to involve himself with her."

"I hope you're correct."

"I am."

She looked as if she was about to argue that Michael was brimming with deception, but Tristan wouldn't listen to any denigrating remarks.

Luckily, he was saved from a quarrel by Rose skipping down the hall.

"Tristan! Tristan! There you are! I've been searching everywhere."

She hurried up, causing Maud to bristle.

"Honestly, Rose," Maud scolded, "where are your manners? Captain Odell and I are talking. It's rude of you to interrupt."

In the months Tristan had lived with the family, he'd never seen Rose so animated, and at Maud's sharp tone, she instantly deflated. Her smile vanished, her shoulders sagged.

"I'm sorry, Tristan."

"Don't be," he declared. "Maud and I were just finished."

He glared at Maud, daring her to disagree.

"We'll continue this conversation later," she said, appearing affronted.

"I eagerly await your comments," he lied, breathing a sigh of relief when she walked on.

He turned his attention back to his sister. She was so lovely with her blond hair and big blue eyes. She was wearing a white dress with a pink ribbon around the waist that matched the one in her hair, and it brought out the rosy hue in her cheeks.

"You're very pretty, Miss Rose," he told her, and he was rewarded with a huge grin.

"I am?"

"Yes. What can I do for you?"

"I had to tell you something important."

"What is it?"

"I am so glad Amelia is staying with us."

"I'm glad, too."

"I've been lonely—what with Father being gone and all."

"I thought that you might be."

"I can't believe that you knew exactly what I wanted."

"What was that?"

"A friend, silly. I've been praying every night, and now—just like magic—Amelia is here!"

With that small announcement, she wrapped her arms around him, her face buried against his chest, and she hugged him with all her might.

He was taken off guard by the sweet gesture, and for a moment, he froze, not sure how to accept it.

Previously, they'd been very formal with one another, and he was delighted to know that she was growing to like him.

He hugged her back, actually planting a kiss on the top of her head.

"Thank you, Tristan," she said. "Thank you so much!"

"You're welcome, Rose. It was my pleasure."

"IT'S four-thirty, Miss Hamilton. You're late."

"I may be late, but I was here at ten this morning, and you weren't here at all."

Helen nearly closed the library door, then decided she shouldn't, so she left it ajar. She marched over to the desk and pulled up a chair.

"Where were you?" she inquired. "I waited an hour."

"I was . . . ah . . . indisposed."

"Hung-over, were you?"

"You'll never get me to admit it."

"You don't have to *admit* it. I saw the proof with my own two eyes."

She blushed, furious that she'd mentioned the torrid episode. She'd been flustered all day, wondering how they'd interact. They were bound in an odd fashion, but that didn't mean she should roll around with him on a bed! What had she been thinking?

Her vehement participation had shocked and frightened her. She'd always suspected that many of her father's disgraceful traits were bubbling just beneath the surface, and her behavior with Odell had confirmed her worst fears: Given the right set of circumstances—and the right man—she was ridiculously loose.

"Are hangovers the norm for you, Captain? If overindulgence is a problem, perhaps we should forego our morning appointments."

"No, it is not the *norm*, Miss Hamilton, and we'll meet as scheduled." He scowled. "You are supposed to call me Tristan when we're alone."

"You shouldn't count on it."

"You are so full of sass. Where do you come by that impertinent tongue?"

"I was born with it."

"I'm certain that's true." He gestured to the door. "Shut it."

"No."

"No?" His scowl deepened. "You seem to be laboring under the mistaken impression that you don't have to do as I say."

"If you expect me to obey, you must give me orders that make sense."

"In your tortured mind, why does it not make sense to shut the door?"

"Because I don't want to be sequestered in here with you. People will talk."

"Let them."

"No. I'm trying to fit in with the other servants and—"

"You are *not* a servant!"

"A semantic difference, Captain."

"It's Tristan, Miss Hamilton."

"I prefer Captain Odell."

He snorted with what might have been either disdain or amusement.

"There must be a reason I put up with you, Miss Hamilton, but I can't figure out what it is."

"I'm sure something will occur to you. Maybe after your hangover wanes, your thought processes will clear."

"I take it back: There's no good reason why I put up with you."

He rose from his chair, and she jumped and pressed into her seat. She was terrified that he would approach her, that he would steal another kiss, and the notion was so electrifying that she couldn't imagine herself refusing.

To her great relief, though, he walked on by, but the instant she relaxed, she realized his intent. She stiffened with alarm.

"Captain!" She stood, planning to stomp over and stop him.

"Be silent."

He closed the door and spun the key.

"I can't be locked in here with you," she hissed.

"You already are."

"I won't allow you to bully me like this."

She stormed over, prepared to wrestle the key away, but he stuck it in a pocket inside his coat. Unless she wanted to grope about under his clothes, she couldn't retrieve it.

"Give it to me," she fumed.

"No."

He took a step toward her, and she took one back. He took another, and she did the same. He was herding her across the room, gradually working her to a rear corner.

"What are you doing?" she blustered.

"What does it look like?"

"Stay right where you are, you bounder."

She held out her palm, as if the small appendage could ward him off.

"Have you had your daily supply of kissing, Miss Hamilton? Has the urge overtaken you?"

"Despite what you suppose, I suffer from no salacious *urges*."

"Last night, if memory serves, I offered to satisfy your need for flirtation."

"Last night, you were drunk."

"But not sufficiently so that I forgot any of the details."

She winced. She'd been hoping he'd have forgotten them all!

"What happened between us," she stammered, "was an . . . aberration."

"Is that what you'd call it?"

"Yes."

"Well, I'd call it incredible."

She gulped with dismay. "You would?"

"Yes, and I want to do it again."

He swooped in and swept her off her feet, depositing her on a nearby divan. He came down on top of her; with the furnishing being very narrow, there was no space to shift away.

She gazed at his handsome face, his blue eyes glittering with merriment, and her heart literally skipped a beat.

"Are you going to kiss me?" She was breathless with anticipation.

"Most definitely, Helen."

"I really wish you wouldn't."

"Now that, my dear, has to be the biggest lie you've ever told."

He narrowed the distance between them, initiating a torrid kiss that was rough and wild and thrilling.

His tongue was in her mouth, his hands in her hair, and he kept on and on till she was dizzy with titillation. He slid to the side, a knee on the floor, as he toyed with her breast, teasing the nipple through the fabric of her dress.

Vaguely, she recognized that he was easing her skirt up her legs. Her calves were bared, then her thighs. He slipped his questing fingers into her drawers and delved into her womanly sheath. They seemed to fit just right, as if he'd been created to caress her that exact way, and she was so surprised that she gasped very loudly.

He chuckled. "I knew you'd be noisy."

"What do you mean?"

"Deep down, you have the temperament of a harlot."

"You're calling me a harlot? Is that what passes for a sailor's flattery? If so, I don't care for it."

"Have any of your *dozens* of swains ever touched you like this?"

"Nary a one."

"Then I am delighted to be the first."

He stroked back and forth, back and forth, as he nibbled a path to her nipple. He bit and sucked at the tiny nub, sending waves of exhilaration shooting through her. She writhed against him, trying to escape the torment, but trying to move nearer to it, too.

Suddenly, she seemed to shatter, and she cried out with an exuberant joy that was shocking in its volume. He captured the sound by smothering it with another kiss.

She spiraled up, then floated down, and she was laughing and sputtering, happier than she could ever remember being.

"Oh, my goodness, Captain Odell, what was that?"

"It's sexual pleasure, you vixen."

"You're a sorcerer."

"There was no magic involved. You are simply too easy for words."

"I am not!"

"Yes, you are. You're loose, too."

"Only because you goad me into misbehavior."

"Trust me: There's been no *goading* on my part."

"Ha! That's what you think."

He kissed her again, and he sighed, murmuring, "What on earth shall I do with you?"

"Why must you *do* anything?"

"I can't stay away from you, but I can't be tumbling you in my library every time you stroll by."

She giggled, loving the notion that he was smitten. How had it happened? *Why* had it happened?

They were playing a dangerous game, and she had to extricate herself, but she didn't want to. She wanted to lie there forever, where she felt safe and beautiful and adored.

She was so wrapped up in her lurid rumination that it took a moment to realize someone was pounding on the door.

"Captain, are you in there?" Mrs. Seymour barked.

Odell's eyes went wide, and he grinned, apparently humored by their predicament. He thrust his loins against hers, setting off a new round of bodily sensation, as Seymour rattled the knob.

Frantically, Helen gestured for him to move off her, but he didn't budge.

"Yes, Maud, what is it?" he queried.

"I was wondering if you could spare me a minute."

"No. I'm having my daily meeting with Miss Hamilton."

There was a lengthy, tense silence as Mrs. Seymour processed the information.

"Will you be long?" she finally asked.

"At least an hour."

Helen vehemently shook her head and whispered, "I'm leaving immediately."

"No, you're not," he countered, whispering too.

"How about if I come back then?" Mrs. Seymour tried again.

"I'll send the butler to notify you when we're finished."

"Miss Hamilton," Mrs. Seymour persisted, "I'll need

to speak with you, as well. About the problem with Rose's clothing."

"I'll find you as soon as the captain lets me go," Helen promised, nearly yelping with indignation as Odell bit her nape. She punched him on the shoulder.

"We must resolve this matter today," Seymour snapped.

Helen held her breath, fuming, as Seymour's footsteps faded.

"You rat!" she hissed, pushing him so that he toppled onto the floor. "You were deliberately trying to compromise me!"

"You're angry? An accomplished flirt such as yourself? This can't be the first time you were caught in a locked parlor, up to no good."

He picked himself up, dusting off his trousers, laughing at her fury, which only increased it. He looked thoroughly composed, not a wrinkle in his coat, not a strand of hair out of place, while she was an utter mess.

Her combs had been dislodged, so her hair was falling down. Her skirt was bunched, her garters undone, her stockings drooping to her ankles. She tugged and straightened and yanked as he calmly observed, but provided no assistance whatsoever.

"You are a menace," she charged.

"And you are cute as the dickens."

"You are a beast, a cad, a . . . a . . . debaucher of innocent women."

"Innocent? You?"

"Yes, me."

He chortled as if she'd told a great joke. "You humor me beyond measure. I thought I hated it here—"

"Where?"

"In this house. In London. But I'm beginning to change my mind."

He hated it in London? He didn't like watching over his siblings?

The gossiping servants hadn't shared this piece of his

story, and she was meddlesome enough to have inquired, but he halted any questions by wrapping an arm around her and kissing her again.

In a trice, she was a muddle of confused yearning, so eager to continue that she was a hairsbreadth away from flopping back onto the divan and dragging him down with her.

She put a hand on his chest and eased him away.

"We didn't discuss any topic of import," she said. "If you keep mauling me, how will we ever get anything accomplished?"

"What did we need to discuss?"

"Rose gave Amelia some of her old dresses to wear."

"I don't care about their girlish games."

"Mrs. Seymour was upset. There was a kerfuffle over it."

"Of minor significance. Rose obviously intended a gift, but how does Amelia feel about receiving Rose's castoffs?"

"She understands that we can't afford to purchase new."

"That reminds me: All three of you need more clothes."

"You've already been more than generous."

Without her having an inkling of his ploy, apparel had been delivered. The outfits weren't the height of fashion, but they were well-sewn and functional, and Helen still couldn't come to grips with his unexpected kindness.

"You're guests," Odell said. "You can't go about like a trio of paupers. It would reflect badly on Lord Hastings."

"Don't buy us anything else," she insisted.

"Don't tell me what I should and shouldn't do. My clerk has made you an appointment with a dressmaker."

"Captain Odell! No. You've done too much."

"It pleases me to see you in pretty gowns. Stop complaining."

"You never listen to me."

"If you called me Tristan, I might."

"Liar."

She started for the door, and he followed her over and gallantly opened it. He peeked out, and with the hallway being empty, he took a parting kiss.

She inhaled sharply, outraged by his brazenness but delighted by it, too. She was in desperate trouble, walking the road that led straight to perdition, but she wasn't concerned in the least.

"We're traveling to the country next week," he mentioned.

"I had heard that you were. Am I going, too?"

"Yes. You and your sisters."

She wasn't sure about making the journey. It would place her in even closer contact with him, and she didn't relish the prospect of constantly hiding, which would be the only way she could force herself to behave.

"Must we go?" she asked.

"Yes, you must, and in the meantime, inform Jane that she must stay away from Lord Hastings. I can't have her flirting with him."

"She wouldn't. She knows better."

"Don't forget that we have a date for supper."

"I'll see you at eight."

"At eight," he murmured.

They stood, staring like two enamored adolescents, until Helen realized how she was mooning over him—in plain sight, where anyone could stumble on them.

Was she insane?

She turned and fled.

"DID you see that?" Rose whispered.

"I did," Amelia whispered in reply.

They were huddled at the top of the stairs, spying on the adults down below.

"He kissed her!"

"I know. I saw!"

Both girls had to stifle giggles.

"Do you think they're in love?" Rose asked.

"Of course they are. They wouldn't be kissing if they weren't."

"Will they get married now?"

"Yes."

"We'll be sisters, won't we? We'll be together forever." They clasped hands and smiled.

Chapter 8

❧

"BONJOUR, *Bonjour!* Please, *mes petites*, come closer. Take a look."

Phillip Dudley laid on thick his French accent, welcoming the group of four young ladies to his wagon. The door was propped wide, his array of bottles and jars carefully arranged for eye-catching effect.

"What may I get for you? A love potion, perhaps?"

The two younger ones giggled, turning toward the oldest one, and he smiled as he saw that he knew her.

"Miss Hamilton?"

"Hello, Mr. Dubois."

"Who are your charming companions?"

"My sisters, Jane and Amelia, and our friend, Lady Rose Seymour."

"I am honored!" He gave a theatrical bow, which initiated another chorus of giggles. "What brings you down to the harbor? Is it because you wish to sample more of my wares?"

"Actually, we're visiting a ship. My employer is a ship's captain, Mr. Tristan Odell. Maybe you've heard of him?"

"I have, as a matter of fact. Isn't he guardian to Lady Rose and her brother?"

"Yes, he is, and he's invited us on board for a tour."

"My," he mused, "aren't you stepping in high company all of a sudden?"

"I certainly am."

"If you're working, you must have had some good luck since we last met."

"My situation has improved dramatically."

He could see that it had. Earlier in the summer, she'd been bedraggled and exhausted and hadn't had a penny in her pocket. He'd feared for her, but over the course of a few weeks, she'd blossomed.

She was brimming with health, her cheeks rosy, her figure pleasingly rounded, and in her fetching green dress, with a matching parasol dangling over her shoulder, she was the very picture of poise, grace, and refinement.

"Does Captain Odell realize how fortunate he is to have you?"

"Yes." She chuckled, oozing confidence, and it was another positive change.

"Vous êtes très jolie," he told her, grinning.

Amelia leaned nearer and explained, "He says you're very pretty."

"It appears," Miss Hamilton said, "that someone has been paying attention to her French lessons. I must be a better teacher than I imagine."

Jane Hamilton was examining his merchandise, and he turned to her.

"I have many excellent remedies," he claimed.

"I can see that." Longingly, she touched a bottle. "How do you know my sister?"

"She stopped by a while back. I gave her a potion."

"Which one?"

"It was my Spinster's Cure—designed to ensure she marries."

Jane glanced over at her sister. "Helen, you didn't tell me you'd been out buying love potions."

"I haven't been." Helen flashed him a killing glare.

"Have you had any luck?" Phillip teased.

"With finding a husband? No, and I haven't been trying, either."

Her protestation elicited snickers and shrewd peeks from Amelia and Rose—as if they shared a secret.

Was romance in the air? He hoped so. When a woman fell in love, he always made money.

"Are you looking for something special?" Phillip asked Jane.

"Do you really sell love potions?"

"I really do."

"Might I have one, Helen?"

Helen seemed alarmed by the prospect. "No, you may not."

"You're such a stick in the mud," Jane complained. "Where's the harm? It's all in good fun."

"I mean no disrespect to Mr. Dubois," Helen stated, "but his tonics are nonsense, and I won't waste a farthing on such foolishness." She spun to Phillip. "Might I speak with you for a moment, Mr. Dubois? In private?"

"*Oui,* mademoiselle."

Furtively, he motioned to his sister, Clarinda, who'd been watching them. While he chatted with Helen, Clarinda would parlay with Jane and give her what she was so anxious to have.

He guided Helen around the wagon, far enough away that she wouldn't hear what Clarinda was saying to her sister.

"What may I do for you?" he queried.

"I must ask you about that Spinster's Cure."

"What about it?"

"Well . . . ah . . . you'd mentioned that it has brought about numerous marriages."

"The potion is packed with powerful magic."

"You're a smart fellow, Mr. Dubois. Do you actually believe that?"

"Yes, and I'm suspecting you do, too, or you wouldn't

be questioning me." He stepped nearer and laid a comforting hand on her arm. He was at his best, his most persuasive, when he was reassuring a worried female. "What is it, *cherie*? You can tell me. Have you taken the potion?"

"I . . . sort of swallowed it by accident."

"By accident?"

"I was merely trying to quench my thirst, but . . . a man walked in front of me, and now . . . oh . . . I don't have the vaguest idea how to explain it."

"What's happened?"

"He's quite infatuated. *Dangerously* infatuated."

"Who is the man? Let me guess: your employer, Captain Odell?"

She frowned, disconcerted by his prescience. "Your deductive abilities are astounding."

"I am famous for them." His smile was smug. "Odell fancies you?"

"Yes."

"He's very dashing, very rich, and handsome?"

"Yes," she said again.

Phillip held out his hands, as if confused. "Then what is the problem?"

"Would he . . . he . . . *marry* me someday?" The instant she voiced the possibility, she waved away her words. "Never mind. I'm being absurd."

He chuckled kindly. "Miss Hamilton, the ways of fate are very strange. If you drank the Spinster's Cure as I instructed, then your destiny has been altered. You will be wed to him very soon. Neither of you will be able to prevent it from occurring."

For just a second, her façade slipped to reveal how lonely she'd been, how beaten down by her recent travails. She was desperate for his comments to be true, desperate to have found a man who loved her, but rational thought quickly settled in, and she scoffed.

"This conversation is ridiculous." She started off toward the girls. "I do *not* believe in magic. I do *not* believe in spells. I do *not* believe in charms . . ."

She muttered the sentences like an incantation, as if convincing herself. He laughed and followed.

"Helen," Lady Rose said, "what were you talking about with Mr. Dubois? Have you bought another love potion?"

"I most certainly have not." She gestured down the street, to where they could see the masts of the tall ships tied up at the dock. "Let's go, shall we? Captain Odell will be wondering where we are."

"WHAT did you need?"

"A love potion."

Clarinda Dudley assessed Jane Hamilton. Since she had always lived with her brother, she scarcely recalled an existence beyond his colorful peddler's wagon.

They traveled constantly, from one end of the country to the other. Their nomadic routine often seemed like a grand lark, particularly in the summer when the days were sunny and warm, but the long, cold winters could be grueling and difficult.

What would it be like to be Jane Hamilton, to wear expensive clothes and reside in a fine house?

Usually, Clarinda enjoyed her itinerant way of life, but lately she'd been restless, and her dour mood was making her question her choices, her decision to remain with Phillip rather than carve out a separate path for herself.

At the advanced age of twenty-five, she dreamed of simple things: a cozy cottage in the country, a garden where she could grow fresh herbs for her tinctures. Perhaps even a husband—if she could ever find a man who wasn't a fool.

"We have various therapies," she informed Jane. "What were you hoping to achieve?"

"Jane!" Amelia scolded. "Helen said *no*."

"She's not my mother, Amelia," Jane replied. "I can buy a blasted potion without begging her permission. Be silent."

Jane grabbed Clarinda's arm and eased her away, and she whispered so that the girls wouldn't overhear.

"There is a gentleman whom I like very much."

"But he doesn't like you in return?"

"I think he does, but I'm afraid it might be temporary."

"Ah . . . I see. You would like his interest to be permanent."

"Yes. He's a terrible flirt, so he's distracted by a pretty face. I'd like his attention to fall on me and stay there. Have you something that will make it happen?"

"Yes," Clarinda lied.

Her medicines were brewed with natural ingredients, and they healed as they were intended, but the elixirs Phillip insisted on selling, too, were trickery pure and simple.

They possessed no magic, and she knew of no special formula to imbue them with supernatural properties. Still, women were desperate, and Clarinda did nothing to discourage them from purchasing Phillip's concoctions. Why should she?

On many occasions, his potions created precisely the result Phillip had claimed they would. Clarinda didn't credit Phillip for the successes, but the human mind, which was powerful beyond their understanding.

If one of Phillip's remedies helped a female to believe that the impossible was possible, Clarinda would never tell her otherwise.

She went to the wagon and poured some powder into a pouch. She handed it to Jane.

"What should I do with it?" Jane asked.

"Put it into his food or drink."

"How many times?"

"Just the once. Are you near enough to him to accomplish it without difficulty?"

"We're living in his home. We dine together every evening."

"That makes it easy."

"Yes, it does." Jane studied the pouch, running her thumb over the leather. "Are you sure it will work?"

The poor girl looked positively miserable, overflowing with unrequited love, and Clarinda sighed, unable to fathom what it was about the feminine condition that turned sane women into such blithering idiots.

She'd never met a man who could make her heart pound, and her charlatan brother was the perfect example of the deviousness of the male species.

"He must be a handsome devil," Clarinda said.

"Very handsome, but he's so far above my station." Jane was quiet, pondering, then she shyly added, "He's old enough to marry. He could marry *me*—if he wanted to."

"And why wouldn't he want to?" Clarinda loyally retorted. "Who could be better than you?"

"I'm not from an aristocratic family, and my father was a renowned scalawag."

Clarinda frowned. "Are we talking about the earl of Hastings? Is that the fellow who's captured your fancy?"

"Yes, but his guardian would never deem me to be appropriate."

Everyone gossiped about the new earl. He was a flirt and a flatterer, his antics bandied about by all of London, and suddenly, Clarinda worried that she shouldn't have encouraged Jane. Wasn't she setting the girl up for heartbreak?

"Do you really suppose he could grow to love you?" Clarinda carefully probed.

"I'm certain of it. Next week, we'll be on holiday at his country property, so we'll be spending significant amounts of time alone. I know I can win him."

Clarinda couldn't bear to contradict her.

"Then I'm sure you will," she kindly agreed.

Phillip's conversation with Helen had ended. She marched toward them, muttering under her breath, and Clarinda motioned to the pouch. Jane stuffed it into her reticule.

"Let's go, shall we?" Helen said. "Captain Odell will be wondering where we are."

"Miss Hamilton," Clarinda called, before they could start off, "your sister tells me that you're off to the earl of Hastings's estate."

"Yes, we are. His tenants are having a celebration to kick off the harvest."

"It's a beautiful spot," Clarinda said. "You'll enjoy yourselves very much."

"You've been there?" Jane queried.

"We were in the area last year. I was up at the manor many times, delivering tonics to the housekeeper."

She had no idea why she'd mentioned the fact. The place had represented an odd sort of harbor for her, and she had such marvelous memories of those visits. She'd become friendly with several of the maids, so there had always been the offer of hot food or a cold beer in the kitchen when she'd stopped by.

In contrast to hers, their lives had seemed so easy. While she had freedom and independence, she'd envied them their structure and routine, their starched clothes and warm beds. She might have stayed there forever, but Phillip had involved himself in a peccadillo with a widow in the village, so they'd had to move on.

It had been the only occasion she'd seriously considered breaking off with him.

"Is the property very grand?" Jane asked.

"As grand as the new earl is said to be," Clarinda replied.

She and Jane exchanged a complicit look as Helen herded her charges down the street.

As Clarinda watched them depart, Phillip came over and put his arm around her.

"Why do pretty girls always depress you?" he inquired.

"Because they make me realize what I don't have."

"What is it that you don't *have* compared to them? Their world is all fussy morals and stuffy rules. If you carried on in the same fashion, you'd go mad in a week."

She didn't think so, but she didn't feel like belaboring the point. He was so vain, so convinced he was right, that she could never win any quarrel.

"What did Miss Hamilton want?" she asked.

"She claims the Spinster's Cure worked."

"Again? What is it with that potion?"

"I don't know."

"Who is the man?"

"Captain Odell, the Scot who came to town to serve as guardian to the earl and his sister."

"Oh, Lord."

"Is Jane Hamilton a satisfied customer?"

"Yes."

"Who's the lucky fellow tormenting her? Anyone I know?"

"Lord Hastings."

"Poor child," Phillip grumbled.

"Do you suppose we ought to . . ." Clarinda's voice trailed off.

"Ought to what? Just say it."

"Should we follow them to Hastings Manor? If the Spinster's Cure has succeeded again, I'd like to figure out why."

"We'd spy on Miss Hamilton and her captain? Don't we have better things to do?"

Not really, she thought, but she said, "Don't pay any attention to me. It was a silly idea."

He shrugged. "There might be some money to be made—selling more tonics and whatnot to the Hamiltons."

"There might be," she concurred. "And I'm worried about Jane chasing after the earl. She's out of her league with him."

"Not our business, Clarinda," he quietly counseled.

"I know, but I still feel guilty about what happened to Lady Redvers. I'd hate to have something awful occur again—especially if we have the means to prevent it."

He pondered, then nodded. "I'll reflect on it. Maybe we will go."

* * *

"You named your ship the *Lord Hastings*?"

"Yes."

"Why?"

"Why not?"

Helen had never been on a ship before, and she gazed at the deck, imagining it skipping across the waves with the sails unfurled. She could picture Odell behind the wheel, barking out orders and saving everyone from peril.

"I believe you're being flip with me," she scolded.

"Perhaps."

He grinned his wicked grin, the one that made her pulse flutter with excitement, and he rested a hand on her back and guided her toward a ladder. The girls had disappeared down a different hatch with his First Mate, and she glared over her shoulder to where they'd gone.

"Where are you taking me?" she asked.

"The governess gets her own private tour—from the captain himself."

"What if the governess doesn't want a private tour?"

"She gets it anyway." Nimble as a monkey, he leapt down and was swallowed up by the dark hold.

She hesitated, anxious about following, when he murmured from below, "Come, Helen. I'll catch you. Don't be afraid."

The coaxing tone was her undoing. She stepped onto the top rung, fussing with her skirt as she dangled a foot to find the next one.

"Don't you dare peek under my dress."

"Too late." His laugh drifted up.

"Ooh, you wretched bounder."

"Your legs are very shapely."

She kicked at him, found nothing but air, and lost her balance. She tumbled down, landing in his arms.

"I thought you'd never get here." He kissed her and set her on her feet.

"Stop that."

"Stop what?"

"Stop kissing me right out in the open where anyone can see."

"But when I'm around you, I'm a sweltering bundle of unassuaged passion."

"You are not."

"I am," he insisted, but she was positive he was joking. She'd never been the type of female who could drive a man wild.

"You kiss me because you can," she said, "because I let you."

"It's definitely a possibility."

"If I had an ounce of moral fiber, there'd be no hanky-panky between us."

"Want to make a wager?"

"With you? Never."

He escorted her down a narrow hallway, halting at the end to usher her into a room that had to be his cabin.

It was small and austere, much as she envisioned a monk's cell might be. There was a table in the middle strewn with maps, shelves along the walls filled with books, a few trunks with closed lids so that she couldn't snoop inside, and his bunk.

The bunk was meant to hold one person, and she considered sitting on it, but as he'd proven with the divan, a carnal escapade could be carried out in very limited conditions.

She didn't care to invite trouble, so she went to the table and plopped down in the only chair. He leaned against the door, watching her, not speaking.

It was a comfortable silence, but she was jumpy, because she couldn't figure out why he'd brought her to his cabin.

"Why call your ship the *Lord Hastings*?" she asked.

"It was a slap at my father," she was surprised to hear him admit.

"You didn't like him?"

"I hardly knew him, but in a fairer world, *I* would be Lord Hastings now."

"Are you bitter that you're not?"

He stood, hands on hips, scowling. "I don't think so."

She chuckled. "You must have some enmity. Anybody would."

"I suppose I do. I never felt he behaved particularly well toward my mother."

"He refused to marry her?"

"He was already married."

"Ah . . ." She studied him, curious about his life, about his upbringing. "Is your mother still alive?"

"No. She died when I was two."

"Have you any other family?"

"Some uncles in Scotland."

"Do they claim you?"

"Barely."

He shoved away from the door, and he proceeded to a bookshelf and riffled through the books. It dawned on her that he was nervous, and the prospect had her smiling.

"You say you hardly knew your father . . ."

"I only spoke to him a handful of times."

"Why would he name you as guardian to Rose and Michael?"

"I have no idea."

"How strange."

"Isn't it, though?" He straightened and peered over at her. "I'm told he was proud of me. He felt I'd substantially advanced myself with very little help."

"So that made you a competent guardian to two children?"

"It's bizarre, I know."

"It certainly is."

"Before I traveled to London last spring, I'd never even met them."

"Your father must have been a very peculiar fellow."

"Now you know where I come by it."

He walked over to her, his hips balanced on the edge of the table. He was hiding something, and when he held it out, she saw it was a hand-painted lady's fan.

She opened it, discovering scenes and shapes that had to be Chinese lettering.

"For you," he said, seeming embarrassed.

"You can't keep giving me gifts."

"Why can't I? It's been collecting dust on that shelf for three years. Would you rather I tossed it out?"

"No. I'll keep it, thank you very much." She traced a finger across the delicate pictures, amazed by the artistic detail. "Have you been to China?"

"Yes."

"You've sailed the globe?"

"Several times."

"I've never been anywhere."

"No you haven't, but that's not necessarily bad."

"My existence has been positively boring compared to yours. I'm jealous."

What would it be like to be him? To have journeyed everywhere and seen everything?

When she was a child, she'd loved to read books about adventurers, and she'd expected that—as an adult—she, herself, would trek off to foreign lands. She had a fond memory of her father asking her who she planned to wed when she was grown. She'd informed him she had no intention of marrying, because she was headed for Egypt to explore the pyramids, and a husband wouldn't permit her to go off on her own.

She could still hear her father's booming laugh.

Of course, she'd never had her adventure. Life had a way of grinding one down. There'd been bills to pay, and a household to run, and sisters to raise, and suddenly, she was twenty-four, having garnered very little reward for her efforts.

He had a wanderlust he'd been able to satisfy, while hers had been driven into the ground by duty and penury.

She'd never done a thing she'd truly wanted to do, and to her astonishment, she yearned to beg him to untie his ship, to take her far away—just the two of them—to some of the exotic places he'd been.

She could practically smell the tropical jungle, the hot ocean breezes, and her old restlessness returned with a vengeance.

"Is it difficult for you," she inquired, "being trapped in London by your family obligations?"

"Yes, it's very difficult."

"Do you like Michael and Rose?"

"They're wonderful."

"How long will you care for them?"

"I'm charged with managing their money until they come of age, then arranging their marriages."

"The end could be years away—especially for Rose."

"I know, and I can't imagine shirking the task. My father left me a letter, with clear instructions for both of them, and it's been the very devil, being burdened with the wishes of a dead man. How could one fail to follow through?"

She gazed at him, realizing why he'd invited her to the ship, to his cabin. It was his quiet way of showing her what mattered to him, of letting her see who he truly was.

"You're a good man, Tristan Odell."

"Why would you say that?"

"Because you are."

He snorted, obviously discomfited by her praise. "I'm just doing what was asked of me."

"What was *asked* and a tad more besides."

"I suppose," he allowed.

He bent down and kissed her, precisely what she'd hoped to avoid, but what she'd secretly craved.

In a thrilling motion, he pulled her out of the chair and laid her down on the table, his maps tumbling to the floor as he came over her. His hands were on her breasts, fussing with the front of her gown, baring her to his eager fingers.

It was the first time he'd touched them without fabric to block sensation, and she felt as if she'd been burned.

He was squeezing her nipples, drawing her skirt up her legs, and her harlot's body rippled with anticipation.

"Something has to be done, Helen," he murmured against her mouth.

"About what?"

"About the passion that keeps flaring between us. I assume you're a virgin?"

The question, so bluntly voiced, took her by surprise, dousing her like a bucket of cold water.

"Yes, I am, you rude oaf."

She was too embarrassed to mention that she hadn't a clue as to how a person's virginity ended up *lost*. She knew it involved a wedding night, a man and a woman, and a physical deed, but whatever it was, it had never happened to her. She was exactly the same as she'd always been.

"If we continue on like this," he said, "you won't be chaste much longer."

"Why is that?"

"Because if you're content to dally, I don't see why I should control myself."

"You're blaming this on me?"

"No. I'm just stating the facts."

She pushed at him, aware that she wasn't strong enough to shove him off, that he'd only move if he wanted to. For a moment he hovered, then he stepped away and she sat up.

Her breasts were hanging out, her hair falling down, and with their ardor waning, her partial nudity was like a slap in the face. What was she thinking?

She straightened her bodice, and as he glared, she glared right back. She didn't understand how, in a smattering of seconds, they'd gone from an episode of wild lust to a vicious quarrel.

"What should we do?" he asked.

"I'm leaving."

"We won't settle anything by you running off."

"I'm not running. I'm furious with you, and I don't want to stay in here."

"Well, don't have a hysterical fit. I won't like it."

"Hyster—" She bit off the remainder of the word, feeling as if she was choking on it.

"Hear me out," he said.

"No."

"You need a man in your bed like nobody's business."

"You nominate yourself?"

"Absolutely," he pompously retorted. "It's clear we're headed to fornication, and we have to recognize the direction we're traveling. Once we start in, there's no going back. That's all I'm saying."

"Message received. Thank you for sharing your concerns."

They might have persisted with their argument, or she might have stormed out, but suddenly the girls were coming down the hall. They were laughing and talking, and someone knocked on the door.

Odell jumped away from her as if she had the plague, and Helen slid from the table and walked to the corner. She turned away, frantically checking to make sure she was presentable.

Without waiting for a summons, the boisterous group burst in, underscoring how reckless Helen had been. What if she and Odell hadn't squabbled? For pity's sake, she was a governess. What if they'd kept on and her charges had seen all? It didn't bear considering.

Helen spun around, somber and sobered and mortified.

"Tristan, Tristan," Rose gushed as she hurried in. "Guess what?"

"What?" he inquired, as usual looking perfectly calm and collected.

"We saw the whole ship. The galley and everything."

"Marvelous."

"Guess what else!"

"I can't imagine."

"On the way here, we stopped by a peddler's wagon, and Helen and Jane both bought love potions."

Tristan raised a brow, his stern scowl shifting from Helen, to Jane, to Helen again.

"I did not!" Jane and Helen hotly said at the same time.

Chapter 9

MICHAEL peered down the darkened hall, ensuring he was unobserved, then spun the knob and slipped into Jane's bedchamber.

He'd never done anything so reckless, had never behaved so badly, but where Jane Hamilton was concerned, he couldn't resist.

He wasn't cruel or stupid. Carnal play was risky, and Jane could wind up pregnant, but as a remedy, he would never marry her. Though she was very sweet, she was beneath him in every way. He couldn't alter that fact, which meant he shouldn't forge ahead, but he was going to anyway.

They were spectacularly attuned, and he was tired of ignoring their attraction. When she was so accessible, and so eager to dally, why shouldn't they?

It was after midnight, but she was up, awaiting him in her sitting room. She was seated in a chair by the hearth. The air was cool, and a fire burned in the grate.

Apparently, there'd been no miscommunication about why he'd come.

She was dressed for an assignation, wearing only a

nightgown and robe, her slender feet bare on the rug. Her striking auburn hair was down and brushed out, hanging to her waist, the long tresses loose with curls. She was lovely and desirable, and his cock leapt to attention.

She stood, appearing young and nervous.

"Hello." An anxious hand gripped the lapels of her robe.

"Hello."

"I'd about given up on you. I was afraid you might have changed your mind."

"Never."

He walked over to her and drew her close, her body pressed to his all the way down, and he kissed her, very sweetly, very tenderly.

"You're so pretty," he murmured.

"Thank you."

"I was hoping you'd let your hair down."

"The naughty side of my personality is guiding my actions."

"I'm glad. I've always found *naughty* to be so much more fun than *nice*."

He kissed her again, more ardently, delighted at how perfectly she fit in his arms. She was just the right height, not too short or too tall. Her delectable breasts were crushed to his chest, her thighs molded to his own. For a brief moment, he caught himself speculating over what it would be like to have her as his wife.

She was so beautiful, and they had so much in common. Every second they spent together was remarkable, but a match between them would never occur. He wasn't ready for matrimony, and when he *did* finally break down and marry, it would be to an appropriate aristocrat's daughter who brought a dowry that would fill the Hastings's coffers to overflowing.

Jane would never be the one he selected, but it was intriguing to imagine her as his countess. Was she imagining the same? The prospect disturbed him. He didn't want to hurt or deceive her, but surely she comprehended the risk she was taking.

A man such as himself would never wed a girl like her. It simply wasn't done, and people on both sides of the social equation were aware of the distinctions. She was merely a pleasant diversion, and for her to anticipate any other conclusion was too bizarre to consider—so he wouldn't.

"Would you like some wine?" she asked.

"I'd rather have a whiskey."

"I don't have whiskey, but I managed to sneak off with a wine decanter after supper."

"You wicked minx!"

"You don't care, do you? It is technically yours, so I suppose it's stealing."

He smiled and shook his head. "Jane, how many times must I tell you? You're a guest in my home. If you want to gorge on a decanter of wine—or anything else—it's fine with me."

"Perhaps I'll become a lush at your behest."

"An adorable lush."

She smiled, too, and she turned to a nearby table and grabbed a glass that had already been poured. She handed it to him, and he took a drink, then wrinkled his nose in distaste.

"You don't like it?" Panic flashed in her eyes.

"It's sour. Is that really from my cellar?"

"I pilfered it from a sideboard down in a rear parlor."

"Maybe I should mention it to the butler. I'd hate to have him serve it to anyone."

Seeming frazzled, she yanked the glass away and took a sip of her own.

"It's not so bad," she claimed. "Try it again; you'll grow accustomed."

He obliged her, still finding it bitter, but she'd gone to so much trouble, and she was so eager for him to like it, that he didn't want to appear rude.

In a quick gulp, he downed the entire contents, deciding it was better to get rid of it all at once and not linger over the harsh flavor.

As the last drop slithered down his throat, he grinned. "I'm a horrible glutton. I didn't leave you any."

"I'm not much of a drinker. I brought it up here for you."

"How thoughtful. What else have you to share that might interest me?"

His lazy gaze meandered down her torso, to her bosom, her waist, her rounded hips, and his intent was very clear. She withstood his avid scrutiny, not shying away, not covering herself, providing blatant confirmation that she knew what he planned.

Since their first meeting, she'd been very forward, had allowed him incalculable liberties. She was playing with fire, but so was he, and he was more than happy to take what she was offering.

Lust swept over him, and he drew her to him once again. He started kissing her, letting her understand that they would proceed in a fashion beyond what they'd dared prior. She reveled in the increasing passion, participating with a dexterity that thrilled and titillated.

Her clever fingers were everywhere, roaming through his hair, across his shoulders, back, and arms. She even dipped down to stroke his buttocks—a brazen deed that made his phallus jerk with anticipation.

Her hips flexed against his erection, obviously recognizing it for what it was, for what it indicated, and he wondered if she actually was a virgin. If she'd previously lain with a fellow or two, she was hardly an innocent, which would certainly solve many of his ethical problems.

He clasped her hand and escorted her to her bedchamber. She didn't hesitate, but confidently walked by his side, equal partners in what could never be an equal act. She had everything to lose, while he had nothing to lose at all.

They reached the bed, and he paused and gestured to her robe.

"May I remove it?"

"Yes."

He tugged it off, elated to note that the nightgown she wore underneath was sewn from a thin, summery fabric. It was pristine white, with thin straps, tiny buttons down the front, and purple flowers stitched along the bodice and hem.

She was trembling, and he rubbed his palms up and down her arms, hoping to warm her, to comfort and fortify her.

"Are you cold?" he asked.

"No." She bit her bottom lip. "Have you ever done this before?"

"Never," he lied. "Have you?"

"No."

"So I'll be your first."

"And you'll be mine."

"Do you know what happens?" he inquired.

"A friend of mine wed last year. She told me."

"It's very physical."

"I heard that it was."

"Are you afraid?"

"I could never be afraid when I am with you."

He eased her onto the mattress and followed her down. They were stretched out, with him on top. He stared at her, his pulse hammering with excitement.

"How are you feeling?" she oddly queried.

"Very grand."

"You don't feel any different?"

"Different than what?"

"The wine didn't . . . ah . . . relax you?"

"No. Should it have?"

She chuckled. "Don't pay any attention to me. I'm a tad overwrought."

"There's no need to be. We don't have to do anything if you don't want to. We can just lie here like this, kissing and talking."

"I don't want to just *lie* here. I'm happy to do whatever you wish."

It was the very worst remark she could have made, for

he persuaded himself that she was cheerfully complicit in her ruination. It was a cad's conduct, a cad's method of avoiding blame and shirking responsibility.

Her green eyes were wide with expectation. She was so trusting, so willing to believe he was the man she assumed, and he wouldn't dissuade her.

He dipped down and kissed her, his fingers kneading her breasts, when suddenly the wine he'd drunk was gurgling in his stomach. He wasn't nauseous, but it was a peculiar stirring, as if butterflies had been released.

The world had narrowed, the area around them darkening so that she was very far away, as if he was viewing her down a long tunnel.

He watched the decades race by. They were married, having children, growing old together. A gentle awareness soothed him, as if he was seeing exactly what was meant to be. If he chose the appropriate route, he could be with her forever.

He opened his mouth, about to utter an inane romantic comment that would convey his heightened sentiment, but a voice of sanity in his head was shouting, *No! No! Don't do it!*

In an instant, the vision blinked out, the present returning with a vengeance. He was in Jane's bedchamber, in her bed.

He shuddered, shaking off the onerous perception.

"What's wrong?" she asked. "For a minute there, it seemed as if you'd . . ."

"As if I'd what?"

"You were . . . lost in a fog. It was very eerie."

The incident was rapidly fading from memory, the details so hazy he could already scarcely recall them.

He flexed, his erection pressing against her loins.

"I'm definitely here," he said.

"You definitely are."

"There's no fog swirling."

She laughed and drew him down for a kiss, fanning the flames of his desire, but the sensations had changed.

He'd planned to have a rough and merry tumble, where he would sweet-talk and flatter, then take what he wanted. But for some reason, he was awash with other feelings, ones that were new and unusual.

If not for her inferior status, she might actually have been his bride, so he needed to make the experience special for her.

"Michael . . . ?" She was patting him on the shoulder.

"What?"

"You are acting so strangely."

"I was thinking about you."

"In a good way, I hope?"

"In a very good way. I'm just so glad to be here with you."

"I'm glad you're here, too. I feel as if I've been waiting for this moment my entire life."

"So do I."

And he was being sincere. Fate had steered her directly into his path, and he was desperate to be joined with her. He couldn't delay another second.

He kissed her with a renewed vigor, fussing with the straps of her nightgown, working it down till the fabric was pooled at her waist.

Her breasts were bare, the pointy tips urging him to misbehave, and he sucked one of them into his mouth. He laved and played, moving back and forth, back and forth, until she was panting and writhing beneath him.

"How do you like it so far?" he teased, as he nibbled across her bosom.

"I'm quite satisfied."

"Ha! I haven't begun to satisfy you."

"You're a man of many talents."

"I certainly am."

He tugged off her nightgown so she was naked, and he stretched out atop her again, giving her no chance to be embarrassed by her nudity.

"You're very beautiful, Jane. I've never met a prettier girl."

"I'm happy to know that I please you."

"You're so right for me. You're my perfect match."

"Yes, I am. I'm so relieved that you realize it."

"We should always be together."

She hugged him as tightly as she could, initiating another torrid kiss, and if he hadn't been so overwhelmed by passion, it might have occurred to him that she was hearing his words in a manner he never intended, but he was too aroused to worry about what she was thinking.

"I want to make love to you, Jane," he murmured, "as a husband does his wife."

"I told you, Michael: Whatever you want is fine with me."

"It will hurt the first time."

"I know."

She spread her legs, her thighs cradling him, welcoming him.

With eager fingers, he opened his trousers and centered himself.

Even though she hadn't had an orgasm, she was wet and relaxed from his ministrations. In any other situation, with any other woman, he might have been more considerate, might have ensured that she found her pleasure before he found his, but with the tip of his phallus wedged into her virginal body, he was consumed by a need to ravish her that was almost feral in its power.

He took a deep breath, fighting for control, but it was no use.

He eased himself in, flexing and flexing, and when his path was finally blocked, when he encountered the evidence of her chastity, he was deluged by such a wave of lust that he gripped her hips and pushed himself in.

She tensed and arched up, crying out in dismay, and he tried to hold himself still, but she was so hot and so tight, that he couldn't prevent the wild ending working its way through his loins.

He impaled himself, once, again, and he came with a

blistering rush, spilling himself far into her womb with nary a thought to the consequences.

Just that fast, it was over, and he buried his face in her nape, mortified that he'd performed as if he was a fourteen-year-old lad and sneaking out behind the stable with Lydia.

He was a more skilled lover than he'd proved himself to be. He knew how to be gentle, how to coax and cajole, but she'd spurred him to a pinnacle beyond what he'd ever achieved with any paramour.

The notion—that she stimulated him to an extreme level—was disturbing. He was afraid he might like her more than he should, which was simply a recipe for frustration and disappointment.

He retreated from her and rolled away, as she winced in pain.

For a long while, they were silent, resting side by side, like two strangers staring at the ceiling.

"Are you all right?" he eventually inquired.

"Yes, I'm all right."

"I hurt you, didn't I?"

"I'll mend." There was another uncomfortable lull, and she said, "Is that all there is to it? I had expected something more . . . romantic."

"I'm sorry. I guess I didn't do it very well. I should have slowed down; I should have helped you through it."

"I'm fine. Don't worry about me. I liked it . . . *really*."

She was lying; he could tell. He'd acted like a bumbling lout, and she'd suffered because of it—though she was too polite to say so.

Glancing over, he was stricken to see that she was crying. He'd fornicated with many women in his short life, but he'd never romped so badly that he'd driven one of them to tears.

He pulled her into his arms, and for a moment she resisted, as if she didn't want to be touched by him, then she snuggled close and sobbed her heart out.

Feeling out of his element, he held her, running a soothing hand up and down her back, whispering words of consolation and support. Ultimately, her weeping ended, and in an exhausted stupor, she fell asleep.

Once he was certain he wouldn't wake her, that he wouldn't be required to hash out the dreadful episode with a distasteful conversation, he slid away. Like the cad he apparently was, he yanked a quilt over her and tiptoed out without a good-bye.

Chapter 10

❦

"MISS Hamilton! In the library. Now!"

"I'm sorry, Captain Odell, but I'm busy. I can't attend you."

Helen stuck her nose up in the air, spun away, and swept up the stairs after Rose and Amelia.

He stood in the foyer of Michael's country house, watching her go, and his fury soared.

The impertinent tart! How dare she refuse his direct order!

It was four o'clock, time for their afternoon meeting, and he wasn't about to let her skip it.

Since their quarrel aboard the *Lord Hastings,* he'd hardly seen her. Their trip to Hastings Manor had been just as hectic as Maud had predicted.

If he had traveled alone, on horseback, he could have arrived after a single lengthy day of riding, but with several carriages lumbering along, loaded down with six females and all their trunks and boxes, it had taken three days.

He was exhausted, his temper flaring, and he was in no mood for sass from his governess.

When they'd fought in his cabin, he'd simply thought he was being prudent, having an adult discussion with an adult woman about sexual behavior. Upon his referring to her virginity, she'd been so offended that one would think he'd asked her to disrobe in front of a group of strangers.

The butler was lurking, pretending not to have noticed Helen's insolence.

"Have tea delivered to the library," Tristan said. "Miss Hamilton will be joining me. She will join me *every* afternoon at four."

"Very good, sir."

"Have tea ready for each appointment."

"I will see to it."

Tristan started off as the other man hid a smirk, obviously skeptical that Helen could be brought to heel, and Tristan, himself, wasn't certain of his options.

Short of picking her up and carrying her to the room, how could he force her to comply? He had no idea.

He stomped up the stairs, winding down the labyrinth of halls that led to the nursery, where the girls would study their lessons and sleep in the adjacent bedchambers.

As he approached, he could hear them talking. He increased his stride, determined to storm in and demand an explanation for Helen's rudeness, but the mention of his name piqued his curiosity. He lagged, then tiptoed closer.

"Do you like Captain Odell?" Rose inquired.

"Of course," Helen glumly responded.

"Would you marry him if you could?"

Helen coughed, as if choking on the prospect. "Definitely not. Why are you two asking all these ridiculous questions?"

"Did Mr. Dubois really give you a love potion?"

"No, he didn't."

"Why would he say such a thing, then?"

"I don't know." Helen sounded unusually exasperated, as if the topic had been incessantly raised.

"Maybe you *should* buy a potion from him," Amelia chimed in.

"Whatever for?"

"To use on Captain Odell, silly."

The comment set off a rash of giggles, which left Tristan disconcerted. He didn't believe in magic; but then again, Helen claimed to have put a spell on him, and he'd been smitten ever since.

"Why on earth," Helen scolded, "would I use a love potion on Captain Odell?"

"So he marries you."

"He's *not* going to marry me. Will you get the notion out of your busy heads?"

"Mr. Dubois's sister gave a love potion to Jane," Amelia tattled.

"When?"

"When you were chatting with Mr. Dubois."

"Why would Jane need a love potion?"

"You never know who might have caught her fancy," Rose mysteriously replied.

"If Jane is willing to try one," Amelia pressed, "why aren't you? I mean, Captain Odell is very nice, and you could—"

"Amelia!" Helen snapped. "Let it go! Please."

Tristan chose this moment to enter. Rose and Amelia grinned, while Helen blushed with embarrassment.

"Hello, girls," he said, and they curtsied.

"Hello, Captain."

They answered together, as if they were one person rather than two. Rose was blooming with happiness, and he was delighted to observe it.

"Will you be all right on your own for a bit?" he asked them.

"Yes, yes . . ." They were glancing back and forth at Helen and himself.

"Miss Hamilton and I will be down in the library."

"We will not," Helen insisted. "Besides, the girls and I need to decide which dresses they'll wear to the village dance on Friday."

"You can decide tomorrow."

"We're scheduled to talk about it now," she mutinously retorted.

Ignoring her, he took her arm and guided her out. Although she wasn't exactly amenable, she wouldn't struggle in front of her charges. She flashed him a look that could have killed, but kept on without verbal complaint.

"I'll send her back in an hour," he said over his shoulder. "You two stay up here till she returns."

He continued on, humored at how he'd manhandled her.

"How long were you standing in the hall?" she muttered through clenched teeth.

"Long enough to hear you gossiping about me."

"We weren't gossiping!" she hotly declared.

"Ha!"

"We weren't!"

"Don't deny it, Helen. My ears are in fine condition."

Apparently, he'd shamed her into silence, and it was a blessed relief. Without another word, he was able to escort her all the way to the library.

The butler was hovering with the tea tray. Tristan deposited Helen in a chair, then went around the desk to sit himself. They stared, an angry, awkward impasse fomenting.

The butler cleared his throat. "Shall I pour, sir?"

"No. Miss Hamilton will do it for me." He glared at Helen, daring her to contradict him. "Won't you, Miss Hamilton?"

For the briefest second, she seethed, appearing as if

she'd decline to obey, but she reined in her temper and gifted the butler with a winning smile.

"I'm happy to oblige the captain in whatever fashion he desires."

"There you have it." Tristan waved the man away. "Miss Hamilton and I have numerous topics about which we must confer. See to it that we're not disturbed."

"I will, Captain."

The butler left, closing the door behind him. Tristan rose and trailed after him to spin the key in the lock. He pulled it out and stuck it in his coat pocket.

They were finally sequestered, and Tristan suffered an emotion that was near to joy. Helen had an entirely different view of the situation.

"Are you insane?" she barked. "Open that door right now."

"No."

He returned to the desk and sat, studying her, curious as to why she caused him to act like such a bully. He'd never previously had to force a woman to endure his company. Then again, no female of his acquaintance would have conducted herself as Helen did.

"The butler will have heard you locking me in," she complained. "In a matter of minutes, the story will be all over the house that I'm in here alone with you, against my will."

"If he tells anyone"—Tristan faced the door so that his voice carried—"he'll be fired, so I'm sure he'll be a veritable fount of discretion."

Someone in the hall—the butler, certainly—tiptoed away.

Tristan smirked. She fumed.

"You are a beast."

He wouldn't dignify the insult with a reply. Instead, he said, "Let's get a few things straight."

"What would those things be?"

"You work for me, Miss Hamilton."

"Yes, I do."

"At the moment, I'm not calling you Helen, because you're behaving like a spoiled child. Perhaps my formality will get your attention, and you'll realize my level of aggravation."

"I've never wanted you to call me Helen."

"Another example of your impossible nature."

"I've been a model employee."

"Except for skipping the meetings I arranged."

"I suppose a person could look at it that way," she grudgingly allowed.

"You don't seem to understand that you must do as I say."

"I think I've been plenty accommodating."

She scowled, vividly reminding him of the failed seduction onboard his ship. He didn't know why he'd invited her for a visit, why he'd taken her to his private quarters. And he definitely didn't know why he'd almost relieved her of her virginity on the table in the middle of the room.

He was lucky they'd quarreled before the girls had burst in.

"Now that we're settled here at the manor, we'll begin having our daily appointments."

"I'm positive my schedule will be much too full."

He sat back, his gaze narrowing with his fiercest ship captain's glower, but it had no effect.

"Why, precisely," he inquired, "do you feel you can counter my wishes?"

"Because—as you just mentioned—I am your employee, but when we're together, we're inclined to mischief."

"I believe I explained as much that day in my cabin."

"Yes, you did. Quite clearly."

"So what is your problem, Miss Hamilton? I'm dizzy from trying to follow your convoluted logic."

"I need this job, and I intend to keep it. If we continue on as we have been, eventually there will be trouble. We'll be discovered by a servant, or Mrs. Seymour will find out, and my reputation would be ruined. I'd no longer be fit to supervise Rose, so you'd have to let me go."

"Can you deem me so fickle that I would fire you over a bit of scandal?"

"You wouldn't have any choice."

"Oh, I always have a *choice*."

"As do I," she said, "and I've made mine. No meetings. Not at ten. Not at four. Not at supper. No meetings."

He'd spent a good share of his life with people telling him what he could and couldn't do. His bastardry had left others with the impression that he could be denied things he wanted or needed, simply because his father hadn't married his mother.

He was prideful and competitive, possessed of his father's aristocratic temperament. He wasn't very proficient at taking orders, that being why he'd mustered out of the Royal Navy as swiftly as he could and, on a wing and a prayer, had started his own shipping enterprise.

When would she learn that he would never do as he was told?

"Miss Hamilton"—he rose from his chair—"is there some reason you imagine that *you* will set the agenda between us?"

"Well, you can't control your baser impulses, so one of us must keep a level head."

"And that would be you?"

"Yes."

He rounded the desk, as she warily watched him. Once she realized he was proceeding directly for her, she made a pathetic attempt to escape, but he was too quick.

He slapped his hands down on the arms of the chair, trapping her.

"What do you want?" she raged.

"Are you drinking love potions again, Miss Hamilton?"

"Not since that first time, and we see what a disaster that turned out to be."

"How was it a disaster?"

"You're awfully taken with me. I wish you wouldn't be."

"We enjoy a physical attraction, Miss Hamilton. Men are powerless against this sort of desire. It's pointless to fight it."

"Try."

"You wouldn't—by any chance—be hoping to ensnare me with magic, would you?"

"As if I could! You're too stubborn for magic to have any effect."

"Now *that* is the smartest thing you've ever said."

He dipped down and kissed her, easing her back with slight pressure. Their lips were softly joined, and she sighed with pleasure. Though she liked to protest and nag, she wasn't immune to him. She rested her palm on his cheek, the sweet gesture thrilling and rattling him.

Kissing her was heaven, and he couldn't fathom why, but once he began, he didn't want to ever stop, which was extremely peculiar.

He'd never been much of a one for kissing. Since his sexual escapades usually involved paid whores, there was no need for wooing. The women with whom he fornicated were reimbursed handsomely to satisfy him, and there was no pretense of affection.

The two parties in the bed—himself and whatever harlot he'd selected—knew what was required and how to get it accomplished in a hurry.

With Helen Hamilton, though, he could have kissed her all day, into the evening, and far into the night, without growing bored.

He bent in, eager to feel his body melded to hers. There was a sofa next to them, and he clasped her waist, intent on swooping her up and laying her down on it, but to his consternation, she managed to wiggle away.

She had him so befuddled with lust that, before he could catch her, she was behind the heavy piece of furniture and using it as a barrier.

Still, he took a menacing step toward it, bizarrely calculating how he might leap over it and grab her—what was *wrong* with him?—but she extended a hand to ward him off.

"Hold it right there, Captain."

"Helen, you exasperate me beyond my limits."

"Not nearly as much as you exasperate me, I'm sure."

"We're simply kissing."

"In the library, in the middle of the afternoon, where anyone could walk in and see."

"The door is locked," he tersely reminded her. "No one can walk in."

"Exactly my point."

"Your *point*? What point is that?"

"I don't suppose you envision *marriage* as your end goal."

"Marriage?" He spit out the word as if it were a tough chunk of meat stuck in his throat. "Don't be absurd. I would never marry you."

"Precisely—which is why I'm leaving, and we are not doing this again."

His remark had sounded like an insult, as if he felt she was beneath him or unsuitable, when in fact, he thought she was very fine, too fine for the likes of him.

He'd made a horrid gaffe, and he couldn't fix it. He wasn't the type to gush with flattery or apologies. Nor would he clarify the comment, for he didn't care to have her discover how incredible he found her to be. If she had a clue as to his high opinion, there'd be no living with her.

She was overly bold, and even the smallest advantage would be wielded to his detriment. Where she was concerned, he'd lost the ability to gain and keep the upper hand. He couldn't be stern, couldn't lay down the law and follow through. In her presence, he'd become a complete and utter milksop, but he was determined that she never know.

"I don't ever plan to wed," he stated, overcome by the need to explain.

"Bully for you."

"It doesn't have anything to do with you personally."

"That certainly makes me feel better."

"I'm a bachelor, and I always will be."

"Just you and your ship, out on all that empty ocean?"

"Well . . . yes."

When she said it like that, it seemed as if she assumed he was lonely, as if she believed his choices had all been bad ones—but they hadn't been.

He was content with his lot, and a bachelor because he enjoyed his independence. He sailed because it was in his blood, because he relished the waves and the water and the sense of freedom it provided.

"Guess what, Captain?" she said.

"What?"

"I *do* plan to wed someday. I want a home of my own, children to mother, and a husband who loves me, and I won't apologize for it."

"I haven't asked you to apologize."

"No you haven't, but I often have the impression that you think I'm desperate, so I'll engage in any loose behavior merely to curry your favor."

"I don't think that about you," he quietly replied.

"I'm a fighter, and I'm going to reclaim the life I used to have. For me, and for my sisters. It was taken from us, but I'll see to it that we get it back."

"I'm betting you will."

"In the meantime, you have these ridiculous ideas about consorting with me in secluded parlors, and you need to rid yourself of them. You're not the marrying kind, and I am."

She skirted the sofa and approached till they were toe-to-toe. Brazenly, she reached into his coat, located the key, and drew it out.

She was so close, her tantalizing scent sweeping over

him, making him anxious to pull her to him, to bury his face at her nape so he could inhale her essence, but he restrained himself, refusing to succumb like the bewitched imbecile he was.

"It's only kissing, Helen," he tried to insist.

"You know that's not true, Tristan."

"We can do it for sport."

"I don't want to do it for *sport*. I want to do it for love."

"We're grown-ups. *Love* is for fools. This is about pleasure."

"You couldn't be more wrong."

"We'll be in the country for several weeks. Won't you be bored?"

"No. I have Rose to look after, as well as my sisters to tend."

She had plenty to keep her busy, chores to accomplish for people she cherished, while he had little to occupy him that was interesting or worthwhile.

The coming days stretched ahead like the road to Hades. He had no one with whom to chat and fraternize, and there was scant satisfaction to be garnered from conferring with tenants or reviewing the estate books with Michael's land agent.

To his horror, he yearned to laugh and play with Helen, and why shouldn't he crave some frivolity? His life was all routine and responsibility, his habits inflexible and ingrained, developed from three decades of fending for himself.

It dawned on him that he'd been anticipating the visit simply because—with the leisurely pace and rural surroundings—he'd expected to have expanded opportunities to sneak off with her. The fact that he wouldn't be able to, that she was ready to sever the tie that bound them, was the most wretched conclusion imaginable.

He might have succumbed to melancholia, but he forced himself to remember that he wasn't hoping for a grand passion. He intended a brief dalliance. Was that too much to ask?

If she declined to proceed with a liaison, what would he do with himself? Mope after her like a whipped dog?

"Stop pestering me," she murmured.

"I've requested an innocent meeting," he grouched. "How is that pestering you?"

"Leave me to my duties. Let me carry on with my assigned tasks."

"I'd rather you spent your time kissing me."

"And I'd rather you turned your attention to someone else."

"Really? That's really what you want?"

"Yes."

He studied her, wondering if she was serious, wondering why it mattered so much. If she didn't care to dally, he could find a woman in the neighborhood to oblige him. Gad, Maud would jump at the chance. He need merely drop a few hints, and she'd welcome him with open arms.

Why put himself through so much misery over Helen?

He was behaving like a buffoon, yet he couldn't get past the notion that if he gave up on her, he'd be relinquishing something fine and rare. There was an ember that sparked when they were together. If he fanned it, if it burned out of control, where would it lead?

How could she not be the least bit curious to learn the answer?

"You're an awful liar," he said, calling her bluff. "You don't want me to seek out another woman. You *can't* want that."

"I'm not lying, Tristan. You're just not listening."

She rose on tiptoe and surprised him by brushing a kiss across his mouth.

Why was it that she could kiss him, but he couldn't kiss her? How was it different?

He grabbed for her, eager to pull her to him, but—as if she were a phantom—she slipped away and went to the door. She stuck the key in the lock and, in a thrice, she was gone, and he was all by himself in the dreary room.

* * *

"WILL we see them kissing again?"

"Of course. Helen drank the potion, so they had must be desperately in love."

Rose and Amelia were sitting on the landing again, spying, waiting on Helen and Tristan. They had been inside the library forever. What were they doing?

"It's so romantic, isn't it?" Amelia asked.

"Like a story in a book."

"Let's pretend they're a prince and princess."

"They were secretly betrothed as children."

"But Helen's wicked stepfather hid her to punish Captain Odell."

"Yes, and Tristan has been searching for her ever since."

"He finally found her."

They both sighed, when suddenly, Helen emerged. They leaned forward, anxious to see without being seen, but the sight that greeted them wasn't what they'd expected.

Helen came out alone, and very quietly, she shut the door. She rested her palm on the center of the wood, her head bowed as if in prayer. She seemed to be reaching out to Captain Odell, or perhaps sending him a visual message.

After a while, she drew away and walked down the hall, but she collapsed against the wall, her legs too wobbly to support her. Her eyes were closed, as if she was in pain, as if she might cry. She hovered, regrouping, gaining strength, then she shook off her unhappiness and kept on.

As Amelia and Rose watched her go, they were stunned.

"What could have happened?" Rose whispered.

"They must have fought."

"Then the potion can't be working."

"I wish Mr. Dubois were here. I'd buy another dose."

"So would I."

"We could put it in his soup."

"We could make him love her. I just know we could."

Disturbed and disheartened, they stood and crept away.

Chapter 11

"WE'RE different from them, aren't we?" Jane glumly inquired.

"Of course we are," Helen replied. "Why would you even ask such a foolish question?"

"Sometimes, it seems as if we belong here, as if it was meant to be. I don't understand why Father's past troubles have to matter so much."

"You can't have imagined we were of the same station as the Seymours. You know better. Our antecedents are much lower, and we can't change that fact."

"It's not fair. We *ought* to belong."

"We don't."

"What's wrong with wishing, though?"

"It can only lead to heartbreak and frustration. That's what's wrong with it."

Helen frowned at Jane, and Jane—not wanting her sister to note any dolor—forced a cheerful expression.

"I know who and what we are," Jane said. "I just thought . . ."

"Thought what?"

"With Captain Odell bringing us into the house as

he did, it skewed my vision of our place in relation to them."

"Well, you need to alter your thinking, and fast. I'm merely the governess—despite how it occasionally seems otherwise."

"We dine at their table, and we wear the pretty clothes he bought. Our bedchambers are in the family wing of the mansion."

"We're the captain's charity case, Jane."

"It doesn't feel like we are."

"Trust me: We are. He was concerned over our plight, and he rectified it by hiring me. I *work* for the man. Don't forget it."

Helen moved off, looking glum herself. She was pale and drawn, her smile having been shoved aside by constant worry, which was odd. Even during their worst period in London, she'd been the eternal optimist, certain that everything would turn out for the best.

And it had—except for the one way that truly counted.

Jane watched in agony as Michael held court in a corner of the crowded parlor. Miriam hung on his arm as he chatted with various neighbors who'd come for supper and cards.

For some reason, after they'd left the city, a barrier had been erected between her and Michael. Miriam had easily assumed the spot at his side, which Jane believed she'd wrangled for her own, and it was pure hell, having to pretend she wasn't devastated.

If she ever saw Miss Dubois again, she'd have a few choice words to share regarding her stupid potion.

Since the night Jane had lain with Michael, they'd had no opportunity for a subsequent assignation. There'd been hectic days of packing, then the trip itself. After they'd arrived, Michael had been swept into the public whirl brought on by his having been installed as the new earl.

Everyone in the area, from beggar to aristocrat, wanted something from him, so he was busy with parties, social calls, and guests.

Through it all, Miriam had been his acknowledged partner. She accompanied him to events at which no one would have considered inviting Jane, the governess's poverty-stricken sister.

Jane was smart and educated. Mentally, she grasped why Michael could never be hers, but emotionally, she was focused on other issues entirely.

She'd been totally convinced of his affection, so positive that she'd surrendered her chastity, but it had all been for naught.

Even though the carnal episode had been distasteful and utterly devoid of romance, she'd do it again in a trice if he but asked it of her.

If only he'd glance in her direction! If only he'd give the tiniest sign that he wanted to be with her! But he didn't notice she existed.

Feeling hurt and betrayed, she seethed with dismay. She was dying to confide in someone, but who could she tell?

Helen was the sole person to whom she could unburden herself, but if Helen had the slightest clue how Jane had been misbehaving with Michael, Helen would take drastic measures. Why, she might even quit her job and relinquish their room and board. Jane would never see Michael again!

She couldn't bear to imagine it, so she suffered in silence.

Her dejected reflections had her so overwhelmed that, before she realized it, Michael was leaving. The vicar and his wife—the evening's honored guests—were departing, and Miriam and Michael were escorting them out.

As they passed, Miriam flashed such a smug look of triumph that Jane yearned to slap it off her plain face. Instead, Jane calmly stood, grinning vapidly, as if her heart wasn't broken into a thousand pieces.

At the last moment, as the rest of the group exited, Michael stepped away from Miriam to set his champagne glass on a waiter's tray. As he did, he was very near to Jane. He winked and mouthed, *May I come to your room?*

Jane nodded, her pulse racing with delirious excitement, as he walked on.

He cared for her! He cared!

She lingered in the parlor as long as she could stand it, then she slipped away without a good-bye to anyone.

She strolled to the grand staircase and climbed gracefully, but once she was out of sight, she ran the remaining distance to her bedchamber. As she hurried in and shut the door, she was laughing, whirling in circles, her arms flung out in celebration, but motion in the inner room had her stumbling to a halt.

Her maid, Lydia, was there, finishing up her chores. She stared at Jane in a blatant fashion that a servant would normally never dare.

Jane reined in her exuberance and studied Lydia in return.

Lydia cleaned Jane's boudoir and assisted her when necessary, but she carried out her duties with minimal competence. She was surly and rude, and could barely conceal how she begrudged Jane her place in the household.

Jane might have spoken to Mrs. Seymour about Lydia's insolence, but Jane was in no position to complain, being lucky to have had a maid assigned to her at all.

"Lydia"—Jane was panicked and wanted the girl gone—"you're up late."

"I can't take to my bed till the party's over."

"It's just ending."

"Will you need help with your dress?" Lydia assessed Jane's torso, as if offended by her pretty gown. "Should I send for a bath?"

She pronounced the word *bath* as if it were an epithet.

"I'm fine. You're excused."

"Are you sure, miss?"

"Yes, quite."

Jane opened the door and gestured to the dark hall, praying that Michael wasn't about to arrive.

Lydia ambled over, slow as molasses, and strutted out. Her gait was so impertinently snotty that Jane was glad she no longer owned any valuables. If she had, she might have searched her jewelry box to see if anything had been stolen.

She waited, hovering, until Lydia's strides faded, then she rushed to the dressing room and scurried about, letting down her hair and yanking off her clothes.

As he quietly entered, she was tugging on her night-gown, pinching her cheeks, then she took a deep breath and went out to the sitting room. Though her stomach felt as if wild horses were galloping through it, she exuded composure, as if his clandestine visit was a common occurrence.

Appearing abashed and uncertain, he dawdled by the door. His coat was off, his golden blond hair gleaming in the candlelight.

He'd brought a single red rose, and he held it out to her.

"For me?" she asked.

"Who else?"

She sauntered over and plucked it from his grasp, pressing the fragrant petals to her nose.

She was awfully nervous, worried that she was doing exactly the wrong thing, that he was taking advantage of her naiveté, of her obvious infatuation, but he smiled at her, and she couldn't help but smile, too.

"I haven't been with you for an eternity," he murmured.

"I know."

"Can you forgive me?"

It was the last comment she'd expected, and she cocked her head, not sure she'd heard him correctly.

"Forgive you? Whatever for?"

"I've been so busy that I haven't been able to sneak away. After what passed between us in London, you must think I'm contemptible."

"No, no, I never could."

He extended his hand, and she dropped the rose and leapt into his arms. Then, he was kissing her and kissing her, and as he picked her up and twirled her round and round, she laughed with joy—and no small amount of relief.

He carried her into the bedchamber, and he deposited her on the mattress and came down after her.

As they began to make love, she understood that it would be completely different from their previous encounter.

He moved effortlessly, showing her how the sexual act was meant to be accomplished. He touched her all over, stripping off her nightgown so she was naked, and he sucked on her nipples, biting and pinching them until she was moaning in agony. She was so happy she wondered if she might die from contentment.

After her initial experience, she was extremely anxious, but thankfully, it was the splendid event her virginal mind had frequently conjured.

There was only pleasure and none of the pain.

When he finally entered her, he slid in easily, their joining so perfect that the Good Lord, Himself, might have specifically created them to fit together.

He thrust meticulously, watching her reactions. Eventually, the sweetest, most exotic wave of ecstasy swept through her. She gasped with surprise, her body tensing, which spurred him to proceed to his own conclusion.

The speed and intensity increased, and very soon, he spilled himself far inside her. Gradually, he relaxed and drew away, stretching out so that they faced each other.

They stared and stared, grinning like fools.

"That was better than the first time, wasn't it?" he asked.

"Much."

"Since then, I haven't thought of anything but you."

"I'm glad."

"I want to be with you as often as I can while we're here in the country."

"I want that, too."

She could hardly keep from squealing with delight. She wouldn't have to fume with resentment, terrified that some other girl had captured his fancy. She wouldn't fret over where he was, because he would be in *her* bed.

"I'll arrive," he said, "as near to midnight as I can manage."

"All right."

"We must be cautious, though."

"Yes, very cautious."

Verbally, she agreed to vigilance, but in all actuality, she was impatient to be discovered. If they were, they'd have to marry immediately. He would be hers forever, but she couldn't risk detection until she was certain he was as madly in love as she. Once she was positive, she would notify the entire world of what they'd done.

"Your reputation mustn't be damaged," he insisted.

"It won't be."

"The village dance is Friday."

"I can't wait."

"I have to show the same amount of attention to everyone; I can't play favorites. Don't be jealous."

"I won't be."

"I would dance every dance with you if I could."

"I know you would."

His respiration was slowing, his eyes drooping. He was dozing off in her bed, and the notion was too thrilling for words.

"Are you tired?" she asked.

"Yes. Let's nap for a while, then we'll do it again."

"I'd like that."

"So would I."

He pulled her close and hugged her, and she lay very still, eager to imprint every detail into her memory so that she would never forget. Yet, even as he drifted off, she was irked to find herself fussing over his presence.

Wasn't this what she wanted from him? Hadn't matters turned out precisely as she'd planned? Why was she so apprehensive?

The pesky morals upon which she'd been raised were niggling at her, and she tried not to heed them, but they wouldn't be silent.

"When you visit me . . ." she murmured.

"Hmm . . . ?"

"My maid is here sometimes. She can't catch you sneaking in. We should probably use some sort of signal to indicate that the coast is clear."

"Your maid is here? At midnight?"

"If I'm up late."

"Who was assigned to you?"

"Her name is Lydia."

"Lydia? Oh, I've known Lydia for ages. Don't worry about her."

His eyes shut, and hers did, too. She slept, cradled in his arms, convinced that she'd made all the right choices.

LYDIA walked down the empty hall, proceeding to her tiny bed in the attic room she shared with three other women. She was grumpy and exhausted and feeling gravely harried at having stayed up merely to tend Jane Hamilton.

The servants were aware of how Captain Odell had rescued the Hamilton sisters from dire straits, how he'd ensconced them alongside the Seymour family when they didn't deserve such an exalted spot.

Lydia was consumed with rage over Jane's good fortune and disturbed by how she constantly threw herself at Lord Hastings.

Over the past few years, he'd showered Lydia with affection, and thus, she had cause to expect that great things were in store for her.

She was buxom and willing, and there was no reason why she couldn't be his mistress. Her mother had been the one to suggest it, and Lydia had quickly decided, *why not?*

Why shouldn't she set her sights so high? A girl could go far by allying herself with such an important man, and she'd just begun hinting at such an arrangement when Jane had arrived on the scene. Where Lydia was concerned, Lord Hastings had been blind ever since.

Lydia hated Jane Hamilton. She hated her pretty hair and big green eyes and willowy figure. She hated the beautiful gowns the captain had bought for her with Lord Hastings's money. Most of all, she hated how Jane was allowed to fritter away the day with no duties or chores, while Lydia had to work like a dog.

In a furious temper, she was marching up the stairs when she heard male footsteps in the hall below. Curiosity had her peeking down, and even though it was very dark, a glimmer of moonlight made it easy to see Lord Hastings as he went by.

Lydia's pulse raced.

It was the perfect occasion to seduce him, and she tiptoed after him and was about to whisper his name, when he stopped at Jane Hamilton's door, spun the knob, and slipped inside.

Lydia was so shocked that she had to count the doorways three times to be positive there was no mistake.

She knew him well; he wasn't in the bloody room to drink tea and eat biscuits! He was having a sexual affair with Jane Hamilton! The rat! And here, Lydia had stupidly thought it was a harmless flirtation.

So . . . Jane Hamilton was putting on airs, prancing about as if she owned the accursed mansion, but when it came right down to it, she was no better than she had to be.

Lydia shook her head with disgust, her mind awhirl with the possibilities presented by Jane's behavior.

How much cash could Helen Hamilton be coerced into

paying so that her sister's folly wasn't revealed? What would it be worth for Helen to save her plush existence?

Even more intriguing, what would Maud Seymour think of Lydia's discovery? Maud had grand plans for Miriam to marry Michael, and she loathed the Hamilton sisters more than Lydia did.

What reward might she offer to be rid of Jane and Helen Hamilton?

Or should Lydia keep the earl's secret for him? Was there an advantage in silence?

She couldn't make a spur-of-the-moment decision on the matter, so she crept to an alcove where she could hide and wait to see what time Lord Hastings emerged. She snuggled down, eager to learn what benefits the night would bring.

Chapter 12

§

"GUESS what I heard?"

"What?"

Clarinda Dudley glanced over at her brother. Their wagon was parked on the lane that led up to Hastings Manor, and she could just see the grand house through the trees. It was a glorious day, the sky so blue, the grass so green.

While she was delighted with their new location, and the world suddenly full of possibilities, his expression was so dour that she laughed.

With their having traveled to the country, chasing after Helen Hamilton, he was in a foul mood. He'd agreed to come, but he was irked over the decision. He insisted that London held better prospects for his personal brand of chicanery, but she didn't care where they camped. One place was the same as the other.

Though she couldn't explain why, it had seemed vital that she tag after the Hamiltons. Silly as it sounded, she felt as if she was destined to befriend them, as if fate had shoved them into her path.

"The housekeeper," Clarinda mentioned, "tells me that they're hiring."

"Why?"

"What with the earl being in residence, they're throwing dozens of parties, and the guest rooms are all occupied. They need extra help."

"Bully for them."

"I thought I might take a job for a bit."

He gaped as if she were insane. "What is wrong with you?"

"It would be fun."

He scoffed with derision. "My sister is not spending the next month cleaning chamber pots for a bunch of rich arseholes."

"We could use the money."

"We have plenty, and besides, with all the people arriving for the harvest festival, we'll make out like bandits. You don't need to work for Lord Hastings."

He looked so stern, as if he were her father and forbidding her from meeting with her favorite beau. He had an intense dislike of the aristocracy and didn't wish to have any interaction with them—unless he was fleecing them out of cash. Then he was happy as a clam.

As for herself, she had no deep feelings one way or another. According to tales told by their long-deceased mother, their father had been the duke of Clarendon, a notorious fiend who had kept their mother as a mistress.

Clarinda didn't know if the story was true, but Phillip was convinced that it was, and he hated all noblemen because of it. To her, it didn't matter if they had been sired by Clarendon or not. It wasn't as if they could show up on his stoop and ask to stay for supper. He was irrelevant.

"Maybe I *want* to work for Lord Hastings," she said, just to needle him. "Maybe I'd enjoy it."

"Don't be absurd. You're too independent, Clarinda. The first time some fussy butler gave you a stupid order, you'd punch him in the nose and quit."

"I might."

She chuckled, absolutely able to imagine it.

She'd been on her own too long, had made her own schedule and followed her own rules, and she wasn't one to suffer fools. Nor was there any reason to waste energy on tasks she loathed.

Yet, as she stared at the manor, the sunlight reflecting off the windows, she was amazed at how desperately she yearned to be inside it, to explore the quiet hallways and study the beautiful things.

"What is our plan while we're here in the country?" she asked him.

"Same as always: Sell, sell, sell to every gullible female who walks by."

"We're low on bottles of Woman's Daily Remedy. Shall I mix up another batch?"

"I will."

It was a fruity alcoholic beverage that they marketed under the guise of it having medicinal qualities. Phillip claimed it eased stress, but mostly it left customers intoxicated so that they didn't worry over their troubles.

Earlier in the summer, Lord Redvers had warned Phillip not to dispense any more of it, but Redvers wasn't present, was he? She and Phillip could do what they liked without the officious aristocrat horning in and telling them how to act.

She was retrieving a basket of empty bottles, and Phillip combining the ingredients, when they heard voices down the road. Shortly, Jane and Helen Hamilton strolled around the bend.

"Look who's here," Phillip murmured.

"Just who I was hoping to meet," Clarinda said.

Phillip scowled. "Why?"

"I like them." She shrugged, perplexed by her interest.

"I swear, you've tipped off your rocker."

"I'm trying to be friendly. Where's the harm?"

"When we saw them down by the harbor in London, didn't you give Jane a potion?"

"Yes."

"We must find out if love has blossomed," Phillip said. "I'll waylay Helen, while you chat with Jane. Perhaps she'll buy something."

With Phillip, it was always about the money. He thrived on the verbal sparring, gleaning an enormous boost from persuading women to purchase items they didn't need. She'd never liked his mercenary tendencies, and though she possessed many of them, she strove valiantly not to let them show.

"Bonjour, bonjour," Phillip gushed, his fake French accent firmly in place as he hurried down the lane to greet them.

Clarinda waved at Jane, and Jane waved back, relief crossing her face, leaving Clarinda with the distinct impression that Jane was very glad to see her.

"Mr. Dubois?" Helen's smile was wide. "What are you doing here?"

"We always travel near Hastings Manor this time of year," he blithely lied. "It's part of our regular route." He was guiding her around the wagon. "I'm mixing a batch of my famous Woman's Daily Remedy. Would you like to try a sample?"

"I might, but I'd have to . . ."

Their words trailed off, and Jane rushed over to Clarinda. She stepped close, their heads together like a pair of conspirators, which Clarinda supposed they were.

"I can't believe you're here," Jane said. "What are you *really* doing?"

"I was worried about you," Clarinda admitted, whispering.

"You came all this way just to check?"

"Yes," Clarinda fibbed, hating that her knack for fabrication was so ingrained. "Our tonics are very powerful. I had to be certain you applied yours correctly. How is Lord Hastings?"

"I gave it to him that very same night, and for a while, it seemed to work."

"He fell in love with you?" Clarinda carefully shielded her incredulity.

"Madly in love, but then, he started avoiding me to spend time with his cousin."

"The swine!"

"I was afraid that the potion had waned or that he didn't swallow enough of it. Do you have some more?"

"Of course."

Clarinda grabbed two vials, and Jane stuck them in her purse.

"Administer a double dose," Clarinda counseled, "to be sure."

"I will. But what about his cousin? The family expects them to marry, and I've been so anxious about it."

Clarinda added another pouch to Jane's burgeoning reticule.

"Slip this powder to her."

"What will it do?"

"It will make blotches break out all over her face."

Jane appeared gleefully horrified. "Will they be permanent?"

"No, but after Lord Hastings sees them, they will have a dampening effect. He'll never gaze at her in a fond manner again."

"That's just the sort of thing I need. Thank you, Miss Dubois. Thank you so much!"

In a burst of youthful exuberance, Jane hugged Clarinda, and Clarinda hugged her back, charmed by the endearing gesture.

"You may call me Clarinda if you like."

"I will," Jane said, but she didn't offer a reciprocal familiarity, and though Clarinda tried not to, she couldn't help but feel annoyed.

She knew who Jane's father was—the disreputable Harry Hamilton—and she supposedly knew who her own was—Duke of Clarendon. Clarinda's blood was much bluer than Jane Hamilton's, but Jane was wearing a pretty dress and residing in the manor, so circumstances set them apart in ways Clarinda couldn't counter.

"Will you be attending the village dance on Friday?" Clarinda inquired.

"Yes. Will you be there, too?"

"Yes. I'll want to hear how well the potions are working."

"I can't wait to tell you everything," Jane replied, and she went to find her sister.

"WHAT is it, *cherie*?" Phillip asked of Helen Hamilton. "When I last spoke with you, you were so happy. Now you are very *triste*, very sad."

"Nonsense," Miss Hamilton responded. "I'm perfectly fine."

"You cannot lie to me, *mon amie*. I see it in your eyes. What has happened?"

"It's nothing."

He moved nearer to encourage confidences.

"Is it your dashing Captain Odell?"

"He's not *my* Captain Odell."

"You lie to me again, mademoiselle. After you drank my tonic, he was completely smitten. You told me so, yourself."

"I did not. I was merely curious about what seemed to be his . . . ah . . . heightened interest."

He studied her, thinking what a shame it was that such a beauty could be so worn down by amour. People always thought Phillip had psychic abilities, but actually he was simply a good judge of human nature.

Women fell in love too easily and when that love was unrequited, their misery was plain for anyone who bothered to look.

"And now?" he queried. "What is your opinion of his affection?"

"I was mistaken. He has no interest in me at all."

"How can that be? He can't have forsaken you. My Spinster's Cure is too strong."

"I don't believe in your potions, Mr. Dubois."

"Just because you don't believe, doesn't mean they don't work."

She sighed, then glanced over at her sister. Evidently she felt that Jane was too close, so she took his arm and led him down the lane. They strolled along, like a pair of sweethearts, until they'd rounded the bend and couldn't see the wagon. She drew him to a halt.

"I have been a bit disconcerted," she confessed.

"Of course you have been."

"I don't know very much about men, Mr. Dubois."

"No female does. We're peculiar creatures."

"Might I ask you a hypothetical question?"

"*Certainement,* Miss Hamilton. I am at your service."

She gazed at him, her expression so touchingly perplexed. "Let's say there was a man—a very handsome, very dynamic man."

"Someone like Captain Odell, perhaps?"

"Yes, someone just like him. Let's also say that he started to fancy a particular woman."

Phillip's mind was spinning as he speculated over what horrid thing Odell had done to her. The rogue was a sailor. What had she expected?

She had to be insane, involving herself with him. Then again, she was Odell's employee and living under his roof. Given her position as governess, it would be difficult to deflect his attention without risking her job.

Phillip's temper boiled. He loved women and hated to see them abused.

"This man," Phillip said. "In what sort of mischief do you imagine he might engage?"

"He might have requested . . . well . . . an illicit liaison." Hurriedly, she added, "The woman knows right from wrong, though, so she refused."

"Let me guess: He's angry at being rebuffed?"

"Yes, and he's forgotten all about her and moved on to another."

All pretense of a hypothetical was abandoned. Her shoulders sagged, and she appeared young and lost. It was all he could do to keep from hugging her.

"Who is he courting?"

"Lord Hastings's cousin Mrs. Seymour. She's resided with the family for years, and she took care of the earl and his sister before Captain Odell arrived."

"He's smitten by this Mrs. Seymour?"

"They're together constantly, like two peas in a pod."

Phillip had never met Odell, but he could vividly picture the horse's ass: rich, powerful, arrogant. Odell's pride would never accept rejection from a lowly servant such as Miss Hamilton. No doubt, he was dabbling with Mrs. Seymour merely to make Miss Hamilton jealous, to grind salt in her wounds.

Odell was a knave!

"Ah, *cherie*, I'm sorry," he murmured.

She stared at the ground. "I'm a fool, aren't I?"

"He's a charming devil, and he helped your sisters. How could you not love him?"

"I'm so stupid."

He patted her shoulder, wishing he could offer useful solace, but he didn't have much to suggest but for a few worthless tonics.

"In romantic affairs," he gently said, "rational people are known to behave irrationally. Be glad you declined his advance. Think where you'd be now if you hadn't."

"I am glad." She peered up at him, her torment clear. "I did the right thing, didn't I? In refusing him? Tell me I did the right thing."

"Yes, you did. You're no match for such a worldly fellow, and he was cruel to have pressured you. Only heartbreak would have resulted."

"Heartbreak resulted anyway."

She chuckled miserably, and he chuckled, too. He slipped her hand into his arm, guiding her back toward the wagon. As they walked, carriage wheels sounded behind them, and they turned to see a sporty gig approaching, a man and woman snuggled on the high, narrow seat.

"Oh no," Miss Hamilton muttered.

"Who is it?"

"Captain Odell and Mrs. Seymour—out for their afternoon drive. They've been taking one every day."

Odell was a handsome bloke, dark-haired and fashionably attired, his broad chest filling out his expensive coat. Phillip detested him on sight.

Mrs. Seymour—with a plain face, mousy hair, and unflattering gown—was no beauty, but she understood the brilliant catch she'd made. The side of her body was wedged to his, and she chatted in his ear, preening like the cat that had found the cream.

Odell saw Miss Hamilton, and he tugged on the reins, the horse lurching to a halt.

"Fancy meeting you here, Miss Hamilton." His demeanor was cold and haughty.

"Captain Odell." She gave the most fleeting curtsy in history.

Odell insolently assessed Phillip, his curiosity as to Phillip's identity blatant and offensive.

"Why are you ambling down the lane?" he barked at Miss Hamilton. "It's the middle of the day. Shouldn't you be at work?"

"I have Wednesday afternoon off."

"Do you? I'd forgotten."

Mrs. Seymour simpered. "You're too lenient with the servants, Captain. An afternoon off? In midweek? Next she'll be wanting paid holidays."

At being reminded of her status as *servant,* Miss Hamilton bristled, but she wasn't cowed by the pair. Her hot, furious gaze locked on Odell, and his cheeks reddened.

Apparently, the obnoxious cad was capable of embarrassment.

"Perhaps I should reconsider her schedule," Odell mused.

"Perhaps you should," Seymour agreed. "She already has Sunday morning off to attend church. How much time does a governess need to herself anyway?"

"Who is your companion?" Odell asked Miss Hamilton. "Have you snagged yourself a beau? I'm not normally one to pry, but in light of your obligations to my ward, it's not appropriate for you to fraternize with bachelors."

Odell's expression was just as furious and just as pained as Miss Hamilton's, and it occurred to Phillip that they were pitifully in love, with Odell as enamored of Miss Hamilton as she was of him.

"I'm Philippe Dubois." Phillip laid on thick his French accent, knowing it was a mannerism Odell would loathe. *"J'ai beaucoup d'affection pour elle."*

"Speak English, you damn Frenchie," Odell snapped.

"As you wish, monsieur. I have been hoping to win Miss Hamilton's affection, but she too much enjoys her duties at the manor. Thus, to my infinite regret, she has declined a deeper attachment."

The remark had Odell so fit to be tied that he nearly leapt out of the carriage to pummel Phillip.

"Will you be staying with us, Miss Hamilton?" Odell snidely seethed. "Or are you running off with your French *suitor*?"

"I'll be staying, Captain. I'm happy at my post."

"We'll be going on then," Odell told her. "I don't suppose that it would be too much to ask that you return to the house at once?"

"I'll rush back immediately. I apologize for causing you any dismay."

Miss Hamilton's tone was sweet and deferential, but there was no concealing the impertinence rippling beneath the words.

Odell studied her, obviously wondering if he should reprimand her or continue to bicker, but his temper was barely controlled. He gave up, not keen on releasing his pent-up emotions in front of Seymour.

"See to it that you're home when I arrive."

He clicked the reins, and the horse clopped on.

"Ooh, that man," she fumed when he was out of sight, and she spun on Phillip. "What were you thinking? You're my beau? You're lucky you didn't get me fired!"

Phillip shrugged, unrepentant. "It seemed the best way to play it."

"To *play* it? This isn't a game, Mr. Dubois. This is my life! It's the difference between my sisters living in a grand mansion or out on the streets with no food in their bellies."

"You asked me for advice about men, Miss Hamilton. Captain Odell is not about to fire you."

"Why not?"

"Because he's in love with you."

She blinked and blinked. "That is the most patently ridiculous thing anyone has ever said to me."

"Trust me on this: He's mad about you, and I was simply fanning his jealousy."

"You are insane."

"Am I?" he smugly posed. "As far as I can tell, my Spinster's Cure is performing precisely as it's meant to. I suspect you'll be wed to him before the month is out."

It was an easy prediction to make. If Odell married her, Phillip would look like a matrimonial genius. If Odell didn't, she'd visit Phillip for more guidance and potions. In both situations, he came out the winner.

He escorted her to the wagon, vaguely listening as she complained about how wrong he was.

"Will you be at the village dance?" he inquired.

"Yes."

"I assume Captain Odell will be there, as well?"

"Yes."

"I suggest you dance with me numerous times."

"Why?"

"So that we can further inflame his passions. A romantic stroll in the dark woods next to the village green probably wouldn't be amiss, either. We'll let him imagine we're engaged in a torrid tryst."

She scoffed. "He doesn't care about me; he wouldn't even notice I was gone."

"We'll see, won't we?" he boasted.

They arrived at the wagon, and he handed her a bottle of red liquid.

"What's this?" she asked.

"It's the Woman's Daily Remedy I mentioned. Have a sample, with my compliments."

"I should drink it . . . why?"

"It will quiet your broken heart—until the Captain comes to his senses."

"My heart is *not* broken."

"Isn't it?"

When she hesitated, he grabbed the bottle and placed it in her purse.

"Everything will be fine," he murmured. "Leave it to me."

Chapter 13

ভ

"WHAT gown have you decided on, Mrs. Seymour?"

"The green one with the matching shawl."

Lydia went to the dressing room and returned with the garment Maud had mentioned. Maud was silent as Lydia helped her into it. As Lydia stepped away, Maud twirled in front of the mirror, admiring herself.

She'd never been a beauty, but it was amazing how a bit of flirtation with a handsome man always made a woman prettier.

Over the past few weeks, Captain Odell had showered Maud with attention, taking her for rides in the carriage, sitting with her at meals, meeting her for drinks late in the afternoon. He'd been the absolute model of chivalry, becoming so indulgent that it seemed as if another person had begun to occupy his body.

She had no idea what had brought about the change. Nor would she question the transformation. The only explanation was that their living together in Michael's home had caused an affection to develop. Why else would he be so intrigued?

He'd invited her to the village dance, and if she was lucky, she might finally wrangle the kiss she'd been seeking. If she was *extremely* lucky, perhaps she'd stir him to a sexual encounter from which he wouldn't be able to extricate himself. After all, he couldn't dabble with a woman of her station unless he married her in the end.

"What do you think of my outfit, Lydia?" she asked the insolent girl. "Is it the appropriate color for me?"

"It's fine."

Maud sat on the stool at the dressing table. "Fix this curl, will you?"

Lydia grumbled to herself as she walked over and laid the curling iron in the fire. She was like an obstinate donkey, always hoping her chores were finished, and being surly when they weren't.

Maud might have fired her years earlier, but Lydia often came in handy. For all her slovenly ways, Lydia was very good with hair and clothes. She was also a veritable fount of information, being content to spy, tattle, or betray anyone if the price was right, so Maud had assigned her to tend Helen and Jane Hamilton.

Maud was eager for facts she could use to the sisters' detriment. She was determined to be shed of them, and with the captain now seeming to regret that he'd hired Helen Hamilton, it wouldn't take much to push him into letting her go.

"I haven't talked with you in ages," Maud said. "How is Jane Hamilton getting on?"

"She's getting on very well."

Lydia spun away, hiding a grin.

"What's that supposed to mean?"

"Nothing."

"Has she scheduled any more of her horseback rides with Lord Hastings?"

"She and the earl have been *riding* quite a lot."

Lydia snickered, and Maud might have remarked on it, but suddenly, a high-pitched howl sounded out in the hall. The door was flung open, and Miriam raced in. She was still in her robe, not yet having dressed for the dance.

"Mother! Mother!"

"What is it?" Maud asked.

"Look at my face!"

"What's the matter with it?"

"I'm covered with blotches!" Miriam moaned.

There was a lamp on the table. Maud lifted it and held it closer. She blanched.

"When did this happen?"

"I was having supper in my room when I noticed I was scratching, then scratching harder, and then . . . this rash popped out everywhere."

Mother and daughter stared in horror at the mirror. Angry welts marred Miriam's cheeks, neck, and arms. Not spots exactly, but not a rash, either. Maud had never seen anything like it.

"Are you feverish?" Maud was terrified that Miriam had contracted an awful new plague that they'd all catch.

"No, just itchy!" Miriam raked her nails over her skin, garnering no relief. "What should I do? Michael asked me to join him in leading off the dancing. You know what an honor it is! The entire village will be watching. I can't go like this!"

"No, you can't. Fetch some cold water!" Maud barked to Lydia. "Wet a cloth!"

"Yes, ma'am."

Maud eased Miriam into a chair, waiting, then observing as Lydia sauntered in with a bowl and pitcher. She poured water into the bowl, dipped a cloth and wrung it out, then she handed it to Maud, who handed it to Miriam.

Maud wasn't the maternal type, and she didn't wish to touch the inflammation. She wasn't about to show up at the dance appearing as if she'd contracted leprosy.

"Is it helping?" Maud inquired.

"Not really," Miriam wailed, "but I can't let it keep me at home. If I do, Jane Hamilton will take my place at Michael's side."

"Over my dead body," Maud seethed.

"Oh, the swelling is getting worse!"

The evening was to have been Maud's crowning achievement, capping years of effort at positioning Miriam so that greatness fell on her.

Michael was at the family seat, for his first visit as earl. Every person for miles around would be at the party, excited to meet the handsome boy who was now responsible for the welfare of so many.

The highlight was always the kick-off to the dancing. Michael had chosen Miriam—his dear cousin, whom he was expected to wed—to parade with him down the center of the village green. The whole world would have seen Miriam basking in his glow.

Wasn't it just like her to wreck everything?

Maud glared at Lydia. "What would you suggest?"

"We could try to conceal it with some of your white facial powder."

"I can't cover my face with powder," Miriam shrieked, appalled. "I'll look like an elderly woman who's hiding her age spots. Michael won't know it's me; he'll think I'm an old hag."

"Have you a better idea?" Maud fumed.

"No," Miriam dolefully replied.

Lydia—with a bit of glee—grabbed the powder and began to dab a heavy coating on Miriam's skin.

"THESE rural celebrations are certainly quaint, aren't they?"

"Yes, very quaint. People seem to be enjoying themselves, though."

Tristan gazed across the grass, studying the large crowd. Everyone was laughing, dancing, eating, and drinking.

Through the throng, he was vaguely aware that Maud was chattering, and her voice was so aggravating, like nails on a chalkboard. Why had he decided to commence a flirtation with her? What insane motive had been driving him?

It was all Helen's fault.

He'd done it to make her jealous, but she hadn't even noticed that Tristan was spending time with Maud. She was so unconcerned, he might have been invisible.

In his entire life, he hadn't encountered a single female who'd told him *no*. He was the bastard son of an earl, a randy Scot, a sailor. Women viewed him as wild and dangerous, and they all wanted him because of it—except Helen Hamilton.

"There goes Miss Hamilton again," Maud complained, yanking him out of his bitter reverie.

"What?"

He could practically smell Maud's desperation to be allied with him, and he could have snapped his fingers and had her in his bed, but he was too obsessed with Helen to bother. He constantly pondered how he could be having sex with *her* instead of Maud. She'd refused him; his pride was bruised, and he was burning with rage.

He'd like to wring her scrawny neck for putting him through such misery.

"She's with that Frenchman," Maud pointed out. "I realize that—initially—you felt some sympathy for her plight, but must we keep her on? Surely, with her involved in this dalliance, she's not an appropriate servant to be caring for Rose."

Helen had been partnered with the blasted foreigner all night, twirling past Tristan over and over. What was his name? Dubois?

Who was he, anyway? Where had Helen met him? Why would Helen prefer him over Tristan?

"Captain," Maud nagged, "did you hear me?"

"What?"

"We were talking about Miss Hamilton."

"We were?"

"Yes, and I sincerely believe that—"

Miriam promenaded by on the arm of a man Tristan didn't know. She had a scarf over her face, and she was ghostly white.

"What is wrong with Miriam?" he asked.

"Nothing. Why?"

"She looks like a damned specter."

"She's fine." Maud forced a smile. "So I was thinking—"

"About what?"

"About Miss Hamilton! Captain, it's so disconcerting when you're distracted. This is important to me. I wish you'd pay attention."

Maud snuggled herself closer, but Helen and her swain had parted company. Tristan watched as the dubious gentleman snuck off behind the blacksmith's barn where the male partygoers were enjoying a whiskey away from the ladies.

"Would you excuse me?"

"What?"

He slipped away and was instantly swallowed up by the crowd.

Maud called, "Captain! Honestly!"

She hurled a few pleading invectives, but he didn't heed them. He was too focused on his goal—that being Helen's beau.

He headed directly to the whiskey keg and filled a glass, needing the liquor to soothe his temper. He sipped it, feigning calm as he scanned the group, locating Dubois off by himself, leaning against a tree and drinking.

Tristan marched over.

"Who the hell are you," he demanded without preamble, "and how do you know Helen Hamilton?"

"Well, well, if it isn't the infamous Captain Odell."

"Answer my question: How are you acquainted with my governess?"

"Helen and I go way back."

"How *far* would that be, precisely?"

"Farther than you'd probably like to imagine," the cheeky fellow retorted in perfectly enunciated English. "Phillip Dudley, at your service."

"What happened to your accent?"

"I'm not French," Dudley boldly admitted. "Helen assumes I am, though. The ladies always find it enchanting, so I like to pretend."

He winked as if they were conspirators in his duplicity toward Helen.

"You're flirting with her because . . . ?"

"Recently she's had some financial trouble, and she's been disowned by her family—because of her dear old da, Harry—but they'll come around eventually. When they do, she'll receive a pot of money. I'll be there to help her spend it."

Tristan was aghast. "You're hoping to marry her in case she inherits some money in the future?"

Dudley chuckled. "Nobody mentioned *marriage*. I simply intend to be her very special friend."

"She's not stupid enough to trust you."

"Isn't she? She's gullible, and she's lonely, and I know just how to play her. In the end, she'll do anything I say." He paused and grinned. "Absolutely anything."

Before Tristan realized what he planned, he punched Dudley as hard as he could, his fist connecting with the man's cheek. Dudley stumbled, but didn't fall to the ground.

"Arrogant bugger," Dudley grumbled, rubbing his jaw.

"Leave her be."

"Why should I?"

"Because I'm ordering you to."

"She's a bloody servant. Why would you care what I do with her? Fire her if you don't want her consorting with me. If she doesn't have a job, she'll be easier to seduce."

Tristan lunged, but Dudley grabbed his wrist, stopping a second blow.

"If you hit me again," Dudley warned, "I'll hit you back. And believe me: With the mood I'm in, I doubt you'll best me."

He was about Tristan's height, with the same muscular

physique. Would they brawl? Tristan would relish a scuf-
fle, and he supposed it would be an even match, with Dudley fighting dirty at every turn. Unfortunately, he didn't
have the chance to learn who would be the victor.

"Hey, you two!" a man hollered from over by the keg.
"There's no quarreling allowed here."

"Save it for another day," someone else counseled.
"Don't spoil the fun for the ladies."

Dudley shoved Tristan's fist away, and Tristan stepped
back, not inclined to continue with so many glaring at
them.

"I'll never fire her," Tristan tersely seethed, "so stay the
hell away from her."

"Damned if I will," Dudley bragged, and he stomped
away before Tristan could reply or react.

"HAVE you seen her?"

"Yes!"

Clarinda and Jane peered over to where Miriam Seymour was hiding behind her mother.

The white cosmetic was appalling. It made her very
pale, but to counter the wan coloring, she'd added bright
red rouge to her mouth and cheeks. In the dim surroundings, she appeared more ghoulish than ghostly.

"I expected your potion to work," Jane whispered, "but
I had no idea!"

"Neither did I," Clarinda mumbled under her breath.

"Were you present for the opening festivities?"

"We arrived too late. The party had already started."

"At the manor, Miriam missed the carriage—
intentionally, I'm sure—so we left without her."

"Which meant Lord Hastings was without a partner for
the first dance."

"Yes, and he asked me to fill in for her! The whole
village saw us. Everyone is gossiping about it. They're all
curious as to why the earl is so fond of me."

"I'm so glad for you."

"When Miriam finally showed up, Lord Hastings took one look at her and nearly fainted—just as you told me he would."

"Did he say anything?"

"No. He's too polite."

"So it all resolved to your benefit."

"Yes. He's danced with me three times. Three!" Jane seized Clarinda's hands and twirled her in a joyous circle. "Can you believe it?"

"Of course I can," Clarinda loyally said. "You're the most beautiful girl here. How could he not want to be with you?"

"He must be falling in love, Clarinda. Don't you imagine he is?"

She seemed so eager that Clarinda could only agree.

"I'm certain of it."

"It's all your doing. How can I ever thank you?"

Be my friend, Clarinda mused. *Let me be part of your world.*

The musicians were striking up the next tune, and a young dandy rushed up to Jane. "Miss Hamilton! Will you do me the honor?"

Jane smiled at Clarinda as she explained, "Since Lord Hastings favored me with his attention, every other boy wants a turn. It's the greatest night of my life!"

Without a good-bye, she pranced off, and Clarinda watched her go, wondering if she'd ever been that young, that imprudently enamored; the answer was a definite no. She would never permit a man to have so much power over her.

From the sidelines, she observed the merriment, deciding she might dance again, too, when she saw her brother limping out from behind the barn.

He scanned the crowd, obviously searching for her, and he hobbled over. As he approached, she noted that someone had hit him. His cheek was swelling, and in the morning, he'd likely have a black eye.

"You were fighting?" she scolded.

"I wouldn't call it a fight, precisely. It was a single punch, thrown before I realized it was coming."

"Honestly," she complained, "I can't take you any-where."

"I know, I know, I act as if I was raised in a cave."

It was one of Clarinda's constant criticisms. "Might I ask the identity of the fellow who caught you unawares? Or were you boxing with strangers?"

"I was giving Captain Odell a piece of my mind, but he replied with his fist."

"Captain Odell? Are you insane? You're lucky he didn't murder you."

"He certainly wanted to."

Phillip grinned in a smug way that indicated he had a scheme fomenting and that it was progressing nicely.

"What are you up to now?"

"I'm just ensuring that the Spinster's Cure has every chance to cast its magic on Helen Hamilton."

"What are you talking about?"

"Odell is convinced I'm an unscrupulous rake and that poor, gullible Miss Hamilton is about to run off with me—to her eternal detriment."

"Why tell him that?"

"The wretched bloke is hopelessly in love with her."

"How do you know?"

"Oh, please," Phillip scoffed. "I am Philippe Dubois, remember? *Amour* is my stock and trade. Odell was so jealous that I thought the top of his head was going to blow off."

As they spoke, Odell strutted out from the shadow of the barn. He stopped near the dais where the musicians were located, and he had a clear view of the festivities. His feet were braced, his hands clasped behind his back as if he was on the deck of his ship and guiding it through rough weather.

He searched the gathering till he found Helen Hamil-ton. She was dancing with the vicar, looking pretty and happy and completely oblivious to Odell, whose fierce focus could have set her on fire.

Clarinda had to admit that Phillip was probably correct: Odell appeared to be wildly jealous.

Phillip studied Helen, then Odell, then Helen again.

"First, it was Lady Redvers," he said, "drinking the Spinster's Cure and ending up married to the viscount. Now it's Helen Hamilton who'll end up with Odell. Didn't you give her sister something, as well?"

"A love potion and a curse."

"I know she felt the potion was effective. How about the curse?"

"Worked like a charm."

Gleefully, he rubbed his palms together as if they were about to be filled with gold coins.

"When word of this gets out, we will make a bloody fortune."

Chapter 14

❦

HELEN knelt in the window seat in her bedchamber, staring out at the starry sky. It was late and quiet, and she felt very lonely, as if she was the last person on earth.

The village dance had been splendid, the music lively and gay, the villagers cordial and boisterous, so why was she moping?

Yes, Captain Odell had forsaken her, but what had she expected?

He was a proud man, and she'd spurned him. Did she suppose he'd sit about, pining over her and trying to win her back?

Sighing with dismay she pulled the cork from the bottle of Woman's Daily Remedy that Mr. Dubois had given her. Though she wasn't much of a drinker, she sensed alcohol in the concoction, the liquor masked by a strong cherry flavoring. She downed a swig, then another, and another, liking how it warmed and relaxed her.

She'd told Mr. Dubois that she wasn't heartbroken, but she'd been lying. She was bereft, exhausted from pretending that all was well, and miserable from acting as if Odell didn't matter.

She slipped from her perch by the window, but she was very dizzy, and she had to grab the dresser to keep her balance.

"Oh my," she breathed.

The remedy was more potent than she'd imagined, and she decided she should ingest some milk to counter its effects, which meant a trip to the kitchen in her nightgown and robe, but what harm could there be? Everyone was asleep, so no one would see her.

Carefully, she started out, finding it easier to walk if her focus was glued to the floor. She stumbled toward the stairs, but with it being so dark, she took a wrong turn, and gradually, she seemed to be winding down a maze of hallways that led nowhere.

At the end of a grand corridor, she halted and frowned, realizing she was lost.

She stood, wondering what to do, when suddenly, the door behind her opened.

"Get your ass in here," a very angry, very stern male said, and she was yanked into the room.

She yelped with surprise, but before she could figure out what had happened, the door slammed shut and was locked.

She whipped around, coming face-to-face with Tristan Odell. He was attired only in his trousers, the top buttons undone, the flap loose, providing tantalizing glimpses of his flat belly and private regions down below.

His black hair was hanging to his shoulders. The gold pirate's earring gleamed in his ear.

His bare shoulders were very wide, his chest very broad, and she gulped with dismay—but with excitement, too.

They were alone! Together! Was she dreaming?

The suite was masculine in its decor, with heavy mahogany furnishings, maroon drapes, and plush carpets. A cozy fire burned in the grate, and he'd been over by it, lounging in a comfortable chair. On a table next to it, there was a glass and decanter of liquor. The decanter was nearly empty.

In the room beyond, she could see his bed. It was massive, as if built for a king.

"Is this your bedchamber?" she stupidly asked.

"As if you didn't know, you little hussy."

"I think I'd best be going."

She spun as if to hurry out but he pointed to a chair and growled, "Sit your ass down."

"I don't believe I ought. I really, really should—"

"Sit down!" he bellowed, and she scurried over and plopped onto the hard seat.

He glared at her, his torrid gaze meandering down her torso, taking in the fact that she wasn't dressed, that her long hair was curling down her back.

His examination was very thorough, as if he was stripping her with his eyes, as if she was naked. Her body rippled with anticipation, her nipples tightening into painful buds that pushed against the fabric of her nightgown.

He didn't speak, but kept looking and looking, and finally she said, "Was there something you wanted?"

"Bloody right there was something I wanted!"

He approached until he was directly in front of her, and he trapped her by slapping his palms down on the arms of the chair.

"You tell that cheeky sister of yours to stay away from my ward."

"What?"

"I see the game she's playing, and it won't work."

"What *game* is that?" She bristled.

"She can flirt and tempt and tease to infinity, but Michael Seymour will never marry her."

"Why, you arrogant wretch! How dare you make insinuations about my sister!"

"When they are fully deserved, I'll say whatever I like."

"When you insult her, you insult me—and my dear, deceased father. I won't stand for it."

"Your *dear father*? Now there was a scoundrel." He flashed a feral grin. "You certainly inherited his tendencies toward duplicity and deceit, didn't you."

"I have no idea what you're talking about."

"Don't you?" He pulled away and stood. "The apple doesn't fall far from the tree, does it, Miss Hamilton? Are you a *Miss*, by the way? Or have you lain with every Tom, Dick, and Philippe in the county?"

She was so furious, she couldn't decide where to begin chastising him.

He hadn't deigned to notice her in weeks, and this was how he chose to act?

She leapt to her feet, ready to slap him silly then storm out, but he shouted again, using his most authoritative ship-captain's roar.

"I told you to *sit down*, Miss Hamilton! What part of that command do you fail to comprehend?"

To her great mortification, she obeyed, her bottom slamming onto the cushion so fast that gravity had to have tugged at an especially quick rate.

She watched, mildly horrified and incredibly intrigued, as he started to pace. She felt as if she was one of his sailors, listening to a list of transgressions that detailed why she was about to be flogged.

"You are not to ever be alone with Mr. Dubois."

"What?"

"You are *not* to be alone with him. Do you hear me?"

It was the strangest edict ever.

"Yes, I hear you, and I think you're out of your mind."

"YOU ARE NOT TO BE ALONE WITH HIM!" he yelled.

He was on the verge of hysterics, and she couldn't fathom why, but she remembered Dubois's assertion that the captain was wild for her.

Could Dubois be correct? Was Odell *jealous*?

A vain thrill coursed through her. What if he was? What did it mean? Where would it take them?

"I can't see," she blithely said, "how my relationship with Philippe is any of your business."

"Philippe?" he gasped, his voice shrill. "You call that blackguard *Philippe*?"

"Why wouldn't I? He's asked me to marry him three times. We're very close, so there's no reason to—"

Before she could finish the sentence, he swooped in and lifted her into his arms, and he turned and marched to the bedroom.

She squealed and fussed and kicked, but it was no use. He was bent on his destination, and he wasn't about to let her escape. Not that she wanted to; it just seemed that a lady should protest.

He dropped her onto the mattress, and though she tried to squirm away, he was on her in an instant, his lean, hard body stretched out the length of hers, pinning her down.

"He is *not* a gentleman," he fumed.

"Maybe I like that about him."

"He's not even French, you little fool. He's a damned Englishman, with a fake accent, who's playing on your gullible nature."

"That can't be. I trust him with my life. He has so many plans for us."

"Oh, he has *plans,* all right. Plans such as planting a babe in your belly, then running off with all your money."

"All my . . . my . . . money?"

She laughed and laughed. She couldn't help it.

Obviously, Mr. Dubois and the captain had conversed. What had Dubois said?

When next they crossed paths, she'd have to profusely thank him.

"What is so funny?" he snapped.

"You. You're absolutely hilarious."

"I'm protecting your virtue and reputation."

"Ha! I may work for you, but you don't own me. I'm an adult woman, and I can consort with whomever I please. It's not your place to order me about."

"Is that really what you suppose?"

"Yes."

"Hear me and hear me well, Miss Hamilton: Dubois's name isn't even *Dubois.* It's Dudley. He is a fraud and a villain, and you are never to speak with him again."

"I'm sorry, but I'm afraid I have to—"

"Aren't you listening? *Never* again!"

TRISTAN felt possessed, as if demons had entered his body and he couldn't expel them.

Ever since he'd met Phillip Dudley, ever since he'd learned Dudley's low intentions toward Helen, he'd been in a fine fettle.

How could she not see Dudley for what he was? How could she fail to detect his dubious character? How could she enjoy his company more than Tristan's?

He'd tried to avoid her. He'd tried to ignore her. He'd tried to pretend she was nothing to him, but he had to face facts: They were bound in ways he didn't like, but there was no setting aside their connection. And he was tired of fighting it.

Since he'd arrived home from the dance, he'd had too much to drink, so he understood that alcohol was spurring him on. In a moment of temporary insanity, he'd decided to stomp to her bedchamber, to demand an apology and an explanation.

If he'd been more sober, he might have reassessed, might have changed his mind, but when he'd opened his door and found her standing there, all sense had flown out the window.

He was a smart man, and he could recognize an important sign when it hit him on the head. Fate had delivered her to him, and he wouldn't decline the sensual gift.

She was meant to be his, and she would be. It was as simple as that. She would forget Dudley. She would give Tristan everything he'd been craving, and they would both be happier for it.

He dipped down and kissed her, and to his surprise, she tasted like alcohol, as if she'd imbibed quite a lot of liquor, too. He sighed with relief. If they were both intoxicated, they could blame their misbehavior on their compromised conditions. In the morning, there'd be a perfectly rational reason why they'd proceeded—they were foxed—and if she was angry, he wouldn't have to feel guilty.

"Have you been drinking, Miss Hamilton?" he asked, wanting to be sure.

"Yes."

"You seem much more . . . *calm* than usual."

"I tried an elixir known as Woman's Daily Remedy. It's relaxed me."

"Has it?"

"Definitely, and since I'm lying beneath you, hadn't you ought to call me Helen?"

"Yes, Helen, I believe I ought."

"I hate how you say *Miss Hamilton*. It always sounds as if you're scolding me."

"That's because I always am. You drive me wild with your foolishness."

He was stunned by how marvelous it felt to be with her. To his mortification, he'd been drowning in despair, lost and miserable without her, and at having the chance to dally, his spirits soared.

He kissed her again, and she joined in with a gusto that seduced and delighted.

Her hands were everywhere, roaming over his shoulders, back, and arms. She stroked her fingers through his hair, played with the earring in his ear.

His own hands explored at will, as he toyed with her breasts, her nipples, her thighs and flanks. Her legs widened, welcoming him to drop between them, but she was still dressed in her nightgown, and in his frantic caressing, he became entangled in the fabric.

He was too impatient to waste time removing the garment, so he grabbed the bodice and ripped it down the center. In an instant, she was naked.

In horror, she shrieked and pulled away.

"Are you mad?" she huffed. "You can't be ripping off my clothes. You've ruined the only nightgown I own. What am I to do now?"

"You could simply sleep in the nude—in case a certain

gentleman visits your bed. He might enjoy finding you in such a naughty state."

"Sleep in the nude? You might as well tell me to shave off my hair."

"Then ask your employer to buy you another."

She snorted with disgust. "He's a cheapskate. I don't imagine he would."

"If you obliged him once in awhile, you might be amazed at his generosity."

"Impossible. He's an ogre. All he does is scream and rant at me."

"He merely wants to be sure you're paying attention."

She looked as if she might continue her complaints, but he wouldn't listen. She'd already said more than he ever cared to hear, and all of it was idiotic and misguided. Her hands were clutched to her bosom as she tried to drag her robe over her naked form, but he wouldn't allow her to hide herself.

The time for virginal games had passed. The time for protests and demurring had ended. He seized her wrists and clasped them over her head, and he was enough of a cad to admit that he liked having her pinned beneath him and at his mercy.

He glanced down her torso, feeling like a conquering Celt about to ravage an innocent maiden. She was perfectly shaped to give a man pleasure: rounded breasts, narrow waist, flared hips. His gaze landed on the triangle of hair between her legs, and a wave of lust shot through him that was so virulent he was glad he was lying down. If he hadn't been, his knees might have buckled.

He began kissing her again, and he kept on and on until she was writhing in agony, then he nibbled her breasts, and he sucked on her nipples, going back and forth, back and forth.

She was such a carnal creature that it was but a simple matter to bring her to orgasm. He slid his fingers into her sheath, and with a few deft flicks of his thumb, she shuddered and cried out.

As she let go, something inside him resolved, as if an argument had been waged and was finally settled.

When he'd initially decided to venture to her bedchamber, he hadn't been certain of his purpose. When he'd found her lurking in the hall, he still hadn't known the precise conclusion he sought. Even when he'd picked her up and carried her to his bed, the goal had been hazy.

Yet now, everything was crystal clear. He would fornicate with her. He didn't care that he shouldn't, didn't care that it was wrong, didn't care that she might not wish to proceed.

He tugged his trousers down to his flanks and wedged the tip of his cock into her sheath. The strange position galvanized her.

She calmed and sobered, her smile fading.

"What are you doing?" she asked.

"I'm going to make love to you—as a husband does his wife."

"Will I lose my virginity? Is that what will occur?"

"Yes."

"I don't want to then."

"I'm going to anyway, Helen. We can't keep dancing around this situation."

"But I thought . . ."

"What?"

"We had to be married before it could happen."

She blushed, her cheeks stained a pretty shade of pink, which underscored how naïve she was. In light of her inexperience, he was behaving like the worst sort of scoundrel. He never despoiled virgins—it wasn't in his nature—and when there were so many loose women in the world, it was totally unnecessary, but he couldn't stop.

Since it was fated for them to be together sexually, it was pointless to fight the inevitable.

"We don't have to be married," he gently said.

He stared at her, sensing the myriad of emotions careening through her. She was scared and worried, but curious, too, eager to try it while yearning for the fortitude to resist.

He kissed her sweetly, tenderly. "Let me do this with you. I want it so badly."

"I don't know . . ." she wavered.

"Don't you see, Helen? It's the only way."

"You make it so hard to say no."

"Then don't. Be happy. Join in."

He pushed with his hips, as she gasped and arched up. To distract her, he clasped her nipple, twirling it between finger and thumb, wrenching her attention away from what was transpiring down below.

He buried his face at her nape, inhaling her lush scent, as he raised the issue that had been eating him alive.

"Tell me you haven't lain with Dubois."

"No, no."

"Swear it to me."

She pulled away so that he had to look at her.

"I barely know him, Tristan. He's a peddler; he has a wagon parked out on the lane. He sells tonics and potions."

"Why was he talking about you?"

"He fancies himself an expert on amour. He had this absurd idea that you were fond of me, that he could make you jealous."

Tristan snorted, but didn't respond. The bastard had made Tristan jealous, all right, having goaded Tristan to fisticuffs, when he'd never previously brawled over any woman.

He began again, diverting her, reveling with her. He kneaded her breasts, relaxing her, so that his phallus could continue its relentless incursion.

"We're almost there," he said, flexing, flexing.

"I'm afraid."

"Don't be. I would never hurt you."

As he voiced the vow, he meant it, but in reality, he

might end up being cruel, might end up hurting her in ways she could never imagine.

"You love me, don't you?" she ludicrously queried.

He nearly replied with, *Love has nothing to do with this,* but before he could, the strangest remark slipped out.

"Of course I love you," he told her. "How could you not know?"

"And you'll marry me after, won't you?"

Even in his aroused state, he was wise enough not to answer. With a groan of pleasure, of extreme need, he impaled her.

At the abrupt penetration, she moaned and tried to wrestle away, but he held her to his chest, her heart fluttering like a frightened bird's.

"It's all right," he whispered. "Everything is all right now."

"You said you would never hurt me."

"The first time is the only time. From here on, it will always be marvelous."

He wanted to give her a chance to acclimate, but he couldn't wait. On finally being joined to her, his body rejoiced, his seed rushing from his loins.

He thrust, and the feel of her—so tight and hot and wet—was too much. With a sudden burst of elation, he spilled himself far inside her, being too overwhelmed to recall that he oughtn't. He'd taken the ultimate liberty, and it was shocking, but incredibly satisfying, too.

He kept on till he was spent, then he slid away and snuggled himself to her. They were quiet, and he thought he should say something, but he couldn't figure out what it should be.

His brain was jumbled not only from the sex, but from the alcohol, too. Already, he was falling asleep. He was being an inconsiderate brute, and he understood that he was, but he couldn't help it.

"I went too fast," he mumbled.

"No you didn't," she politely claimed.

"It will be better next time."

"It was fine this time."

"Rest with me for a bit," he urged.

"I can't. I have to return to my room."

"I want to do it again. Unless you're too sore?"

"No, I'm not too sore."

An awkward silence descended, and since she was an incessant talker, it was obvious she was troubled or that she'd hoped for more from him than he'd given her. But he was a man of few words, and he never wasted any of them on frivolous matters such as romance.

Surely she knew that about him?

He was dozing off, and in his lethargy, he heard her say, "You promised, remember?"

"Yes, I did," he replied, in his muddled condition, having no clue to what she referred.

"You'll follow through?"

It was a question, but a prayer, too, and he lied, "Yes, I will."

Her worries assuaged, she sighed and nestled closer, and he drifted off, with her in his arms and content in a manner he'd never been.

When he roused, it was morning.

His head pounded from a hangover, and the sunlight streaming in the window was inordinately bright. He moaned and rubbed his temples as he glanced to the side.

She was gone, not so much as a dent in the pillow to indicate that she'd been with him. The air was so still that, for a moment, he wondered if—in a drunken stupor—he'd dreamed the encounter, but there was blood on the sheet, on his phallus, proving that his memories were accurate. She had been there.

A flap of fabric stuck out from under her pillow. He lifted it and saw her shredded nightgown folded into a tidy square.

He pressed the garment to his nose and inhaled deeply,

detecting her scent, liking to be reminded—immediately on awakening—so vividly of her.

Smiling, he rose to face the day, his first order of business to find her and let her know that she would be his—until he tired of her and moved on to another.

Chapter 15

❦

"EVERYONE noticed."

"So what?"

Michael glared at Tristan, who was sitting like a king on a throne at his library desk.

"We've been through this a hundred times," Tristan scolded. "Must we go through it a hundred and one?"

"I'm a bloody earl," Michael snapped. "If I want to dance three times with the same girl, I don't see how it's anybody's business but my own."

"It's because you *are* an earl that it matters."

Michael turned to the window, his attention captured by the sight outside. Jane was walking across the garden. She'd paused to remove her bonnet, and it dangled at her thigh, the ribbons threaded in her slender fingers. Standing as she was, with the sun shining down and the green colors of the park spread behind her, she looked so pretty that his heart pounded with pleasure.

"I've explained this to you over and over," Tristan said. "I don't know how to make you understand."

"Try again."

Michael was being deliberately obtuse.

He was aware that a man of his station had to be cautious with women. Until he was ready to wed, he could dabble with whores, but that was as far as his amorous adventures could take him. If he showed too much interest in any one female, hopes were raised; and in his world, expectations had to be acted upon.

Jane Hamilton was the sort of person any fellow would love to have as a mistress—but not as a wife. Never a wife.

Her ancestry alone kept her from being suitable. Then there was her father's scandal, her poverty, her lack of a dowry. She brought nothing to the table. No money. No property. A bad reputation and no influence.

The worst strike against her was their affair. Though he had been the one to suggest and pursue it, her deficient virtue ensured that she could never be his countess.

He knew all these things. He realized all these things. And they galled him.

He liked everything about Jane, and while she wasn't from the upper echelons of society, she was hardly a tramp, and he couldn't treat her as he would a doxy. Rules had to be followed, customs maintained.

Jane had never mentioned the subject, but it was obvious she imagined he would shuck off the shackles that bound him to an aristocratic marriage. He wished he was that brave and chivalrous, but the sad fact was that he was the earl of Hastings and a peer of the realm. He would do what was best for the title, for the family, and for the heritage he'd inherited from his father and his father's father before him.

But he couldn't stop dallying with her, couldn't stop wanting to be with her. He was in deep trouble, charmed and smitten and besotted, and he yearned to confide in Tristan, to ask his advice, but Michael didn't dare confess what he'd done.

Tristan would be furious, and he'd send the Hamiltons away. Michael would never see Jane again.

"It was foolish of you," Tristan nagged, "to dote on her."

Michael whirled to face him. "It was a country dance, in a rural village. Who cares?"

"Maud cares. She's been pestering me all day."

"So don't listen to her."

"She knows more about these situations than I do. She saw you, and there were other people—people who matter—who saw you, too."

"Name one."

"I won't debate the issue. You were in the wrong. Don't pretend you weren't."

Michael shrugged, weary of defending himself. He wouldn't be admonished as if he was still a lad in short pants.

"What about Miriam?" Tristan inquired. "Have you given any thought to how she must have felt?"

"She wasn't ready to go on time, and Maud insisted we leave without her."

"After she arrived, you didn't ask her to dance a single dance."

"She looked like a damned ghost, and I wasn't about to parade her in front of my tenants."

"I'm told you hurt her feelings."

"She'll get over it," Michael replied coldly.

He was exhausted by Miriam and the charade Maud forced him to play. He would never marry Miriam, and Maud needed to stop encouraging her.

"I'm sure she will—eventually. You're missing the point."

"What is the *point*? I'm tired of waiting for it."

"You behaved inappropriately. You're held to a different standard now."

"I like Jane," Michael quietly stated. "I like her very much."

"It doesn't mean you can have her lead off the dancing."

"Who should I have asked?"

"Anyone but Harry Hamilton's daughter. She's a perfect candidate to tarnish your reputation, and I won't have it."

"Maybe it's not up to you."

"It bloody well is," Tristan seethed, "as our dear father guaranteed by how he drafted his will."

Michael pushed away from the window, and he walked over to the desk, studying Tristan across the long expanse of oak.

Usually, he was glad of Tristan's friendship and guidance, glad for his sense of obligation that had brought him into their lives. Tristan kept him focused, kept him humble, kept him wise in his decisions.

It was no secret that Tristan would rather be anywhere else, and he stayed because he'd been pressured into it by their father. Tristan never shirked a task, never reneged on a promise, and generally, Michael was happy for his loyalty.

Yet Michael was overly enamored of Jane, and as a boy—now a man—who'd always been showered with everything he ever wanted, he found Tristan's harangue infuriating. Michael's temper flared, making him uncharacteristically insolent and out of sorts.

"You like to remind me," Michael bristled, "that you're my brother, but you forget that you're only my *half* brother, and a bastard one at that. Father may have begged you to come here, but that was his choice, not mine. Don't presume to command me over issues that don't concern you."

If Tristan was offended by the awful comment, he didn't reveal it with so much as the blink of an eye. He was used to dealing with dangerous ruffians, with pirates and criminals and sailors, and Michael's paltry attempt at bravado was probably laughable to the older, more worldly man.

Still, Michael was delighted to have stood his ground. He was the earl, and it was about time Tristan remembered it.

Tristan rose from his chair, meeting Michael's gaze with a bored one of his own.

"I've given up much to assist you," Tristan calmly declared, "and I have treated you with civility and respect. I lecture you for your own good—to guide you as you assume your responsibilities."

"That's not how I see it on my end," Michael hotly retorted, but Tristan kept on as if Michael hadn't uttered a word.

"In all circumstances," Tristan said, "you will afford me the courtesy I am due, as a man, as your guardian, as your brother, as your elder. If you ever speak to me so rudely again, I will beat you to a pulp."

He rounded the desk, and he approached Michael until they were toe-to-toe.

"Do I make myself clear?" Tristan softly asked.

They were the same height, but Tristan was all brawn and muscle, his body honed from years of hard work. He had sailed the seven seas, fighting brigands and battling foreign navies.

If he ever stooped to violence, he would tear Michael limb from limb without breaking a sweat, and Michael wouldn't land a single blow, even though he wished he could brawl like an experienced pugilist.

He was angry and confused and worried about Jane, but he couldn't tell Tristan the reason for his foul mood.

Backing down, he murmured, "Yes, you've made yourself very clear. My apologies. I overstepped my bounds."

Tristan marched out, leaving Michael to fume like a chastened child.

He lingered, letting his rage cool, and as it did, he was desperate to be with Jane. Was she still out in the park? He left the library and headed for the rear servants' entrance.

Quietly, he hurried along, not wanting to bump into Miriam or Maud. Miriam would be sad and fawning, while Maud would be shrewish and irate. He'd endured enough of a tirade from Tristan. He couldn't abide one from her, too.

When he turned the corner that led to the door, he stumbled to a halt. Tristan was there—with Helen Hamilton.

They weren't doing anything improper, but their placement and demeanor told a story that words never could have.

Tristan was at the foot of the stairs, with Miss Hamilton on the first step. He leaned in and whispered a remark Michael couldn't hear, and she chuckled and replied, "Perhaps later. If you're very, very nice to me."

Tristan reached out and furtively squeezed her fingers, then she continued up. He watched her go, focused on her shapely backside in a fashion that no employer should ever exhibit toward an employee. His expression was a display of such affection and longing that it almost hurt to observe it.

She disappeared from sight, and Tristan let out a heavy breath, his shoulders sagging—as if with regret.

He spun around, only to find himself confronting Michael. His eyes widened imperceptibly, but otherwise, he was his usual composed self.

Michael's temper was boiling again. Tristan had been vociferous in his chastisement. At all costs, Michael had to stay away from Jane, but Tristan found it perfectly acceptable to dally with her sister.

What gall! What cheek!

"Having a few tumbles with Miss Hamilton, are you?" Michael chided.

"Just helping her up the stairs," Tristan fibbed.

"Really? You're an honorable man, Tristan, and lying doesn't become you. Would you like to amend your response?"

Apparently Tristan was still smarting from Michael's earlier insult.

"As a matter of fact, I would," he tersely said. "How about this: My personal affairs are none of your business."

Michael scoffed. "You have the nerve to lecture me— when you're doing exactly the same thing?"

"It's not the same," Tristan tried to claim. "Not even close."

"No, it never is."

"You're an earl. I'm not. I am a commoner and a bachelor, and thus, I can carry on however I please."

"But she's a young lady, living under your protection. You have a heightened duty to her. Isn't that what you always tell me?"

Two slashes of color stained Tristan's cheeks. "Point taken. Now, if you'll excuse me."

"Hypocrite," Michael seethed, and he pushed past Tristan and stormed outside.

"SNEAK away with me for a bit."

Jane heard the question whispered from behind her, and she grinned, recognizing the voice as Michael's.

"When?" she whispered back, without looking at him.

"Fifteen minutes."

"At our special spot?"

"Yes. I'll meet you there."

She was thrilled that they had a *special* spot, that they shared secrets.

The Seymours were hosting a garden party, so the entire grounds were packed with people. Neighbors were eating and drinking, chatting and socializing. Children ran and wrestled on the swathed grass. A quartet of musicians filled the air with lively tunes.

It would be dangerous for Michael to vanish, and Jane took it as a sign of his burgeoning affection that he would risk so much.

After he'd moved away from her, she tarried a few minutes, then entered the house, planning to dash in the front then tiptoe out the back. She'd proceed on to the woods on the other side of the park, to an ancient maze that had gone to ruin, but as she hurried into the foyer, Mrs. Seymour was marching down the stairs. Jane made the mistake of glancing up, so she couldn't pretend she hadn't seen her.

"Where are you off to, Miss Hamilton?" Mrs. Seymour

asked, and she gestured to the open door. "The party is that way. I wouldn't think you'd miss a single moment of it."

"I need to check . . . my hair. I lost a comb; I thought it might fall."

Jane had never been a good liar, and she was sure the comment sounded false.

"Your hair is fine," Mrs. Seymour said. "I believe your sister is searching for you."

"Helen?"

"Yes."

"I'll find her."

Jane started down the hall, when Mrs. Seymour called, "Miss Hamilton?"

"What is it?" She spun, her impatience to be away barely controlled.

"Isn't your bedchamber in this direction?" Seymour pointed up the stairs. "Your . . . hair. You have to fuss with it, remember?"

Something flashed in Seymour's gaze. A warning? A glimmer of distaste?

"How silly of me!" Jane smiled and laughed. "I'm going the wrong way. I can be such a scatterbrain."

She came to the stairs and climbed, slithering past Seymour and keeping on up to the landing. With Seymour's hot glare cutting into her like a knife, she hid around the corner, watching until Seymour descended and went outside. Breathing a sigh of relief, she raced back down, eager to reach her destination.

Michael had shown her the entrance to the maze, had taught her to maneuver the path to the bench in the middle. They often trysted in the spot when they wanted privacy during the day. Since Jane was an avid walker, no one noticed when she ambled off, and as Michael's interest in her spiraled, her trips increased in frequency.

She was convinced he was falling in love with her, that it wouldn't be long before a proposal was tendered. After all they'd done, no other conclusion was possible.

Quickly, she was through the hedge and sitting on the bench. She waited and waited, excitement altering to anxiety, then dismay, then fury. How could he have failed to arrive?

She was weary of their clandestine arrangement. Why wouldn't he claim her? Why couldn't he shout his fondness to the world? If he'd admit what they both knew, everything would be so simple.

She'd like to raise the forbidden subject, to probe his intentions and garner a firm commitment, but she had no idea how.

An eternity had passed, and the sun was setting in the western sky. Once it grew darker, the dancing would begin. Should she continue to dawdle? Should she leave? She didn't want to be out in the woods at night, but she didn't want to miss him, either.

The temperature was dropping, and she shivered, deciding that she couldn't remain. She'd just stood to depart, when his strides pounded through the brambles.

"Can you forgive me?" he begged as he burst into the clearing.

"Always."

He rushed to her, hands extended, and she clasped hold.

"Maud accosted me. I didn't think I'd ever escape."

"You're here now. That's all that counts."

"But I can't stay. She delayed me too long, and I have to lead the dancing."

He sat on the bench, and he pulled her onto his lap, giving her the sweetest kiss ever. As he drew away, she snuggled herself to his chest, her ear over his heart so she could hear its steady beating.

They were quiet, with Michael stroking up and down her back.

"You're freezing," he murmured.

"I'm fine," she insisted, biting down on all the words that were trying to spill out.

She yearned to tell him how worried she'd been, how

nervously she'd fretted over the encroaching darkness, but she would never complain.

The interval was extremely intimate, and she was positive he'd declare himself, but he'd never remarked on his feelings for her, and this time was no different.

"When will we return to London?" she finally asked.

She was desperate to have her future settled, and she hated having such a terrible secret from Helen.

"As soon as all the harvest parties are over."

"What will happen then? Between us, I mean. Will we keep on as we have been?"

"Of course."

It wasn't anywhere near the assurance she'd been seeking, and her spirits sank.

"We've been carrying on quite outrageously here in the country," she mentioned. "Won't it be more difficult at your town house?"

"We'll figure it out. We're inventive; we haven't let circumstances foil us so far."

"No, we haven't."

She tried to sound chipper, but with each opening she gave him, it seemed less likely that she would receive the answer she craved.

She gazed at him, her fondness shining through. In the waning light, the colors were so vivid. He looked dynamic and magnificent, like an angel who'd flown down from heaven. His golden hair shimmered; his eyes were very blue.

He stared at her, neither of them speaking, then he took her hand and kissed each of her fingertips—as if in farewell. Her pulse thudded with dread.

"I'd be with you if I could," he ventured. "You know that, don't you?"

"Yes, I know."

"If there was any way for us to be together . . ."

"There's always a way," she cheerily retorted.

When he didn't jump to agree, she held very still, praying for a promise, a vow. But he was silent, appearing sad and pensive. He gripped her waist and stood her on her feet, then he stood, too.

"I have to get back to the party," he said.

"All right."

"You leave first, and I'll watch to be certain you're safe."

His expression was impossible to read, and she knew she should go, but she had the oddest feeling that this was good-bye, that she'd never be alone with him again.

"Will you dance with me?" she humiliated herself by asking.

"I won't be able to this evening."

"Why not?"

"We were too obvious the other night in the village."

"Yes, I suppose we were." She was dying inside. "Will you visit me later?"

"I can't sneak away. I have so many responsibilities—what with all our guests."

She forced a chuckle. "Duty calls!"

"Yes, it does."

"Well, I'll keep a candle burning—just in case."

She started off, and when she would have vanished into the maze of branches, he softly said, "Jane?"

"Yes?" On tenterhooks, she whipped around.

"I'll . . . ah . . . talk to you tomorrow."

"I can't wait."

She gave him a saucy wink, and with a brash flick of her skirt, she spun and ran so he wouldn't see her tears.

"WILL you join me?"

"I'd be delighted."

Maud observed as Michael offered his hand to Miriam, as he led the dancing. He was very smooth about it, not evincing the slightest hint of how he'd previously embarrassed her, and Miriam was so besotted that there was no question of her forgiving him.

Maud climbed up onto the front steps of the mansion,

the higher vantage point providing a fuller view of the festivities. Miriam's rash had cleared, and she looked as fetching as she ever would, given her plain features. As the musicians struck up a chord and the lines formed— with Michael and Miriam at the head—Maud swelled with pride.

She scanned the crowd until she espied Jane Hamilton. The girl had crept out of the shadows, and with her having the morals of a strumpet, she might have been off cavorting with any village boy.

Maud was fixated on the dancing, but Jane was, too. She followed Miriam's every move, envy written all over her face. No doubt she was remembering the prior dance, how Michael had singled her out. She'd made a spectacle of herself, but Tristan had put a stop to her nonsense quickly enough.

Michael passed directly by Jane, Miriam twirling on his arm, and he didn't so much as glance at Jane. She might have been invisible.

At the snub, Jane appeared stricken, and Maud's smile was grim, but satisfied.

Jane Hamilton had no concept of rank or station, so she was learning a hard lesson: She would never be one of them.

Someone exited the house, and she peered behind her to see that it was Tristan. Jane Hamilton was instantly forgotten.

Maud wasn't certain what had happened with him. For several glorious weeks, he'd showered her with attention. Then, nothing. He'd reverted to his usual courteous demeanor.

She had been slow to realize that he no longer wished to consort with her, so she'd posed numerous invitations to fraternize—invitations that had been politely rebuffed— before it dawned on her that she was making a fool of herself.

With anyone else, she might have simply been furious, but she was aghast to admit that she was crushed by the change. A match between them would have solved so many financial problems.

She had no idea what she'd done to push him away, and she was a teeming wreck, spending her days in useless contemplation as she tried to figure out how he could once again be bewitched by her.

Since she had no clue how she'd managed it the first time, her mental castigation was a futile exercise in frustration.

"Captain"—she struggled to be cordial—"I was wondering where you were."

"Hello, Maud."

He came down the stairs to stand next to her, and he studied the crowd as if he was searching for someone. A woman was walking down by the lake, and he was like a dog on the hunt, completely focused on her and oblivious to Maud.

She pretended not to notice, but she was livid that a female strolling hundreds of yards away—in the dark—could intrigue him while she, Maud, could not.

"The dancing just started," she said, pointing out the obvious.

"Are people enjoying themselves?"

"They seem to be."

"Good." He was very distracted, his disinterest annoying.

"Michael asked Miriam to lead the opening set."

"Marvelous."

"I guess he listened to you, after all."

"I guess he did."

She had had a lengthy chat with him about Michael and his friendship with Jane Hamilton. Maud had assumed the private discussion had placed her on solid ground with him again, where she was an equal partner, reviewing family issues, but apparently, it had been a wasted effort.

"Will you be dancing?" She sounded pitifully anxious for him to ask her.

"Not tonight. I'm weary of all this socializing. It's such a beautiful evening; I thought I'd row the boat across the lake."

"Row the boat?"

"The moon is up, and I'm having the worst craving to be out on the water." He turned to her, as it occurred to him that he should invite her. With visible distaste, he offered, "Would you like to join me?"

In a rowboat? Out in the water?

Of all the things he could have suggested! She was wearing her best gown, her most expensive pair of shoes.

The request was too ridiculous to consider.

"I'd better not."

"Are you sure? We could have a . . . talk."

The word *talk* rang like a death knell.

"I'm afraid of the water," she wanly said. "I fell in as a child, and . . . well . . ."

She trailed off, making a dismissive gesture with her hand, and he scrutinized her, glaring as if he finally understood what was wrong with her.

"You should probably stay and dance then." At her refusal, he looked relieved.

"Yes, I probably should."

"Have fun. The men will be lining up to partner with you."

He continued on, giving no explanation for the past few weeks, and her temper sizzled.

How dare he treat her so shabbily! How dare he tempt and tease, then ignore!

He'd been so blatant in his flirtation that even dense, self-centered Miriam was aware of their brief alliance, and the abrupt ending. She'd asked Maud about it, but what was Maud supposed to tell her?

Maud climbed nearer the door, so that she could see all the way to the lake.

As he moved out into the park, he bumped into the woman he'd been watching. He'd stopped under a lamp that was hanging from a tree, and the woman stopped, too, so her identity was perfectly clear.

Helen Hamilton! Ooh!

Tristan smiled and murmured something, which made Hamilton grin. She sidled closer, not touching him, but acting in a very familiar manner.

He extended an arm, and she grabbed hold, their heads pressed together in conversation. Then he escorted her toward the lake, toward the intimate boat ride that could have been Maud's if she'd been braver.

Darkness swallowed them up, and Maud tarried, speculating, enraged, and plotting how Helen Hamilton could be most swiftly dispatched from their lives.

Chapter 16

❦

"HELLO, Captain Odell."

"Hello, Miss Hamilton. Fancy meeting you here."

"Yes, fancy that."

Helen smiled at Tristan, her heart jumping with the silly fluttering motion it always made when he was near.

The party was exhausting, so she'd taken a walk for some quiet contemplation, but there was scant privacy to be had.

There were people everywhere, exploring the lighted paths through the massive gardens. Music and laughter rippled across the grass, disturbing the calm evening air.

She was weary of the festivities, of the unending flow of visitors, many of whom were staying at the manor. In some ways, it was like living in a grand hotel, where she would come down to breakfast but never know who would be sitting at the dining table with her.

"Why aren't you dancing?" she asked.

"Why aren't you?"

"Haven't you heard? I'm extremely popular, so I've been run ragged with partners. I needed to rest."

"Should I be jealous?"

"Yes, absolutely."

She grinned, and he chuckled.

They stared at each other like besotted fools, and it was a good thing night had fallen. Anyone watching them would have noted their heightened affection.

"You still didn't tell me," she said, "why you're not dancing."

"Because I'm terrible at it."

"You are not. I've seen you; you're graceful as a ballerina."

"As I deem myself to be a very masculine fellow, I'm not certain that's a compliment."

She glanced about, and since no one was close enough to observe them, she grabbed the lapels of his coat and shook him. "Tell me the real reason."

"I'm tired of all these blasted parties."

"So am I."

"I just don't know how long a man is supposed to smile and bow and engage in vapid conversation with the ladies."

"Or how long the poor ladies are supposed to fuss and flatter and flirt with the gouty, drunken men."

"Precisely. I miss my ship," he surprised her by saying, and he sighed as if he'd lost his last friend.

He rarely offered a personal comment, and she held onto it like a precious memento.

"I know you do."

"I can't stand it that I'm never out on the water anymore, so I've decided to do the next best thing."

"What is that?"

"I'm taking the rowboat out to the center of the lake, so I can gaze up at the stars and feel sorry for myself."

"Why are you woebegone? Is it because you reside in an enormous mansion and have fine clothes to wear and plenty of food to eat?"

"Yes. Will you join me?"

"Out on the lake? Or in feeling sorry for yourself?"

"If you come with me, I won't be quite so glum."

She pretended to consider, then took his arm. "Oh, I imagine I can make the sacrifice."

They strolled along like sweethearts who were courting. The moon was bright, the weather balmy. The sounds of celebration faded until it seemed they were very much alone.

It was the most romantic moment of her life, and she knew she ought to be more circumspect, that she should be worried about propriety, but it was a party. Surely, the social rules had been relaxed.

They arrived at the lake's edge, and he guided her out onto a wooden dock. A small boat was tied to a piling, and it floated several feet lower than the spot where she was standing. How exactly was a female in a pretty dress and slippers to maneuver herself into it?

She hesitated, turning to look at him. He was very close, peering at her with such an intense expression that it made her knees weak. She was positive he would kiss her, right out in the open, where anyone could see, but he didn't, and she couldn't decide if she was relieved or disappointed.

"Have you changed your mind?" he asked.

"About getting in the boat? Are you joking?"

"Some women are afraid of the water."

"Not me."

"Can you swim?"

"Probably better than you."

He laughed. "Let me help you down."

In a swift move, he lifted her and plopped her onto the wooden seat. The vessel rocked wildly, and she squealed with alarm.

"I thought you said you could swim," he complained from up above.

"I can, but that doesn't mean I want a dousing in my party clothes."

"Maybe I'd enjoy seeing you all wet. The damp fabric would outline some very interesting attributes."

"Would you forget about my anatomy?"

"An impossible task." He shrugged out of his coat and laid it on the dock. "You won't swoon, will you, if I'm in my shirtsleeves?"

"I'll try not to."

He snorted, then untied the boat and, like a nimble cat, he hopped down into it, causing it to pitch precariously again. She grabbed the sides, as if a firm grip could prevent them from tipping over.

He sat across from her and clutched the two oars.

"You're awfully jumpy," he said.

"You make me nervous."

"I do? Why?"

"I always presume you're up to no good."

"You might be correct."

He leaned forward and squeezed her hand, a furtive gesture hidden from people strolling the banks.

"I'm glad you came with me," he murmured.

"I'm glad, too."

"I can't abide a timid female."

"I know that about you."

"You're not timid."

"Definitely not."

For a long while, he studied her, and she held her breath, convinced he would say something relevant to her situation, but he was annoyingly silent.

Since the night she'd stumbled into his bedchamber, when they'd both been too intoxicated to think clearly, she'd been waiting for a certain conversation to ensue, but it hadn't, and she hadn't a clue how to initiate it herself.

If her father had been alive, she'd have gone to him immediately, would have advised him that a marriage proposal needed to be tendered, and he'd have seen to it at once.

Dear Harry wouldn't have judged or condemned. He, himself, had eloped with Helen's mother, much to the horror of her mother's parents, which was why Helen's relatives wouldn't claim her. All these years later, they were still bitter.

In an instant, Harry would have helped her, but without his presence by her side, she had no idea how to raise the issue, how to force Tristan to behave properly.

There was no one else to speak for her, and while she'd flirted with the notion of proposing, herself, she never would. A woman simply didn't ask a man to marry her—the prospect was outrageous—so she had to be content in the knowledge that he'd said he loved her, that he'd promised they would wed. It had been a drunken vow, uttered in the heat of passion, but it had been uttered none-theless.

Eventually, he would do the right thing. He always did, and she wouldn't consider, not for the merest second, that he might not.

He pulled on the oars, his strong arms working them away from the dock. She watched him, his chest muscles flexing, as he tilted nearer, as he bent away.

She remembered that chest, bared, pressed to her naked torso, and heat shot through her.

Glancing away, she trailed her fingers in the cool water. She drew them out, droplets careening off, and she flicked at him, wetting his face and shirt.

"Minx!" he teased, but he kept rowing.

They'd traveled far from the shore, and he paused in his movements, the boat drifting to a stop. It was so still, the stars a dazzling canopy overhead. Back at the party, a bonfire had been lit and sparks glimmered like fireflies.

"Penny for your thoughts," he said.

"Actually, I was thinking of you and how lucky I am that we met."

"You're very beautiful tonight—with the moon shining on your hair."

"Thank you."

"I'm pretending you're my very own mermaid."

"I'm wearing entirely too many clothes to be any such thing."

He laid a finger on her lips. "Sound carries out here. We must be cautious with what we say."

Which meant that there would be no declaration of amour, no intimate discussion of their future.

They were quiet again, and she tolerated it as long as she could, but his reticence was driving her mad. She wanted him talking and talking, hoping that if sufficient words tumbled from his mouth, he might ultimately mention the right ones.

"What about you?" she asked. "I'd give a penny for *your* thoughts, but I don't have a penny."

Unable to look at her, he peered up at the sky. "I might leave for a bit."

"Leave?"

"Yes. My crew is taking my ship to Scotland, to deliver some cargo. I might climb aboard for the ride."

"How long would you be gone?"

"A few weeks. A month maybe." He met her gaze. "Would you miss me?"

"No," she petulantly replied.

"Liar."

Something was wrong, but she wasn't certain how to learn what it was.

Warily, she broached, "It's been so enjoyable here in the country. Are you unhappy?"

For an eternity, he was mute, scrutinizing her. Then he said, "No, I'm not unhappy."

"Good."

Was this really happening? With how close they'd grown, how could he pick up and go? Clearly, he wanted to be away from *her*, and at the realization, she was hurt and furious. Why would he simply flit off? Was it his opinion that he had no reason worth staying?

"I feel as if I'm bursting out of my skin," he tried to explain, "with all these people and these parties and these meetings with agents and tenants. I just need some breathing room."

"It has been hectic," she evenly concurred. "I've often wished I could sneak away. You're fortunate that you can."

It was a tiny opening, and she'd foolishly imagined he might ask her to accompany him—an arrangement that would be completely improper and to which she would never agree. But still, the prospect tantalized, and she was crushed when he didn't extend the offer.

"You seem to have settled in with the family," he said instead.

Settled wasn't exactly the word she would use. "Yes, I have."

"You're doing well."

"I am."

"So you'd be all right while I was away?"

"Of course, I'd be all *right*." That wasn't the point. The point was his leaving her. "I'm an adult woman. I've been taking care of myself since I was a baby."

He assessed her features as if memorizing the details, as if this was good-bye. "You're always so strong."

"I've had to be."

"You're a survivor."

"Yes, I am."

"I like that about you. I'm a survivor, too."

"Kindred spirits."

He frowned as if it had just occurred to him that they had traits in common. Then without further comment, he grabbed the oars and tugged on them, deftly turning them around. Within minutes, he was tying the rope to the piling.

He reached down, clasped her hand, and with a quick yank, she was on the dock.

Her head was spinning with questions as she tried to deduce the precise purpose of their conversation. Was he hinting that their affair was over? Was he merely apprising her of his plans? Was he sending a message that there would be no proposal?

He was a male, so he wasn't very adept at discussing personal matters. Did he need time away in order to arrive at a decision?

If so, why not just admit it? Why keep her in limbo, her mind in turmoil, her heart aching?

He picked up his coat and pulled it on, and she was a hairsbreadth away from seizing him by the lapels and shaking him till his teeth rattled.

He guided her to the rocky bank and made a show of helping her gain her balance. It gave him the opportunity to hover close and whisper in her ear.

"I want to come to your room. Later tonight."

Her eyes widened with surprise, but she couldn't reply. Another couple was strolling down the path and might overhear.

"Let me," he mouthed, and she nodded and stepped away.

"Thank you for the boat ride, Captain Odell," she said, imposing distance. "It was lovely."

"My pleasure, Miss Hamilton."

He flashed a hot, torrid look, filled with sexual promise, then she blinked, and it was gone. He stared at her with the cool expression he displayed to the world.

"May I escort you back to the party?"

"There's no need. I'm sure you're busy with the guests. I can find my own way."

She stumbled off, struggling to appear calm and composed, but inside she was reeling.

What did he want? Why had she acceded to the rendezvous? Would he propose? What if he didn't?

Since she'd surrendered her chastity, her position was extremely precarious. If he wasn't contemplating marriage, if he'd seduced her with wicked intent . . .

No, she wouldn't consider it. She knew him. She understood him. He would do what was required.

Yet what if she was pregnant? What if—at that very instant—his child was growing in her belly? What then? What then?

She and her sisters would be back on the streets, with no money and nowhere to go.

In a terror, she skirted the crowd and fled to her room,

where she paced and paced, her dread mounting, her panic increasing by the minute.

Finally, she noticed what remained of the bottle of Woman's Daily Remedy that Mr. Dubois had given to her. She drew out the cork and gulped the contents, then she went to the window seat and gazed out, wishing she could see the lake, wishing she could see if he was still there, but her bedchamber was located on the wrong side of the house.

"All will be well," she muttered. "All will be well."

He was coming to propose. She would accept no other possibility.

She walked to the dressing room, took down her hair and brushed it out, then slipped into her robe. She was anxious to look as pretty as she was able from the moment he arrived.

"WHAT'S going on here?"

Clarinda stepped off the path and into a hedge where she could see the shoes and petticoats of two girls.

Lady Rose Seymour and Amelia Hamilton peeked out.

"Miss Dubois? Hello," Amelia said.

"Hello, yourselves. Are you enjoying the party?"

"It's been very exciting," Rose answered. "Tristan allowed us to stay up late so we could dance and everything!"

"Lucky you."

"How about you, Miss Dubois? Are you having fun?"

"Yes, I'm having quite a lot of fun, and actually, my name is Miss Dudley. My brother likes to play games. He likes to pretend our name is Dubois to fool people, but it's not Dubois."

She neared, curious as to why they were huddled in the bushes in the dark.

"What are you doing?" she asked.

They glanced at each other, a silent communication

being exchanged, then Amelia said, "Will you promise not to tell?"

"Absolutely."

"We're spying on Captain Odell and my sister Helen."

"You scamps. Whatever for?"

"We're trying to decide," Rose explained, "whether they're in love. We thought they were, but now, we're not sure."

"They keep fighting," Amelia clarified.

"Ah . . ." Clarinda mused.

She peered through the bushes to find the girls had an excellent view of the lake. The moon was full, so it was easy to see Helen and Odell out in the middle in a small rowboat. The scene appeared entirely innocent. They were sitting apart, on opposite benches, and Odell had the oars in his hands, but Clarinda was aware that something more serious might be occurring.

"What do you think?" Amelia queried as Clarinda drew away.

"I don't know."

"She drank a love potion, though, right?"

"She might have," Clarinda carefully replied.

"So it's probably love, isn't it?" Rose pressed. "I mean, Tristan hasn't ever invited any other woman to go out on the lake with him."

"Perhaps it is love," Clarinda agreed.

The girls grinned, delighted to have their suspicions confirmed.

"Then why are they fighting?" Amelia asked.

"Adults quarrel occasionally," Clarinda said. "It's very common."

"Have you another potion we could apply?" Rose inquired. "One that would make them live happily ever after?"

"We want them to marry," Amelia said, "because we'd be sisters."

"We've already administered plenty of potions," Clarinda advised. "Now, we simply have to wait for the magic to work."

"WILL that be all, Miss Hamilton?"

"Yes."

"I could fetch some hot water if you'd like."

"No, no. Please go!"

Lydia bit down a chuckle. Jane Hamilton was frantic to get Lydia out of the room, so Lydia was determined to remain. Obviously Hamilton believed Lord Hastings was about to visit her, but he would never risk it when there were so many guests in the house.

"I could bring a warming pan for the sheets."

"No! Thank you!"

Lydia smirked and left. She never curtsied to Jane Hamilton, and if she was being disrespectful, Hamilton was in no position to complain.

Who would she speak to? Mrs. Seymour?

Ha! The prospect was laughable. Seymour hated her and would never listen.

She descended to where she could see the foyer, to where she could watch the front door. If Lord Hastings came in, Lydia would waylay him and initiate the tryst that was long overdue. She would restore herself in his life, while gleaning enormous satisfaction in stealing him back from Jane Hamilton.

He arrived much sooner than she might have predicted. After tiptoeing in, he scanned the area, checking that he was alone, then he started up the stairs.

Lydia moved into his path, tugging on the bodice of her dress, unbuttoning a button or two to reveal more cleavage. As he rounded the corner, he practically bumped into her.

"Well, well," she greeted, "if it isn't my favorite earl."

"Lydia, you're up late."

"I'm finishing my chores." Her gaze meandered to his

crotch, and she was thrilled to note the bulge in his trousers. So he was glad to see her.

"Is there anything I can do for you," she seductively said, "before I retire?"

Her message was clear, and he definitely received it. She stepped closer, not touching him, but near enough that she could feel his bodily heat.

"I just came inside to retrieve a warmer coat from my bedchamber," he lied. "I only have a few minutes."

"If memory serves," she teased, "we only need a *few* minutes."

He smiled. "I don't think so. Not tonight."

"The parlor behind you is empty."

"Is it?"

He peered over his shoulder, staring, considering.

"I know what you like better than anyone." She recalled how often she'd sucked him into her mouth and was confident that he recalled it, too. "Should I refresh your memory?"

"My memory is extremely vivid."

He hesitated then pulled away, his interest waning like water rushing down a drain. "I'm tempted, but I can't," he insisted, though he did take a naughty swipe across her breast.

What could she say? She couldn't argue or beg.

She shrugged and grinned, hoping she looked flirtatious and bored.

"Maybe next time," she breezily said.

"Yes, maybe."

He walked on, and she headed for the stairs as if to go down, but as soon as she safely could, she spun and sneaked after him.

As she'd suspected, he proceeded directly to Jane Hamilton's room, and once he was inside, there was no need to dawdle. She knew what was happening.

Her fury soared. How dare he spurn her! How dare he choose Hamilton!

Lydia was less restrained than Hamilton and more amenable to doing what he liked. What could skinny, fussy Jane Hamilton give to him that she, Lydia, could not?

Lydia had been patient, had kept his secret, expecting he would tire of Hamilton and focus on Lydia again, but his insult was too great to be borne.

He didn't realize that his fixation with Hamilton would bring disaster and scandal, and he had to be protected from her. Hamilton had to be exposed, then sent away. For Lord Hastings's own good.

The only question was: Who should first learn of the affair, and how could Lydia inflict the most damage?

Chapter 17

TRISTAN slipped into Helen's bedchamber, and she was over in the window seat, staring out at the stars. Her auburn hair was down, and she wore only her robe.

A frisson of lust shot through him, his cock hardening. The unruly rod knew what would transpire, how exquisite it would be, and he could scarcely stand the notion of any delay, but delay there would be.

He wouldn't jump on her like a sex-starved maniac.

A candle burned on the writing desk, an empty liquor bottle next to it. He clearly recollected the trouble they'd gotten into with previous intoxication. Luckily, he was sober, so one of them would keep a level head.

"Drinking again, Miss Hamilton?"

"Yes, as a matter of fact."

She glanced over her shoulder. For a moment, he couldn't read her expression, couldn't deduce if she was glad to see him or not, but then she smiled, the sight of it lighting up the room.

"What do you enjoy in an alcoholic beverage?" he asked.

"It's the Woman's Daily Remedy that Mr. Dubois sells."

Dubois again? To his relief, he hadn't crossed paths with the arrogant oaf since he'd punched him at the village dance.

"Must Dubois be part of this conversation? And he's Phillip Dudley, not Philippe Dubois. He's an Englishman."

"You certainly spend an awful lot of time fretting over him. It's enough to make me wonder if you're jealous."

"If I was, I'd never admit it."

She laughed, and the happy sound had him grinning like a halfwit.

"Are you foxed?" he inquired.

"I don't believe so."

It was his turn to laugh. "You're imbibing, so why lie about it? Tell me why you're drinking."

"I was lonely. I was beginning to think you weren't coming."

"Not come? Are you mad? Wild horses couldn't have kept me away."

He pushed away from the door and walked to her. With her on the cushion, on her knees, they were eye to eye, and she wrapped her arms around him, surprising him by pulling him close and initiating a kiss in which he readily participated.

Her body was crushed to his, and he hugged her tight as they reveled in the embrace, hands roaming, torsos shifting.

He lifted her and carried her to her bed, dropping her onto the mattress and tumbling down with her.

The carnal encounter that followed was unlike anything he'd ever experienced. Nothing made it especially different from prior trysts. There was no excess of passion, no riotously naughty acts. They simply established an intimacy he hadn't thought possible between a man and a woman.

He kissed and caressed and nibbled, quickly stripping her of her robe, so that she was nude. Then she did the same to him, removing his coat and shirt, his boots and trousers.

It was the first time she'd seen him naked, and though she was only a few steps beyond her virginity, she handled it well. She fondled and explored with an innocence that charmed and titillated.

As he came over her and their torsos melded, he was overcome by how perfect it felt to be with her. His heart actually ached with gladness.

There were so many words on the tip of his tongue that he was afraid to open his mouth, afraid to hear what might spill out. He wanted to divulge how much he cared about her, but he didn't dare.

He'd promised to marry her, and he wished he could retract the vow, which was the reason he was leaving for Scotland. He had to get his priorities straight, had to remember what was important and what wasn't. If they were apart for a while, perhaps she'd cease to matter so much.

Throughout his life, he'd tried to show the world that he wasn't like his philandering father, that he would never impregnate a woman and blithely walk away. What if he had? Yes, he was a confirmed bachelor, determined never to wed. But what if she was pregnant? What then?

She was gazing at him, patiently waiting for him to say what he was supposed to say, but he simply couldn't. He'd never pegged himself as a coward, but apparently, he was.

She must have sensed his distress, for she rested a palm on his cheek and murmured, "It will be all right, Tristan. Don't worry."

She always knew just how to please him, to calm him. Her affection stirred his masculine instincts, making him eager to conquer, to claim, and he began kissing her in earnest, being pitifully desperate to be inside her. Yet he wanted the coupling to be joyous and romantic, so she would realize how much he cherished her.

He wasn't good at confessions, couldn't confide what he was thinking or feeling—hell, he didn't even *know* what he was feeling—but he could certainly show her how much she meant to him.

By the time he entered her, she was wet and relaxed, ready for him and the pleasure he would give her.

He started to flex, gradually increasing the pace, their ardor rising. She met him thrust for thrust, her elation evident, her bliss extreme. An orgasm swept over her, and he let loose, too, and they raced to oblivion together. He'd never previously joined a woman in orgasm, and he found it to be the sweetest, most thrilling thing that had ever happened to him.

As his cock softened, he pulled away and tugged her near so she was facing him. She smiled, her fondness washing over him like a gentle rain.

"You're leaving me," she said.

"Just for a while."

"Why?"

"I need to get away."

His lie had failed to persuade her, and she shook her head.

"Tell me the truth."

He was ashamed to have discovered that he was too spineless to propose, to follow through, so he wondered what excuse he should give.

He had no idea how to be a husband or a father, and he had a wanderlust that couldn't be sated. If he bound himself to her, eventually he'd sail away, and he might never return. Who would want such an unreliable man as a spouse?

"I have to go," he said.

"Swear to me that you'll come back."

"Of course I will. I have to. Rose and Michael are here."

The instant he voiced the comment, he regretted it. Her smile faded.

"Yes, Rose and Michael."

"You'll be here, too," he hastily added. "I could never stay away from you for long."

Wearily, she chuckled. "You already hurt my feelings. It's too late to fix it. Don't try."

"I'm sorry; I'm not very good at this."

"I know."

She rolled onto her back, studying the ceiling, and he hated that he'd upset her. He didn't understand why their sexual encounters had to be fraught with such drama.

Why couldn't they just experience moments of passion and merriment? Why was their relationship riddled with emotion?

She reached over and squeezed his hand.

"Would you take me with you to Scotland?"

He was startled by the query, a spurt of ecstasy rushing through him at the notion, but he tamped it down.

"I couldn't."

"Why not?"

"A sailing ship is no place for a lady."

She scowled and shrugged. "It was worth asking."

"I wish I could take you. It's so beautiful out on the water. You'd love it."

"I'm sure I would," she agreed. They were silent, then she said, "I'll miss you."

"I'll miss you, too."

"What will I do all day—and all night—while you're gone?"

"I don't know, but promise me you won't spend any time with that Phillip Dudley character."

"I like that Dudley character. He amuses me."

"I don't care if you like him. Just don't spend any time with him."

Her smile was back.

"You're jealous; I'm certain of it."

"Perhaps."

She sighed. "It will be so quiet without you here."

"Really?"

"Yes, really. Don't look so surprised."

"But I am surprised."

"Why?"

"I don't believe anyone has ever missed me before."

At the admission, an odd sorrow inundated him, pricking at the lonely little boy, the lonely young man he'd been.

With his mother deceased and his father barely acknowledging him, he'd never had a family or a home. After he'd matured and was traveling the oceans, his isolated existence had become ingrained.

He'd never dwelled on the fact that he didn't belong anywhere, that he had no *people* to call his own, and suddenly, it seemed like the saddest thing in the world.

She leaned over and kissed him. "Will you stay the night with me?"

"I thought you'd never ask."

"I want to be paid ten pounds."

"Ten! You're mad."

Maud glared at Lydia as if she'd escaped from an asylum.

"Plus I want two new dresses, and a new uniform."

"An outrageous demand."

"And I want to be permanently assigned to duties upstairs. No more scrubbing pots in the kitchen when Cook needs extra help."

"Go back to work, Lydia. You annoy me."

"When you're so eager to be shed of the Hamilton sisters, ten pounds isn't much—if it will guarantee you get your wish."

Maud paused, pondering her reply.

Lydia had a knack for spying, for listening when she shouldn't and seeing what she oughtn't. What could she have discovered?

"How do I know your information is worth so much money?"

"It's worth it, all right. I'll bet you can have them out of here by tomorrow morning."

"Fine, then. We have a deal. What is it that you've learned?"

"Give me the money first."

Maud seethed, hating to be bested by a servant and inclined to refuse just on principle, but she was desperate to hear Lydia's gossip.

She went to her desk and opened her strongbox, extracted the cash, and handed it over. Lydia stuck it into her cleavage.

"Write me a note that I can take to the seamstress in the village," Lydia pressed.

"About what?"

"About the dresses. Beg pardon, Mrs. Seymour, but I won't have you claiming you don't owe them to me."

Maud gnawed on her lip, wondering if she shouldn't fire the cheeky girl, but in the end, she dipped her quill in the ink pot and penned the voucher for Lydia's clothes.

"I can read, Mrs. Seymour," Lydia mentioned, "so don't try any funny business. I'll know if you've allowed the sewing or not."

Maud seethed again. She'd planned to scribble a few sentences of gibberish. How was it that Lydia understood her so completely? They were possessed of the same penchant for deceit, so perhaps Lydia recognized treachery when she stumbled on it.

Maud finished the letter, waiting impatiently as Lydia read every word. Satisfied, Lydia tucked it into her cleavage, too.

"What is it?" Maud said. "I'm all ears."

"It's about Jane Hamilton. Where would you like me to start?"

HELEN walked into Maud Seymour's sitting room, struggling not to appear nervous, but she couldn't help it. She'd never previously been invited to Seymour's private quarters, and the summons boded ill.

The furniture had been oddly situated, with Seymour seated in a large, comfortable chair, but another chair—a hard, straight-backed one—had been set across from it. Apparently, an interrogation was about to commence, with Helen the person who would be questioned.

What was her crime? She couldn't imagine.

Thank heavens Tristan hadn't yet left for Scotland. She was amazed that—whatever her transgression—Mrs. Seymour hadn't delayed until he was gone so that Helen would be unprotected.

"Yes, Mrs. Seymour?" Helen smiled, hoping she looked amiable. "You asked to see me?"

The woman gestured to the empty chair, and Helen sat.

"I've never been one to beat around the bush," Seymour began, "so I won't hesitate to reveal that I never wanted you in this house."

At the vicious remark, Helen was taken aback. She was silent, grappling with how to respond.

Courtesy won out.

"I'm very sorry to hear that," Helen evenly stated, "for I've been happy in my position."

"I'll bet you have. It's easy to be content when you've glommed on to your betters like a leech on a thigh. Do you enjoy being a charity case? With your antecedents, it must come naturally."

Helen inhaled a deep breath, counted to ten, then let it out. She stood.

"If you have a specific complaint, I suggest you discuss it with Captain Odell."

"I intend to." Seymour's tone threatened enormous trouble. "In the meantime, we're not finished. Sit down."

"I'd rather not."

She turned to go, when Seymour bellowed, "Sit down, Miss Hamilton!"

Helen was so furious, she was trembling, but she complied, positive that Seymour wouldn't desist until she said what she was dying to say.

"I don't answer to you, Mrs. Seymour, despite how

you wish it were otherwise. Captain Odell has been very clear that I should only take orders from him, but I try to be agreeable. I will listen to you, but I will not be insulted."

"The captain may be your employer," Seymour retorted, "but if you think you can stay here without my approval, you should think again. Tell me about your sister's relationship with the earl."

The query was so unexpected that, initially, Helen had no idea to whom she referred.

"My sister Jane," she asked, "and Lord Hastings?"

"Yes."

"They're cordial. They're friends. They ride horses every day. They've danced at some of the parties. Why?"

"Is she pregnant?"

Helen came halfway to her feet. "What?"

"Is she? Don't lie to me. The truth will emerge—sooner rather than later."

"You have some gall, making unfounded accusations."

Seymour scoffed. "Was pregnancy your game all along? I've been curious about your motive in being here. Maybe I've finally exposed it. After all, a bastard baby would bring good fortune to a trio of homeless, disowned females."

"You believe that we . . . that I . . . that she . . ."

Helen was so enraged that she couldn't complete a thought. The allegation left her dazed. Her legs gave out and she sank into the chair.

"Are you planning to demand a stipend?" Seymour continued. "A trust fund? A house for the little bugger? All at Michael's expense, of course."

Seymour's cruel character—which she typically sought to conceal—was fully unmasked. Helen's loathing was unleashed, too, and for the first time in her life, she worried that she might attack another person. Her fists were actually itching to land a few blows.

"How dare you slander us!"

"Slander? Last I heard, truth was a defense."

Helen rose and stormed out, but before she made it to the hall, Seymour called, "You haven't answered me, Miss Hamilton. Is she pregnant or not?"

Helen whipped around. "If she was, I would never discuss it with you."

"I wonder what the captain will have to say," Seymour pretended to muse. "I can't wait to find out."

Seymour was very relaxed, looking every inch the rich, privileged matron she was. She was too calm, too sure of herself, and her certainty alarmed Helen.

What had Jane done?

Helen had been so busy with Amelia and Rose, with Tristan, that she'd had scant opportunity to fret about Jane, but Jane was older and possessed of a strong moral constitution. She was aware of the strictures by which she was to conduct herself, and she knew better than to become involved with Lord Hastings.

As you knew better with Tristan? a niggling voice pestered, but she shoved it away. Her situation with Tristan was nothing like an affair between Jane and Lord Hastings. Hastings was bound by rules and restrictions that would never apply to Tristan. Would Jane have crossed such a forbidden line?

Her sister had always been enamored of Michael Seymour. Even when they'd been destitute, with not a bite of food in the cupboard or a penny in their pockets, she'd been fascinated.

Had her girlish attraction metamorphosed into a dangerous liaison?

Helen spun away and raced for the stairs, heading directly to Jane's bedchamber.

She knocked once and turned the knob, but the door was locked, so she knocked again, louder. When there was no reply, she knocked a third time and a fourth.

Ultimately, Jane asked, "Who is it?"

"It's Helen, Jane. Let me in."

After much foot dragging and delay, Jane opened the

door, and though she hurriedly whirled away, Helen saw that she'd been crying.

Her back to Helen, she went to the window and peered outside.

"What's the matter?" Helen inquired.

"I'm just feeling a bit low." Jane had a kerchief clutched in her hand, and she furtively swiped at her eyes.

Helen grabbed two chairs and set them facing each other. She plopped down in one.

"Jane, come," she gently coaxed. "We need to talk."

"Can't we put it off till I'm in a better mood?"

"No, we can't."

Jane sighed, but she trudged over and sat. She stared at the floor.

"What is it?" Jane queried.

"I have to ask you a question, and you must tell me the truth."

"I'm always honest with you. Why would you even say such a thing?"

Helen studied Jane, assessing her slumped shoulders, her mottled cheeks. Her morose condition provided damning evidence, and Helen hated to pry, but she had to hear the facts from Jane's own mouth.

"I won't be angry," Helen pressed, "but you can't lie to me."

"I won't!"

"I don't know how to delve into this with any aplomb, so here it is: Are you having an affair with Lord Hastings?"

Jane drew in a sharp breath and started to weep. "Why would you ask me that?"

"Someone told me, Jane—someone who was very sure—so you can't deny it."

Jane kept staring at the floor, pulling the kerchief through her fingers. Finally, she whispered, "Yes."

Helen sagged with defeat. "How long has it been going on?"

"Since we moved into his London house."

"Did he . . . force himself on you?"

"No, no. I wanted it to happen."

"Oh, Jane . . ."

They were silent, downcast and despondent.

"Are you pregnant?"

"I'm not certain how I'd know."

"You miss your monthly courses."

There was a lengthy, pained pause, then Jane shuddered and admitted, "I might be. I'm a tad late."

"How late?"

"Two weeks?"

Helen calculated the days, the months. Would it be an April baby? A May one?

"Look at me, Jane," she said.

Jane glanced up, her woe plainly visible.

"Why are you crying?" Helen inquired.

"Because . . . because . . ."—she choked down a sob—"I love him and I've been expecting him to propose, but he hasn't yet, and I'm beginning to fear that he never will."

Helen fumed, her temper boiling, and she leaned forward and patted Jane's hand. "We'll see about that."

"What can you do?"

"You're not some scullery maid he seduced in the kitchen. You're Jane Hamilton. Your grandfather was a man of great repute. Lord Hastings can't have ruined you without there being consequences."

"What consequences?"

"He has to marry you. He has no choice."

"How will you make him?"

"The captain is his guardian. I'll speak to him; I'll demand it."

"Will he listen to you?"

"Yes, he will. He and I are friends, and he's extremely honorable. He'll order Lord Hastings to wed you."

Jane gazed at her lap, the kerchief being tugged with a renewed vengeance.

"I hope you're correct."

"Why wouldn't I be?"

"It's just that Mrs. Seymour has been fanatical about letting us know how we don't belong."

"Don't worry about her," Helen scoffed. "I'll talk to the captain immediately. We'll have it all arranged before supper."

"Do you really think so?"

"Yes." Helen's mind was spinning with plans. "We'll apply for a Special License, and we should be able to hold the wedding in a few days."

Jane's relief was palpable. "I'm so glad; I've been so afraid."

"Don't be." Helen started out.

"Where are you going?" Jane asked.

"I have to find Captain Odell. You stay here till I return. I'll be back with good news. I promise."

Helen opened the door to slip out, when Jane said, "Helen?"

Helen peered over her shoulder. "Yes?"

"I've made a mess of things, haven't I?"

"A bit of a one, but we'll have it fixed in a trice."

"I didn't mean to. I just . . . just . . ."

She appeared so young and so lost, and Helen's heart melted.

"You're not the first girl who was charmed by a handsome boy. It happens all the time."

"I never thought it would happen to *me,* though. I'm sorry. I wanted to tell you about it, but I didn't know how."

"It's all right, Jane. You both should have behaved better, but I blame Lord Hastings for the entire debacle."

"It wasn't his fault."

Helen could have argued the point, could have condemned the philandering rogue. From her initial meeting with Hastings, his flirtatious nature had been clear, and she had no doubt that he'd meticulously plotted Jane's fall from grace.

But Jane was too besotted, and she wouldn't heed any criticism, so it would be a waste of breath. Helen would save her fury for the conversation she was about to have with Tristan.

"It doesn't matter how it occurred," Helen insisted. "Captain Odell will give you the resolution you're due."

Chapter 18

❦

"CAPTAIN," the butler announced, "Miss Hamilton requests an audience."

"Thank you. I'll see her now."

The butler held open the library door, and Helen entered.

Tristan had been sequestered in a private appointment, and for more than an hour, she'd cooled her heels in the hall. She hurried in, ready to burst out with the fact that there was terrible trouble, when she noticed he wasn't alone.

Maud Seymour was seated across from him.

Helen should have realized that Seymour would rush to tattle, but she'd been so frantic about Jane that the obvious hadn't occurred to her.

She stumbled to a halt, recollecting Jane's comment about how they'd never truly been welcome. Suddenly, she wasn't nearly as sure as she had been of Tristan's support.

"I . . . I . . . have to talk to you," she stammered.

"I believe I know the subject." He gestured to the chair next to Seymour, indicating she should sit.

Helen wanted to beg him to order Seymour out, but she couldn't. Their affair was a secret, so he couldn't show her any special favor, and she couldn't demand it. As far as Seymour was aware, Helen was a servant.

Still, Helen asked, "May I speak with you privately?"

"There's no need for a private discussion."

"Please?"

"This is a family issue," Seymour chimed in, "and the earl is likely to wed my daughter. What concerns him, concerns me. If I am not the person who should be present during this conversation, who is?"

Tristan pointed to the chair again, and Helen marched over, feeling as if she was about to face a firing squad.

She studied him, trying to glean some hint of his opinion, some evidence that she had an ally in the room, but he glared back with an unruffled, imperious expression.

"Mrs. Seymour has shared the pertinent details with me," he started.

"Has she?" Helen hotly said.

"Yes, and we've decided how to proceed."

"How to *proceed*? It seems easy enough to me: There must be a wedding, and from what Jane just confided, I'd say the sooner the better."

Tristan stiffened as Seymour scoffed, "Why would you suppose there should be a wedding?"

"Jane isn't some doxy. She's a gently bred girl, from a good family, and—"

"Harry Hamilton's daughter?" Seymour interrupted. "You have some nerve if you think she's entitled to any heightened regard."

"Maud," Tristan scolded, "there's no need for insults."

"Well, she is Harry's daughter. What did you expect would happen, with Michael being allowed to socialize with a child like her? She's been throwing herself at him all summer."

"Maud!" he said more sharply. "I insist you be courteous, or you'll have to leave."

"As you wish," Seymour yielded. "I wouldn't miss this chat for the world."

Refusing to back down, Helen persisted with her argument.

"Despite Mrs. Seymour's remarks about my father, Jane *is* from a good family, and Lord Hastings can't use her like this without consequence. Marriage is the only solution we'll accept."

For a moment, Tristan looked pained, and he shut his eyes, pressing finger and thumb on the bridge of his nose. When he sighed and straightened, he gazed at her with regret.

"Here is what we'll do," he gently advised.

"*We*, being you and Mrs. Seymour? You've settled everything without asking me?"

"You're the governess," Seymour snapped. "Why would you have been consulted?"

Many livid replies could have been hurled: *Because I'm not just the governess; because I love Tristan Odell and I thought he loved me; because I assumed I mattered to him!*

But she couldn't allude to any of them.

"I want to speak with Lord Hastings," Helen declared. "I want to hear—from his own mouth—that he concurs with this hideous insult."

"I'm afraid that won't be possible," Tristan responded.

She was silent, stunned, aggrieved beyond words.

"Miss Hamilton . . ." Tristan stopped, then began again. "Helen, listen to me."

"Give me a reason why I should."

"Miss Hamilton!" Seymour chided. "Honestly. Remember your place."

"In a situation such as this," Tristan continued, ignoring Seymour, "there are many factors to consider."

"I can think of only one," Helen said. "A young lady has been callously ruined by Lord Hastings and amends must be made. Immediately."

"Yes, amends must be made," Tristan agreed. "But first, the liaison has to be severed, so Lord Hastings and I will be departing the property at once. Our horses are already being saddled."

"He's leaving? No. I want a wedding. I *demand* a wedding!"

Tristan shook his head. "It's not going to happen, Helen. I'm sorry."

Seymour added, "I can't believe you'd expect such an outrageous conclusion, Miss Hamilton." She peered at Tristan. "Since you graced her with your favor, Captain, she's lost all sense of rank and station."

Helen kept her attention focused on Tristan. He was stern and implacable, exhibiting none of the endearing traits he'd permitted her to see during their more intimate encounters.

She couldn't reconcile this ruthless, obstinate person with the supportive friend she'd come to cherish. He was no longer Tristan Odell, the man who made her pulse race and her spirits soar. He was every inch *Captain* Odell, the uncompromising, merciless autocrat whom he'd appeared to be when they'd initially met.

"She's my sister," Helen futilely pointed out.

"I realize that."

"She's an impressionable eighteen-year-old girl."

"I know how old she is."

"She loves him! She's positive he loves her, too. This is breaking her heart. It's breaking mine."

"I'm sorry," he repeated, though he didn't look as if he was.

Seymour cut in. "With each statement you utter, Miss Hamilton, you sound more deranged. Cease your begging and heed Captain Odell. He's trying to inform you of your arrangements, but you keep interrupting."

At the comment, Helen was so incensed that she wanted to charge Seymour and pound her to the floor till she was a bloody heap on the rug. She glared at Odell, waiting for him to reprimand Seymour, or at least attempt to smooth over her harsh tone.

Instead, he killed Helen a bit by saying, "Yes, Miss Hamilton, let's finish this, shall we? The entire business is distasteful, and I intend to resolve it with a minimal amount of unpleasantness."

"By all means," Helen seethed, "don't let my petty troubles keep you from your more urgent affairs."

His cheeks flushed as if with chagrin, but he forged on, ever the dutiful guardian to his ward.

"We feel there should be a cooling-off period, that time and distance will make the affection wane."

"Lord Hastings is a renowned libertine," Helen retorted. "I'm sure he'll get over Jane very quickly. His roving eye has probably already landed on the next girl he plans to seduce."

Odell fumed, but pushed on. "He will accompany me on my trip to Scotland, then he will stay in Scotland with some Seymour relatives for six months."

"Six months . . ." Helen muttered, recognizing how inconsolable Jane would be. "What is to become of my sister?"

"The three of you—yourself, Jane, and Amelia—will return to London. I will have a house rented for you, and you'll reside there till we learn if there is a babe."

Several of his remarks were important, but only one struck her as being worthy of a response. "Am I being dismissed from my post?"

"Not dismissed, precisely," he hedged.

"Then what, *precisely*, is occurring?"

"For now, you'll receive an allowance. Future decisions will be made once we know whether or not your sister is increasing."

Meaning: If there was a babe, the Seymours would take it and have it raised by trusted servants on a rural estate. Jane would be paid a nominal sum as damages, which they could live on until Helen found another job.

If there was no baby, their situation was very dire, indeed.

"If she's not pregnant," Helen inquired, "will we be tossed out on the street to fend for ourselves?"

"I'm certain we'll be able to reach an accommodation."

The offer was kindly tendered, but in light of how much Helen had cared about him, it was the coldest, cruelest thing anyone had ever said to her.

To her horror, tears welled into her eyes and dripped down her cheeks. She didn't even try to swipe them away. She was too astonished, and it was a sign of how far they'd moved beyond their prior relationship that he displayed no reaction to her obvious sadness.

"Will I ever see Lady Rose again? Will Amelia?"

"Really, Miss Hamilton," Seymour nagged. "As if we would let Rose consort with Amelia after this scandal!"

"I'm done working for you, aren't I?" Helen's gaze was locked on Odell.

"How can you imagine we'd still want you?" Seymour replied for him. "Your sister didn't have any better sense as to the consequences of her behavior, but you surely do. Rose is the daughter of the earl of Hastings, the sister of the earl of Hastings, yet you assume you could remain as her governess? Jane is completely disgraced, and her disgrace is yours. You will never work for us again. Not as long as I draw breath."

A heavy, humiliating silence festered, fraught with rage and betrayal. The spark that had once sizzled inside of Helen, the ember that had been lit when she'd first grown to love Odell, was extinguished.

Rage metamorphosed to hurt, then to hatred. Animosity wafted from her posture, her very soul.

"I presume you concur with Mrs. Seymour?" Helen tightly queried.

He was too much of a coward to answer. "Why don't you go speak with Jane?" he urged. "Notify her of what will be expected."

"Then we will send up the maids," Seymour mentioned, "to pack your bags for the trip to London."

"I ask," Odell said, "that Jane stay in her room until the earl and I have departed. We won't allow any further contact between them."

"Not even a simple good-bye?" Helen pleaded. "Where's the harm in that?"

"A clean break," Seymour explained, "is for the best. She'll get over him faster."

They presented such a united front. There was a wall that separated her from them—a wall of rank and wealth and status—but due to her fondness for Odell, Helen had forgotten that it existed. She'd forgotten where she stood in the world, but they had reminded her swiftly enough.

Reeling with dismay, she rose and left.

As she headed for the stairs, she wondered why she'd involved herself with him. In an instant, her safe, secure spot had vanished. All that she'd built through the summer and into the autumn was wrecked.

She'd trusted him, had loved him, had even believed he would eventually marry her, but it had been a chimera.

She was a fool. A gullible, impetuous, stupid fool.

They were at his mercy, a step away from the streets again, and all depended on whether a babe was about to be born. Until the matter was resolved, they would be in limbo, and once it was finally settled, only bad choices faced them.

There'd be no wedding, no happy ending.

What was she supposed to tell Jane?

"WHAT were you thinking?"

"I guess I wasn't."

Michael glanced away, too ashamed to look at Tristan.

"How many times have I lectured you about this?" Tristan inquired. "How many times have I warned you?"

"Too many."

Tristan was angry enough to spit nails, and he whirled away and went to the sideboard to pour himself a glass of whiskey. He glowered at Michael in a way that made Michael feel petty and small.

Michael had known better than to ruin Jane, but he'd selfishly proceeded anyway. Though he'd been aware that discovery could occur, it had been a vague notion, lost in a hazy future. He'd never imagined such an abrupt exposure of the affair, hadn't anticipated such a wrenching conclusion.

"Have you spoken to her?" Michael asked.

"No, and you're not going to either."

"She has to be told what's happening."

"Her sister is handling it."

"She should hear it from me."

"Hear what? That you've destroyed her life, and you'll pay her a few pounds' reparation?"

Tristan gulped down his whiskey, and Michael was surprised to note that his hand was shaking. Evidently, he was more distraught than he let on.

"You're making too much of this," Michael tried to protest.

"Too much? Are you mad? At the very least—the very least!—you will have to support that girl for the rest of her days. If she has a baby, you'll have to support it, too. There will be trust funds to manage; schooling to provide; and the bitter, rare visits with a child you'll hardly know— one who will never forgive you for how you treated his mother."

After their own father's shenanigans with Tristan's mother, he knew of such things, and Michael panicked.

What if Jane was pregnant? What if they had a son and Michael never saw him? The prospect was too depressing to consider.

When he was with Jane, it always seemed so right, as if it was fated, so he hadn't thought through the ramifications. He hadn't peered down the road to this horrid moment, where he was dishonored and she was disgraced.

"You could fix this so she and I could be together," Michael said. "Why are you being so difficult?"

"Can you actually assume it would be appropriate to continue the relationship?"

"I love her," he was stunned to find himself declaring.

"Love, bah!" Tristan scoffed. "When did *love* ever have any bearing on marriage?"

"If you won't let me marry her, she could be my mistress."

"Yes, she could be, and you might sire several children with her. How would you explain them to your wife at your wedding?"

"Oh."

"Are you proud of the trouble you've caused? Was it worth lifting her skirt?"

"It wasn't like that."

"Really? Why don't you tell me how it *was*?"

"I care about her."

"Big bloody deal. She's still ruined, and you're still a scoundrel."

Michael was about to comment when Tristan held up a hand, halting him.

"If you're about to claim that she was complicit, or that she wanted it, too, I swear to God that I will march across the room and pummel you to the floor."

"I wouldn't claim any such thing."

"Good, because I won't listen to any of your nonsense."

"I always liked her—from the very beginning. She's a very fine girl. Very fine."

"So you deflowered her? Is that how you treat a woman you view as remarkable?"

"It's not any different from what you've been doing with her sister."

Tristan bristled. "Don't drag Helen into this mess."

"Nobody is screaming at you for being a lout. Why must I be castigated but not you?"

"Because I'm not an earl, and you are! You're in the wrong. Admit it for once, would you?"

"Yes, I was wrong. I'm sorry."

They sighed, then sat in silence, both morose and miserable. Tristan poured another drink and swallowed it down, the alcohol relieving some of his distress.

"What now?" Michael inquired.

"I told you: We're leaving for London immediately, and we're traveling on to Scotland."

In other circumstances, Michael would have jumped at the chance for such an adventure, but he couldn't accept the fact that he wouldn't see Jane for six months. And if Tristan had his way, he would never be with her again.

Tristan kept ranting that separation was for the best, but why did it have to be so? Yes, Michael had behaved badly, but scandals could be smoothed over.

He just had to get a message to Jane, had to learn where she'd be and devise a method to secretly correspond. They could plan for when he returned to England.

Surely, she'd still be fond of him in six months. Wouldn't she be?

The butler knocked on the door and peeked in.

"Your horses are ready, Captain Odell. You may depart whenever you are so inclined."

"Thank you."

Tristan finished his whiskey and pushed away from the sideboard.

"Let's go."

"I have to talk to Jane first."

"No."

Michael's temper flared.

Normally, he was content to do as Tristan bid him; Michael was amenable simply because he didn't care overly much as to the result of Tristan's decisions. But they'd finally arrived at a spot where the outcome mattered very much.

He stomped over to Tristan, knowing his brother was stronger and tougher, that if they came to blows, Tristan would win any battle, but this time, Michael wouldn't back down as he always had in the past.

"I have tolerated your harangue," Michael said, "and I've apologized. Yes, I failed to heed your warnings, and now a girl—one whom I love very much—has been harmed. I've listened to you and listened, but I've heard enough. I will talk to Jane, or I will not leave."

"Jane vacated the premises an hour ago. I sent her away before I summoned you to the library."

Michael felt as if he'd been punched in the stomach.

"Where is she?" he bellowed.

"I will never tell you, and there's no reason for you to ever know."

Tristan went to the door and gestured to the hall.

"Go to the stables. Check the horses and the saddle-bags. I have to fetch my coat and pistol up in my bed-chamber. I'll be out in a few minutes."

Michael glared at Tristan, yearning to hit his brother and to keep on hitting him until his smug face was a mass of bruises. But what good would it do?

Jane was gone, and Michael had been vanquished at every turn.

He shoved Tristan aside and stormed out.

"GET out of here!"

Helen shouted the command, being far beyond the time when she would have practiced discretion about Tristan coming to her room, but Tristan ignored her.

Michael was out in the barn, leading the horses around to the front, and Tristan was determined to be away before Michael had any notion that Jane was still in the house.

Once Maud had revealed the affair, Tristan had been at a loss as to how to proceed. To his surprise, she'd had the exact answers he'd needed, and he was amazed at how sensible she'd seemed. After a lengthy discussion, he'd decided to follow nearly all of her advice.

Though Helen had been crushed, marriage between Michael and Jane wasn't an option Tristan had considered for a single second. During their meeting in the library, he'd hated appearing so callous, but adolescent romance was potent, and the infatuation had to be stamped out.

"Get out!" she shouted again.

"I have to talk to you."

"You've made your position perfectly clear."

"I haven't said what I wanted to say."

"Believe me: You've said plenty. Now go away, or I'll start screaming, and I'll continue screaming until someone comes to help me."

He marched over until they were toe-to-toe. She was enraged, but he wasn't in the best mood, either.

Did she think this was easy for him? Did she think he relished hurting her? If so, she had to suppose he was an unfeeling monster, when in fact, the debacle had left him extremely distraught.

Michael had ruined Jane, but Tristan had ruined Helen, too. What kind of brothers were they? What kind of men? Apparently, their father's blood ran strong in their veins, and Tristan was very ashamed.

Why couldn't she be more sympathetic? Why couldn't she understand his point of view? He hoped to soothe her sufficiently that they could have a decent farewell.

"I'll be leaving shortly."

"Marvelous. I'll be glad to see the last of you."

"You're angry; you don't mean that."

"Oh, I do! I really, really do. You are the most despicable, disloyal—"

He grabbed her by the forearms and shook her.

"What did you expect me to do?" he demanded.

"I expected you to help my sister." She pushed him away, seeming as if she couldn't bear his touch. "I expected you to make Lord Hastings do the right thing."

"He could not marry her!"

"According to whom? You and Maud Seymour?"

"Yes, according to us. I'm his guardian, for pity's sake. I would not permit it, and I will not apologize to you."

"Why wouldn't you *permit* it, Mr. High-and-Mighty

Captain Odell? Are you of the opinion that she's not good enough for him? Is that what you're telling me?"

"She is *not* good enough for him. He is a peer of the realm, one of the largest landowners in the kingdom, one of the richest men. He will wed as is appropriate to his rank and station. You're a rational person. You know this to be true, and I have no idea why you're raising such a fuss."

"You could actually say that to my face?" she hissed. "You could actually claim that Jane is not worthy to marry into your family?"

"Yes."

Before he realized what was happening, she slapped him as hard as she could.

It was a powerful blow that staggered him, and as he straightened, he was rubbing his cheek, his eyes cold with fury.

He'd rarely been hit in his life. With men, he was always on guard against it, and no woman had ever previously dared.

"If you were a man," he seethed, "I'd hit you back."

"If I were a man, it would be pistols at dawn."

He frowned, wondering if this was the last time he would ever see her and not able to abide the notion that it might be.

He would stop in London and instruct his clerk to rent lodging for her before proceeding on to Scotland. Even if all went smoothly, he would be gone for several weeks.

Would she still be in London when he returned? If she fled, how would he ever locate her? Yet in light of all that had transpired, why would he want to find her?

Since the moment they'd met, she'd been trouble, and now, with her sister's fiasco, his decision to assist her was coming back to haunt him in spades.

"Promise me"—he struggled for calm—"that you will move into the house my clerk rents for you. Promise me that you will wait while I travel to Scotland."

"Why would it matter to you where I might be?"

"Promise me!" he roared. "I have to know you are safe until I can make other arrangements for you."

"What might those arrangements be? Will you marry me? Will we all live together, just one big happy family? I can picture us in our tidy home: you and me and my sister, who is not 'good enough' for you."

They stared and stared, a chasm opening between them, and he felt as if he was falling into it, as if he'd never claw his way out.

"I didn't deserve that," he quietly said.

"Didn't you?"

"I've tried to reach an acceptable conclusion."

"Acceptable for whom?"

Why was she behaving like this? She knew who Michael was. The standards were different; the stakes were different. Michael wasn't some neighborhood lad who, when caught in a peccadillo, could wed the girl next door. He was the *earl* of Hastings.

His father had written to Tristan—on his deathbed, no less!—charging Tristan to select the best bride possible. By any measure, Jane was not the *best,* and she would never be Countess of Hastings.

It was as simple and as heartless as that.

Exhaustion swept over him, the weight of the world on his shoulders. "What do you want from me?"

"I don't want anything from you," she insisted. "I just want you to go away, then I never want to see you again."

"Oh, Helen . . ."

He held out his hand, stupidly supposing that she might take it, that they might somehow bridge the gap separating them, but she gaped as if he was insane.

"Isn't your brother waiting for you?"

"Yes, he is."

"You probably ought to hurry, or the earl will be delayed. We can't be upsetting the poor, cosseted child."

Tristan was silent, a thousand comments coursing

through his head. He yearned to confide how devastated he was, how sad and overwhelmed.

When he'd agreed to care for Michael and Rose, he'd known he didn't possess the necessary skills to deal with the problems that might arise, but he'd had no idea how wretched it might truly become.

He needed Helen's guidance and support, her friendship and counsel, but she was acting like a stranger, as foreign to him as if he'd just bumped into her on the street.

"I'll be back in a few weeks," he said. "I hope you're still in London. I hope I can find you."

"I wouldn't count on it."

"I'm sorry it ended like this."

"Are you?"

"Yes."

"You have a funny way of showing it."

She appeared brittle, as if she was frozen on the inside. The sparkle in her eye was gone. The smile on her lips had vanished.

He'd simply been trying to do what was right for everyone concerned, but he hadn't a clue how to convince her, how to make her love him again.

Feeling bereft, as if his heart was broken, he spun and left.

"TRISTAN! Tristan!"

Rose flew out the front door of the manor to see him fussing with the stirrup on his saddle. Michael was with him, already mounted and about to ride away. At her frantic cry, Tristan whipped around.

"Rose? What is it? What's wrong?"

She ran to him.

"You're leaving," she accused. "Why?"

"I have to go to Scotland."

"Without saying good-bye?"

"I've had a lot on my mind," Tristan claimed, "and I completely forgot."

"I want to know what's happening," she demanded. "I'm not a child, so don't treat me like one."

Tristan glanced at Michael, and they exchanged a look that Rose couldn't decipher.

"We have business in Scotland," Michael said. "It's important, so we have to deal with it immediately."

"You are such a liar," Rose charged. "The servants were talking. You did something horrid to Jane Hamilton."

"They're mistaken, Rose," Michael contended. "I didn't do anything to Jane. I like her very much."

Rose turned her furious attention to Tristan. "Miss Hamilton has been fired, hasn't she?"

Michael glowered at Tristan. "How interesting that you didn't bother to mention it."

"She hasn't been fired," Tristan maintained. "She's just . . . just . . ." On the spur of the moment, he couldn't devise a suitable fabrication. "I'll explain when I get back."

"Explain it now!" Rose commanded.

"There's no time, Rose."

"She's the best governess I've ever had. There's no reason for her to lose her job."

"She hasn't."

"If she goes, Amelia will have to go, too. The maids are in Amelia's room. They're packing her bags!"

"She and her sister will . . . ah . . . be in London," Tristan asserted. "You'll see her again very soon."

"Swear it to me!"

Tristan hesitated, his vacillation providing all the information she needed. He prided himself on his honor, and he would never offer a vow that wasn't true.

He came over to her, and he rested a hand on her shoulder, as if the paltry gesture would make things better.

"There's been some trouble," he admitted.

"What is it? Maybe I can fix it for you."

"It's adult trouble. It wouldn't be appropriate to discuss it with you."

Rose peered up at Michael, and from his sheepish expression, she realized that the servants' gossip was correct. Michael had committed a terrible deed, but she and Amelia would suffer for it.

"They're packing Amelia's bags," she repeated.

"I know." Tristan seemed embarrassed by the fact.

"I'll never see her again, will I? You're making her go, and I'll never see her."

"Rose, let me—"

"She's the only friend I ever had!" Rose shouted, shoving him away. "You may not take her from me! I forbid it!"

She wished she were a man, that she was bigger and taller, that she could force him to listen, that she could force him to do what she said.

Tristan sighed. "It's not up to you, Rose. If there were any other way . . ."

"I'll be alone with Maud and Miriam."

"Just for a while. I'll hurry home as fast as I can."

"When you first arrived, you told me you'd always be here—till I was a grown-up. You're not coming back, are you?"

"Of course I am. Why would you say such a thing?"

"What about Michael? When will he be back?"

"He'll be away a bit longer than me," Tristan hedged.

"How long is that?"

Tristan didn't reply. Instead, he said to Michael, "Let me get her in the house."

As if she were a baby, he tried to push her toward the door, but she wrestled out of his grasp.

She gazed at Michael. "Don't allow him to do this," she begged. "Order him to let Amelia stay with me. I'll die if she goes!"

"It's not up to me," Michael asserted.

"You can stop him. You're the earl"—she pointed at

Tristan—"and who is he? He's no one, that's who! He came here where he wasn't wanted or needed, and he thinks he can wreck everything. Stop him!"

"You're acting like a baby. Go inside," Michael scolded, imagining she'd heed him when he had failed her so miserably.

She was so angry that she didn't care if she ever spoke to either of them again. She hoped they left and never returned.

Shaking from head to toe, she studied Tristan, her rage uncontrollable, her heart broken.

"If Amelia leaves," she said, "I will never forgive you as long as I live."

She whirled around and raced into the house.

Chapter 19

"WHERE are you going?"

"I'm off to visit Helen Hamilton."

"You are not. I forbid it."

Clarinda glared at her brother.

"You forbid it?"

"Yes."

"You're not serious."

"Keep walking, and you'll discover how serious I am."

Clarinda rolled her eyes. "Don't nag as if I was still ten years old."

"If you don't want me nagging, don't act like a child."

Clarinda spun around and proceeded down the lane.

"Excuse me!" Phillip snapped. "Aren't you listening? I said that you are *not* to go up to the manor."

"I heard you. I'm simply ignoring you, which I understand will be a shock when you're so enormously conceited, but you'll get over it."

She continued on, pleased that she'd finally forged ahead.

She was determined to befriend Helen Hamilton, and why shouldn't she?

They had much in common: They were the same age, and they had dubious antecedents. Hamilton worked as a governess, and Clarinda worked, too. Not at a lofty position in a fancy house, but they were both employed females.

Because of her itinerant wanderings, Clarinda had never had any friends. Whenever she met a woman she liked, they moved on before a bond could form. She'd resolved to change her life, and she thought Miss Hamilton might welcome an overture.

Hamilton wasn't a servant or a member of the Seymour family, so she didn't belong to any of the established hierarchies in the mansion. She was probably lonely, and Clarinda was vain enough to suppose that Hamilton could greatly benefit from an association.

Clarinda remembered her first encounter with Miss Hamilton, when she'd been poor and hungry and desperate. She'd managed to secure a post with Odell, but if anything happened and she lost it, she was awful at taking care of herself.

She hadn't any of the common sense that came naturally to Clarinda. Clarinda's younger years had been filled with toil and struggle, but she'd learned how to fend for herself, how to land on her feet. Along the way, she'd had her dear, larcenous brother to teach her the ropes, but Miss Hamilton had had no one like that.

When times were hard, Hamilton hadn't a clue of how to get on.

Clarinda possessed some of her mother's clairvoyance, and she perceived adversity brewing for Hamilton as clearly as if she were sniffing smoke on the wind.

Miss Hamilton was involved with the captain, and Jane with the earl, but if either of the affairs was exposed, Miss Hamilton's job would vanish. What Hamilton didn't realize, but what Clarinda fathomed all too well, was that Odell would never side with her in any genuine dispute. Within hours, she'd be out on the streets, her sisters trailing after her, so she needed Clarinda.

Clarinda planned to call on her. She'd be cordial and helpful, and hopefully she'd create a connection so that Hamilton would allow her to assist once calamity struck.

"Clarinda!" Phillip barked, marching after her. Shortly, he caught up.

"Why are you in such a snit?" she demanded. "Am I not permitted to have any friends? Am I not permitted an existence beyond this wagon?"

"You may have as many friends as you like. I just don't want you rubbing elbows with those rich snobs."

"I'll do my best to avoid them."

"Nothing but trouble will come from it."

"I'm visiting Miss Hamilton. Why would I even see any of the Seymours? From the way you're acting, you'd think I was off to entice the earl into my bed."

"He's been known to turn a few girls' heads."

"As if I would be tempted by a boy like him! Honestly, Phillip. Get a grip on yourself."

"I have a bad feeling about all this. What with the potions we gave them and the secret romances that are festering, I'm worried that we've stirred a hornet's nest."

"Really? So am I."

They stared, identical dark eyes brimming with concern. They would never discount such a mutual insight. Their acuity was usually spot-on, and their ability to judge people and situations had frequently saved them from disaster.

"I'd better hurry over there," Clarinda said.

"Don't you dare come back with any grand ideas."

"I wouldn't dream of it."

She strolled off, feeling liberated and carefree.

It was a beautiful autumn day, the sky blue and the temperature warm but with a hint of crispness in the air. The leaves were beginning to change, and as she entered the park that led up to the mansion, the trees were a dazzling canopy of red and gold.

She was nearly skipping, delighted to be wearing a pretty dress, to be making a social call, and she was so swept up in being glad that she almost didn't notice Miss Hamilton, who was walking directly toward her. Peering at the ground, she trudged along, looking as if she'd been tortured on the rack. Her morose condition provided ample evidence that the catastrophe Clarinda envisioned had already occurred.

Clarinda stopped and waited until the other woman was several yards away, then she hailed, "Miss Hamilton?"

Hamilton glanced up and frowned, having been so lost in dismal rumination that she didn't appear to recognize Clarinda.

"Miss Dubois? Or is it Dudley? Someone told me you're not French."

"I'm very English, and yes, it's Dudley."

"So your brother is a charlatan?"

"The very worst kind, but he means well."

The remark was a paltry attempt at a joke, intended to lighten the mood, but it failed. Not so much as a flicker of a smile crossed Hamilton's face.

"I was coming to see you," Clarinda said.

"Me? Why?"

In for a penny, in for a pound. "I thought you might need a friend."

"It's been a long time since I've had one of those," Miss Hamilton admitted.

"I realize this will sound terribly forward of me, but what's happened? I can see that it's taken a toll on you."

Clarinda went over and took her hand, and Hamilton collapsed slightly, her knees unable to support her weight. She felt insubstantial, as if her body had no mass.

Frantically, Clarinda gazed around, searching for somewhere to sit. On a nearby path, she espied a garden bench in a shelter of trees. She guided Miss Hamilton to it and eased her down. Hamilton followed without a murmur of complaint, being visibly overwrought and relieved to have Clarinda in charge.

"What is it?" Clarinda pressed. "You can tell me."

"It's the very worst thing," Hamilton mumbled. "The very worst . . ."

At any other period in Hamilton's life, Clarinda knew Hamilton wouldn't have breathed a word of shame or disgrace, but she was bewildered and shocked and had no one in whom to confide.

Clarinda had arrived at a propitious moment, content to listen and empathize, to share Hamilton's sense of offense, and there was plenty about which to be outraged.

Tragedy never touched men like Odell or Hastings. They skated through the world, secure in their positions, in their power over others. It was women who paid the price.

"I don't know what to do now," Hamilton said. "I was so sure of him. I was positive he'd take my side."

"You were mad to think so," Clarinda advised. "A man will gravitate to his own kind. He would always have allied himself with the earl, without ever considering what you might need."

"Jane is absolutely inconsolable. She believed the earl loved her, but he up and left without a good-bye. Can you imagine her despair?"

"Yes, I can." At being reminded of how foolish a female could be, Clarinda sighed. "What about your bodily situation, Miss Hamilton?"

"What do you mean?"

"You're worried that your sister might be pregnant, but what if you are, too?"

The notion must not have occurred to her, or perhaps she had been so distressed over Jane that she hadn't fretted over her own predicament.

Clarinda had herbs in the wagon that could bring on a woman's courses to flush out the womb so a babe never became reality. She wondered if she should offer them to Helen and Jane.

Some might argue that it was wrong to use such a remedy, but when Clarinda pondered the fate of an unwed mother, with the Hamiltons destined to survive on whatever dubious charity Odell decided to provide, Clarinda would never judge what was best.

"If I am pregnant," Hamilton seethed, "I'll buy a gun. A very big gun, then I will hunt him down and shoot him dead."

"That's the spirit!" Clarinda said, witnessing the first spark of fury in Hamilton. "But let's not kill him. Let's make him pay through the nose. Let's make Hastings pay, too. The bastards—pardon my language—shouldn't be allowed to get away with such cruel mischief."

"No, they shouldn't."

"There are standards of decency by which men are expected to behave. If they won't marry, as is proper, they can cough up money damages."

"I wouldn't have the faintest idea how to make them. I'm so overwhelmed. I feel as if I've fallen into a dark pit that's filled with poisonous snakes and I can't climb out."

"Have you no relatives who might speak to Odell on your behalf?"

"No."

"When do you leave for London?"

"Tomorrow morning." Hamilton peered down the pretty, leaf-strewn lane, but didn't really see it. "What will happen to us there? If Jane is increasing, we'll probably receive some cash to tide us over till the baby is born, but if she's not, we'll be tossed out on the street in a few weeks."

"I wouldn't put it past them."

"It was so difficult to find a job this last time, and I can't imagine my luck will have improved."

Clarinda tried to picture Hamilton in London, fending for herself. She was smart and educated, but she wasn't competent in any way that mattered. She hadn't a clue how to barter, how to lie or cheat or steal.

"If you're leaving for London in the morning," Clarinda said, "I'm coming with you to be certain you're safe. I won't hear any argument."

Phillip would be angry, but then, Phillip didn't need to

know. Clarinda would write a note and slip away before he even realized she was gone.

"Why would you help me?" Hamilton asked, appearing stunned.

"It just seems as if I should." Clarinda couldn't explain it any better than that. "How are you feeling?"

"You've comforted me enormously. Thank you."

"Then let's get you back to the manor." Clarinda stood and pulled her to her feet. "I want you to buck up. You and your sister aren't the first women to be duped by a handsome scoundrel."

"No, we're not."

"You won't be the last, either. Go into the house with your head high and your temper blazing. Show that witch, Maud Seymour, why she should be wary of crossing you."

"I will." Hamilton was growing more confident by the second.

"I'll see you in the morning. I'll be in the village, at the blacksmith's barn. Tell your driver to stop for me."

"COME in, Miss Hamilton."

Helen entered the library, where a few hours earlier she'd permitted Captain Odell to insult and shame her. She glared at Maud Seymour, refusing to be cowed, refusing to have her perceive any upset.

Seymour was seated behind the massive desk, in the chair Odell had used, and Helen sat across from her.

She wasn't sure why she'd obeyed Seymour's summons. In light of all that had transpired, there weren't any consequences that might arise from being rude to her. What more could Seymour do? Fire Helen—again?

"What now?" Helen snapped, not displaying a shred of courtesy.

"Let's get something straight."

"Fine. What is it?"

"I assume you wish to follow the path Captain Odell laid out, where you'd continue to wallow in our charity by loitering in the earl's town house until the captain's clerk arranges your lodging and allowance."

"Yes, that's exactly what I intend. You despicable people owe it to me."

"Well, I'm not about to proceed with the captain's plan, so let me explain what we'll do instead."

"I can't wait to hear."

"I will travel to London before you. I insist on being present when you arrive so I can guarantee you don't take any valuables."

"You presume I would . . . *steal* from Lord Hastings?"

"Why would I trust a servant who has been terminated?"

"Of all the cheeky, impudent, outrageous—"

Helen had started to rise from her chair, and Seymour calmly said, "Sit down, Miss Hamilton, so that I may apprise you of the rest of it."

"I never liked you," Helen fumed, standing. "Since the day I was hired, you've been awful to me. You're vicious, and you're cruel, and I won't tolerate any more of your hate-filled diatribes."

"Your sexual affair with Captain Odell has been exposed."

The comment was so casually voiced, and so unexpected, that Helen blanched and sank into the chair before she could hide her reaction.

"I have no idea what you're talking about," she tried to claim.

"Don't you?"

"You accuse me of being a thief. You accuse me of being a harlot. What next? Armed robbery? Premeditated murder?"

"So you deny the relationship?"

"Yes, I do."

As if Helen hadn't rebuffed the charge, Seymour kept on, apparently possessed of many secrets to which Helen wasn't privy.

"You need to learn a few details about your precious captain."

"I won't listen to any gossip, and you have an incredible amount of gall to denigrate him when he's not here to defend himself."

"I'm not disparaging him. He personally provided this information to me when he first came to stay. There wasn't much I could do about it, so I felt forced to agree."

Seymour rang a bell, and a rear door opened. The maid Lydia entered.

"You've met Lydia, haven't you?" Seymour inquired. "She tended your rooms."

"Yes, I know Lydia."

Seymour gestured to the sullen, buxom girl, and as she approached the desk, Helen's panic flared.

Lydia was attired in a new dress, one that had to have cost much more than a servant could ever afford. Her hair was styled in a flattering fashion, and she'd applied a rosy cosmetic to her cheeks and lips.

In the fetching gown, and with her face and hair arranged, she was downright pretty.

Why had she been summoned? Had she been spying for Seymour? If so, what might she have discovered?

"I doubt you'll believe me," Seymour contended, "but I'm telling you this for your own good."

"Oh, I'm sure you are. You've been a veritable saint in worrying about me."

"The captain is a handsome, virile rascal who could charm any female. I don't blame you for becoming involved with him."

"We were not involved!" Helen insisted.

"At the moment, you're angry with him, but eventually, he'll return from Scotland, and when he does, he'll try to seduce you again. He'll ply you with money and other support, and ultimately, you'll succumb. He's very adept that way, so he's hard to resist."

"You have a point to make. Please get to it."

"You must understand why you should go away and never see him again. I realize this will hurt you, but I don't know how to reveal it without being bluntly clear."

"What is it?" Helen sneered, exasperated beyond her limit.

Seymour gestured to Lydia again. "How are you acquainted with Captain Odell?"

Lydia stared at the floor. "I have two children by him."

Helen gasped.

"What are their names?" Seymour asked.

"Tim and Ruth."

"And what was the news you just shared with me?"

"I . . . I . . . may have a third on the way."

"When were you last intimate with Captain Odell?"

"Yesterday, ma'am," Lydia whispered so softly that Helen had to lean forward to catch the words.

The room was so quiet that Helen could have heard a pin drop. Time seemed to have halted. The earth had stopped spinning on its axis.

Could Tristan Odell have acted so brazenly? Could he have dallied with Helen and another servant under the very same roof? Was it possible?

What did she really know about him? On the night he'd hired her, she'd been in a brothel, but he'd been in a brothel, too, and she always managed to forget that fact.

He had a lusty sexual appetite—as his conduct toward Helen had shown. Why assume she was the only woman to tickle his fancy?

Still, he was an honorable man, driven by duty and responsibility. Despite how enraged Helen was over Jane, he would have viewed himself as doing what he had to for Lord Hastings.

Could that sort of man—one who was loyal and devoted—change his stripes so rapidly? It seemed unlikely.

"She's lying," Helen scoffed.

"Is she?" Seymour glared at Lydia. "Lydia, how was it that you initially came to be seduced by Captain Odell?"

"I was . . . was . . ."

She couldn't say it, and Seymour snapped, "Spit it out, you wretched girl. I haven't got all day!"

"I was governess to his nephew. At his house in Edinburgh."

"Your dress is lovely. Where did you get it?"

"The captain bought it for me." Lydia was still staring at the floor. "He favors seeing me in blue."

"You're wearing a locket. From him, I suppose?"

"To remember him by—while he's away."

She pulled it from the bodice of her gown, where it had been dangling between her breasts on a gold chain. For the briefest instant, she peeked up, her eyes locking with Helen's, and Helen saw what had to be jealousy and malice.

Lydia looked as if she hated Helen, as if she'd like to do her harm.

Was she fond of Odell? Could her story be true?

"That will be all," Seymour said.

Lydia scowled but didn't leave, appearing as if she was anxious to spew a few more horrid comments, and Seymour barked, "Lydia! You're excused."

Lydia nodded, then left without uttering whatever it was she was hoping to impart.

Helen was stunned speechless, and she yearned to pack her bags and flee immediately, but she couldn't go till morning, when the carriage was ready.

"He brought her with him," Seymour said, "when he came to take control of Rose and Michael. He advised me that she would live with us, as a kind of private consort"—she snorted at this—"but I had no idea how to explain such a tawdry situation. I insisted she at least make a pretense of being a housemaid, and ultimately, he agreed."

"Is that why she's so sullen in her duties?"

"Yes. She deems them beneath her, and why shouldn't she? She's enjoyed his attention for years, and you—better than anyone—understand how elevating it can be to a woman's life."

"I certainly do."

Helen glanced down at her hands, trying to work it out, trying to decide what to believe. How could she discount what she'd just witnessed? How could she refuse to see what was right before her very eyes?

If Lydia was practically Odell's common law wife, what had Helen been?

Was she merely another naïve, lonely governess who'd crossed his path? Had he viewed her as an easy mark?

It was all too much to absorb, and she rubbed her temples, wishing she could massage away the terrible questions that were roiling inside her head.

"He's not who he seems to be, Miss Hamilton."

"Perhaps not," Helen equivocated.

"You imagine I'm fabricating all this?"

"Maybe."

"You stupid fool," Seymour seethed. "Guess where he plans to stop before he proceeds on to Scotland? He has a mistress in London. He has one in Scotland, too. He keeps them both, so he can be entertained no matter where he is."

"And Lydia? He keeps her, too? Is that what you're saying?"

"Yes, that's precisely what I'm saying."

"How is it that you know all this? Why would you have been apprised?"

"When he showed up on our stoop, you think I wasn't wary? Michael's father had turned over vast properties and hundreds of thousands of pounds to a virtual stranger, so I hired a Bow Street runner to investigate him." She opened a desk drawer and withdrew a file. "Would you like to read the report?"

The file lay there between them, like a talisman daring Helen to pick it up. She couldn't. What if she perused it and all of Seymour's accusations were proved true?

Helen wouldn't be able to bear it.

"I can't look," she murmured.

At Helen's cowardice, Seymour smirked.

"There's one more thing you should also know."

"What?"

"Before Michael left, he proposed to Miriam. She accepted."

"No, no . . ."

"We've decided on a winter wedding, around Yuletide."

"You'll never persuade me that Lord Hastings agreed."

"It wasn't up to him. With your sister's unfortunate disgrace, Captain Odell felt that marriage would rein in Michael's wilder tendencies. We're simply moving forward with what was arranged years ago."

"You're lying. You have to be!"

"Am I? Find her. She's wearing his mother's engagement ring. She'd be delighted to give you a word-by-word description of her discussion with him."

Helen was reeling.

Jane was convinced that Hastings would make everything right in the end. She'd been so confident that Helen had allowed her own spark of hope to ignite. She'd told herself that scandal could still be avoided, that the earl might urge the captain to relent.

Helen had actually invented a scenario where Odell came to her and profusely apologized, where he begged her forgiveness, and they went on as before. Only better. Only happier. Out in the open, with a future ahead of them. But—apparently—she was simply the governess he'd seduced between mistresses.

Had any woman in all of history ever been so badly used? Had any woman ever been so stupidly trusting? So blind?

What was she to do now?

The walls were closing in, and she couldn't catch her breath. If she swooned, who could blame her? Her poor heart was beating so hard that she wouldn't have been surprised if it had burst out of her chest.

Dizzy with dismay, she staggered to her feet, needing the strength of both arms to push herself up, and she stumbled toward the door.

"You can't stay on the fringe of our lives, Miss Hamilton," Seymour needled from behind her. "We don't want you there."

"Be silent! I've heard enough!"

"You'll go to our London house tomorrow to retrieve your belongings, then I never want to see any of you ever again. Do I make myself clear?"

"Yes, very clear."

Helen felt as if she was swimming through water, as if the door was at the end of a narrow tunnel and, with each step she took, it moved farther away. Finally, she reached it, and she lurched out into the hall. She sagged against the wall, tears dripping down her cheeks.

She'd just tried to keep her sisters safe. By allying herself with Odell, she'd thought she'd succeeded. How could she have been so mistaken?

Everything was ruined. Everything! And it was all her fault.

Her bedchamber was the only place where she could hide from the contemptible people who inhabited the manor. She gazed about, as if lost and trying to get her bearings.

With a huge effort, she straightened and ran for the stairs.

MAUD listened to Helen Hamilton's unsteady strides as she hurried off.

She grinned.

Maud had merely pretended to support Odell in his ridiculous plan to rent a house for Jane Hamilton, but she had no intention of acquiescing to such preposterous behavior.

She would not have Jane flitting about on the edge of Michael's life. Nor would she accept Odell's infatuation with Helen. Maud wanted Odell for herself, so she couldn't risk that Hamilton might dawdle and rekindle his interest.

She had one more surprise in store for Hamilton, but it would happen in London, which was the reason Maud had offered Hamilton a coach ride to the city.

In their rural community, neighbors were nosy and observant. Events were noticed and remarked upon. But in the teeming metropolis, any tragedy could transpire. A woman could disappear and never be found. Even a thrifty fellow such as Captain Odell couldn't locate a female who vanished without a trace.

Behind her, Lydia entered and walked over.

"How did I do, ma'am?"

"I swear, Lydia, you might have had a career on the stage."

"We tricked her?"

"You were marvelous. She was completely fooled."

Lydia chuckled. "Do you have my money?"

"Oh yes, and I consider it well earned."

"Thank you."

Maud drew out her strongbox and handed over the cash. It was an enormous amount, but when Lydia had suggested the ruse, Maud had been happy to pay the price she'd demanded.

"You're accumulating a small fortune," Maud mentioned.

"A girl can't ever have enough."

"Too true. What will you do with it?"

"I haven't decided, but it will be something grand."

Not if I have anything to say about it, Maud mused.

Lydia had great skills, and initially, she'd been an asset, but at her involvement in duping Hamilton, she'd become a liability—one that Maud couldn't afford. Lydia knew too much, so she'd have to go, as Hamilton had to go. Maud would simply have to find the best method of parting with her.

Lydia wouldn't be deceived as easily as Hamilton had been. Maud would have to be careful and bide her time, but Lydia's employment with the Seymour family was over.

"Are you still leaving for London tomorrow?" Lydia asked.

"At first light."

"I'm traveling with you, aren't I? I'm riding in your carriage as your personal maid."

"I promised, didn't I?"

"You surely did, ma'am." Lydia curtsied. "I'll see you in the morning."

"I'm looking forward to it."

Lydia slinked out and Maud went to the sideboard and poured herself a brandy. She sipped it, congratulating herself on a fine day's work.

MIRIAM sat at the dining table. She'd been waiting for hours for Jane Hamilton to come down, but Jane had been sequestered in her room. Sooner or later, she would have to eat, and hunger would drive her to the dining room.

Miriam was perched in a perfect position, her chin balanced on her hand to emphasize the fabulous emerald ring on her finger. Her mother had retrieved it from the safe, and when Maud had explained her scheme, Miriam had eagerly joined in.

She wasn't exactly certain what Jane Hamilton had done to Michael, but Michael had been sent away because of it, so Jane Hamilton would pay and pay dearly.

Footsteps sounded in the hall, and Jane finally wobbled in. She was pale and drawn, and it was obvious she'd been crying.

Ha! She wasn't so pretty now.

"Hello, Miss Hamilton." Miriam grinned maliciously.

"Hello."

Jane was very quiet, the merriment gone from her usually vibrant green eyes. She plodded to the buffet and filled a plate with food. Then she sat and picked at it.

Though she was trying to ignore Miriam, she kept

peeking over. Miriam was waving her fingers, blowing on the emerald and burnishing it on the fabric of her gown.

When Hamilton didn't comment, Miriam extended her hand, pushing the large gemstone under Hamilton's nose.

"Isn't it lovely?" Miriam gushed.

"Yes, lovely," Jane muttered.

"I told Michael I didn't need anything so extravagant— I would have been happy with a simple gold band—but he insisted on his mother's ring. He said it was tradition."

Hamilton froze. "What was . . . tradition?"

"The earls of Hastings always use the same ring when they become engaged. They've used it for centuries."

"Are you saying . . . that you're betrothed to Lord Hastings?"

"He proposed this morning before he departed. Since you've been in your bedchamber, I suppose you wouldn't have heard the news."

"No, no." Hamilton started to tremble, and as she came to her feet, she was shaking her head and babbling to herself.

The false revelation had rattled her till she appeared quite mad, and after spending such a wretched summer watching Jane flirt with Michael, Miriam was thrilled to see her reduced condition.

Miriam twisted the knife, amazed that she had such a knack for duplicity and cruelty.

"Mother asked me to be courteous and invite you to the wedding, but I'm not going to. I don't like you, and I don't want you to attend."

Hamilton staggered as if Miriam had struck her, then suddenly, she began to scream and scream and scream.

Calmly, Miriam rose and strolled out, and as she reached the stairs and climbed, she realized that Hamilton's shrieks were wafting throughout the mansion.

As she passed her mother's room, Maud peered out the door.

"What is that infernal racket?" Maud inquired.

"It's just Jane Hamilton, learning her lesson." Miriam pulled off the ring and gave it to her mother. "You can put this back in the safe. It's served its purpose, and I won't be needing it for a while."

Chapter 20

❦

"Why can't I talk to Rose?"

"Because Mrs. Seymour won't let you."

"I won't leave unless I can say good-bye to her."

Amelia sat on the bottom stair and wrapped her arms around the newel post as if she was a prisoner in chains. It would require an enormous amount of coaxing to pry her away, and from her mutinous attitude, any attempt would involve clawing and shouting.

Clarinda glanced over at Helen, who was too dazed to notice the drama occurring with her little sister on the other side of the foyer.

After a horrendous two-day coach ride to town, Helen was completely bedraggled. She looked like a war refu-gee, Odell's betrayals a yoke too heavy to bear, and Clarinda was glad she'd insisted on coming along.

Evening was approaching, the waning hours making decisions imperative, but Helen was unable to make them, and Clarinda wasn't sure what Helen wanted to do.

Maud and Miriam Seymour, together with a recalci-trant, livid Lady Rose, had traveled in a lighter, faster carriage, so Maud had been waiting for them. She'd had their bags packed and stacked by the door, planning that the Hamiltons take them and depart, the question being where they were supposed to go.

The last of Helen's trunks were being loaded into a rented hackney out in the drive. They contained all her worldly possessions, the final few items she'd managed to salvage after her father's death.

What must it be like to be Helen? To have been raised in a grand house in the country, to have been a member of the neighborhood gentry, but to have lost it all?

Hers was a brutal society. No one had come forward to help. Not even her blood relatives. Only Captain Odell had expended any effort, and his assistance had been a disaster.

Clarinda sat, too, and gazed at Amelia.

"Do you recall what I told you, Amelia?"

"Yes. Mrs. Seymour is angry at Helen and Jane, but I don't see why that means I can't say good-bye to Rose. How can that hurt anybody?"

"Mrs. Seymour is a witch."

"Yes, she is," Amelia fumed.

"And since she's a witch, we should make her resemble one."

"How?"

"We'll slip her a potion so that warts grow on her nose."

Amelia's eyes widened with wicked fury. "Have you such a thing?"

"Not with me. I left my supplies in my brother's wagon, but I promise I'll get even with her someday."

"I want to accompany you when you trick her into drinking it. I want to watch her suffer."

Footsteps sounded above them, and Clarinda stood to move out of the way. Grudgingly, Amelia stood, too.

They peered up to see Mrs. Seymour descending. She was very smug, exhibiting not a hint of embarrassment that she was tossing three destitute females out on the street, one of them being only twelve years old.

Seymour walked over to Helen and extended a small leather pouch.

"What's in it?" Jane snidely asked. "Poison? Should we swallow it before or after we leave?"

"If I deemed you worthy of a reply," Seymour retorted, "I would speak to you. As it is, this is my home, and you're a disgraced harlot. I don't have to listen to you, so shut your mouth."

"I hate you," Jane seethed, "and the best part of this eviction is that I never have to see you ever again. Please tell your daughter that I think she's fat, stupid, and ugly."

"How dare you!"

Jane stormed out onto the stoop as Seymour shrieked, "Get back here, you pathetic ingrate!"

Jane had no intention of obeying, and Helen distracted Seymour by saying, "I assume you came down for a reason. What is it?"

"I'm paying you your wages. I won't have you running about town claiming you were cheated."

Clarinda breathed a sigh of relief. She had brought a full purse of her own, so they'd hardly starve, but until Helen could land on her feet, every penny was vital.

Without comment, Helen snatched the pouch away and stuffed it in her reticule. She didn't count the coins, but it would have been pointless to quibble. If Seymour hadn't provided the amount owed, who could force her to cough it up?

"I'll give your regrets to Captain Odell," Seymour taunted. "I'll inform him that you were weary of living off his charity, so you made other arrangements."

"You do that." Helen turned to Amelia. "Come, Amelia, let's go."

Amelia ignored Helen and marched over to Seymour.

"I want to talk to Rose," Amelia boldly declared.

"That won't be possible," Seymour tightly responded.

"You're the cruelest person I've ever met," Amelia charged. "I'm going to find Captain Odell and tell him how you treated us."

"He already knows," Seymour fibbed. "Weren't you aware? This was his decision. He was tired of supporting you."

"You are such a liar!" Amelia spun and stomped out.

In light of Amelia's youth and friendship with Rose, Seymour's remark was particularly vicious. What was the woman's problem? Her behavior enraged Clarinda as nothing had in ages.

Helen followed Amelia out, but Clarinda dawdled until she and Seymour were alone.

"Who are you," Seymour snapped, "and why are you in my home?"

In reply, Clarinda mumbled a mouthful of gibberish, a nonsensical mixture of Latin and French that seemed important and grave and scary.

"What are you saying?" Seymour scowled, looking a tad unsettled. "Speak English—if you know any of the language."

Clarinda held out her index and pinkie fingers, a pair of horns, indicating the sign of the devil. Seymour recognized it and stumbled back.

"I am a white witch," Clarinda boasted.

"There's no such thing," Seymour countered, but her alarm was obvious.

"Isn't there?"

"No."

"Occasionally, I dabble in the black arts." Clarinda uttered more rubbish, then clapped her hands three times, the sound echoing off the high ceiling, giving it an extremely portentous flair.

Seymour jumped. "Stop that!"

"It's too late," Clarinda hissed.

"Too late for what?"

"Too late for you."

"What are you blathering about?"

"I've cursed you. It's already taking effect."

"Are you insane? You can't just come into a woman's residence and . . . and . . . curse her."

"I can, and I have. Beware."

"Beware! Of what?"

"There's been wicked business carried out this day."

"The only *wicked business* is my listening to you. Get out!"

She hurried over and flung the door wide, pointing to the street.

Clarinda studied her, then she approached until they were toe-to-toe. Seymour was trying to stand firm and not retreat, but she was superstitious, and thus, very afraid.

"Whatever plans you have for yourself," Clarinda warned, "or for your daughter, they will never come to fruition."

"Be silent."

"Your fate has been altered. I can't stop it now; it's out of my hands."

Seymour pushed her outside and slammed the door, the key spinning in the lock. Clarinda chuckled and went to join Helen.

"What did you say to her?" Helen asked.

"I put a curse on her."

"You didn't!"

"I did."

Clarinda hadn't actually done anything, but Seymour thought she had, and that's what mattered. In the future, whenever Seymour suffered the slightest mishap, she'd remember Clarinda and wonder if the curse was working. The more she fretted, the more her troubles would increase.

"Thank you," Helen said.

"You're welcome. I'll avenge you in other ways, too. I just need some time to ponder my retribution."

From above them, a window was thrown open, and Rose called, "Amelia, up here! It's me!"

They all glanced at her, and Amelia waved and jumped up and down.

"I asked to say good-bye," Amelia told her, "but Mrs. Seymour wouldn't let me."

"She wouldn't let me, either. When I tried to come downstairs, she locked me in my room!"

"She didn't!"

"Just wait till my brother gets back and discovers what she—"

She was grabbed from behind and yanked inside, the window banged shut, and she appeared to be wrestling with someone, but they were powerless to intervene. None of them was related to Lady Rose, and they had no authority to defy Seymour. Clarinda hoped that Odell wasn't in Scotland too awfully long, that Rose wouldn't be imprisoned for months.

"Can't we help her, Helen?" Amelia pleaded. "There must be something we can do."

"There's nothing, Amelia. It's not our business anymore. Let's go."

Helen herded them into the rented hackney, with Amelia balking and Helen having to lift her in. As they settled on the hard seat, they were a sullen, depressed group.

"At least we have some money," Clarinda mentioned.

"It's more than I had when I arrived," Helen responded.

The driver stuck his head in. "Where to, ladies?"

Helen was at a loss, and Clarinda offered, "I know of a lodging house, out on the edge of the city. It's clean and affordable."

"Fine," Helen murmured.

Clarinda gave him the directions, and he climbed onto the box and clicked the reins. They started off, and as they rattled away, Jane was the only one who gazed out at the mansion.

"I can't believe it's ending this way," she said. "I can't believe he did this to me."

"Let it be a lesson to you," Clarinda counseled. "You should be wary of men and their promises."

"I thought he was different," Jane insisted.

"He wasn't."

Helen snorted but didn't remark.

They rode along, miserable and brooding, when suddenly, the carriage slowed and was eased off to the side of the street.

"What is it?" Helen asked.

Amelia peeked out. "Some men are talking to the driver."

The door was yanked open, and a burly fellow loomed in. He was blond and tough-looking, dressed in a gentleman's coat and trousers, but he exuded menace. He might have been a pugilist or a criminal.

"Are you Helen Hamilton?" he inquired.

"Yes."

"You're Jane Hamilton?"

"Yes."

The two sisters frowned with concern.

"Would you step out, please?"

"Why?" Helen demanded. "What's wrong?"

"Get out, ma'am."

"Who are you," Clarinda asked, "and what do you want with us?"

"I am Mr. Mick Rafferty. Who are you?"

"I am a friend of the family."

"And *I* am not. I must speak with the Misses Hamilton on a rather delicate matter. If you'll humor me for a moment . . . ?"

He gestured for them to debark, his demeanor indicating that refusal was not an option. If they didn't comply of their own volition, would he drag them out?

Helen scowled at Clarinda, then shrugged.

She went first, Mr. Rafferty assisting her as if he was a gallant. Jane and Amelia came next, with Clarinda bringing up the rear.

"Miss Hamilton," he said to Helen, "were you previously employed by Michael Seymour, Lord Hastings?"

"I was."

"Is it true you recently left under less than *satisfactory* circumstances?"

"You could say so."

From behind the hackney, a man called, "I've got it. It's here."

Clarinda shifted over to see that another ruffian had been searching Helen's trunks. Clothes and shoes were scattered on the cobbles. A crowd had gathered to watch, and people parted as the oaf pushed toward Rafferty.

He brandished a gold ring with a large emerald in the center, waving it like a prize.

"Look at this beauty!" he exclaimed as he placed it in Rafferty's palm.

"Would you like to explain this?" Rafferty asked Helen.

"I can't."

"Is it your contention that you have no idea whose it is?"

"Yes, that's exactly my contention."

"And I suppose you haven't a clue why it's in your luggage."

"No!"

"A likely story," a bystander muttered.

Jane neared to get a better view. "It's the betrothal ring Lord Hastings gave to Miriam."

"So you admit it!" Rafferty crowed.

"It certainly seems to be the same one," Jane affirmed.

"May I see your purse, Miss Hamilton?" he said to Helen.

"No, you may not."

Rafferty's accomplice, the swine who'd riffled through their trunks, stepped in so that Helen was trapped between the two men. Rafferty plucked the purse from her grasp, and though she lunged to retrieve it, his partner clutched her arms and restrained her.

Rafferty opened her bag and removed the pouch that Maud Seymour had given to Helen—almost as if he knew it would be there. He loosened the string and dumped out the contents. A pile of shiny gold coins clinked out.

The spectators gasped.

"Miss Helen Hamilton," Rafferty announced with great

formality, "and Miss Jane Hamilton, I arrest you for committing grand theft against Lord Hastings."

"You're mad!" Helen fumed. "Mrs. Seymour paid me that money herself!"

"I'll just bet she did," Rafferty sneered.

"She did!" Helen insisted, but denial was pointless.

"I'm afraid you're going to have to come with me."

"I won't!"

Helen tried to walk away, but she was immediately seized. Jane tried to flee, too, but she met the same fate.

Clarinda had observed the encounter with a horrid fascination, and as she saw where the cards were falling, she let herself be swallowed by the mob of passersby. She had a tight grip on Amelia, and she pulled her away. Amelia frowned at Clarinda, but Clarinda motioned for silence.

Helen's and Jane's hands were being bound with ropes, the onlookers mesmerized by the spectacle, as Rafferty said, "Where's the little one?"

"She was here a minute ago," his companion answered.

"We've got to locate her. We were supposed to nab all three."

At hearing the threat, Amelia and Clarinda ran. There were too many people blocking Rafferty's path, so he couldn't chase after them. Plus, he didn't dare abandon Helen and Jane, for they would be unguarded if he and his minion raced off.

Clarinda and Amelia wound through the streets, and once Clarinda deemed it safe to stop, they huddled together in an alley.

"Who was that man?" Amelia queried.

"He's a criminal," Clarinda replied. "Now, listen to me. I need you to be very brave. Can you be?"

"Yes, I'm very brave."

Clarinda drew out some cash and gave it to her.

"What's this for?" Amelia inquired.

"I may be gone for a day or two."

"Gone!"

"Use it to eat."

"All right," she hesitantly agreed.

"Can you find your way back to the earl's house?"

"I think so."

"Wait till dark, then sneak in, so you can tell Rose what happened."

"What *did* happen?"

"Mrs. Seymour is pretending Helen and Jane stole that ring."

"The money, too?"

"Yes."

"Ooh, that lying witch!"

"Your sisters are in terrible trouble. We have to help them."

"I will do anything!" Amelia vowed.

"Rose must inform Captain Odell about Mrs. Seymour—the instant he returns from Scotland."

"It might be ages!"

"I know, but at the moment I can't figure out what else to do. After you speak with her, you must hide yourself somewhere nearby."

"For how long?"

"Until I come for you."

"Where will you be?"

"I'm going to follow Mr. Rafferty. We have to learn where he's taking them. The second I find out, I'll be back."

Amelia gazed at her. "I'm scared."

"No, you're not. You can't be. There's no time. Helen and Jane are counting on you."

Clarinda shoved her toward the street, but Amelia wouldn't budge.

"Are you sure this is the only way?"

"Yes, I'm sure."

"But . . . but . . ."

"Amelia, please. I have to get back to Rafferty before he leaves. If he's already gone, we might never locate them."

The prospect galvanized Amelia, and she nodded.

"Swear that you'll come for me," she begged.

"I swear."

"I don't know how to live on my own. I don't know how to take care of myself."

"You won't have to. I'll be there in a few hours."

Amelia chewed on her bottom lip, about to burst into tears, but she took a deep breath, and she straightened.

"I'm Harry Hamilton's daughter," she firmly said, brimming with ire, "and I've had about all of this I can stand."

"That's the spirit."

"I'll see you very soon."

"Yes, you will. I promise."

Amelia reached out and squeezed Clarinda's hands, as if sealing the pledge. Then she raced off in one direction, and Clarinda raced off in the other.

"WHAT is this one called?"

"Passion's Flower."

"What does it do?"

"It brings on amour—when the gentleman in question is disinterested."

Phillip smiled at his female customer. With her big blue eyes and delectable curves, she was lovely. Usually, he enjoyed chatting with a pretty girl, but he was worried about Clarinda.

When he'd awakened, she'd been gone, and he'd told himself that she was at Hastings Manor, delivering tonics, but she hadn't returned.

Where was the blasted woman?

"Mr. Dubois?"

From what seemed a long distance, he realized that his customer was talking.

"What did you ask me, Mademoiselle Lambert?"

"What is this?"

"It is my famous elixir, Woman's Daily Remedy. It calms body and soul, being especially beneficial when you are distressed."

She pulled the cork and sniffed the contents.

"May I have a little taste?"

"Certainement."

She took a sip, but as the intoxicating brew slid down her throat, she coughed and coughed.

"Oh my," she sputtered. "It's quite potent."

"It definitely is."

"With where I'm going, though, it might be just what I need."

"Are you off on a journey, *cherie*?"

"To Scotland—as companion to the two most horrid twins you've ever met." She paused, chagrined. "I can't believe I said that. You won't tell anyone, will you?"

"I am the very model of discretion."

"Good, because my employer is a beast. If he learned that I was complaining, I'd be fired before I ever started working."

"No one will hear a word from me, mademoiselle."

She pointed to the label on the bottle, which included a picture of a lily. "I think it's my destiny to purchase this."

"Why?"

"My Christian name is Lily. Lily Lambert."

"Then by all means, you must have it."

Pert dimples creased her cheeks. "Yes, I must."

She gave him her money, and he gave her the remedy.

"Would you like to take two?" he suggested. "If the trip turns out to be as bad as you imagine, you might go through the first one rather fast."

"I might indeed. I'd better have another."

She put both bottles into her bag, then examined more of his merchandise. A curious sort, she liked to smell and touch and feel, and she actually had cash to spend. At any other time, he would have been ecstatic, but where the hell was Clarinda?

"Mr. Dubois! I swear you're woolgathering."

"Pardon, cherie. You are correct. I am concerned about my sister. She's off on an errand, and she is late in coming home."

"Your anxiety is understandable." She held up a vial. "What's this?"

"Ah . . ."—he had to force himself to focus—"it is my biggest seller, my Spinster's Cure."

"It *cures* spinsters? Of what?"

"If you swallow it while staring at the man you hope to marry, you will be wed within the month."

She chuckled. "You're joking."

"Je suis serieux!"

"You seem like such a sane fellow. Surely you're not claiming it has magical powers?"

He raised a finger in the air, trying to look stern and wise. "You have heard of the great lord Viscount Redvers. *Non?*"

"No."

"His bride, Mary, was a spinster, but she drank the tonic as I instructed, and *voila,* she is now Viscountess Redvers and happily wed to the infamous nobleman."

"Well, then, if it worked for her, who am I to quibble? I should have my own supply."

She was smart and pragmatic, so she found him to be hilarious, deeming his assertions to be nonsense, but he didn't particularly care if she believed or not.

Still, he said, "You laugh at me."

"I laugh *with* you. I'm having fun."

"You suppose my medicine is *faux*—false—but you will see."

"I'm certain I will."

"My Spinster's Cure will aid you in fulfilling your wish to be married. You crave a husband, yes?"

"Of course. How did you know?"

"It is my job to know. You would like to have a home of your own, a cozy cottage in the country, with dogs and cats and three"—he halted and studied her—"no, *four* children."

"You are absolutely amazing."

"Aren't I, though?"

"I'll take two vials."

"A prudent choice. A double dose can never hurt."

He knelt under the shelf to retrieve a second vial when, to his surprise, he discovered a folded piece of paper stuffed between the jars. His name was on it, Clarinda's handwriting clearly visible.

"What the devil?" he muttered.

He grabbed it and stood, banging his head as he rose.

"Ouch," Miss Lambert commiserated, but he ignored her.

He ripped open the note, and as he read it, his temper flared.

"Oh, for pity's sake." He crumpled it into a ball and tossed it on the ground. "She is out of her bloody mind."

"Who? Your sister?"

"Yes."

"What's she done?"

"She's on her way to London"—he was so furious that his French accent was forgotten—"chasing after those accursed Hamilton sisters."

"Honestly!" Miss Lambert said, as if they'd been discussing the Hamiltons all along. "What was she thinking?"

"I don't know, but when I catch up with her, she'll be sorry."

"You won't resort to violence, will you, Mr. Dubois? Not against your sister!"

"Not against her, but if I run into that arrogant Captain Odell, I will beat him to a pulp."

"I'm sure he deserves it."

"Trust me: He does. This is all his fault, hiring that Hamilton woman, then Hamilton putting ideas in Clarinda's head. Didn't we follow them here? For no good purpose, at all!"

He stomped off down the lane.

"Mr. Dubois!" Miss Lambert called. "Where are you going?"

"I'm off to the village to rent the fastest horse I can find. I must get to London right away."

"What about your wagon?"

"I can't worry about it at a time like this. Not when Clarinda could be in danger." He gestured to the bottles and jars. "You may have whatever you'd like. Be my guest."

For a moment she was taken aback, then she grinned. "Thank you. I will."

He spun away and hurried on.

Chapter 21

❦

"SIT down and shut up."

"I don't feel like shutting up."

"Well, I'm weary of listening to you, so be silent."

Tristan stared at Michael, and he was an inch away from stuffing a stocking in his mouth to keep him quiet.

He went to the sideboard to pour himself a drink, glad to learn that Lauretta Bainbridge stocked an excellent brandy. They were back at her brothel where it had all started, where—earlier in the summer—he'd stumbled on a desperate Helen Hamilton trying to sell herself.

After so much time had passed, it was either the perfect conclusion or the ideal punishment. Perhaps it was merely a pathetic attempt to convince himself that he hadn't cared about her.

Tristan had meant to sail for Scotland immediately, to whisk Michael out of the country and have him far away from England and the trouble he'd caused, but there had been a delay in loading the cargo.

With Michael moping in Tristan's small cabin, and Tristan fretting over Helen and the choices he'd made,

Tristan had been at his wit's end. A trip to the bawdy house seemed the best way to ease their stress.

Tristan was determined to prove that his sexual affair with Helen had been just that: a sexual affair. He refused to believe that there had been more to it, that he might have . . . *loved* her.

"You can pretend," Michael nagged, "that you've fixed everything by dragging me off, but you haven't."

"For the time being, I've gotten you away from Jane. That's enough for me. We'll work out the rest as we go along."

"You can take me to Scotland. You can leave me there with no money and no acquaintances. You can even lock me in a dungeon under some old castle, but the moment I can arrange it, I'll come back and find her."

A muscle ticked in Tristan's cheek, his temper flaring.

Since they'd left Hastings Manor, Michael had been complaining about Tristan's autocratic nature, about Jane's predicament, about Tristan's decisions.

The entire debacle was a nightmare!

"Why would you come back and find her?" Tristan asked.

"Because I love her."

"You do not."

"I do!"

"You're too young to know if you're in love."

"Don't tell me what I'm feeling. I'm not a child. Stop acting as if I am."

"All right, all right! You're in love. How can it matter? You can't marry her, so it's pointless to wallow in this adolescent infatuation."

Michael whipped around and stomped over until they were toe-to-toe. With each minute the debate continued, it grew more heated, and they were closer to exchanging blows.

Tristan would win any fight, but he didn't want them to brawl.

"It's not an *infatuation*," Michael seethed. "Don't call it that. I won't have you demeaning my connection to her."

"Fine! It's not an infatuation. It's the greatest amour in all of recorded history. So bloody what?"

The boy was eighteen years old. What did he know about anything?

Once he'd copulated with a few eager harlots, Jane would be but a distant memory.

Michael flopped down on the sofa and glared at the door.

"I hate being here," he protested.

"Trust me: There's nothing going on with you that a bit of illicit fornication can't cure. A tumble with a pretty whore always puts things in perspective."

"What would Helen think if she discovered you were already off visiting prostitutes?"

"Leave Miss Hamilton out of this, would you?"

Michael constantly raised Helen as an issue, while Tristan insisted that they'd enjoyed no heightened relationship. Though he felt like a heel for denying his affection, what purpose would be served by announcing her ruination?

Some conduct was meant to be private, and a gentleman's seduction of a lady definitely qualified for discretion. He'd behaved like a despicable cad. What would he be labeled if he talked about it, too?

"I saw you that day on the stairs," Michael scolded. "She's in love with you, and she'll never forgive you for keeping me away from Jane. You realize that, don't you?"

"Give it a rest, Michael. Please!"

Tristan went to the window to gaze out at the night sky, but there wasn't much to see. Lauretta's footman had deposited them in a room that looked out over an alley. The sky wept with rain, and the dreary weather matched his mood.

Surely Helen would forgive him—wouldn't she? After

a few weeks or months had passed, she'd calm. She'd accept that he'd done what was best for Jane and Michael. He'd apologize, and they would start in where they'd left off.

But where, precisely, would that be?

What with the attraction between her sister and his brother, she could never work for Tristan again. Nor could she reside in the Seymour household.

Yet even if Tristan provided a separate lodging for her, where she could live with her sisters, he couldn't pop in for a quick dalliance, and he most certainly could never crawl into her bed.

If he didn't support her financially, she'd have to take a job as a nanny or a governess, and any position would prevent them from resuming their affair. At the slightest whiff of a romance, she'd be terminated, so there was no place for him in her life, and at the notion, he was unaccountably distraught.

Yes, they'd quarreled that last morning at Hastings Manor, but he'd told himself she'd get over it. What if she didn't? Or what if—when he returned from Scotland—she'd vanished and he couldn't locate her?

What then? What then?

The frantic query raced through his head. His pulse hammered in his chest, and he began to perspire.

Not see her again? Was that what he wanted? Dare he risk it?

To hell with Michael! To hell with Scotland!

He had to speak with Helen, had to beg her forgiveness, and if she declined to give it, he'd kidnap her and abscond with her to the South Seas. He'd keep her on a hot, secluded beach, spoiling and making love to her until she relented.

He was about to spin toward Michael, ready to tell him to do whatever he wanted, to marry or not, to have Jane as his mistress or not, to jump off a cliff—or not. Tristan had never sought the burden of caring for Michael anyway, but before he could move, the door opened.

Lauretta waltzed in, followed by the whore Jo who'd serviced Michael the prior time they'd visited.

Their arrival landed on him like an icy pail of water, dampening his spurt of anxiety, his absurd—almost maniacal—need for Helen.

Why was he always so overwhelmed by her?

She made him angry and drove him crazy, and it was impossible to deal with her. She'd presumed on his good nature, had treated him like a milksop, like a belea-guered husband. When he'd refused to come to heel, she'd screamed and accused and blamed, but he didn't regret his actions.

He'd had enough of her nonsense, and he was actually lucky that he'd departed when he had. If he'd stayed on, she might have wound up pregnant. Then he'd have had to marry her. He ought to be celebrating his escape from the marital noose.

He *would* celebrate his escape—with Mrs. Bainbridge and any other female in the house who tickled his fancy.

"Hello, Captain." Lauretta was beaming, glad to have him back.

"Hello, Lauretta."

"Lord Hastings," she said, "I've asked Jo to attend you. You had seemed to enjoy yourself so much the last time that I thought we'd begin with her." When Michael didn't hurry to agree, she hastily added, "I assume that's all right?"

"Yes, it's fine." Michael was coolly detached, exhibit-ing none of the enthusiasm he'd shown when Tristan had first brought him to the brothel.

The two women exchanged a nervous glance. Jo ap-proached and curtsied low, her negligee flopping loose, exposing her to her navel.

"I have a grand evening planned for you, milord."

"Let's get at it." He stood and took her hand. "The sooner we're finished, the sooner I can go."

"Don't mind him," Tristan grumbled. "He's been in a sour mood all day."

"Jo will be just the ticket to cheer him!" Lauretta gushed, smiling.

The young couple walked out, with Michael glowering at Tristan as if he was about to be boiled in oil. The door closed behind them, leaving Tristan alone with Lauretta.

"What about you, Captain?" she inquired. "Can I interest you in any entertainment while you wait for your ward?"

He studied her, admiring her lush auburn hair and curvaceous figure. She was very beautiful, dressed in a flowing red gown, a flimsy robe overtop bared acres of creamy skin.

His lust flared.

Why not? he asked himself.

Before meeting Helen, he'd been celibate for months, then he'd spent the summer in misery, chasing after her and luring her into bed. Their few carnal encounters had been extremely endearing, but also extremely tepid considering his typical salacious fare.

Lauretta could provide hours of naughty amusement, and when they finished, if he hadn't managed to purge himself of his ludicrous longing for Helen, he'd start in with another girl. Then another and another. He'd keep at it until he was too drained to remember Helen's name.

"As a matter of fact," he said, "I would like some company."

Her smile widened, and she neared, her nipples brushing his shirt, her thigh his leg.

His cock sprang to attention.

"Would you like anyone in particular"—her voice was husky and breathless—"or will I do? I don't usually service my customers, but for you, I'd make an exception."

"You'll be perfect."

"I was hoping you'd say so."

She guided him to the boudoir at the end of the hallway. It was an exotic place, designed for seduction. There were crimson drapes and rugs, plush red pillows on the floor, a comfortable divan in front of the hearth. A cozy fire burned in the grate.

A huge bed was positioned in the center, and he escorted her to it. He lay down and pulled her down on top of him, and he tugged on the bodice of her negligee, a plump breast popping into view.

For a brief instant, he thought about kissing her, as he would have with Helen, or perhaps snuggling and talking, which was what he'd relished most about his time with her. He'd found it so easy to talk to her, and he'd always . . .

He wouldn't think about Helen! Not when he was about to fornicate with a whore. Helen shouldn't be crossing his mind at all.

Lauretta Bainbridge was good for one thing and one thing only—rough, raucous sex—and that was the purpose for which he would utilize her.

There'd be no virginal sensibilities to worry about as had been the case with Helen. There'd be no fretting over how he was hurting her. There would be no . . .

Helen! Ah!

She was like a brain disease, a malignant tumor growing bigger and bigger. Despite how he tried, he couldn't stop ruminating over her. She'd ruined so much for him already, and she was *not* going to ruin this!

He yanked at Lauretta's robe, ripping it off her shoulders like a wild man.

Oddly, he was terrified that if he didn't get to it, he might chicken out altogether. Michael's remark—that they shouldn't be doing this—made him feel ridiculously guilty, as if he was . . . cheating on Helen.

"Are you in a hurry, Captain?" Lauretta asked.

"Ah . . . no."

"Then what's the rush? We have all night."

She rolled them so that he was on his back, and she stretched out, her palm on his chest, rubbing in slow circles.

"You're awfully tense," she said. "How about if I relax you?"

"An excellent idea."

She unbuttoned his trousers and slipped her curious fingers inside, and she stroked him, using tantalizing movements that demonstrated her prowess.

But as she began nibbling a trail down his stomach, her destination obvious, a vision of Helen swamped him. He recalled that final evening at Hastings Manor, when they'd been out in the boat on the lake. The stars had been so bright, the air so fresh, and she'd been so pretty.

It was the damnedest thing, but his heart ached at the memory, and to his eternal disgust, his erection waned.

How embarrassing!

Of course, Lauretta—being a skilled courtesan—noticed immediately. She frowned, clearly disconcerted and wondering if she should comment.

A limp rod would reflect badly on her expertise, and his reputation for virility would suffer.

She forced a smile. "Let me try a little trick you might enjoy."

Her tongue flicked out and teased the tip of his cock, and he should have been jolted by sensation, but he wasn't. He sighed and eased her away, and he sat up, his legs dangling over the edge of the mattress.

"I don't really want to do this," he said.

"Don't worry about it. Every fellow has the same problem occasionally. It's much more common than you realize."

His brows shot up. "There's nothing wrong with my phallus."

"Oh! Oh! Absolutely not. I didn't mean to imply . . . that is I . . . uh . . ."

He sighed again. "Michael told me we shouldn't be here, and he was correct. I'd best go fetch him. I doubt Jo is having any more luck with him than you are with me."

He stood, straightening his clothes, and she stood, too. She was wringing her hands with concern.

"You won't mention this to anyone, will you?" she asked. "I can't have rumors circulating that I couldn't . . . you know."

"You're very beautiful and very seductive, Lauretta. My lack of interest has nothing to do with you."

She blew out a relieved breath. "Thank God."

"I'm just distracted. I've had a lot on my mind."

"You certainly have, you poor dear. What with Lord Hastings and Lady Rose and dealing with your father's estate, you've assumed the burdens of ten men."

"And now, I guess I'm getting married as well. If she'll have me, that is."

He'd finally declared his intentions toward Helen, and he'd done it before a notorious madam. He'd shocked himself, but he'd shocked her more.

"Married! Isn't this rather sudden?"

"Yes, very sudden."

"I hadn't heard a word about it, and I'm usually privy to all the gossip."

"I just decided myself."

"It's not Maud Seymour, is it?"

"No, not her. I might be mad as a hatter, but I'm still possessed of a few of my faculties."

"Whew! You've dodged a bullet." Still a tad unsettled by events, she chuckled nervously. "Who is it, then? If I might be so bold as to inquire?"

"Helen Hamilton."

She paused, recollecting. "*That* Helen Hamilton? The woman you bought from me last summer?"

"The very one, and if you ever tell a single soul, I'll have to kill you."

"My lips are sealed."

"They'd better be."

She studied him, then laughed. "Harry Hamilton's daughter! I can't believe it."

"It's insane, I know."

"Not necessarily. Harry was a friend of mine. If she's anything like him, you're in for a grand ride."

"You could be right about that." He went out into the hall. "Where is Michael?"

"Third door down. On your left."

He proceeded to the room she'd indicated, while speculating over what was happening inside and how rude it would be to interrupt.

He pressed his ear to the wood as Michael was saying, "I love her, but he won't listen to me."

"Who does he think he is?" Jo commiserated. "Your bloody da?"

"Yes, that's precisely what he thinks."

"Why not tell him to sod off?"

"I'm about to. I've had enough of his bullying."

Tristan knocked twice, then entered, hoping he wouldn't go blind from witnessing some particularly indecent act. To his surprise, Michael was sitting in a chair, and Jo on the bed. Jo was still wearing her robe and negligee, and Michael was fully dressed, with not so much as his coat having been removed.

"What now?" Michael snapped. "Can't I even copulate without your butting in and ordering me how to accomplish it?"

"Let's get out of here."

Michael cocked his head, confused, as if Tristan's words had been jumbled.

"You want to leave?"

"Yes."

"You're sure?"

"Yes. You were correct: We shouldn't be here."

"Well . . . good."

"I love Helen," Tristan proudly announced.

"It's about time you admitted it," Michael said.

"It certainly is, so we're not sailing to Scotland. Helen and Jane were traveling back to London, and they should be at the town house. Let's go home and see if we can fix this mess."

"Are you telling me I can wed Jane?"

"You can do whatever you want. I don't care."

Michael grinned at Jo. "I retract everything I just said about him."

"You lucky dog." Jo clapped her hands. "Marrying for love! How utterly brilliant."

"Isn't it, though?" Michael agreed. He grabbed Tristan by the arm and dragged him out before Tristan could change his mind.

"I didn't steal that ring!" Jane fumed.

"A likely story," Mr. Rafferty chided.

"And I didn't steal that money," Helen added.

"I've heard it all before, Miss Hamilton," Mr. Rafferty replied. "Didn't you know? Everyone in prison is innocent."

"You're making a huge mistake."

"Notify the warden," Mr. Rafferty retorted.

"When Captain Odell learns how you treated us, you'll be so sorry."

"Which Captain Odell would that be? Would it be the same captain who swore out an oath against you?"

"What?" Helen gasped.

"The complaint came from Odell, himself. I guess he'd been suspicious of you for some time, and in light of what I discovered in your luggage, his fears appear to have been well-founded."

Could Odell have done this to her?

He'd wanted to protect Michael from scandal, but how far would he go to achieve his goal? With Helen and Jane locked away, there would be no chance of an unsuitable marriage or a bastard baby to drain the family coffers.

Was he capable of such duplicity?

If she'd been asked that question the previous week, she'd have bristled at the notion. But now?

Every single thing Helen believed about him had turned out to be a lie.

He seduced his servants. He kept mistresses. He had sired at least two illegitimate children—perhaps more.

Why should she be surprised by another betrayal?

"Don't listen to him, Helen," Jane seethed. "This is Seymour's scheme and hers alone."

"Listen or don't," Rafferty responded. "I have his affidavit right here."

Rafferty waved a sheath of official-looking papers, but he didn't offer to show them to Helen. What good would it have done anyway?

If the documents were forged, she couldn't prove it.

"What will happen to us?" Jane inquired.

"You'll be tried and convicted. Then you'll either be hanged or transported to Australia."

"Hanged!"

"It's the usual sentence for desperate felons."

"You could be wrong," Jane insisted. "We could be proclaimed innocent—since we *are* innocent."

"With me testifying against you?" Rafferty laughed and laughed. "In my entire life, I haven't seen a thief judged not guilty. Is this your first offense?"

"Of course. Why would you even have to ask?"

"If it is, you'll probably be transported, but if you have a habit of committing crimes, your days are numbered. Best make peace with your maker."

Jane was on the verge of charging him, but with their hands still bound behind their backs, she could fall and be injured. Plus, Rafferty seemed the sort who might hit a woman. Helen stepped in between them.

"Why did you do this to us?" she queried.

"For money, Miss Hamilton. Why would you suppose?"

"Whatever Mrs. Seymour paid you, I'll pay you more."

"I've peeked in your purse. It's empty."

The prison gate opened, and at the sound, Helen shuddered.

Rafferty grabbed her and spun her, removing the ropes on her wrists, as his partner did the same to Jane. They were shoved inside, the heavy gate clanging shut.

He started to walk away, and on watching him go, Helen felt as if she'd lost her last friend. He was the only person who knew where they were. If he never told anyone, if he never came back, they could die in this foul place.

Where was Amelia? How would she get on by herself?

They'd been separated in the crowd, and Helen wanted to beg Rafferty to find her, but should she?

Was Amelia better off alone on the streets or incarcerated with Helen and Jane?

Jails were ripe with disease, with starvation and violence, but the streets would be even more dangerous.

"Rafferty!" she called.

"What?" He whipped around.

"If you cross paths with my sister Amelia, would you bring her here so I can keep her with me?"

"Absolutely. The little bugger should have been captured with you. She slipped away, but I'll locate her."

He strutted off again, and Helen panicked.

"Rafferty! We don't have any money."

"No, you don't."

"How are we to eat? How are we to keep warm?"

"That, Miss Hamilton, is not my problem."

He gave a jaunty salute, then sauntered away.

Helen and Jane stood, huddled together, peering after him till he disappeared.

"I can't believe this," Jane muttered. "I simply can't. What are we to do? Are we to perish in here?"

Helen scoffed. "Not if I have anything to say about it."

"Where could Amelia have gone?"

"I'm hoping she's with Clarinda."

"I hope so, too."

They dawdled, waiting, wondering what catastrophe would befall them next.

"I'm sorry," Jane said, and she burst into tears.

"Why would you be sorry?"

"This is all my fault. If I hadn't dallied with Lord Hastings—"

"This is *not* your fault. I blame the entire debacle on

Captain Odell, and I will get even with him if it's the last thing I do."

A guard shuffled up. He was filthy and obese; his clothes reeked, his teeth were black stumps.

He carried a stick, and he brandished it at them.

"What are ya doing out here?" he snapped. "No prisoners allowed by the gate! You have to stay in the courtyard."

They turned and proceeded down a dark hall, which she assumed led deeper into the facility.

Helen didn't know much about penal routines except that you needed cash to survive. You had to buy your food, your blankets, your fire. If you were rich, you could purchase a private cell, could have food delivered and your servants attend you.

If you had nothing and no one, you slept on the ground. You starved. You grew ill and died.

She stumbled to a halt.

"Damn . . ." she mumbled, cursing for the first time ever.

"What is it?" Jane asked.

"I didn't see Rafferty fill out any papers or sign a manifest with our names on it. Did you?"

"No, why?"

"If anyone ever came to check, there'd be no record of us arriving."

"No. There'd be no record," Jane gloomily concurred. "It doesn't matter, though, does it?"

"Why wouldn't it?"

"Who would ever search for us?"

"Who, indeed?"

Chapter 22

❦

"CAPTAIN! Michael!" Maud forced a smile, tamping down her spurt of alarm. "What are you doing home? I thought you'd be halfway to Scotland by now."

"We had a change of plans," Tristan said.

"Is anything the matter? I trust there were no difficulties with the ship?"

"No. I need to take care of some unfinished business. Where is Miss Hamilton?"

"Miss . . . Hamilton?"

"Yes."

"She's not here."

Michael and Tristan froze.

"What do you mean?" Tristan asked.

"She stopped by with her sisters to retrieve their belongings, but they hired a hackney, loaded their trunks, and left."

"Left!" Michael looked stricken. "Jane, too?"

"Yes, not that she is any of your concern."

"I specifically ordered her to come here," Tristan growled. "I told her to wait till my clerk rented her a house."

"She claimed she didn't want the house," Maud lied.

"Do you know where they went? Did they provide a forwarding address?"

"No, and I didn't inquire. Good riddance, I say."

"But . . . but . . . I have to talk to her," Tristan said. "She must have said something. What about her bedchamber? Perhaps she wrote me a note."

"The entire suite has been cleaned from top to bottom. There was no note."

She gestured to the front parlor, urging them in to where a toasty fire burned in the grate. "Now then, Miriam and I were about to sit down to a quiet supper. You'll join us, of course, so you can tell us what's happening. Captain, let's get you a brandy while I instruct the staff to set two more plates."

She spun away, but Michael and Tristan didn't move.

"I'll check their rooms," Tristan advised Michael, and he dashed up the stairs.

Michael proceeded into the parlor to warm his hands by the fire, which gave Maud the opportunity to confer with Lydia, who was hovering down the hall.

Loudly enough for Michael to hear, Maud said, "Please notify Cook that Captain Odell and Michael have returned. We'll dine in half an hour."

"Yes, ma'am." Lydia was craning her neck, watching Michael.

Maud leaned closer and whispered, "First, though, run up and unlock Lady Rose's door. Don't let anyone see you."

Lydia nodded and scurried away, as Maud tarried with Michael, both of them waiting for Tristan.

Thank God she'd had the foresight to act swiftly with regard to the Hamiltons! What if she'd delayed? Tristan and Michael would have strolled in to find the women still squarely wedged in the center of their lives. Due to Maud's shrewd planning, they'd vanished without a trace.

The only problematic detail was Rose and her temper. If Tristan had stayed away as he was supposed to, Maud would have had plenty of time to calm Rose, to convince her that Amelia hadn't been much of a friend after all.

As it was, Rose's pique was still fresh, so she'd be difficult, but Maud was adept at handling an unruly child.

The butler was lurking, and Maud had him pour her a sherry, which she was sipping as Tristan entered.

"Well . . . ?" Michael asked him.

"Completely empty. They didn't leave so much as a lock of hair."

"Damn," Michael muttered, then he apologized. "Sorry, Maud."

"Apology accepted, but Captain, what is going on? We agreed that Michael would travel to Scotland and remain there."

Tristan ignored her and spoke to Michael. "Think back. Did she ever mention a relative? Maybe an acquaintance in the city?"

"No one that I remember, and there was just her mother's family, but they wouldn't assist Helen or Jane—no matter how desperate they were."

"Bastards," Tristan grumbled.

"Captain!" Maud scolded. "Honestly. What is it? You're scaring me."

"Did you give her any money when she left?" Tristan absurdly probed.

"Why would I have?" Maud scoffed. "If she needed cash, she should have saved the wages you paid her. You did *pay* her, I assume?"

"Yes, but not an amount sufficient to see her through this debacle."

"So," Michael mused, "they're broke and on the streets again. I'm very worried."

"So am I," Tristan concurred. "Why would Helen go? Why would she place her sisters in jeopardy? I realize she was angry with me, but she wouldn't have deliberately endangered Amelia. I offered her lodging and an allowance. Why choose the streets, instead?"

"I don't understand it," Michael said. "What should we do?"

"I won't have you fretting over it now," Maud interrupted, intent on dissuading any rash pursuit while the trail was hot. "You'll wash up and eat, you'll have a good night's sleep, and your options will be clearer in the morning."

"I want to take action," Michael insisted. "I can't dawdle, wondering if Jane is all right."

Maud was incensed, and she stomped over to him.

"You are not to speak that girl's name."

"It's not up to you," he retorted.

"It certainly is. You've caused enough trouble. We contained the scandal at Hastings Manor, and I won't have you stirring it up in the city. If you start chasing around after her, what will people say?

"And you!" she fumed at Tristan. "What were you thinking, bringing him here? We had it all arranged."

"I decided that separation was pointless," he maddeningly stated. "Michael is old enough to make his own mistakes. I'm not the man to baby-sit him."

"You're permitting him to . . . to . . . *involve* himself with her?"

"If that's what he wishes."

"Oh, for pity's sake!"

Maud was so irate that little red circles formed at the corners of her vision, and she truly thought she was about to suffer an apoplexy.

There was a sofa behind her, and she sagged down onto it.

What a disaster!

For a moment, her alarm returned as it seemed everything was ruined, but then, she recollected how perfectly her scheme had been implemented.

Rafferty had already contacted her. The Hamilton sisters were the newest tenants in Newgate Prison, and when a woman went inside, she rarely came out again.

Maud's panic was ridiculous. She'd never be found out, and she might have relaxed, but she'd forgotten about Rose.

Suddenly, a pair of determined footsteps pounded down the hall.

"Tristan! Tristan!" Rose called as she ran in.

When he saw her livid face, he frowned. "What's wrong?"

"Ask *her* what's wrong," Rose charged, advancing on Maud. "You evil, wicked witch!"

Rose lunged, as if she might attack, and Maud squealed with fright and jumped behind the sofa, using it as a barrier.

"Whoa!" Tristan said, and he grabbed Rose around the waist, holding her as she fought and kicked, trying to escape so she could assault Maud.

"Let me go! Let me go!"

"Rose!" Michael admonished. "What are you doing?"

"She locked me in my room!" Rose told him. "The whole time I've been home, I've been locked in."

"*What?*" Michael glared at Maud.

"I couldn't say good-bye to Amelia," Rose whined.

"You saw Amelia?" Tristan inquired.

"Through the upstairs window. Maud wouldn't let me come down." Her struggles had ceased, and she grew limp in his arms, her burst of fury spent.

"But you talked to her?"

"Only for a second."

"Was she with Helen and Jane?"

"Yes. Amelia was very distressed. Maud did something terrible to them. I just know it!"

Both men glowered at Maud, and she huffed, "Rose Seymour, your imagination is outrageous. How dare you level false allegations! You're lucky I'm not the type to have you whipped for telling tales. And where are your manners? Your brothers have just arrived, yet you're screeching like a banshee."

"What did you do to them?" Rose yelled.

"Rose!" Maud snapped. "I won't put up with such discourtesy!"

Rose couldn't be allowed to hurl dangerous accusations. Maud approached her and eased her away from Tristan.

"Let's get you up to your bedchamber," Maud said. "You may come back down when you're more yourself."

Rose wrestled away and gazed up at Tristan. "You never listen to me. You never help me when it's important."

"I just walked in the door, Rose. Give me a few minutes. Michael and I will sort it out."

"Don't bother," Rose angrily fumed. "You never cared about Amelia. *I* am the one who loved her. I'll find out what happened to her on my own. I don't need you!"

She stormed out, and as her strides faded, there was an awkward silence.

"At her age," Maud counseled, "a girl can be so volatile. Let me pour you that brandy."

She gestured to the butler, as Tristan stared out in the hall, focused on the spot where Rose had vanished.

"Maybe I should go after her," he murmured.

"Absolutely not!" Maud insisted. "You'd be encouraging her in her rude behavior. She'll assume she can act that way and get away with it."

"I hate to have her so upset."

"For now, we'll leave her be. After she's calmed, she'll apologize to us. Only then will we converse with her on any topic."

He might have continued to vacillate, but she was saved by Miriam hurrying in.

"Michael, you're home!" she said, beaming.

"Hello, Miriam." His tone was cool and ominously polite.

"I thought you were off to Scotland."

"No," was all he said.

"Let's go in to supper, shall we? I want to hear of your adventures so far."

Without waiting for his reply, she deftly guided him to the dining room.

"You must be starving, too," Maud remarked to Tristan, and she motioned after them, urging him to follow.

"I am hungry, now that you mention it."

He went easily, any concern over Rose temporarily forgotten.

Disaster averted!

With Rose sent away in disgrace, Maud had the opportunity to convince him that the girl was completely mistaken about everything.

"We can discuss Rose after the meal," she suggested. "We have to figure out what's to be done with her."

"She's distraught because she's missing Amelia, and I expect she will keep on missing her for quite some time."

"Yes, she will, poor child, but she'll get over it. We'll see to it, hmm?"

Tristan held her chair, and she smiled.

TAP! Tap! Tap!

At first, Rose didn't realize that the noise was anything special. She imagined it was tree branches scraping the house, and she was too enraged to pay attention. During her imprisonment, with that sneaky Lydia delivering her food, Rose had planned the revenge she'd have once her brothers returned, but she'd confessed every indignity, and they wouldn't listen.

They *never* listened.

The noise came again.

Tap! Tap! Tap!

She walked over to the window and threw it open. The night was very dark, so it was difficult to see.

"Who is it?" she asked. "Who's there?"

To her surprise, Amelia stepped out of the shadows, and when Rose almost called out to her, she pressed a finger to her lips, indicating Rose should be silent.

Let me in! Amelia mouthed.

Rose pointed to the servants' entrance, and she raced

down the rear stairs. In a matter of minutes, they were in her room, with no one the wiser as to Amelia's arrival.

They huddled on the floor in Rose's closet, behind her rows and rows of dresses, and on studying her friend, Rose bristled with temper.

Amelia's face and hands were dirty, her shoes scuffed, her hair straggly. Her stockings were torn at the knees, as if she'd fallen.

"Where are your sisters?" Rose whispered.

"You won't believe what happened to us!"

"Yes, I will."

As Amelia recounted her tale of treachery and arrest, Rose was so furious that she thought she might explode.

"We can't let Maud get away with this!" Rose said.

"No, we can't."

"What should we do?"

"I was hoping we could talk to Captain Odell or Lord Hastings."

"I already tried. They ignored me."

At the news, Amelia looked deflated and very near to tears.

"I'm supposed to meet Miss Dudley very soon," Amelia mentioned. "What will I tell her?"

"You'll tell her Captain Odell is a cruel blowhard and that he won't help us. She'll understand."

"She'll know where Helen and Jane are, though. Perhaps we could rescue them ourselves!"

"Yes, perhaps we could."

Rose stood and grabbed a shawl, and she made a sort of sack and started stuffing various items into it.

"What are you doing?" Amelia inquired.

"I'm running away. I'm going to live with you and Miss Dudley."

"We don't have a home for you."

"Then we'll live on the streets, but we'll be together. I hate it here, and I refuse to remain another second. Maud will never lock me in again."

She tugged Amelia to her feet, and they riffled through

Rose's clothes and pulled out her two warmest cloaks. They drew them on, then tiptoed to the door and peeked out. It was late and very quiet.

"We can sneak out the kitchen," Rose murmured. "We'll take some food with us."

"We should bring extra. Miss Dudley will be hungry."

Holding hands, they crept to the stairs.

TRISTAN sat at his desk in the library. He leaned back in the chair and rubbed his eyes.

Everyone was in bed, and he should have been, too, but he kept thinking about Helen and where she might have gone. There must have been a detail he'd missed, some hint of where to begin his search.

He picked up the folder he'd been perusing, scrutinized it again, then dropped it onto the polished wood. It contained the original letter sent over from Mrs. Ford's employment agency when Helen had come for her interview.

Helen Hamilton, age twenty-four, proficient in French, Italian, pianoforte, geography, mathematics. Especially good with comportment and social graces.

He'd read the lines a hundred times, as if the paltry narrative could offer a clue as to where she was.

In the morning, he'd visit Mrs. Ford, as well as the decrepit boardinghouse where Helen had previously stayed. He'd even call on her despicable relatives.

Someone, somewhere, had to know what had happened to her.

He was so engrossed in his miserable musings that when a commotion commenced out in the drive, he couldn't make sense of what it was.

Gradually, it dawned on him that a man was shouting, raising a ruckus.

"Odell, you bloody fool! Answer your bloody door!"

Tristan frowned, trying to place the voice, trying to remember who he might have enraged sufficiently that the person would seek him out in the middle of the night. He hadn't been in London in weeks. Who could it be?

He couldn't have the oaf waking the entire neighborhood, and he'd just risen to tell him so, when a sleepy footman beat him to it.

"Is there a problem, sir?" the fellow said. His tone was sarcastic, but who could blame him? It was one o'clock in the morning.

"Yes, there's a problem!" From the stomping of feet, it was clear the man had blustered his way into the foyer. "Where is Odell?"

"Really, sir, you can't—"

"Odell, you bastard! Get your ass down here!"

Would the crazed maniac race through the mansion? Would he search the bedchambers? What sort of lunatic had arrived?

Tristan went over and peered down the long hallway; as he recognized the interloper, he blanched with disgust.

"Phillip Dudley?" Tristan groused as Dudley barked, "Odell!"

Without invitation, Dudley marched toward him, the footman hot on his heels.

"Sir! Sir!"

The footman grabbed at Dudley's coat, but was unable to slow him, and Dudley approached until they were toe-to-toe.

"Where is my sister?"

"Your . . . sister? Who is your sister, and why would I know where she is?"

Tristan glared at Dudley as if he was a madman, and he was close to throwing him—bodily—out into the yard, but the footman was all ears, and if there was a brawl, the gossip would be all over town the next day.

"I won't need you anymore this evening," Tristan told the servant, who bowed and disappeared. Tristan pointed into the library and gestured to Dudley. "In here. Now."

Tristan walked over and sat down behind the desk, as Dudley pulled up the chair across from him.

"Mr. Dudley, I will ask this once, and I expect you to be brief. What the hell are you thinking?"

"I'm taking my sister out of this accursed place."

"This *place* being the dwelling in which we're currently located?"

"Don't play dumb with me, Odell. I won't have her fraternizing with you people."

"You seem to be laboring under the strangest impression that I'm acquainted with your sister and that I've given her shelter."

"Are you claiming you're unaware of this?"

Dudley tossed a letter onto the desktop, and Tristan picked it up, learning that Dudley's sister—one Clarinda Dudley—had traveled to London with Helen.

"Ah, I see," Tristan mumbled.

"She's not an unprotected female like poor Miss Hamilton. Clarinda has *me* to speak up for her. If you've laid a finger on her, we'll be having a quick wedding first thing tomorrow."

A muscle ticked in Tristan's cheek. In a smattering of sentences, so many insults had been hurled that he couldn't tabulate them all.

"Are you a drinking man, Dudley?"

"Yes, why?"

"I believe we'd better have a whiskey."

"If you imagine you can ply me with alcohol so you can—"

"You make my head pound with your complaints. Be silent."

Tristan proceeded to the sideboard and poured two stout glasses. He handed one to Dudley. Dudley kicked his back in a single swallow, shuddered, then licked his lips.

"Not bad," he said. "Now, where is my sister?"

"If she was with Helen, they've vanished."

"What?"

"Helen stopped by here while I was away. She packed her belongings and left in a rented cab with Jane and Amelia."

"What was her destination?"

"She didn't say."

"Was Clarinda with her?"

"If she was, I haven't been informed."

The exchange eased some of Dudley's bluster.

"Well . . . shit," he muttered.

"My feelings exactly."

Dudley rose and helped himself to another whiskey. He downed it as he had the first: in one gulp. Then he started for the door.

"Where are you going?" Tristan asked.

"There's no reason to hang about, begging for answers when you obviously don't have any."

Tristan was correct: The man was insane.

"What if your sister shows up?"

"She won't."

"Humor me, though. What if I see her?"

"Tell her I'm in London. She'll know where I'm staying."

He kept on, and Tristan suffered from the most peculiar urge to stop him. Dudley had a confidence and brusque edge that—Tristan was mortified to admit—reminded him of himself. If he had to launch a massive search for Helen, Dudley would be a great asset.

"How well do you know Miss Hamilton?" Tristan queried.

"I crawled into her bed every night, you wretch. How well do you think?"

"Would you be serious? I'm trying to learn if she has a friend in London who might have taken her in. I was hoping she might have said something to you."

"In all the times you tumbled her, you never bothered to inquire about her background? Her people?" Dudley studied him, his disdain clear. "I guess a man of your station would have been too busy. You'd have been focused on other . . . *things*."

Tristan flushed with embarrassment. He'd never probed for details about Helen because he'd simply assumed she

would always be with him. He'd never looked down the
road to the day when she might leave, and at being con-
fronted with more of his failings toward her—by Dudley,
no less!—he blazed with temper.

"Watch your rude tongue, Dudley," he quietly warned.
"I won't have you slandering her."

"That's fine talk from the scoundrel who ruined her."

There was nothing Tristan could say in his defense, for
he *had* ruined her. Any denial of an affair would be a betrayal, and any acknowledgment of it would be wrong and
further damage her reputation.

Hadn't Tristan done enough?

"I just want to find her," he said. "I want to bring her
home."

"It better be because you've come to your senses and
decided to marry her."

"It is."

"About bloody time," Dudley snorted. "Miss Hamilton
drank my Spinster's Cure potion ages ago. What took you
so long to make up your mind?"

"Don't drag your blasted potion into this."

"Why shouldn't I? It works."

It was Tristan's turn to snort. "Will you help me hunt
for her?"

"No, but if I stumble on her, I'll let you know."

He marched out, and once again, Tristan was unaccountably dismayed to see him go. Like a buffoon, he
chased after the man.

"If I need to get ahold of you," Tristan inquired, "where
will you be?"

"I can't imagine why you'd have to contact me."

"If you locate your sister, I want to ask her about
Helen."

"*When* I locate my sister, if she has any pertinent information, I'll send you a note."

He paused, scowling at Tristan with what seemed close
to an evil eye.

"Marry that girl, would you?" Dudley pressed. "Don't be an idiot."

With that, he left, and Tristan loitered on the stoop as he vanished into the night. Dudley hadn't taken a dozen steps when he halted and murmured, "Well, well, what have we here?"

Dudley glanced at Tristan over his shoulder. "Come have a look."

"At what?"

"Just come. You won't believe it."

Tristan pushed away from the door and went down into the street.

There, outlined in the shadows, were Amelia, Rose, and a dark-haired woman whom he didn't know.

"Miss Dudley, I presume?" Tristan said.

"Yes, Captain."

"Where the devil have you been?" Dudley snapped at her.

"If you're going to take that tone with me," she replied, "then it's none of your business."

Dudley and Clarinda engaged in a staring match, while Tristan frowned at Amelia and Rose. He assessed their warm cloaks, the sack Rose had slung over her back. Amelia was carrying some bread and cheese. Were they running away?

At the prospect, he was aghast.

"Rose, are you leaving me?" Tristan demanded, wanting to appear stern rather than terrified by her rash behavior.

"I'm going to live with Amelia," she announced.

"I assume you have a good explanation for your decision."

"Not that you'd ever listen to it."

Tristan nodded, evaluating her furious stance, her mutinous expression. Earlier in the evening, she'd been so angry, but he'd discounted her rage. He hadn't a clue how to care for a child, and where she was concerned, he was always making stupid choices.

He'd let Maud convince him that Rose's upset wasn't important. He'd been exhausted and worried about Helen, so he'd ignored Rose when she'd desperately needed him. How many times would he fail her? How was he to regain her trust?

"I'm listening now, Rose," he told her.

Miss Dudley stepped forward. "There's something you should know. Something bad."

Tristan's heart fluttered with panic. "Helen's not . . . not . . . dead, is she?"

"Physically, she's fine, but it's still bad." Miss Dudley gestured to the door. "May we come in?"

"Yes, of course. Please."

He led the way into the mansion, the odd group trailing after him like ducks in a row.

Chapter 23

❦

"WE'VE come to retrieve Miss Helen Hamilton and Miss Jane Hamilton. We won't leave without them."

"I realize that you are anxious over their fate, but I've scanned the list three times. There are no women here by that name."

"Look again," Tristan said.

He stepped nearer to Warden Bromley so as to intimidate him with his greater size, and he tapped his riding crop on his thigh. The incessant snap was a curt reminder that he could just as easily slap it across Bromley's leg as his own.

With trembling hands, the smaller man searched for a misspelling or a clerical error that would indicate their identities had been incorrectly logged.

A clerk rushed in and spread even more pages on the desk.

"This is a file of yesterday's arrivals." Bromley ran a finger down the lengthy columns. "There was no Helen or Jane Hamilton brought in. Are you sure they were delivered to this institution?"

"We have an eyewitness who saw the gate clang shut behind them."

Michael was sitting in a chair, and so far, he'd been silent. He was dressed to the nines, wearing his most expensive coat, his most intricate cravat, and presenting himself as a bored, pompous aristocrat.

They hadn't known what type of welcome they'd receive at the prison, hadn't known if—short of engaging in a lengthy legal process—they'd be able to walk out with Helen and Jane. As insurance, they'd decided to use Michael's position as leverage.

He flicked at the lace on his cuff. "I've heard that there is graft in the prisons. I've even heard that bribery is common."

"Not in my facility," Bromley huffed, but he appeared nervous.

"I don't suppose money could have been paid to make them vanish."

"Certainly not," Bromley insisted.

"Because if I ever found out that had happened"— Michael flashed a lethal grin—"I would be extremely angry." He glanced around the tidy office. "Yours seems a rather good job. I would hate to have you lose it over such a trivial matter."

Bromley gulped. Michael was one of the most influential men in the land. If he chose to wield his power, he could have Bromley fired in an instant.

"Who is Mr. Rafferty?" Tristan asked.

"I've told you, Captain," Bromley complained, "I don't know. Perhaps we could question some of the guards."

"Yes, let's do."

Michael stood. "While we wait for you to assemble them, I would like a tour."

"A tour?" Bromley was horrified.

"I'm about to begin my duties in parliament, so a visit would be highly informational."

"Lord Hastings, I really don't think you ought to—"

"Is there some reason I shouldn't explore? If I didn't know better, I might imagine that you didn't want me to see the condition of the place."

"It's not that. It's just . . . just . . ."

"Just what?" Michael snapped, his impatience clear.

Boots sounded in the hall, and Tristan whipped around as the door was flung open. A ruffian was pushed into the room, and Phillip Dudley followed him in.

"Meet Mr. Rafferty," Dudley said without preamble.

"How did you locate him?"

"I bribed a guard."

Michael and Tristan turned to glare at Bromley, and he protested, "I can't fathom how that would be possible."

"I just bet you can't," Tristan seethed.

"He's a local reprobate," Dudley explained, "known to every criminal in the area." He whacked Rafferty in the back. "Tell the captain what you told me."

"They're here. I brought them in myself."

"On what grounds?"

"Theft. What else? Why are you raising such a fuss? I was acting on your orders."

Tristan frowned. "*My* orders?"

Rafferty pulled some papers from his coat and Tristan snatched them out of his hand. As he perused them, his temper boiled over.

"What do they say?" Michael asked.

"It's an affidavit," Rafferty responded, "that accuses the ladies of stealing a valuable emerald ring and a pouch of gold coins. It was sworn to by the captain. His signature is there, plain as day."

Tristan shook his head. "No, Mr. Rafferty, not *my* signature."

Tristan scowled at Michael, and in unison, they muttered, "Maud."

Michael glowered at Bromley. "I demand that you escort us personally. We don't have time to waste."

HELEN leaned against the wall, enjoying the sun that shone on her face. She shut her eyes to block out the miserable souls around her, and she whispered a prayer for

Amelia. That she was with Clarinda Dudley. That Helen would see her again.

She and Jane had survived their first night. It had been cold and scary, and sleep difficult. She was exhausted—and hungry—but alive and in one piece.

She'd worried over the sorts of treacherous felons they might encounter, but her fellow inmates were a mix of desperate people from all walks of life—the common factor being their poverty. Men, women, and many mothers with their children huddled together, so no one had bothered her.

Fleetingly, she thought of Captain Odell. Was he aware of what had transpired? Would he ever learn of it?

Most likely, he was glad of her and Jane's disappearance. It would solve many of his problems. He was probably celebrating!

"No, you may not have it!"

Jane's terse voice echoed through Helen's reverie, and Helen lurched up and peered about, finding her sister surrounded by three burly, filthy brigands.

Jane had heard that soup was being dispensed, and she'd gone to look, while Helen had stayed behind to keep their spot along the wall. Jane was carrying a bowl and crust of bread, and the men yanked them away.

"Leave the poor girl alone," an older gentleman scolded.

"Mind your own business," one of the criminals retorted.

The older man stood, as if to argue with the trio, but he was shoved to the ground and landed hard on the bricks.

With his assistance so easily foiled, everyone in the crowd glanced away, not eager to be dragged into the mess.

Helen was afraid, but she couldn't sit by and allow Jane to be abused.

"Jane, come here," she said.

"But he took our food," she complained, "and I'm famished."

"It's just food, Jane. It's not worth fighting over."

"He can stand in line like everybody else; he can get his own."

"He could, but he won't. Come away from there. Now."

Helen approached them, as the trio spun to see who'd had the gall to interfere. They were tall and frightening, and she and Jane were in terrible danger, but Helen couldn't back down.

She pasted on her most stern governess frown. "You have her food, so please go away. We don't want any trouble."

"Aren't you a sassy wench?" the largest man jeered, and he reached out and mussed Helen's hair.

She batted him away.

"Don't touch me," she said very quietly. "Don't touch my sister."

"Blimey, boys. She's givin' me orders!"

"Will you obey, Harry?"

"Not bloody likely."

"Let's show her what's done to those what tries to boss us about."

"A grand idea, gents, but let's find a place that's a tad more private."

Before Helen realized his plan, she was grabbed by the waist and swooped off her feet. The man—Harry—carted her off, as if she was a sack of potatoes. Out of the corner of her eye, she saw that Jane had been seized in the same despicable way.

"Help! Help us!" Helen screamed, fully expecting others to leap up and rescue her, but no one did.

From up above on a rampart, several guards watched the fracas, as well, and she called out to them, too, but they blithely observed, as unmoved as if they were ancient Romans and she a Christian that had been thrown to the lions.

Helen kicked and clawed but made no progress in stopping him. Harry quickly marched toward a dark corridor, and Helen could only imagine what fate awaited them when they vanished from view.

Harry stepped into the hallway, the sunlight fading, his

strides increasing in speed when, to her surprise, a man emerged from the shadows and blocked their path.

"Put her down," he curtly said.

"You can have a turn when I'm finished," Harry replied.

"Put her down or I'll kill you where you stand."

"Did you hear that, lads?" Harry sneered over his shoulder at his companions. "The fool thinks to kill me."

They laughed and laughed, as if Harry was immortal. He tried to push past the brave fellow, but a skirmish broke out, though Helen was unsure who hit whom. It all happened so fast.

Harry's arms went slack, and he dropped her. Panicked, on her hands and knees, she crawled toward the open area among the other prisoners. She was completely rattled, trembling, crying, reaching out for Jane, but unable to locate her.

Behind her, the sounds of fighting were brutally clear. Bone cracked on bone, body parts smacking stone, and much sooner than seemed possible, all was silent.

She skittered into the courtyard and huddled in a ball, taking deep breaths, wondering if she would ever calm. It was only her second day in the accursed jail! How would she survive? How would she keep her sanity?

Suddenly, a pair of strong arms encircled her. For a moment, deeming it the miscreant Harry again, she lashed out. She bit and scratched, but gradually, the man managed to clasp hold of her wrists and halt her struggles. She was immobilized, and a male voice crooned words of comfort.

"Helen . . . Helen . . ." he was saying. "You're all right now."

Confused, she pulled away and gaped at him. Was she dreaming? Was she hallucinating?

"Tristan?"

"Yes, Helen, it's me. I've come for you. I've come, and you're safe."

"Where is Jane?" she frantically inquired.

"She's fine. Michael is here, too. He's with her."

"I was so afraid," she murmured.

"I know you were."

He drew her to his chest, and she nestled with him, her ear over his heart. Her pulse was thundering like a war cannon, while his was hardly elevated, providing no evidence that he'd just thwarted three combatants.

He stroked her hair, her back, her shoulders, as he repeated that she was all right, all right, all right.

After such trial and tribulation, the solace was exactly what she needed. For a time, she wallowed in his embrace, enjoying the realization that he'd been distraught over her plight, that he'd searched for her. But as she relaxed, she remembered who *he* was, and who *she* was. She remembered what he'd done to her, how he'd insulted her family, her father, her sisters, herself.

She recalled Maud and Lydia, his mistresses and illicit children, and she eased away, forcing a cool, bland expression onto her face.

"Thank you, Captain Odell. I appreciate your assistance."

"Oh, Helen, when I returned to London and you weren't at the town house, I was so frightened."

"You needn't have been."

"I'm so glad I found you."

He moved as if to hug her again, but she jumped away and stood.

"I must check on my sister."

She walked into the dim corridor, her last sight of him on his knees, his hand stretched out to her in supplication.

He looked hurt and perplexed by her detachment.

What had he expected? Had he presumed she would immediately fall for him again?

Apparently so.

He was insane, and her days of playing the gullible fool were over.

She hurried to Jane's side.

* * *

"CAPTAIN, you wished to speak with us?"

"Actually, Maud, Michael summoned you. Come in."

Maud entered the library, Miriam trailing after her. Tristan gestured for them to sit, and as Maud neared, she was unnerved.

Michael was seated behind the desk, and Tristan was standing at his right hand—as if Michael was in charge and Tristan merely a valued advisor.

It was a minor modification, but the implications were monumental. Michael was indicating that he'd assumed the reins of power. A message was being sent that he was in control and his commands would be paramount.

Maud should have been excited about the change. After all, she'd always been able to manipulate Michael, but his tense gaze boded ill.

"There appears to have been some trouble," Maud pointed out, intending to steer the conversation in a direction to her liking. "A maid told me that the Hamiltons have returned. Is it true?"

Neither man replied, and Maud panicked. How had the women been located? Why had Tristan brought them home? What had they revealed?

Tristan waved toward the corner, and Lydia approached, her head down, as if she was terrified or ashamed. Nothing in her demeanor signified that she was acting. She seemed genuinely cowed.

"You know Lydia, of course," Tristan said.

"Yes. I hired her."

Maud glared a visual warning that Lydia should keep her mouth shut and all would be well, but Lydia was too much of a coward to peek up.

"Miss Hamilton and Rose both suggested that Michael and I have a long chat with Lydia," Tristan said. "So we did. Before we begin, Maud, is there anything you'd like to say to me?"

Maud's mind whirred over what her answer should be.

What had Lydia confessed? How should Maud handle the situation?

When she failed to respond, Tristan focused on Miriam. "How about you, Miriam? Is there anything you'd like to say?"

"Honestly, Captain," Miriam scoffed, "I have no idea why we're here, and I most especially have no idea why I should care that you've been talking with a housemaid."

Tristan nodded as if the snotty comment was precisely what he'd anticipated.

"Michael," Miriam implored, "why are you letting him treat us this way? He shouldn't be allowed to."

"Be quiet, Miriam." Michael's tone was even and restrained, but underneath, there was a hint of steel.

Tristan stared at Lydia.

"Who locked Lady Rose in her room?"

"I did, Captain," she replied.

"On whose orders?"

"Mrs. Seymour's, sir."

"Who hid the emerald ring in Miss Hamilton's luggage?"

"I did, sir."

"On whose orders?"

"Mrs. Seymour's."

The interrogation went on in a similar fashion, with Lydia candidly giving an account of every task she'd carried out at Maud's behest. Maud fumed, reflecting on how—when the examination was ended—she would have Lydia flogged, then fired.

Maud had known better than to trust Lydia, and she couldn't fathom why Lydia would jeopardize her position with Maud. Maud had never taken her for an idiot.

Tristan's inquiry concluded, but Maud was still in a dither, her thoughts careening between fury and dread, as she struggled to decide what her strategy should be. Defiance seemed best.

"What have you to say now?" Tristan demanded of Maud.

"Lydia is a liar. She always has been. She's on probation and about to be terminated, and she knows it. This is her revenge."

"None of what she's just confided is true?"

"Not a word."

"So everyone is lying?" Tristan queried. "The servants, Rose, Lydia, Jane Hamilton, Mick Rafferty. All of them are lying, but *you*—and you alone—are telling the truth?"

At hearing Rafferty's name—how had the rogue been exposed?—she nearly blanched with astonishment, but she controlled herself and waved Lydia away as if she was a bad odor Maud couldn't abide.

"You insult me by asking the question, Captain. May we get back to discussing the Hamilton sisters? After the scandal involving Jane, I refuse to have them in our midst."

As if she hadn't spoken, Michael scowled at Miriam, his rage palpable.

"You told Jane Hamilton that you and I were betrothed."

"I did not!" Miriam had the good sense to respond. "If she said so, bring her in here, and I'll call her a liar to her face!"

"Several servants saw you wearing my mother's engagement ring. You deny it?"

"No, I don't deny it. Mother allowed me to. It's a very beautiful piece of jewelry, and it's wrong to keep it locked away."

"You're claiming it was a harmless prank?"

"Not a *prank*. It matched my dress, and it looked pretty on my finger."

"Lydia, you're excused," Michael stated. "Go wait in the hall."

Lydia slithered out, managing a quick glance at Maud as she passed, but Maud couldn't decipher her expression. Was she gloating? Was she smug? Was she afraid? Was it a warning of even more trouble to come?

Lydia exited, the door closing behind her, and an awkward silence ensued. Maud rushed to fill the void.

"*Now* may we discuss the Hamiltons?"

"No, we may not," Michael snapped. "We have more important matters to cover."

"Such as?"

"My father was fond of you, so I have permitted you to live in my home. I have supported you financially and been your most steadfast friend, and this is how you repay me? With treachery and deceit?"

"Treachery!" Maud huffed. "Don't be ridiculous."

"Maud, I have grudgingly accepted your guidance and constantly acceded to your wishes, but the situation is ending. Right here. Right now."

"What are you saying?" Maud was growing angry. "So what if a few disgruntled employees have made allegations? You can't possibly—"

"Miriam," Michael interrupted, "let me be perfectly clear: I will never marry you. You will never be my countess. Despite how long you've planned on ensnaring me, it will not occur."

At first, Miriam simply gaped at him. Then she started to tremble, and she was shaking her head from side to side.

"No, no, you don't mean it. You can't mean it! Mother promised me! We're destined to be together."

"Tell me that you understand." Michael was stoic, dispassionate, ignoring her emotional entreaty. "Tell me that we will have no further miscommunication on this issue."

Miriam leapt up and ran around the desk. She fell to her knees and grabbed his coat.

"Please, Michael," she begged, shaming herself. "I've been so patient. Whatever I did, whatever you *think* I did, I did it for you! Please!"

Michael was still as a statue, and Tristan leaned down and pried her away. She fought to escape, anxious to prostrate herself again.

"Miriam!" Maud scolded. "Remember yourself."

Maud wanted to intervene but wasn't certain how. Michael was unreachable, and Odell intent on embarrassing them.

Odell wrestled Miriam out, and two footmen stood in the hall, as if the moment had been prearranged.

"Escort Miss Seymour to her bedchamber," Tristan commanded. "See that she stays there. If she attempts to leave, prevent any departure and notify me at once."

"You have no authority over me," Miriam seethed.

"You may proceed of your own accord," Tristan said, "or I shall bind your hands and feet and have you carried there."

They engaged in a staring match that Miriam could never win, and she turned to Maud.

"Mother! You can't let him get away with this!"

"Go to your room, Miriam. I'll be up in a few minutes."

"Mother!" Miriam tried again.

"Go!" Maud hissed.

Miriam stomped off, and Odell shut the door. He came back to stand behind Michael.

"How dare you, Odell!" Maud raged, rising, quaking with fury. "You lowborn scoundrel! How dare you disrespect my daughter! How dare you disrespect me! Michael Seymour, if I had a whip, I would use it on you for permitting such a disgusting display."

Michael rose, too. He seemed different somehow, powerful and confident as he'd never been. Her mistake, she suddenly realized, was that she still thought of him as a malleable boy. Apparently, when she hadn't been paying attention, he'd metamorphosed into someone she didn't know.

"You're leaving for the country," he announced. "You and Miriam both. Immediately."

"I am not. Your father charged me with watching over you, which I have done—thanklessly, it seems—for over a decade. You cannot be alone and at Odell's mercy."

"My father is deceased," Michael roared, "and I am

Earl of Hastings! You will obey me, or you will regret it till your dying day."

"Don't raise your voice to me, young man."

Her bravado was forced. She was stunned by his behavior and wondering how to counter it.

Since the instant Odell had arrived on the scene, she'd battled him for Michael's affection and deference. They appeared to be in the final skirmish, and Odell would not emerge the victor!

She was about to admonish and chastise, then coax and cajole, as she would have in the past, but before she could say a word, Michael spoke again.

"I have decided to marry."

"What? No, that can't be right." When he said nothing, she frantically asked, "Who? Who have you selected?"

"Who would you suppose? It's Jane Hamilton. We will hold the ceremony as soon as the Special License is delivered."

"No, no, I forbid it!"

"To my great relief, it's no longer up to you."

Michael rounded the desk and walked out.

Her head spinning, her knees weak, she sank into her chair. She felt dizzy, as if she might lose her balance and slide to the rug.

All the wasted years! All her plotting and scheming! For naught! She'd been so sure he would pick Miriam, and now that he hadn't, what good was any of it?

"Although I advised a contrary approach"—Odell's remark seemed to emanate from far away—"the earl is willing to be generous. Here is how he has commanded you to proceed."

"I won't listen to you." She clasped her hands over her ears, as if she could block out her fate.

Odell came over, and he pulled her hands away, pinning them behind her back. He loomed over her.

"Your bags are being packed. You will depart—within the hour."

"Bound for where? I have no money but for the tiny

stipend I received from my late husband. What is to be done with us? Shall we be put out on the streets?"

"Had it been left up to me, that is precisely what would have happened. Instead, the earl is offering you the Dower House at his property in Yorkshire. But only the house. For your financial needs, you will have to survive on your stipend."

Maud had been to the property once. It was a cold, dreary residence located at the end of the earth. She would be broke and isolated, with boring, fussy Miriam as a companion. The resolution was the cruelest one imaginable.

She wrestled away and stood.

"I won't go."

"Fine. You may fend for yourself, and if that is your choice, you should expect no compassion—or support—from Lord Hastings."

"You are trying to be rid of us."

"Yes, we are. We make no bones about it. We won't have you on the premises and creating mischief."

Maud teemed with rage. If she were a man, she'd pummel him into the ground. He'd stolen everything from her: her home, her authority, her position in the family. Most despicably, he'd diverted Michael's esteem, and without it, all was lost.

"This is because of Helen Hamilton, isn't it?" she sneered. "You've caused all this trouble just so you can lift her skirt a few more times."

"Be silent."

"I won't be! She came here as a beggar, as a charity case, and you raised her up above everybody. She is a—"

In a flash, he grabbed her by the throat, his large palm applying pressure, cutting off her air. She scratched at him, struggling to escape, but she couldn't fight him off.

"I haven't implemented the punishment I wished," he whispered in her ear, "because Lord Hastings asked me not to, but hear me and hear me well, Maud Seymour: If you ever mention Helen Hamilton's name again, I will sneak into your bedchamber in the middle of the night and smother you in your sleep."

He pushed her toward the door.

"You sicken me," he said. "Get out of my sight."

Maud staggered away and went into the hall, where she was irked to find Lydia dawdling. As Maud started for the stairs, Lydia followed, dogging her heels.

Maud swatted at her. "Leave me be, you wretched girl."

"The captain ordered me to watch you pack—so that you don't steal anything."

Maud inhaled a sharp breath, and she glanced over to see Odell casually loitering in the library doorway, observing all.

"I won't have this unfaithful tattle near me," Maud declared.

"She is rather fickle in her loyalties, isn't she?"

Lydia absurdly proclaimed, "I'm accompanying you to Yorkshire, too."

"You are not. I never intend to set eyes on you again, and you are most certainly not welcome in my new home."

Slyly, Lydia grinned. "Ask the captain. He'll explain it to you."

"I gave Lydia a choice," Odell said. "I could have her arrested, or she could indenture herself to me for the next seven years."

"I chose the seven years," Lydia bragged. "It was a better conclusion than prison."

"She's indentured to you?" Maud was aghast.

"Yes," Odell admitted.

"In what capacity?"

"She will be employed at the Dower House, where you will be residing, and her main duty will be to report on your conduct. I won't have you meddling in Lord Hastings's affairs, so her presence will guarantee that you're behaving yourself."

With Maud reduced to penury, there would be no way

to sway Lydia, no way to bribe her. She would make Maud's life a living hell.

"Seven years!" Maud wheezed. "She will spy on me for seven years?"

"Yes."

It was the ultimate humiliation, the ultimate insult.

"No, absolutely not. She will not come; she will not report."

"Then you will not have the house."

Maud stared at Odell, wondering how she could ever have fancied him, how she could ever have assumed they might have had a future together.

"I'll talk to Michael," she threatened. "He'll over-rule you."

"The arrangement was his idea."

Odell strutted away, while Lydia gestured for Maud to hurry.

"The captain is having the coach brought 'round," Lydia nagged. "We mustn't keep him waiting."

"Your precious captain can sod off."

"I'll be sure to tell him you said so."

Chapter 24

🙰

JANE sat at her dressing table, brushing her hair.

She'd been fed, and she'd bathed—three times—but she didn't think she'd ever feel completely clean again.

Odell had retrieved their clothes from Rafferty, so she was bundled in a comfortable nightgown and a warm robe, with thick woolen socks on her feet.

The horrid ordeal was at an end. She and Helen were safe. Amelia was with them. Clarinda, too. They were in Michael's town house, and she was settled in her bedchamber, but for how long? What would happen next?

Michael and Captain Odell had whisked them out of the prison, and Michael had escorted her to his mansion, but she hadn't spoken to him since. Now, it was evening, and she was waiting.

For what, she wasn't sure.

What was her position in the household? What was Helen's? How was Jane's relationship with Michael to proceed? Would they even have a future?

She was terrified that Odell had brought them home merely to be shed of them again. Most likely, he'd shuttle them off to a cottage in the country, with a tiny allowance and the scandal squelched, which Jane couldn't bear to imagine.

She wanted to take action, to assert herself and make her opinions known, but instead, she was loitering in her room like a frightened mouse.

Suddenly, to her great surprise, she heard someone out on the balcony. She whipped around, seeing a man attired all in black, but she wasn't alarmed. With that blond hair and lanky physique, she knew exactly who it was, and her heart thudded with joy.

She jumped up and hurried over as Michael opened the door and entered, the cold night air whooshing in behind him. He swooped her into his arms, then he was kissing her and kissing her as rapturously as if they'd never been separated a single second.

"Oh, Jane," he murmured, "I thought we'd lost you. I thought I'd never see you again. I'm so sorry."

"You're forgiven. For everything."

"I can't believe Maud did this."

"She always loathed us."

"I realized it, but I didn't understand the danger she posed."

He broke away and led her over to a chair. He helped her to sit, then he pulled up a chair and sat, too.

"I hate to seem so rushed," he said, looking grim, "but we need to talk. Fast. There's something you have to know."

She took a deep breath, let it out slowly. Was this goodbye? After all she'd been through, it couldn't be over. Not like this.

"What is it?" she cautiously asked.

"I haven't behaved very well toward you."

"No, you haven't," she dared to reply.

"Initially, I told myself we were engaged in an innocent flirtation."

"It was never innocent—not from the very first day."

"Then, as we became more involved, I wanted to bind myself to you in some way, but I couldn't figure out how."

"And now?"

"Now I want you to know that I . . . I . . . love you."

She gasped. "You do?"

"Yes, so very much."

She smiled, unable to hide her relief. "I love you, too."

He dropped to one knee and clasped her hand.

"Will you marry me?"

She started to tremble. From the moment she'd met him, she'd dreamed of hearing that very question, but in light of all that had occurred, she'd been forced to accept that it would never come to fruition.

She didn't have to mull over her response. She knew what she wanted, what she'd always wanted.

"Yes, yes, of course I will."

He was trembling, too, and he leaned in and kissed her.

"I was so afraid you would say no."

"Are you mad? I never would have."

"At Hastings Manor, I asked Tristan if I could propose, but he wouldn't let me."

"What changed his mind?"

"I have no idea. Out of the blue, he said I was old enough to make my own choices—and my own mistakes."

"This will never be a mistake."

"No, it won't."

"I swear I will make you happy every day for the rest of your life. It will be my only goal."

He eased away and sat in his chair again.

"We still have a problem, though," he insisted.

"I thought Captain Odell had decided it was all right."

"Tristan is fine with it. It's your sister Helen who's balking."

"Helen?"

"Yes. Just after supper, I spoke to her and requested your hand in marriage, but she—most regretfully—refused my suit."

"She didn't."

"She did."

"I am absolutely mortified." Jane flushed with embarrassment. "Did she give you a reason?"

"She believes I'm a philandering roué who's not ready to settle down and who will bring you decades of misery."

"She said that?"

"Well, not that precisely, but her underlying message was loud and clear. I might have fared better if Tristan hadn't been present. She's very angry with him, and I think she declined the match just to spite him."

The news had Jane in a furious temper. Didn't Helen comprehend that marriage to Michael was the answer to all their prayers? It would provide Helen and Amelia with financial security, and since Jane was ecstatically in love with Michael, it was the perfect conclusion.

She stood, prepared to march down the hall to give Helen a tongue-lashing.

"Where are you going?" Michael inquired, pushing her down into her seat.

"To punch my sister in the nose for insulting you."

"Don't worry about her."

"But I don't want to spend weeks or months begging her to relent."

"Neither do I. So I have a suggestion."

"Anything," Jane vowed. "I will do anything you ask."

"Good girl." He turned her hands, palms up, and he kissed the centers. "I would like us to elope to Scotland."

"Elope!"

"If we ride on horseback, we can travel fast, and no one will be able to stop us."

"When would we leave?"

"Right now. I have two mounts saddled and waiting out in the stable."

"We'd simply gallop away?"

"Yes. It's a scandalous way to start out, but when we came back, the deed would be done, and Helen couldn't prevent the union."

"I've always dreamed of having a big church wedding. Could we have one when we return?"

"Certainly."

Jane walked over and opened her desk, yanking out ink pot, paper, and quill.

"What are you doing?" Michael queried.

"I have to write a letter to Helen, informing her of where I've gone." She grinned. "Then I'll need a minute to change my clothes and pack a bag."

ROSE peeked in Amelia's room, checking to ensure that her friend was sleeping soundly. Amelia had been so exhausted that she'd dozed off over her supper tray. Rose had tucked her into bed, and she hadn't stirred.

Rose smiled with satisfaction, feeling that all was right with the world again, then she tiptoed to her own room. As she entered, she was aggravated to note that Tristan was in a chair over by the window.

Since he'd discovered her sneaking away, they hadn't spoken. He'd been busy with Helen, with Maud and Miriam and Michael. Everyone had priority over Rose, so she hadn't been able to ask what had transpired at the prison, how he'd rescued Helen and Jane or, most important, what would happen now.

She knew she should thank him for helping Amelia, for finally listening and intervening, but she was enraged that it had taken a grown-up—namely, Clarinda Dudley—to convince him of Maud's duplicity.

When he'd first arrived in London, she'd been so happy, but he'd proved himself no different than the other adults in her life who'd ignored her and discounted her wishes.

She stared at him, her expression defiant so that he would understand he wasn't welcome and she wasn't glad to see him.

"Where have you been?" he inquired.

"I was checking on Amelia."

"Is she sleeping?"

"Yes."

"You've been a good friend to her. I'm proud of you for that."

The compliment pleased her, but she didn't want him to know. She merely shrugged.

"I knocked," he said, "but you weren't here. I was worried."

"I doubt it," she scoffed.

"I thought perhaps you'd left me again."

"What if I had? Why would you care?"

She went to her dresser and straightened items that didn't need straightening. She could feel him observing her, his probing gaze annoying and disconcerting.

"If you ran away," he claimed, "it would hurt me."

"I expect you'd get over it."

"You're wrong. I'd hunt for you forever. I'd never quit searching."

She hated it when he pretended to be kind, and she whirled around and glared at him.

"What do you want? Why are you in here?"

"I came to say that I'm sorry."

"Fine. You're sorry." She gestured to the hall. "Now you can go."

"You tried to tell me what Maud was like, but I wouldn't listen."

"No, you wouldn't, and look at all the awful events that occurred because you didn't."

"I'm ashamed of how I acted. Will you ever forgive me?"

"Someday . . . maybe."

Tears flooded her eyes. To hide them, she walked over to the wardrobe and pulled the doors open and closed, open and closed.

"I sent Maud and Miriam away."

"Good."

"They're never coming back. Maud will never harm you or Amelia again."

Rose shook with relief. It was the very best news she'd ever had, the most wonderful thing he could possibly have done.

"Thank you."

"I don't suppose you'll believe me, Rose, but after Father died, and I found out he wanted me to watch over you, I was afraid."

She snorted. "Why would you be afraid of anything?"

"I don't know much about little girls or what they need. I felt I was a terrible choice." He paused, as if struggling over his words. "What's your opinion of how I've behaved as your guardian?"

"You're pretty bad at it."

He'd brought Amelia to reside with them, but other than that one brilliant decision, he'd failed Rose over and over.

"Turn around, Rose," he urged. "Look at me."

"No."

"Rose!"

With that hint of command in his voice, it was difficult to refuse. She spun toward him, swiping at the tears that had dribbled down her cheeks.

"How should we proceed," he asked, "with you and Amelia and me?"

"I want Amelia to remain with us. Always."

"Miss Hamilton won't agree. She's anxious to have her own home, her own place."

"You could make her stay. You could order it."

"I doubt she'd obey me."

"If you were nicer to her, she'd stay."

He chuckled, but not in a happy way. "She's very angry, and she needs some time to calm down."

"If she leaves with Amelia, I want to go with them. I want to live where Amelia lives. I want to be with Miss Hamilton."

"Rather than me?"

"Yes."

"I don't know if I could allow it."

"Why couldn't you? You never wanted to take care of me; you said so yourself."

"That's not true!" He appeared furious, as if she'd insulted him. "You're my sister. I *do* want to take care of you. I just don't think I've done a very good job of it so far."

"No, you haven't."

She began to weep, hating to be so sad, but she'd pinned so many hopes on him, and they'd all been dashed.

"Oh no," he murmured. "Don't tell me I've made you cry."

"I'm not crying," she fibbed. "I'm just tired."

"Come here." He extended his hand.

She was dying to walk over and clasp hold, to sit on his lap as if she was a young child while he told her everything would be all right, but she wasn't young anymore, and things might never be right again.

"Rose, come!"

When he spoke that way, being imposing and strong, she couldn't ignore him.

She took a step, then another, and once she was near enough, he grabbed her wrist and tugged her onto his lap as she'd been secretly wishing he would do.

He nestled her to his chest, as he rubbed a comforting hand up and down her back. He smelled marvelous: like leather and brandy and horses, how she'd imagined her father would have smelled if she'd ever been permitted to snuggle with him.

"It seems," he said, "that all I do is make the women I love cry."

"If you don't want us to cry, you shouldn't be so mean to us."

"Out of the mouth of babes." He chuckled again, and he sounded better, as if his mood was improving. He dried her tears with his thumb. "We'll figure it out, Rose. I'll reflect on a solution, then I'll talk to Miss Hamilton about you and Amelia."

"Could I live with them?"

It wasn't what she actually wanted. She wanted to stay

with him so that they could change their house into the home it had never been, but he probably wouldn't be interested.

"We'll see," he hedged.

She might have pressed him, might have asked if he was serious, but if he swore, then failed to follow through, she'd be more forlorn than she already was.

"Would you mind," he asked, "if I looked in on you during the night?"

She drew away and gazed into his blue eyes that were so much like her own. "How often would you?"

"How about every half an hour?"

"Till morning?"

"Yes, till morning."

"I suppose that would be all right."

He hugged her.

"Don't ever run away again," he whispered. "I couldn't bear it if you left."

"I won't run away."

"Promise?"

"Promise."

She smiled, and immediately, she fell asleep, the steady beating of her brother's heart a soothing rhythm in her ear.

"HELEN?"

"Hello, Captain Odell."

Tristan bit down a grimace, depressed to hear that he was still *Captain* Odell and not Tristan. He'd completely squandered her affection, so he didn't know why he expected the other mode of address, but he wished he could put them on a more cordial footing.

He was a cad, an oaf, a scapegrace. He admitted it, and he was trying to make amends. Why wouldn't she let him?

Timidly, he entered the parlor, uncertain of his welcome, but fairly positive that she'd rather speak to a snake-oil salesman.

"I've been searching for you everywhere."

"Have you?"

She was over by the window, staring out. It was cold and rainy, the gray sky giving a hint of the winter weather that would arrive all too soon.

A smart man would be headed south, with the wind at his back and the salt spray in his face. A smart man would shuck off his responsibilities and do whatever the hell he wanted. A smart man would leave all this feminine drama behind.

He'd never been hailed as being particularly smart.

She spun around, her expression cool and detached, as if he was a stranger to whom she'd just been introduced. She was pale and brittle, as if—with the slightest harsh word—she might shatter into a thousand pieces.

"Have you seen Jane?" she inquired. "She never came down to breakfast, and she's not in her room. I'm worried about her."

"She's not here."

"Where did she go?"

"She's with Michael."

"I apologize." She pursed her lips, her fury clear. "I specifically ordered her to stay away from him, but it seems I have little control over her."

He approached, loathing how she stiffened, as if she didn't want him too near.

"Actually, she wrote you a note. Michael left it on my desk in the library. It's addressed to both of us."

He held it out and she snatched it away, being careful that their fingers didn't touch. As she read the curt missive, explaining their elopement, she snorted with disgust.

"Well," she fumed, "I guess there's not much more to say. Again, I apologize."

"I don't mind that they wed." She appeared skeptical, and he hastily added, "Truly, I don't. Last evening, when he asked you for her hand, I came with him so you'd know he had my blessing."

"You claimed you were amenable, Captain, but at the moment, Lord Hastings isn't present, so you don't have to lie to me. We both realize that this is the very worst ending imaginable."

"Why would you think that?"

"Jane is a hopeless romantic, and she's immersed herself in a dangerous affair with a foolish, immature boy. The conclusion will be awful. Don't try to tell me any differently."

"What if you're wrong?" he queried, sounding like a hopeless romantic himself. "What if he loves her till his dying day?"

"I'm not wrong."

She crumpled Jane's letter, marched over to the hearth, and threw it in the fire. Stoically resigned, she watched as the flames consumed it.

She was such a tragic figure, so bereft and alone, as if she didn't have a friend in the world. He wanted to break through her wall of reserve, wanted to persuade her that everything would be fine, but she wouldn't listen.

He couldn't bear to see her so unhappy, to recognize that he'd been the cause. And now that Michael and Jane had eloped, what purpose was served by her rage? He'd hurt her by refusing to let the pair wed, but he'd relented.

Surely the concession counted for something. Didn't it?

"Have you considered my suggestion?" he asked.

"What suggestion is that?"

"You and Amelia should remain here."

"Here!" She was appalled.

"Yes. Maud and Miriam are gone. When Michael and Jane return from Scotland, this will be Jane's home, so you needn't leave."

"I would *never* stay in this house."

He couldn't stand to be so far away from her, and he went over and laid a hand on her shoulder. She didn't exactly flinch, but there was no mistaking that she detested his touch. She whirled to face him, accusation in her gaze.

"Helen, please forgive me," he begged, his heart on his sleeve. "I understand that you were upset with me—I made a stupid decision, and I'm sorry for it—but Michael and Jane will be wed shortly. The source of our discord is over."

"Over? Because they're marrying?"

"Yes."

"What does their marriage have to do with anything?"

Utterly confused, he gaped at her.

Weren't they fighting because Michael had ruined Jane and he—Tristan—wouldn't force Michael to wed her? Hadn't the entire quarrel commenced because Tristan had been an insensitive ass?

"I thought you'd be glad they were marrying. I thought it would fix the rift between us."

"Really? Is that what you suppose? That you can offer a bland apology, and we'll take up where we left off?"

"Why couldn't it happen? You were fond of me once. Tell me how I can regain your affection."

"You can't."

"You don't mean that."

"I mean it very, very much."

She walked away, keeping a sofa between them as a barrier.

He sighed. "What should I do, Helen? If you could have anything you wanted, what would it be? Let me give it to you."

"I heard from the housekeeper that Lord Hastings owns an empty apartment on the other side of town."

"He owns many properties."

"I would like to learn which one is vacant, then Amelia and I will reside there while I search for a job."

He tamped down a spurt of temper, aware that anger would get him nowhere with her. "You're about to be sister to the countess of Hastings. You can't . . . *work* . . . for a living."

"Then what would you propose I do?"

"Just wait till Jane returns. We'll sit down and talk it through."

"I don't want Lord Hastings's charity. I don't want him having to support me merely because he wed my sister. It wouldn't be fair to him."

"He's a very rich man, and he'll want Jane to be happy. Let *him* judge what he deems to be fair."

"Fine." She looked as weary of their bickering as he was. Her shoulders drooped, her legs seeming to give out, and she slid into a nearby chair. "How would I move in to the apartment I mentioned?"

"I'll simply ask my clerk as to availability, then I'll have the housekeeper send over some servants to ensure it's ready for you. I'll need a few hours."

"I'll be in my bedchamber. Have someone notify me when we may depart."

"May Rose come with you for a bit? She's worried about Amelia. It would be a comfort to her if they could be together."

"Of course. Rose is always welcome."

"I'll only arrange this if you promise to remain there— and rest from your ordeal. I won't have you gallivanting around the city, seeking employment. It would embarrass Lord Hastings."

"I will wallow in his generosity. I will be completely idle; I will become a veritable sloth."

He stared and stared, wishing she'd smile so he could smile, too.

Once, she'd been so enamored of him, and he'd been vain enough to assume that she might even have loved him. How had such strident regard vanished practically overnight? A spark had to still burn deep inside. How was he to rekindle it?

With great effort, she pushed herself to her feet, and she started for the door, the route taking her directly past him. She was prepared to stroll by as if she didn't see him, as if he were invisible.

He stepped in, wanting to rattle her and eager to elicit a reaction. At this desperate point, he'd settle for a snide remark.

"Helen . . ." he murmured, relishing the chance to speak her name.

"What?"

"You seem very exhausted. May I escort you to your room?"

She gawked at him as if he'd ordered her to swallow poison.

"No, you may not."

"Why are you behaving like this? I simply can't fathom why you're so enraged."

"You can't?"

"No."

"Shouldn't you check on Tim and Ruth? They must be missing you."

"Tim and Ruth? Who the hell are Tim and Ruth?"

"As if you didn't know," she scoffed. "And where is Lydia? In light of her delicate condition, she must be missing you, too." A burst of hurt and fury flashed in her eyes, then she spun and stomped out.

He dawdled in the quiet parlor, scratching his head and struggling to figure out what she'd been trying to say.

Chapter 25

"I hope you've learned your lesson."

"That depends. To what lesson are you referring?"

Clarinda stared at her brother, humored by his ill mood. He was still furious that she'd run off with Helen, but his pique was driven by the fact that he'd been afraid for her safety. He hadn't calmed, and he was trying to hide his alarm by blustering and ranting.

"You have the gall to ask me what *lesson*?" he demanded. "How about this one: People like us aren't meant to rub elbows with the aristocracy."

"Why shouldn't we? If our father was actually Duke of Clarendon, then our blood is bluer than Captain Odell's."

"Even if Mother's tales were true—which I seriously doubt—we don't need to court trouble. The rich have their own problems, and we shouldn't meddle in them."

Clarinda laughed. If Phillip found some benefit in claiming an exalted sire, he was the first to brag, but if he was making a different sort of point, they might have been street urchins who'd sprung from nowhere at all.

"I had a grand time," she told him. "Quit fussing."

He was standing by the wagon, labeling bottles of Woman's Daily Remedy. In his race to locate her in London, he'd left the wagon unattended. When he'd returned to fetch it, most of their potions and herbs were gone. It was a sore spot for which she was being blamed.

He slammed down a jar and glared at her.

"As Miss Hamilton was being arrested, what if you hadn't been able to slip away? What if that ass, Rafferty, had absconded with you, too? You'd have vanished into thin air, and I'd have spent the rest of my life wondering where you were."

"Give me some credit, would you? I'm your sister. You taught me every devious trick I know. You think I couldn't have sneaked out? Or that I couldn't have gotten a message to you?"

"I'm not certain what I think anymore." He took a deep breath and let it out slowly. Very quietly, he said, "You scared me half to death."

"I'm sorry." She walked over and kissed him on the cheek. "Am I forgiven?"

"Yes, you're forgiven. I'm just glad I'm your brother and not your father. You'd push me to an early grave. You might anyway."

Clarinda hugged him, then grabbed an empty bottle and started filling it. They were down by the harbor, where they always did a brisk business. What with so many travelers leaving the country, women were especially anxious to bring along tonics.

"Mr. Dubois!" a voice called from the crowd. "Fancy meeting you here."

A blond female hustled up, appearing harried and harassed.

"Bonjour, bonjour." Instantly, Phillip adopted his French accent. "Mademoiselle Lambert, isn't it?"

"How lovely that you remembered."

"She stopped by when we were back at Hastings

Manor," Phillip explained to Clarinda. "On the day I went searching for you."

"It was quite exciting," Miss Lambert said, smiling at Clarinda. "I trust you're his sister and that all has ended well?"

"Yes, everything is fine," Clarinda replied.

"How did your wagon fare, Mr. Dubois? I was worried about you abandoning so many supplies."

"We lost a few items," Phillip stated, "but nothing that couldn't be replaced. "Why are you in London, *cherie*?"

"We're sailing for Scotland." She pointed to a ship where several passengers were climbing the gangplank, their trunks and boxes waiting to be loaded behind them.

"Scotland? In the autumn?"

"Hunting." She pronounced it like a dirty word, and she wrinkled her nose in distaste as she indicated a tall, dark-haired man leaning against the ship's rail. She whispered, "It's Lord Penworth, my employer—the ogre I mentioned."

"Ah," Phillip commiserated. "He looks pleasant enough."

"Only on the outside. On the inside, he's a brute."

"You'd better have some more of my Woman's Daily Remedy for the journey."

"I'd better. The first two bottles were extremely . . . invigorating."

Phillip handed over more of the elixir, and she slipped it into her reticule.

"Do you have the Spinster's Cure I gave you?" he asked.

"Both vials."

"Drink them as soon as you stumble on an interesting fellow with a steady income. You'll be wed in no time flat, so you'll be able to tell your tyrant of a boss to stuff it because you quit."

"That's my plan. Wish me luck!" She walked on, grinning and waving good-bye as if they were old friends.

They were so caught up in her happy farewell that they failed to discern the approach of another person. Clarinda turned away to discover that Captain Odell was standing directly behind her. She jumped.

"You might give a body a bit of notice," she griped.

"Miss Dudley," he curtly greeted. "Mr. Dudley."

He was handsome as ever, attired in a blue coat and tan trousers, his black boots polished to a shine, but he was his usual taciturn, grumpy self.

Though he'd rescued Helen and Jane, Clarinda couldn't move beyond the part he'd initially played in setting off the debacle.

He'd been eager to ruin Helen, but when push had come to shove, he'd deserted her like the worst cad. As far as Clarinda was concerned, he and his snotty ward, the exalted Earl of Hastings, could choke on a crow.

"What do you want, Odell?" Phillip snarled, not liking him any more than Clarinda did.

Odell flushed, as if he was embarrassed to be visiting them.

Arrogant bastard!

"I need to talk to your sister."

"There she is." Phillip gestured to Clarinda. "Have at it."

"Privately," Odell snapped.

"Anything you have to say to Clarinda, you can say in front of me."

"It's all right, Phillip," Clarinda insisted. "I doubt he bites, and I'm dying to hear what it is."

"Fine," Phillip fumed, "but one wrong word, Odell, and I will beat you to a pulp."

"You and what army?" Odell scoffed.

To prevent any fisticuffs, Clarinda grabbed Odell by the arm and dragged him away from Phillip. She kept on until she was certain Phillip couldn't eavesdrop, then she whipped around.

"What is it?" she inquired.

"During your recent adventures, I'm assuming you spoke at length with Helen."

"What of it?"

"I'm merely confused over . . . over . . ." He stopped, flummoxed and unable to spit it out. "She's very furious with me."

"Of course she is. You behaved despicably."

"Thank you, Miss Dudley. I'm aware of my shortcomings. I don't need you enumerating them."

"If you're about to ask me to plead your case with her, I won't. She's better off without you."

A muscle ticked in his cheek. "Your intervention is not necessary. I'm perfectly capable of resolving this on my own."

"Are you?" Clarinda raised a brow, silently informing him that she deemed him a total incompetent.

"It's just that Helen said the strangest comments to me, and I'm mystified by them. She mentioned three people— Ruth, Tim, and Lydia—and how they'd probably been *missing* me."

"Good for her. I'm glad she found the temerity to accuse you to your face."

"She acted as if I should know Tim and Ruth, but I don't. And the only Lydia of my acquaintance is a former housemaid who worked for Lord Hastings. Have you any idea what she meant?"

Clarinda studied him carefully, taking in his candid gaze, his open posture. She was adept at reading emotion, her skill as ingrained as her brother's. Odell was genuinely perplexed, and another layer of Maud Seymour's cruelty was heaped on the top of the pile.

"By any chance, Captain, do you keep two mistresses, one in London and one in Edinburgh?"

"No."

"I don't suppose you have any illegitimate children?"

"No. Who told you I had?"

"The witch!" Clarinda muttered. She peered about and

saw a crate nearby, and she led him over to it. "I have a story to tell you. It's rather long. Let's sit down, shall we?"

"All right."

As she seated herself, she scowled at him. "Why are you so curious about Helen? What's it to you if she's angry?"

"I'm planning to marry her—if she'll have me."

Clarinda sighed. "Obviously, there's a pertinent detail you haven't heard about her relationship with Maud Seymour."

"Oh no . . ." he breathed. "I imagine this will be awful."

"Very awful, but once you learn the truth, you'll know exactly what to do."

"ARE you still here?"

"Barely. I'm on my way to visit my ship."

Phillip glared at Odell, wanting him to go away. By his very presence, he tempted Clarinda into a world that Phillip was determined she would never inhabit.

"I assume you're finished with my sister?" Phillip asked. "I won't have you pestering us."

"Yes, I'm finished with her, but I have something I need to say to you."

"What is it?" Phillip jeered, braced for an insult.

"Thank you."

"Thank you?" It was the last remark Phillip had expected. "What for?"

"You helped Helen."

Phillip glanced away, embarrassed. "I wasn't helping *her*, precisely. I was simply searching for Clarinda."

"Shut up, Dudley. Accept a compliment when it's been offered and skip the obnoxious attitude."

"Compliment accepted. Now bugger off, you rich oaf."

"There are a few other things I have to get off my chest."

"Such as?"

"I'm grateful to you for your assistance, so I'd like to show my appreciation."

"How? Will you pat me on the back and buy me a pint?"

"No. Actually, I own a home in Scotland, but I'm staying in England for a time. Hopefully, I'm marrying, so I've purchased a small property here."

"And . . . ?"

"My house outside Edinburgh is empty, and I thought maybe you and your sister could move in and watch over the place. I'd pay you."

Phillip's initial response was to refuse, but he saw Clarinda over on the wharf, chatting with a pair of drunken sailors. He hated having her fraternize with the likes of Odell, but he hated her mingling with the dregs of society even more.

She was a duke's daughter. Didn't she deserve a fine house in a fancy neighborhood? After the itinerant life they'd led, he didn't suppose she'd acclimate to four walls and planting roots, but shouldn't she have the opportunity to decide for herself?

"We might be interested," Phillip casually said.

"You know where my ship is docked, don't you?"

"Yes."

"We're taking up a load of cargo. You could sail with me, and my clerk in Edinburgh would get you settled. I need your answer by Thursday."

"I'll speak with Clarinda and let you know."

The conversation should have been concluded, but Odell didn't leave. They were by the wagon, the doors open to display Phillip's merchandise. Odell was studying it intently.

"Was there something else?" Phillip inquired.

"I was . . . ah . . . wondering . . . ah . . ." Odell halted and shook his head. "Never mind. It was a stupid idea."

"What was? Tell me."

"Would you have a . . . a . . . love potion you could recommend?"

Poor Odell blushed from the tips of his hair to the tips

of his toes, growing so red that he might have been roasting over a hot fire.

"Don't say a word," Odell barked. "Give me a blasted potion—if you have one—or be silent."

"Are you going to marry that girl?"

"It's up in the air. I need a little help to persuade her."

"You need more than a little *help*. You need a bloody miracle."

Phillip pulled out a vial of his favorite potion and handed it over.

"What should I do with it?" Odell asked.

"Slip it into her tea. She won't stand a chance."

"Are you sure?"

"I am Philippe Dubois." He laid on thick his French accent. "*Je guarantee!*"

Odell snorted with disgust. "Charlatan."

"I'll bet you ten pounds that I'll be dancing at your wedding next week; then we'll discuss whether I'm a fraud or not."

"If you tell anyone about this," Odell threatened, "I'll have to kill you."

"Don't worry about me. Worry about yourself and how you'll wear her down."

"I plan to flatter and sweet-talk. She's a pushover for that sort of thing."

"If that doesn't work?"

"I'll beg."

"And if that doesn't work?"

Odell waved the vial. "A little magic should be just the ticket."

"HELEN, have you finished your tea?"

A flurry of giggles followed the question, and Helen scowled at Rose and Amelia. They were out in the hall and peeking into Helen's sitting room as if they were spying on her.

It was the fourth time they'd pestered her about the tea,

and she knew they were up to mischief, but she couldn't figure out what plot they were hatching.

"Yes, I'm finished."

"Would you like some more?"

"I've had plenty."

The reply brought on another spate of giggles, which was interrupted by a knock on the front door.

"Who could that be?" Amelia was all wide-eyed innocence.

"I can't imagine." Rose looked just as guilty.

As they raced down the stairs to learn the identity of their visitor, Helen went to the window and peered down in the street, curious herself as to who had arrived. There was a horse tethered to the fence, but it provided no clue as to its rider. With all the merchants who had been stopping by, checking to be certain she had all she required, it could be anyone.

Captain Odell had been good at his word. He'd arranged a small house in a quiet neighborhood. It was comfortable and cozy, fully furnished, and staffed by a competent group of servants. She even had a carriage and driver at her disposal if she had errands to run.

Helen understood how the world worked: When your sister wed a rich man, your fortunes improved dramatically, but still, she felt like an intruder.

She kept expecting to be tossed out into the road, and she spent hours every day staring outside. She watched the people passing by, and it seemed as if everybody was moving forward except her.

She had nothing to do. The servants needed no supervision. She prepared lessons for Rose and Amelia, but both girls were so smart that classes were short and instruction limited. She'd promised Odell that she wouldn't search for a job.

So she was . . . waiting . . . for something to happen.

She wished Jane would return from Scotland so that Helen could resolve how she was to carry on.

In the hectic interval surrounding the elopement, a brutal and unwelcome detail had been overlooked: Jane was now wife to Captain Odell's brother, and the ramifications for Helen were monumental. For the rest of Helen's life, she would be thrust into social situations with Odell, and she couldn't bear the notion.

After reviewing her options, it was apparent that she had to retire to the country so she would be far away from events. She hoped Lord Hastings had a tenant's cottage where she could live like a hermit, cut off from news and family.

At the prospect of being separated from Jane, of being alone and isolated, she was overcome by a wave of dizziness. Suddenly, she was very hot, the tea she'd ingested gurgling in her stomach. It tickled her innards, and she laughed at the sensation, as if she was slightly intoxicated. She sank into a chair and grabbed a napkin from the tea tray, and she vigorously fanned her heated face.

The girls scampered up the stairs, and Amelia poked her head in.

"You have a caller."

"*I* do?"

"Yes. Guess who it is."

"I haven't a clue."

Amelia opened the door, and Captain Odell stepped through. On observing him, Helen's heart did a little flip-flop, and she was greatly annoyed by it.

She wasn't a lovestruck adolescent. She wasn't like Jane, who'd been swept off her feet and was too overwhelmed to think logically. She was a pragmatic, rational adult who knew better than to be thrilled, yet she was delighted by his arrival.

Since she'd moved out of Lord Hastings's town house, she hadn't seen Odell. He hadn't visited or sent any notes of inquiry as to her condition. Initially, she'd been hurt by his disregard, but then, she'd realized that there was no reason for him to check on her.

In their last conversation, she'd been very clear.

He wasn't the man she'd presumed him to be, and

though he'd been eager to continue their illicit affair, she would countenance no further association. She'd sufficiently humiliated herself over him, and her ridiculous infatuation was at an end.

"She's had her tea," Amelia mysteriously informed him, "but there's still some in the pot, if you decide she needs more."

Amelia winked, and he winked back, and she shut the door and left. A silence descended that was so intense it was almost frightening.

She gathered her wits and stumbled to her feet, the peculiar dizziness keeping her off balance as she gestured to a chair.

"Won't you sit?"

"No, thank you," which meant she couldn't sit, either.

"Why have you come?" she asked. "Is there a problem?"

He approached until he was directly in front of her, and she didn't like him to be so close. Oddly, since she'd drunk her tea, her senses were heightened. She could smell his skin, and the fact that she could reminded her of *why* she knew his scent so well: Knowledge had been gained through immoral contact.

Her cheeks flushed with chagrin.

"I'm leaving London," he said without warning.

"Leaving?"

"Yes."

"When?"

"Today. I'm traveling to the country to inspect a property I just purchased, then I'm off to Scotland."

"I see."

She tried to maintain a bland expression, but detachment was difficult. The announcement was distressing, but she couldn't figure out why it would be. What was it to her if he departed? She should be glad. She should be celebrating.

"I wanted you to hear some important news from me," he kept on, "before you hear it from anyone else."

"What is it?"

"I bought your father's estate, the one where you grew up."

"From the duke?"

"Yes."

He'd bought her childhood home? He'd done business with the man who had killed her father in a duel? Who had acquired all of Harry's debts and foreclosed? Who had thrown Harry's indigent daughters out on the road?

He'd bought it from *that* man?

"How . . . marvelous for you."

"I rather thought so. I got an especially good deal on it, too. The pompous ass didn't really want it, and I expect—when he finds out who I'm bringing to live there with me—it will gall him to infinity."

Was he referring to Lydia? To one of his mistresses?

Helen was so stunned that she worried she might faint.

"I purchased it sight unseen," he said, "but it's supposed to be lovely."

"Yes, it's very lovely," she tightly replied.

"I'm in a rush to take possession, but before I go, I have a few things to tell you."

The spurt of euphoria she'd suffered when he'd entered the room had vanished. She felt ill and simply wished he would leave and never return.

"There's nothing you could say that I would care to hear."

"I'm going to talk anyway, and you're going to listen."

She recognized his mulish attitude. He wouldn't desist till he'd gotten his way.

"All right," she fumed. "Please be brief."

"When I'm finished, don't you dare say that you don't believe me."

"I'll believe you if I deem you to be credible, but you should know that your reputation for veracity is on thin ice with me."

"So I've been told."

He looked very much the ship's captain he was, feet braced, hands clasped behind his back. His gaze was very powerful, very hypnotic. She wanted to glance away, but couldn't.

That pesky tea sloshed in her stomach again, her surroundings fading into the distance until there was only him and her and no one else in the whole world.

"I understand," he said, "that you had some unpleasant communications with Maud Seymour to which I wasn't privy."

"I did."

"I also understand that she might have insinuated several details about my character that you chose to believe—without asking me if they were true."

"I didn't need to ask you. There was a witness to verify Seymour's account."

"First of all," he seethed, his temper sparking, "while I've never claimed to be a saint, I have never kept a mistress. Not in London. Not in Edinburgh. Not anywhere."

"A likely story," she scoffed.

"Be silent!" he commanded. "Over the past few weeks, you've ranted and raved and insulted me, and I've bit my tongue through every lashing. Now it's my turn."

"Fine. Have at it."

"I have no children." He started counting on his fingers, tabulating the sins she'd committed against him. "I have no idea who Tim and Ruth are. I met the housemaid Lydia when I arrived in London last winter. Other than the fact that she was a servant, whom I occasionally caught flirting with Lord Hastings, I scarcely know her. She was never my governess, and I have no nephew in Edinburgh."

She studied his eyes, his posture, his demeanor. Not by the slightest sign was there any indication of deceit. Her head began to pound as she tried to unravel his words.

She remembered that day in the library at Hastings Manor. Seymour had been so sure, Lydia so convincing.

Seymour had produced a . . . file assembled by a Bow
Street runner. Who wouldn't have believed them?

"You're saying it was all a lie?"

"Yes, that's exactly what I'm saying. If you'd had the
courtesy to ask me, instead of skulking around and imagining the worst, we could have avoided all this turmoil."

"You didn't travel to London to visit your mistress?"

"No."

"You weren't going to Edinburgh to visit your other
one?"

"No," he said more forcefully. "When Michael and I
came to London, I went straight to my ship, to wait for cargo
to be loaded, but we didn't leave for Scotland." He paused.
"I *couldn't* leave."

"Why not?"

"Because I'm getting married. Why do you suppose I
bought a house?"

"For your bride?"

"Yes, if she'll have me."

In light of how much she'd once cared about him, it
was a cruel blow. She was aghast and couldn't hide her
dismay.

"You have someone in mind?"

"Yes. It's the reason I purchased the property—so that
I have a benefit to offer besides myself. I don't presume
I'm much of a prospect as a husband, so I wanted to put
more on the table during any proposal."

She tried to compute the number of hours that had
passed since she'd assumed he loved her, to this horrid
moment where he'd already moved on to someone else—
someone he was eager to . . . to . . . *wed*.

There was a chair directly behind her, and she plopped
down into it and stared at the floor, feeling again as if she
might faint.

"You're looking a bit peaked, Miss Hamilton."

"My stomach is upset. It must be something I ate."

"Why don't you have more tea? Monsieur Dubois insists that it will cure what ails you, while Mr. Dudley simply nags that I should hurry up and do the right thing."

She frowned and peered up at him. "What did you say?"

"I said: Have some more tea. Dudley claims it will work wonders for your disposition."

He poured her a cup and held it out to her. With trembling hands, she took it. A shushed giggle whispered by, as if Rose and Amelia were peeking through the keyhole.

"You seem distraught," he mentioned. "Why are you? Might it be because you don't like to learn that I'm marrying?"

"It doesn't really matter to me one way or another."

"Liar. If I didn't know better, I'd suspect you were jealous, and you could only be jealous if you still had feelings for me."

"I don't," she fibbed. "I don't have any feelings for you at all."

Yet as she spoke the falsehood, the room faded again, and she experienced the strangest vision, a compendium of scenes from earlier in the summer: afternoons spent watching for him, hoping to see him down the hall or to hear his tread on the stair; nights of torrid passion, when she'd felt so vibrant and joyful, as if she might live forever.

How had she lost it all? Could she get it back?

"Drink the rest of your tea, Helen." His voice came from far away.

As if she were paralyzed, he pressed the cup to her lips, and he tipped it until she'd downed the entire contents.

Gradually, the odd dimming waned. Reality returned, and he took her hand and went down on bended knee.

"There is one other thing I need to say," he told her.

"What is it?"

"I love you."

"You what?"

"I love you. Will you marry me?"

She gasped. "You want to marry *me*?"

"Yes."

"*I* am the bride you're talking about?"

"Yes, you silly girl. Who did you think I meant?"

"I had no idea."

"It's always been you—from the moment we met."

"My childhood home, my *father's* house, you bought it for me? So that I could reside there with you?"

"Yes."

"But . . . why?"

"Because I knew it would make you happy."

"Oh . . . oh . . ."

"I've been searching for your furniture, and I've found a lot of it, but if you assist me, we'll recover even more."

"You've been out hunting for my old furniture?"

"Yes, as well as the rugs and artwork and clothes and such. Most of it was sitting in a warehouse. I haven't had it unpacked; I need you to show me where everything goes."

She was shaking, astonished by his generosity.

"You did all that for me?"

"Yes."

"But . . . but . . . why?" she asked again.

"I love you, Helen. I love you more than my life."

She started to cry. She hadn't planned to; she was just so overwhelmed. Tears dripped down her cheeks, and at the sight, he appeared stricken.

"Don't cry," he said. "You know I hate it when you're sad."

"I can't help it."

"I'm only returning what never should have been taken from you in the first place."

She cried harder.

When the duke's men had come with their wagons, when Helen had tarried with Jane and Amelia, observing as they'd emptied room after room, she'd convinced herself that her possessions were just *things*.

How could it matter if someone took them? They could buy new, when times improved, but she'd been lying to herself.

The loss of her home, where her father's laughter still rang in the halls, had been a crushing blow, and she hadn't realized that there was a single person who understood how devastating it had been.

Tristan Odell had understood, and he'd expended the effort to repair the damage that had been inflicted. While she'd been hiding in her temporary apartment, bemoaning her lot and feeling sorry for herself, he'd been quietly fixing all that was wrong.

Her sister was wife to an earl. Her family's estate had been restored to her. She could wed—if she dared—and have the children she craved. And she could have a handsome, kind, and considerate husband to boot.

He came up off his knees, and he sat in the chair next to her. He pulled her onto his lap so she could cry on his shoulder.

"I didn't think you loved me," she wept. "I didn't think you cared."

"You blasted woman! Of course I love you. I've always loved you."

"You never said anything."

"I was too much of a coward."

"You bought my father's house!"

"Yes, I did."

"You bought it for me!"

"To make you happy."

"The gesture is too sweet for words."

"I was hoping you'd feel that way."

"I don't know what to say."

"How about yes?" he asked. "In case you've forgotten, there's a proposal on the table, and you haven't replied."

She smiled, unable to speak, the tears still flowing, and he swiped them away.

"Stop your blubbering, Helen. You're ruining my best coat."

"I'm sorry I believed all those awful stories they told about you. I shouldn't have. I was just so afraid. I thought I was all alone again. I thought you'd forsaken me."

"Never," he vowed. "I never would. Now what is your answer?"

"Yes, yes, yes, I'll marry you. In a second. In an instant. Immediately and eternally."

"Are you sure? Because with me, it's forever. I won't have you changing your mind before we can get it accomplished."

She gazed into his blue, blue eyes, captivated by how remarkable he was, how strong and steadfast and true. He would be her husband, her lover, her friend. For the remainder of her days, he'd be by her side, her most devoted companion, her most reliable ally.

"I will never change my mind."

"Then I am the luckiest man in the world."

He let out a whoop of elation and—given his usual stoic manner—it was completely out of character. He leapt to his feet with her in his arms, and he twirled in circles, kissing her as they spun round and round.

The door banged open, and Rose and Amelia rushed in.

"What happened, Captain?" Amelia queried. "Why were you yelling?"

"We were trying to listen," Rose added, "but we couldn't hear you at the very last."

Tristan stood Helen on the floor, and he smiled at the two girls.

"Let's just say that I owe Phillip Dudley ten pounds."

"Whatever for?" Helen inquired.

"He bet me that he'd be dancing at my wedding next week."

"Have you scalawags slipped me a love potion?"

"Yes," they all retorted at once.

Helen grinned at Tristan. "Since I am suddenly, wildly, and madly in love, I guess he won that wager hands down."

"I guess he did, too. I will never doubt the man again."

"You're getting married?" Amelia asked. "You're serious?"

"Yes, we're serious," Helen responded.

"And we'll all be together," Rose chimed in, "like a real family?"

"Yes," Tristan said, "like a *real* family."

Rose and Amelia squealed with joy, then raced over to join Helen. The three females in Tristan's life hugged him as tightly as they could.

Chapter 1

❦

"I might deign to hire you, Miss Lambert."

"I hope you will, Lord Penworth."

"But you would be expected to exhibit the utmost decorum at all times."

"Oh, absolutely. I wouldn't have it any other way."

Lily Lambert sat in her chair, staring across the massive oak desk at the arrogant, officious aristocrat John Middleton, Earl of Penworth.

He was extremely handsome, with dark hair, piercing blue eyes, broad shoulders, and excessive height, but good looks couldn't mask the fact that he was an overbearing boor.

She'd been eager to serve as companion to his two wards and his fiancée, but now she wasn't so sure.

When she'd agreed to come for the interview, Mrs. Ford—owner of the Ford Employment Agency—had warned her that Penworth could be fussy and domineering, but no amount of notice could have prepared Lily for how unpleasant he would truly be.

She'd been in his presence for all of five minutes, and he'd done nothing but chastise and complain. What an onerous boss he would be! He didn't appear to like servants very much. Or females. Perhaps it was simply *female* servants whom he detested.

She kept her expression blank, not by so much as the quiver of a brow providing any evidence of her own level of aversion to his rank and status.

For the prior decade, she'd been nanny, governess, and companion to the spoiled offspring of nobles just like him, and she'd endured plenty of nonsense. Because of her dismal history, her opinion of him was very low—even though she scarcely knew him.

She wondered if he was the sort to seduce his maids, but she thought he wouldn't be. He was too conceited, too set on being marvelous. He'd never stoop to fraternization.

"I'm a hard taskmaster," he said, intoning it like a threat.

"And I'm a dedicated worker."

"If I issue orders, they must be instantly obeyed."

"I would be yours to command."

"I'll brook no sloth or insubordination."

"I wouldn't dream of idleness or rebellion."

He snorted at that. "I won't have you down in the kitchen, criticizing me over your supper—a supper I have supplied in my own house."

"I am loyalty personified."

"I demand fidelity and constancy."

"I'm constant as the day is long."

"But are you devoted? Can you be trusted?"

"Of course I can be trusted."

He meticulously studied her, as if she were an agitator bent on causing trouble. Then he held up the thick file Mrs. Ford had sent. It was filled with glowing letters of recommendation, but all of them were forged. Lily had written them herself.

She was petite and pretty, and she labored in grand mansions that were occupied by toplofty husbands who were used to taking whatever they wanted, so she'd fended off many advances. With mischief exposed, the wife of the miscreant was never inclined to be rational.

Lily had been fired—through no fault of her own— more times than she could count, and she refused to starve merely because an oblivious noblewoman couldn't make her spouse behave.

Being all alone in the world, Lily had no family to lean on for support, so she had to do what was necessary to get by. If financial security meant drafting a few fake letters, so be it, and the positive reports weren't really false.

She *was* a dedicated worker. She *was* reliable and steady. She *was* kind and courteous, so she suffered no qualms about furthering her claims of proficiency, and she'd never been caught.

In her experience, the person hiring was always in a hurry, needing someone to start immediately, so references were never checked. Lily acted competent, thrifty, and educated, so people were easily convinced that she was precisely who she said she was.

"You have an impressive resume," Penworth remarked.

"I try."

"Yet I must admit that I'm wary."

"Of what?" she snapped before she could stop herself.

He'd flustered her, and her composure slipped. She hastened to shield any reaction.

"How old are you, Miss Lambert?"

"Twenty-five, milord."

"You've had numerous positions. Why so many? Are you prone to quitting? Will you pack your bags after a few weeks? Will you leave me in the lurch? I would hate to find myself trapped in Scotland with my wards unattended."

He was guardian to eighteen-year-old twins, Miss Miranda and Miss Melanie Newton. They were daughters of a friend who'd perished from fast living.

They were accompanying Penworth on his annual hunting excursion to his castle in Scotland, as was his fiancée, Lady Violet Howard. She was the same age as the twins and making the journey north as well.

Of all the dreadful situations for which Lily was remotely qualified, having to spend the autumn traipsing after a trio of rich, indolent adolescents had to be the worst available option. She viewed the coming ordeal with a nauseating resignation, but while she didn't particularly want the job, she couldn't afford to decline it.

After the disaster at her last post—what she referred to as the *incident* with her employer's husband—she was anxious to flee London for a bit. In case any gossip leaked out, she had to be far from Town so stories could fade before she returned.

Her ability to obtain work was dependent on a stellar reputation, and she was determined to hide until the storm had passed.

"Your questions are understandable, Lord Penworth, but if you look closely, you'll see that I have perfectly logical reasons for my frequent moves."

"Those being?"

"I was companion to several elderly ladies who died, so the jobs ended."

"I suppose," he allowed, as if she should have been so accursedly loyal as to have stayed on after her employer was deceased.

The man was an idiot.

"I was also governess," she said, "to various girls who went on to marry. Once they were wed, my services were no longer required."

At this news, he harrumphed as if her charges had done something shocking by marrying, and she could barely contain her exasperation.

What sort of woman was he seeking? A saint?

He opened the file and began to read, poring over every detail, as she fidgeted and fumed in her seat.

Ultimately, he exhaled a heavy sigh. "Fine. You're hired."

The remark was the exact opposite of what she'd expected, and she gaped at him. "What did you say?"

"You're hired."

"Oh."

She'd been so sure of rejection that acceptance was almost a letdown.

"You don't seem very excited," he mentioned.

She flashed a tight smile. "I'm positively ecstatic."

He barked out a laugh, the sound rusty, as if it didn't happen often.

"Is this you in *ecstasy,* Miss Lambert?"

She couldn't abide his condescending tone and answered more sarcastically than she should have. "Would you like me to leap up and twirl in circles?"

"I doubt my poor heart could stand the sight. A simple *thank-you* will suffice."

"Thank you."

His chin balanced on his hand, he leaned back in his chair and assessed her. She scrutinized him in return.

He was thirty, so there was only a five-year difference in their ages, but he was so urbane, so patronizing and sophisticated, that he seemed decades older. Wealth, station, and life experience separated them as clearly as if a line had been drawn.

His long legs were stretched out, one foot crossed over the other. Even though he had slouched down, he appeared to be uncomfortable, and she wondered if he ever relaxed.

"You're very interesting, Miss Lambert."

"Why do you say so?"

"I've given you a place in my household, but you're not gushing. Most females—when I take the time to personally interview them—are a tad more obsequious."

"I offered to rejoice, but you said you'd rather I didn't."

"So I did."

"Have you changed your mind? Would you like me to flatter and compliment? I certainly can if it will make you happy."

"Don't you dare go all sycophantic on me. We're merely completing a business transaction." He tapped a pensive finger against his lips, and he scowled. "There's just one problem."

"What is it?"

"You're very pretty. It worries me."

On hearing the comment, she felt as if they'd stepped into a murky bog.

She didn't consider it vanity when she admitted to being pretty. There was nothing wrong with her vision, and she could see her reflection in a mirror. She was blond and blue-eyed, with a heart-shaped face and pouting lips. Her high cheekbones and dimples had driven several aristocratic sons to write absurd, unwanted poetry about her.

In addition to her comely features, she was pleasingly plump, rounded in the right spots, with a bosom that was fuller than it should be, a small waist, and curvaceous hips. Her shapely figure attracted male attention that she didn't solicit or condone, and she occasionally received risqué proposals that involved her posing in the nude.

"My looks are . . . *worrying* to you?" she tentatively ventured.

"Yes, so I'm afraid I have to set some ground rules."

"Ground rules?"

"Yes."

"Such as?"

"There will be no flirting with the footmen."

"Definitely not."

"Nor can I permit drinking or cavorting. No frolicking with boys in the village. No late night dips in the pond in your undergarments."

She was so insulted she couldn't think straight.

"Anything else?"

"No gambling. I absolutely draw the line at wagering."

"I'll do my best to avoid it."

He raised an imperious brow. "Are you mocking me, Miss Lambert?"

"I wouldn't dream of it."

"Recently, we've had a rash of untoward behavior, and it's my opinion that much unpleasantness could have been averted if I'd been clearer from the start as to the conduct required."

"Your housemaids have been disruptive? They've been swimming in the pond and dallying with the footmen?"

"Not my maids. The companions I've hired for my wards."

"How many have you hired?"

"In the past year? Seven."

His cheeks flushed as she gawked at him, trying to make sense of the information. Why would so many have come and gone over such a short period? Was he just particularly bad at choosing capable people? Or was he an impossible brute?

Lily was acquainted with many of the women from Mrs. Ford's agency, and there was no more boring, humdrum group in existence. She couldn't imagine any of them instigating the type of trouble he'd described.

Suddenly, she was swamped with misgivings, and an alarm bell began to chime.

"You've had *seven* companions?"

"Yes, and none of them has had the fortitude to stick it out."

"May I inquire as to why?"

"No, you may not. Suffice it to say that it was a lack of character on their parts."

"On *all* their parts?"

"Yes," he haughtily insisted. "I asked of them what I ask of myself. I maintain the highest standards of decency and decorum. I would never cause a scandal, initiate gossip, or involve myself in an immoral situation. I demand the same of my servants."

What a dreadfully dull household it must be, she mused. Then again, it had to be better than being groped in a dark hallway or having your employer's husband sneak into your bed in the middle of the night.

"I don't suppose any of this was due to mischief by your wards?"

"My wards? Why would you even suggest such a thing? Their reputations are beyond reproach."

"So . . . it was simply a scourge of amorous, flighty ladies' companions?"

That imperious brow was raised again. "You doubt me?"

It would be completely impolitic to answer *yes,* so instead, she stood.

"I had said *thank you,*" she told him, "but I must change my reply to *no* thank you."

"What do you mean?"

"This job sounds to be quite above my level of competency. I'm sorry, but I wouldn't be right for it."

Cursing herself for a fool, she started out. They were at his country manor, Penworth Hall, a two-day journey from the city. Mrs. Ford had loaned her coach fare to attend the interview, with the understanding that Lily would pay her back from her first month's wages.

If she walked out, how would she square the debt? And if she snubbed the Earl, why would Mrs. Ford place her at another post? Lily had lost many of the positions Mrs. Ford had found for her. Why would Mrs. Ford keep Lily on?

She'd almost made it to the door when Penworth barked, "Miss Lambert, sit down."

"I can't. I really must—"

"Miss Lambert!" he stated more fiercely. "I haven't given you permission to leave."

"I didn't realize I needed it. I believe our appointment is concluded."

"It's not concluded until I say it is. Sit down!"

Brooking no argument, he gestured to her chair, and she vacillated, then slinked to her seat. He grinned malevolently, delighted to have his authority so blatantly demonstrated.

"You've been hired," he declared, "and you will not refuse me."

"As you wish," she tersely retorted.

"We depart for Scotland on Saturday, and I don't have time to interview anyone else."

"Lucky me."

"Your ungrateful attitude will not help matters, Miss Lambert."

"I apologize for my discourtesy," she insincerely muttered.

"Mrs. Ford assures me that you're ready to commence your duties."

"I am."

"We're sailing from London. I trust that mode of travel won't be a problem for you?"

She'd never been on a ship and had no idea how she'd weather the voyage, but when he was such an ass, she felt justified in being contrary.

"I get seasick," she said, lying.

"I don't care," he rudely responded. "It's a minor distance, so your discomfort will be brief."

"I'll try not to be ill in your presence."

He ignored her snide remark and continued. "I've been informed that you booked lodging at the inn in the village."

"Yes, milord."

"I will send for your bags. A chamber will be prepared for you, and you'll join us for supper so you can be introduced to the twins. Tomorrow, you'll assist them in their packing so that the three of you can become acquainted."

"I can't wait," she lied again, and she couldn't shield her distaste.

"You have a sharp tongue, Miss Lambert. I don't like it."

"Then perhaps you should reassess your decision."

"No. I enjoy getting my way, and the more you protest, the more insistent I shall be that you do as I bid you. Might I suggest that—in our future dealings—you keep that fact in mind?"

"I will."

"You may proceed to the foyer. The butler will meet you there and have a maid show you to your bedroom. We have drinks at seven and supper at eight. Be prompt and dress appropriately."

There were a thousand replies she could have made, but what was the point? He hated to be denied, and she was no better. Nothing galled her more than having an arrogant male ordering her about, which certainly had her questioning her choice of career.

She imagined thwarting him, watching until he was off the property, then running away. Would he chase her down as if she was a feudal serf? Would he call out the hounds? Would she be dragged back in chains?

He was such a conceited beast that he just might, so

she'd bite the bullet and obey, but she would loathe her job—and him—every second.

Why couldn't she have had a different type of life?

Her parents had died when she was a baby, and she didn't remember them. She'd had no relatives to take her in, so she'd been shuffled among the neighbors until there was no one left.

Since she was twelve, she'd supported herself. She struggled and toiled, but she couldn't find a place where she belonged. It was her greatest dream to marry, to have a kind husband and a home of her own.

Instead, she had to rely on the whims of a man like Penworth.

They stared and stared, his snooty expression letting her know how futile her spurt of rebellion had been. Her wishes were trivial compared to his, and she sighed and nodded, reluctantly acknowledging his power.

Without further disagreement or complaint, she stood and went to locate the butler so she could learn where her bedchamber would be.

Enter the rich world of
historical romance
with Berkley Books.

Lynn Kurland

Patricia Potter

Betina Krahn

Jodi Thomas

Anne Gracie

Love is timeless.
penguin.com

M9G0907